"DON'T YOU THINK THIS HAS GONE FAR ENOUGH?"

Transfixed, Sydney watched Mike walk toward her. "You're going about it all wrong, Delaney," he said.

He slid his arm around her waist and drew her against him. "Body contact first, Delaney."

His hands glided up to the middle of her back, pressing her even tighter against the hard, muscled length of him. His mouth closed over hers. She parted her lips in acceptance and from the first second, he proved to be the master, she the novice. And what had begun tenderly soon deepened. Passion surged through her as she molded to his body.

When his mouth freed hers, she remained in his arms, breathless and drained of resistance.

"Now *that*, Delaney, is how to kiss. And you don't learn it from any book."

TENDER IS THE TOUCH

ANA LEIGH

AVON BOOKS ◭ NEW YORK

TENDER IS THE TOUCH is an original publication of Avon Books. This work has never before appeared in book form. This work is a novel. Any similarity to actual persons or events is purely coincidental.

AVON BOOKS
A division of
The Hearst Corporation
1350 Avenue of the Americas
New York, New York 10019

Copyright © 1994 by Ana Leigh
Inside cover author photograph courtesy of Fantasies Photography Studio
Published by arrangement with the author
Library of Congress Catalog Card Number: 93-91664
ISBN: 0-380-77350-3

First Avon Books Printing: February 1994

AVON TRADEMARK REG. U.S. PAT. OFF. AND IN OTHER COUNTRIES, MARCA REGISTRADA, HECHO EN U.S.A.

Printed in the U.S.A.

RA   10   9   8   7   6   5   4   3   2   1

To Betsy and Margaret—
and the hope of new beginnings

There is a tide in the affairs of men,
Which, taken at the flood, leads on to fortune;
Omitted, all the voyage of their life
Is bound in shallows and in miseries.
On such a full sea are we now afloat;
And we must take the current when it serves,
Or lose our ventures.

WILLIAM SHAKESPEARE

Chapter 1

Seattle
August 1882

"**M**iss Delaney."

Only noon, and the little toad has already driven her to distraction.

"Miss Delaney!" the odious assistant editor repeated in a voice Sydney swore had yet to transcend pubescence. The six men seated at the other desks in the room simultaneously raised their heads and glanced in her direction. Sighing, Sydney Delaney shoved back her chair.

With a confident step and a mass of auburn hair swept up into a neat chignon at the back of her head, Sydney presented a stately bearing in spite of her moderate five-foot, two-inch stature. Her demeanor, coupled with the no-nonsense, tailored look of the black coat bodice and box-pleated skirt she wore, indicated that her purpose in life was something more than the mere pursuit of a man, an aspect further evidenced by the fact that the twenty-four-year-old had already reached the age of spinsterhood.

"You called, Mr. Curtis?"

A young man with sandy hair and an acne-blemished face shoved a typed sheet of paper across a desk piled high with neglected, month-old editions of the *New York Times*, the *Boston Herald*, the *Chicago Tribune*, and the *St. Louis Dispatch*. "Did you type this, Miss Delaney?"

Sydney thought the question superfluous, inasmuch

as she was the only person in the office capable of using a typewriter. "Yes, I did, sir."

"And who wrote this piece of drivel?"

"I did, Mr. Curtis."

She clenched her hands behind her back in an effort to maintain her composure when his mouth curled into a smirk. "I suspected as much."

"Well, Mr. Curtis, both of these men died earlier this year, and I thought their deaths warranted an editorial."

"You thought!" Curtis emitted a sarcastic laugh. "This is 1882, Miss Delaney. Exciting things are happening all over the world. What makes you think anyone is interested in reading your eulogy to a couple of poets who died seven or eight months ago?"

"Mr. Curtis, Henry Wadsworth Longfellow and Ralph Waldo Emerson are two of America's most renowned and loved poets. Both of these distinguished gentlemen have made a decided contribution to American literature."

"Miss Delaney, when will you realize you have no feel for what is news and leave the editorials to those who do? I remember last year you wanted us to print your boring editorial against the banning of some indecent poems by another one of those . . . poets."

"The poems were *Leaves of Grass*, Mr. Curtis. They were not indecent. And the poet was Walt Whitman."

"It doesn't matter," he declared impatiently. "I want you to stop wasting my time. You are not qualified to be a journalist, Miss Delaney."

"Yes, sir. I see." Her better judgment could not suppress an added thought. "Then why do you have me modify your editorials, sir?"

Although politely asked, her bold question was answered by an impatient glare. "You are a clerk and typewriter, Miss Delaney. Accept your position. In the future, devote the time spent in this office to what you are paid to do, or I shall be forced to dismiss you. Do you understand?"

"Yes, sir."

Returning to her desk, Sydney picked up an envelope from the morning's mail, noting with interest the return address.

MacAllister Alaskan Freight Line, Territory of Alaska.

Sydney opened the envelope and found a brief letter requesting the *Puget Sound Monitor* to post a help-wanted ad in the newspaper.

After putting aside an enclosed check to cover the cost of the ad, Sydney reread the specifications, inserted paper in her typewriter, and began to compose the ad.

Wanted: Office Assistant. Competent person needed for accounting and correspondence. Position offers starting salary of $15.00 per week plus lodging. In addition, the employee will receive $1,000.00 bonus if he remains on the job for one full year. Please send letter of application to—

She stopped typing for a moment to check the address. *Solitary, Alaska? Solitary, indeed. Surely the name would be appropriate for any town in that remote wilderness,* Sydney thought to herself.

Smiling, she finished the ad, wondering about the person who would take the job even for the generous salary. As for the bonus, that promise seemed more like a bet.

One thousand dollars . . .

She propped her elbows on the desk and cupped her face between her hands. Wistfully, she mused on the thought of what she could do if she had one thousand dollars. Why, with that much money, she could open the bookstore she and her father had always dreamed of owning. Needless to say, she could never do so on the six dollars a week she earned at the newspaper.

With a sigh of desolation, she returned to her work.

The next day the city awoke to a downpour that had begun during the night and continued throughout the morning. Near midday, Sydney was at her desk.

"Miss Delaney!" The familiar shout rang out. Ignoring the summons, she resumed typing the classified ad she had begun the previous day.

"Miss Delaney, come here, at once!"

No doubt about it . . . this is going to be another one of those days. She rose to her feet.

"I would like to eat my lunch, Miss Delaney," Billy Curtis complained. "I asked you over fifteen minutes ago to go to the pharmacy and get me a pint of root beer."

Gritting her teeth, Sydney glanced out the window at the rain. Why hadn't the little toad mentioned the beverage when he sent her out earlier in the pouring rain?

"I was waiting for the rain to let up, Mr. Curtis," she answered politely. "My mantle and hair are still damp from the last errand." To strengthen her argument, she tucked several strands of red hair back into the chignon on her head.

Curtis glanced up with a patronizing smirk. "Mind over matter, Miss Delaney. If you have the mind, a bit more dampness won't matter, will it?"

"It *matters* to me, Mr. Curtis, and furthermore, I do have the *mind* to mention I am not employed to run errands in the rain." Though annoyed, she smiled innocently to soften the blow of her objection.

"You, Miss Delaney, are employed to follow my orders," the ill-tempered man shot back.

"Yes, sir!" she answered respectfully. But somehow her tone conveyed a twinge of insubordination.

As she expected, the subtlety was lost on the toad. He had already returned to the enormous responsibility of running the newspaper; leaning back in his swivel chair, he lit a cigar and closed his eyes. "Now, Miss Delaney. I want my beverage now."

Once back at her desk, Sydney decided to risk one further attempt to avoid going out in the downpour. She picked up the tin container of milk intended for her own lunch. "You're welcome to this milk, Mr. Curtis." She placed the tin on his desk.

His quick, ferretlike glance darted up to her. "I don't want milk; I want root beer, Miss Delaney." He spoke each word slowly and precisely, as if speaking to a child. Then he lowered his head.

No, not a toad; the man is definitely a weasel, Sydney reflected.

When the obnoxious young man had become assistant editor the previous year, Sydney had recognized that her intelligence and capabilities far exceeded those of the whiney and insipid nineteen-year-old, whose only qualification for the position was his bloodline— nephew of the owner of the newspaper.

"Mr. Curtis," Sydney began with calm resolve, "section one of the Thirteenth Amendment to the Constitution clearly states, 'Neither slavery nor involuntary servitude shall exist within the United States, or any place subject to their jurisdiction.' I should remind you that the Territory of Washington does fall under that jurisdiction."

His impatient glance encountered an intrepid pair of green eyes. "What are you prattling about this time, Miss Delaney?"

"The Constitution, Mr. Curtis. Slavery no longer exists."

Heaving a sigh of sufferance, he took a puff of his cigar, leaned forward in his chair, and slammed his hand on the desk. "Miss Delaney, I am tired of these petty objections when you are asked to run an errand. You *are* being paid for your services."

"True, Mr. Curtis. I am being paid, but for my typewriting and spelling skills. I am *not* being paid to chase out in rainstorms to procure your lunch or refreshments. So, I suggest if you want root beer, go out in the rain and get it yourself."

Billy's eyes seemed to bulge out of his head. "I shall write my uncle immediately to inform him of your insubordination, Miss Delaney."

"Insubordination." Sydney considered the word for a minute. "Would you like me to spell it for you?"

Unrestrained snickering rose up from the room. The assistant editor jumped to his feet. "This time you have done it, Miss Delaney." His voice rose even higher. "This time you have carried your insubordination to the limit. You are a disruptive force in this office. Therefore, you are fired, Miss Delaney." Billy Curtis pulled out a heavy set of keys, unlocked a bottom drawer, and extracted a metal box.

Chagrined, Sydney now regretted her injudicious outburst. She knew full well that she could not afford the luxury of speaking her mind; jobs were not plentiful for women in Seattle.

"I'm sorry if I've offended you, Mr. Curtis."

Curtis smiled smugly and put a tiny key in the lock of the strongbox. "And well you should be, Miss Delaney, because now you will have plenty of time to regret overstepping your bounds, won't you?"

He carefully counted out several coins. "Here is two dollars and fifty cents to pay you in full through noon today. Do not expect a reference from me. Please remove your presence from this office since you are no longer employed here." He leaned forward. "And be sure to take the ghosts of all your dead poets with you as well as your . . . milk." He pushed the tin toward her with the back of his hand.

Humiliated, Sydney snatched up the money and the tin of milk. For a long moment she waged a silent battle. Oh, how much pleasure she would derive from dumping the contents of the tin over his head and watching the milk run down his smirky face. But her dignity prevailed. Instead, she spun on her heel and returned to her desk.

As Sydney retrieved her gloves, her glance fell on the envelope from Alaska. Impetuously, she picked it up, pulled the sheet from the typewriter, and tucked the papers into a skirt pocket.

Stopping at the door only long enough to pin on her hat and fling her damp mantle around her shoulders, Sydney walked briskly out of the office.

At this time of day, the street bustled with activity. Horse-drawn carriages rambled over watery ruts. People hurried past one another without so much as a side glance, trying to stay dry as they huddled under umbrellas.

The steady rain had created narrow rivulets that intersected and joined one another to form swirling patterns on the road. As Sydney hopped over a ditch, a carriage sped past, sending clods of mud spattering in all directions.

Grumbling, she crossed the street to Pioneer Square and scurried through the small, triangular-shaped park.

Stopping to count her change, she reflected on her plight. Every cent would be precious now. Dare she waste one of the much-needed coins on an omnibus? She tightened her mantle around her and decided to walk.

Undaunted by the relentlessly falling rain, Sydney hastened past the docks and up a steep hillside. After several blocks, she passed through the gate of a wrought-iron fence and into a cemetery, toward the headstone that marked her father's grave.

"Well, Father, this has been an unfortunate day for me," she whispered. She sat down and started her weekly ritual of wiping off the dirt that had accumulated on the stone since her last visit.

Her father had been dead for six years, but she still

missed him terribly. It seemed to Sydney that their family had had more than its fair share of tragedy. . . .

In 1871 George Delaney had lost his wife and home in the great Chicago fire. With no other relatives, the bereaved widower and his broken-hearted, thirteen-year-old daughter headed west on the Union Pacific. He had been a professor at Chicago State University, and so he decided to accept a position teaching English literature at a small academy in Seattle. After several years, George Delaney was forced to take to his bed after an attack of influenza further complicated by a lung injury he received during the Civil War.

Sydney lovingly nursed her ailing father. She had willingly forsaken the company of the young beaux who had courted her so that she could sit at her father's bedside reading to him or chatting about their dream of opening a bookstore.

When she was eighteen, at her father's insistence Sydney took a thirty-day business course to learn secretarial skills—primarily the operation of the typewriter, the office machine the famous Remington Company had begun to manufacture two years earlier in 1874.

The infirm man had lingered for three years, finally going to his reward when Sydney was nineteen. With medical bills having depleted his funds, George Delaney could not leave his orphaned daughter any worldly assets other than an extensive education and cartons of books.

Her dire straits forced her to move from their rented house to a cheaper, furnished room in a boarding house. During the year that followed, Sydney worked at assorted odd jobs such as tutoring children or clerking in the newly opened Woolworth Five and Dime until she had been fortunate enough to find steady employment as a clerk and typewriter on the *Puget Sound Monitor.*

The patter of the rain on the granite stone provided a soothing accompaniment to her thoughts. *I lost my job today, Father, or do you know that already? It wasn't very practical of me to put myself in such a vulnerable position, but you know how impetuous I am.* She sighed deeply. *I always seem to be my own worst enemy.*

Then she allowed herself to consider the thought that had been nagging at her since the previous afternoon. *I've been thinking about applying for a position in Alaska. I don't know very much about the land . . . and the thought of it scares me . . . but I could earn over twice as much as I made at the newspaper, and the job offers a thousand-dollar bonus.* Her eyes misted with unshed tears. *I would have to leave you, though, Father. But it would only be for a year,* she added hastily. *And then, when I get back, I would have enough money to open the bookstore we've always talked about owning.*

Sydney paused, as if expecting a response. Glancing heavenward, she realized the rain had suddenly stopped.

It was enough of a sign to convince her.

Darkness had descended on the city by the time Sydney hurried past the Masonic Hall near her boarding house. The sound of organ music filtered through an open window of the neighboring Methodist church as the choir practiced for Sunday morning service.

She offered a friendly hello to the lamplighter who was making his evening rounds. He doffed a worn, stovepipe hat, then lit the gaslight, which cast a shimmering glow on the rain-washed sidewalk and street.

The rain resumed by the time Sydney turned up the path leading to a white frame house. The dim light concealed the peeling paint on the porch and battered eaves. Thoroughly drenched, but feeling elated nonetheless, she climbed the stairs that led to her small room on the second floor.

As she shook off her mantle, Sydney cheerily greeted her roommate. "Hail to thee, Brutus, my blithe spirit."

The red and blue parrot cocked its head as she shook the water from her bonnet and hung it on a wall peg.

She walked over to the cage and patted the bird. "It's miserable outside. I lost my job today, and I'm happy as a lark."

"Sydney's right. Sydney's right," the parrot squawked, following with two shrill whistles.

"You're just lucky you don't have to go out in that downpour," she added, making quick work of removing the rest of her damp clothing. "And much to your pleasure, I am sure, my dear *Bruté*, you have heard the last of the horror tales concerning the dubious deeds of Billy the Kid. The scoundrel and I have parted company. Tell me what you think about that?"

"Sydney's right. Sydney's right," came the response and whistles.

Within minutes, snuggled in the warmth of a flannel dressing gown, she cleaned the cage and fed the bird while she waited for a pot of tea to brew on the small stove in her tiny, one-room flat.

Soon the soothing effects of the hot liquid had alleviated any lingering chill from the rain, and she sat down at a battered desk to reread the letter from Michael MacAllister.

Alaska. She knew so little about the mysterious land. Why, she had been only nine when the United States purchased the territory. Was it really the bitterly cold, worthless expanse of frozen glaciers and barren tundra that some claimed it to be? She studied the big expanse on a map of the world. Ridiculed as Seward's Folly at the time of its purchase in 1867, the United States had paid the Russian government $7,200,000 for the 586,400 square miles of this vast and unexplored region.

"Well, I don't know too much about it, Brutus, except that it looks far away," she said without her earlier bravado.

"Sydney's right. Sydney's right," Brutus replied, adding the usual double whistle.

Her fingers dawdled with MacAllister's letter as she

now wrestled with her doubts. Damnation! Could this be the opportunity she had been waiting for? There certainly weren't too many options for a woman in Seattle, short of marriage—which was not even a consideration for Sydney. Her younger courting days had come and gone while she nursed her father, and she always managed to find shortcomings in the few men who now tried to court her.

She walked over to the birdcage. "What do *you* think I should do, Brutus? If the land is so barren and insufferable, how is it this MacAllister has such a flourishing freight line that he can afford to offer a one thousand dollar bonus?"

She shook her head at the bird. "On the other hand, Brutus, if the land weren't so barren and insufferable, MacAllister wouldn't *need* to offer a one thousand dollar bonus, would he?"

The parrot offered its usual response, hopping from foot to foot along its perch.

"You're certainly no help," she murmured affectionately. "But I would like that bookstore, Brutus. I may never have an opportunity like this again."

Moving back to the desk, she picked up a small framed picture of her parents. Inexplicably, the lines from one of her father's favorite passages drifted through her thoughts. *"And we must take the current when it serves, Or lose our ventures."*

A worried frown revealed her inner struggle. "I don't want to drown in that current, Brutus, but after all, other people live in Alaska. If they can do it, why can't I?" The bird cocked its head as she stared for a long moment into its black-rimmed eyes. Finally, with a determined nod of her head, she declared, "Let's do it."

Picking up the pen, she dipped the nib into the inkwell and wrote a reply.

Chapter 2

October 1, 1882

As Sydney stood at the rail of the tramp steamer, her gaze remained fixed on a snowcapped peak as she watched two eagles swirl and glide in a graceful pas de deux against a brilliant blue sky. She sighed in disappointment when they dipped from sight.

Suddenly she gasped. Like silent sentinels, three sheep stood motionless on the rocky ledge, staring at the passing ship. The shaggy white-furred animals had magnificent curved horns that reminded her of the bighorn sheep she had once glimpsed as a young girl while crossing the Rocky Mountains.

The sudden blast of the ship's foghorn startled the sheep, and they bounded from one ledge to the next as gracefully as deer in a fen.

Her earlier misconceptions of a barren land had been quickly dispelled as the ship sailed along a coastline densely covered with spruce-lined slopes, alpine meadows, and the wondrous splendor of cascading waterfalls plunging into the ocean. Clouds hovered like halos over distant, snowcapped mountain peaks, and glacier walls sparkled with blue ice. *It should be called Paradise, not Alaska,* she thought with awe.

For nine days the freighter had followed the inland passage along the coastline of British Columbia and Alaska, stopping at several of the seaports to take on or deliver freight. But Sydney had been so enthralled with the sights that the days had passed swiftly, the crude facilities on the freighter a minor inconvenience.

Now, three days after leaving Juneau, the freighter neared her destination, a tiny seaport located between the Alaskan panhandle and the town of Seward. Sydney leaned over the rail to watch two porpoises swimming near the bow of the ship. At the sound of a loud splash, her glance shifted to where a sleek black and white whale breached the surface of the water to breathe, blowing a cloud of steam fifteen feet in the air. The porpoises quickly dove and swam away.

From the time the ship had entered the Gulf of Alaska, the temperature had dropped slightly, but the thin drizzle that plagued them throughout the voyage had been left behind. She felt the autumn chill through her serge skirt, and Sydney tightened her mantle around her, then tucked her hands back into her muff.

She knew her clothing would be inadequate for the severe Alaskan winter, but the money Mr. MacAllister mailed to her for the passage fare had been used to pay the final rent on her room and the cartage for shipping her books. Barely enough remained to obtain cheap passage on the tramp steamer.

Sydney trembled, but not from the cold—she trembled with excitement at the thought of her new beginning.

From the day she had sealed and posted the letter to Michael MacAllister, she waited impatiently for his reply. As the weeks passed, and her meager funds dwindled, she began to doubt the wisdom of insisting he sign a contract legalizing the terms of employment. Then, when she had just about given up hope, the packet arrived with the signed contract and passage money.

And now with the port of Solitary just ahead of her, the daring move had reached fruition.

Two blasts sounded from the ship's horn as the steamer entered the cove of a narrow inlet. At her first glimpse of Solitary, her heart seemed to leap into her throat. Tucked in the base of a coastal ridge, the town looked tiny from the ship.

"As you know, my dear, I am going on to Kodiak, so I fear this is vhere ve must say good-bye."

Smiling, Sydney turned to the tall man who had moved to her side. "I'm so grateful to you, Colonel Kherkov. You've been a wonderful raconteur. Thanks to you, I think I know this country as well as my own."

"Vell, ve Russians did settle the territory long before you Americans arrived. And so I travel by steamer around Alaska at the behest of the Russian government—visiting towns, trying to keep the peace between the two groups."

"Why, Colonel Kherkov, do I detect a note of nationalism in that remark?" she teased.

"Perhaps." He reached for her hand. "But, beautiful as Alaska may be, don't trust her, my little Sydney. For like a voman, she has many shifting moods and vill turn on you vithout varning."

"You make the place sound heartless, Yuri."

For a long moment she regarded the tall, distinguished man intently. Dark, penetrating eyes immediately drew her attention to the handsome face embellished by a neatly trimmed goatee. A black sealskin hat covered dark hair streaked with gray at the temples. The mien of this cultured Russian diplomat reminded her so much of her father, it was not surprising Sydney had become good friends with Yuri on the voyage from Seattle.

"I vish you luck in your new venture, my dear." Kherkov bowed and kissed her hand. "I am sure you vill need it ven you meet Michael MacAllister."

Shocked, she glanced up at him. Kherkov flashed a secretive smile and walked away.

Yuri's puzzling remark was quickly forgotten when Sydney stepped ashore. She stood still, gazing around in disbelief that she was actually here in Solitary. Several dozen wooden buildings were crowded between the sea and the tree-clad slopes. She offered a nervous smile to two Tlingit Indian boys who were watching her inquisitively. She was about to ask them if they spoke English, when the two boys dashed away.

Several males were occupied unloading freight. Thanks to Yuri Kherkov's instruction, Sydney recognized them as Tlingit Indians. Short and stocky, with broad shoulders and muscular chests, the natives had the features and dark, coarse hair of Indians she had seen on the western plains; but unlike the American Indians, these natives were light-skinned and many were dressed in the pants and shirts of the white man.

Her eyes swept the bleak huddle of buildings. On a sign tacked to a wooden structure in the center of the town, she noticed the words "MacAllister Alaskan Freight Line." An unaccountable feeling of trepidation came over her. She shivered.

"Don't worry, Brutus. Just 'screw your courage to the sticking-place. And we'll not fail.' "

Carrying her valise in one hand and Brutus' plaid wool-covered cage in the other, Sydney headed for the building.

A handsome, dark-haired young man jumped to his feet when Sydney walked into the office. "Yes, m-ma'am?"

Settling the birdcage firmly on a chair, she put down her valise. "Good afternoon. I'm looking for Mr. Michael MacAllister."

"Mike's n-not here. He'll be back t-tonight," the young man said.

"Oh," Sydney sighed, unable to disguise her disappointment. "Not until tonight?" Her disheartened glance appeared to strike a chord of sympathy in the young man because she saw his dark eyes deepen with concern.

"M-maybe I can h-help you," he said.

Sydney did not wish to burden this man with her

problems, but she was in a quandary. Where could she go until Michael MacAllister returned?

She smiled nervously. "I'm Sydney Delaney. Mr. MacAllister hired me as an assistant."

The compassion she had seen in his eyes now turned to shock. "I'm B-Brandon Mac-MacAllister," the young man said shyly.

"Are you Mr. MacAllister's son?"

He shook his head. "B-b-brother."

"Well, your brother indicated that lodging would be provided with the position. Perhaps I could go there and await his arrival."

"I g-g-guess so," he said, frowning.

He grabbed a jacket from a wall peg and picked up her valise. "I'll take you."

When he reached for the birdcage, Sydney stopped him. "No, I'll carry that." She could hardly trust Brutus' welfare to a stranger.

She followed Brandon MacAllister to a house immediately next door. Appalled, she looked about at the large room that evidently served as a combination parlor and kitchen. The floor boards were sanded but unpolished. Other than a crudely constructed bow-back bench and chair near the fireplace, the parlor end of the room was drab—not a rug on the floor, picture on the wall, or curtain at the window. Two oil-burning lamps, garishly painted with pink flowers, stood on a trestle table behind the settle.

Stacked on the floor next to the table was a pile of newspapers. Sydney stole a glance when passing and smiled when she saw the familiar *Puget Sound Monitor* blazoned across the top.

The kitchen was considerably nicer, offering a copper dry sink, a black, cast-iron cookstove, and a pine table with two backless benches. Sydney peeked into the doorless chamber of a small walk-in pantry that smelled of spices and onions. The three walls were lined with shelves holding an assortment of stoneware, copper bowls, and tin-lidded canning jars filled with spiced crab apples, jams, and pickled vegetables. Huge tin canisters, wooden barrels, and stone crocks containing apples, onions, vegetables, and dried meats were kept cool on the dirt floor.

Well, at least it appears to be tidy, Sydney thought with relief.

The original house had been enlarged, and when Brandon led her through a door into the addition, she saw four more doors that opened onto the hallway.

"You c-can use this room," he said, taking her to a rear bedroom. After depositing her bag on the floor, he nodded politely. "I'll build a fire, and there's p-p-plenty of food. The water b-barrel's outside the door, and the p-privy's in the back."

Sydney thought he certainly appeared to be a pleasant enough young man, and she smiled gratefully. "Thank you, Mr. MacAllister."

"If you need anything else, I'll b-be at the office."

"There is one other thing you can do for me," she added when he started to edge away. "I have several cartons of personal effects on the ship."

"No problem, m-ma'am. I'll take c-care of them." Despite his willingness to be helpful, it seemed he couldn't get away fast enough.

Once alone, Sydney put aside her thoughts of Brandon MacAllister and glanced around at what would be her new home for the next year. Like the main room, the bedroom was utterly lacking in decor. But she would soon change that, Sydney reflected with her usual optimism.

Setting the birdcage on a chest, she removed the protective covering. "I'd say some lacy curtains and a bright bedspread will make all the difference in the world. Don't you agree, Brutus?"

"Sydney's right. Sydney's right," the parrot piped, then whistled.

As Sydney unpacked her valise and put away her

clothing, she noticed the intricate carvings on the chest, an unusual touch to the spartan room.

She decided to ask Brandon MacAllister about the interesting woodwork and returned to the main room. There was no sign of him; however, true to his word, a fire now burned in the fireplace.

She heard nothing but the fire's crackle. Deciding that the house must be deserted except for herself, Sydney tapped on one of the closed doors. Receiving no reply, she opened it and peeked into the room.

The room was much like her own. She closed the door quickly, not wishing to snoop further. She repeated the action on the opposite door and met with the same result. The last door at the end of the hallway opened to the outside.

Returning to the kitchen, Sydney remembered Brandon's earlier invitation and looked for something to eat. If nothing else, she needed a cup of tea. She investigated the contents of the tall canisters and discovered flour in one, sugar in another, and cornmeal in still another. On one of the shelves beside a wooden box of matches, she found a tin with Oriental drawings and painted symbols. Sydney removed the lid and took a deep sniff.

"Hmmm . . . looks like tea. Smells like tea. Hence . . . it must be tea. Right, Brutus?" She looked around when there was no reply and realized she had left his cage in the bedroom.

She had fallen into the habit of talking to her beloved companion in the confines of the room they had shared together. "Looks like I'll have to cure myself of that habit," she said aloud. "Or people will think I talk to myself."

Venturing outside, she filled a jug with water, then ladled several cups into a brightly painted enamel kettle. A further search produced half a loaf of bread in a wooden bread box, and the remains of a fish in the box out on the window sill, in which the MacAllisters kept food that required refrigeration. A cautious sampling proved the fish to be a smoked salmon, so Sydney spread a small quantity on the bread.

Night had descended by the time she had finished off her meal with an apple from one of the barrels that stood in the corner.

Still no one had returned to the house and her curiosity about the other two roomers sharply increased.

Hoping that someone would arrive before she went to bed, Sydney changed into her nightgown, donned her green flannel robe, and sat down on the floor before the fireplace to brush out her hair.

The warm fire soon lulled her into a state of drowsy meditation as she slowly dragged a brush through long, thick strands of hair that hung past her shoulders. Many times since deciding to uproot her life, Sydney had suffered doubts. Now alone in the strange house, she further questioned the wisdom of her impulsive decision. The country was breathtaking; however, from the little she had seen of Solitary, the town appeared to be more primitive than she had imagined.

But as always, her courage buoyed her up, and she felt a rush of excitement.

Lost in her thoughts, Sydney did not hear the door open, and turned around only when she felt the cold chill that swept across the floor.

For several seconds Mike MacAllister stood staring at the unexpected sight of the ravishing beauty.

Sitting in the glow of the fireplace, she reminded him of the northern lights—a shimmering, swirling merge of reds and greens.

"Well, hello!" Mike said, finding his voice.

Sydney smiled warmly. "Hello."

His lingering glance swept over her appreciatively. He could not imagine why this beautiful woman would be in Solitary, let alone sitting on his very hearth.

"Did Bran bring you here?" he asked curiously.

"Yes, he did," she said, rising to her feet.

Mike smiled in amazement. Apparently, he had considerably underestimated the prowess of his younger brother. When she continued to stare, he arched a brow inquisitively and removed a wool jacket, tossing the garment on the chair. "Bran around?"

Sydney wondered if he was one of the roomers. She had the pleasant impression of stature, broad shoulders, dark hair, a rugged face, and a deep, resonant voice. Feeling awkward, she heard her voice come out in a husky whisper. "No, I haven't seen Brandon since he brought me here earlier. I've been waiting for Michael MacAllister."

"Well, honey, you've found him," Mike said. Moving to the kitchen, he located a bottle of whiskey.

Mike had not anticipated ending the day with such an unexpected delight and figured he owed Bran a big favor. "I haven't seen you in town before."

"I just arrived today, Mr. MacAllister. I'm Sydney Delaney."

Her announcement hit him like a cold blast of Arctic air, instantly cooling his ardor. Good God, he had been planning on going to bed with the wife of his new assistant!

"I apologize, Mrs. Delaney. Your husband never mentioned that he was married."

"It's *Miss* Delaney, Mr. MacAllister. I have no husband."

"*You're* Sydney Delaney?" At her nod, he poured himself a shot of whiskey and downed it quickly. In his embarrassment at having mistaken her for a new girl at Claire's, Mike had not taken in her first name. Then remembering his manners, he picked up the bottle and silently offered her a drink. She shook her head.

He cleared his throat. "I'm afraid there's been a misunderstanding, Miss Delaney. Hiring a female would be out of the question. The position requires the services of a man."

"Mr. MacAllister, my qualifications were impressive enough for you to hire me. Why have they changed since you discovered that Sydney Delaney is a female?" Sydney challenged.

"I'm sure you would be competent at handling many of the office functions, Miss Delaney—"

"Then let me do so, Mr. MacAllister," Sydney interrupted. "If you just give me the chance, you'll discover that my intelligence is equal to that of any man, sir."

"Miss Delaney, if you had any intelligence, you would know Alaska is no place for a woman." He spoke lightly, trying to ease the tension.

Mike could understand why the woman would be upset at being turned down for the position after making the long trip to Alaska, but there were aspects of the job too grueling and dangerous for a woman. Allowing her to remain was out of the question.

"Certain requirements for the position are beyond the capabilities of a female."

The same old argument she had heard more often than she cared to count . . . a woman's capabilities were *never* equal to a man's. Just another Billy Curtis, Sydney thought with disgust. Only the face and voice were different.

"Capabilities? Such as what, sir?" she angrily levied.

"What difference does it make, Miss Delaney? My mind is made up. You cannot remain."

At this unlikely moment, Brandon MacAllister entered the house. Frustrated by the unexpected turn of events, Mike cast a swift glare at his brother. "This isn't a set-up, is it, Bran? I'm not in the mood for stupid tricks."

Brandon MacAllister shook his head. "I don't kn-know anything about it. I-I'll t-talk t-to you l-l-later." He hastened out the door he had just entered.

"Do you always bully your brother like that? No wonder he stutters," she declared.

Mike had been as reasonable with her as he intended

to be. If she wanted to trade insults, she would find out he could give as well as take. "It's no business of yours, lady. You should concern yourself with how you lied to me."

"Lied to you?" Indignant, she challenged, "In what way, may I ask?"

"Sydney Delaney is supposed to be male, not female," he accused.

"Hah! Because you say so," she scoffed.

Sydney realized she was in for a battle royal with the bombastic Michael MacAllister. Recalling Colonel Kherkov's baffling remark when they parted, she now understood the prudence in Yuri's warning. Deciding that discretion was, indeed, the better part of valor, she decided to retreat to her room to plot her strategy.

"I propose we postpone this conversation until morning, sir. Perhaps we'll both be capable of a more rational discussion at that time." She turned and walked back to her room.

But once there, she discovered to her dismay that he had followed her. "Mr. MacAllister, I am tired. I am anxious to retire."

"What I have to say will take only a minute, Miss Delaney. It is out of the question for you to remain here in Alaska."

"Sydney's right. Sydney's right." Brutus' strident chirrup and whistle sounded from the corner.

Mike swung his glance toward the commotion. "What in hell is that?"

Undaunted, Sydney thrust up her delicate but determined chin. *"That,* sir, is my parrot."

"A parrot! You brought a tropical bird to Alaska?" he asked aghast. Carting the idiotic, feathered creature to the territory was very evidence of the woman's lack of sense. Incredulous, he threw up his hands. "That bird's presence here is as absurd as *yours."*

Determined not to say something she'd regret later,

Sydney walked over to the door and held it open. "I would appreciate your leaving, sir."

Seething, Mike stopped and shook his finger in her face. "Lady, come Saturday when the steamer returns from Kodiak, you're hauling your trim little . . . posterior . . . along with that birdcage, right back onto the boat."

"We'll just see about that," she challenged and closed the door in his face.

Mike thundered down the hall, and the house shook when he slammed the front door on his way out.

Her aplomb shaken, Sydney sat down in the center of the bed with her legs crossed and her chin resting in her hands. "Well, Brutus, it appears that Solitary is even more . . . primitive . . . than I feared."

Brutus hopped along his perch. "Sydney's right."

Frowning, Sydney ignored him.

Late into the evening, at the nearby brothel where Claire Montrell had acquired her earthly riches, Mike MacAllister sat alone in brooding silence at a corner table. Across the room, Bran and Pasha, an older Russian gentleman, had been playing Red Dog for a couple of hours, until Bran got tired and left. Ultimately Pasha had wandered away, too. Lily and Sal, the two prostitutes who worked for Claire, had approached him separately, but he had declined their services. Sex was the last thing on his mind tonight.

Even Claire had stayed behind the bar and left him alone.

And that was the way he wanted it.

Finally, nearing midnight, with Mike the only remaining customer in the bar, Claire Montrell walked over to his table carrying a whiskey bottle and a glass.

"What's on your mind, Mike?" She put the bottle and glass on the table and sat down, then refilled his shot glass and poured herself a drink.

Although life had not been kind to the blonde madame, nature had been benevolent. The hard knocks she had endured had left no scars—neither physical nor psychological. And despite having passed her fortieth birthday, Claire still had the face and body of a young woman and the serenity of a saint.

Mike had known Claire Montrell for thirteen years; and with the exception of his brother, he considered her his best friend.

He picked up the tiny glass and for a lengthy moment stared at the amber liquid. "Sixteen years is too young for a girl to die. Don't you think, Claire?"

"Sixteen is too young for anyone to die, Mike."

"Yeah." He downed the shot.

She picked up the bottle and refilled his glass again. "This about Beth?"

"Yeah," he said. "This is about Beth." He raised the glass and swallowed the drink.

This time Claire was not quick to refill his glass. "So what about Beth, Mike?"

"Beth would have been twenty-nine by now if she'd have lived. And she would have lived if I hadn't brought her to this wilderness."

"You don't know that, Mike. Beth might have been run over by a train, could have died givin' birth, or even fallen off the top of one of those four-story buildings they have in San Francisco."

He flared in anger, slamming his hand down on the table. "But she didn't, did she? She froze to death in an Alaskan wilderness." He rifled his fingers through his hair and sat with his head propped in his hand. "Don't make light of it, Claire. You know this territory's no place for a woman. The land's too hard on women. I've seen more than my share of them die because of it. My wife . . . one of them."

She reached out and grasped his hand. "And I've seen twice as many good men die here, Mike," she said kindly. "But I don't blame the land for it. Lord, honey, I'm not tryin' to make light of Beth's death. Or your brother's either. Losin' someone we love touches everybody's life at one time or another. But you gotta put it behind you, honey, 'cause it'll eat you alive if you try to dwell on the whys of it."

Then she offered a saucy grin. "Besides, quit badmouthin' Alaska. She sure's been good to me. I'm a rich woman, Mike. I got more money than I can spend in my lifetime. So I've got no complaints."

"You never do, Claire." His gloom had passed. Either the whiskey had done it—or Claire.

Walking in and unexpectedly finding a beautiful woman sitting on his hearth had completely unnerved him. Seeing the tiny, defenseless woman had resurrected painful memories for him—and with those memories had come the reminder of the vulnerability of a woman in Alaska.

"Claire, why don't you find yourself a good man, marry him, and start spending some of that money you've got? Take a cruise around the world, why don't you?"

"If I did that, who would take care of Pasha? That Russian may be older than me, but he'll never really grow up," she said lightly. Smiling, she leaned across the table. "Don't suppose the new gal you hired had anythin' to do with that mood you were in."

Mike jerked his head up in surprise. "How'd you hear about her?"

Claire chuckled. "Word gets around fast in a town this size."

Mike buried his head in his hands. "That redhead is trouble with a capital *T.* "

"I hear she's pretty too," Claire said slyly, her blue eyes alight with amusement.

"Pretty! What's pretty about a wildcat snarling in your face? Miss Sydney Delaney is going to be on the next ship out of here."

He shoved back his chair and stood up. Leaning down, he kissed the top of her head. "Good night, sweetheart."

"Good night, Mike." She watched him stride away with his hands in his pockets. "Hmmm ... Miss Sydney Delaney, is it?" Her mouth curved in a smile.

Chapter 3

As she dressed the next morning, Sydney primed for battle, rehearsing the arguments she would present to defend her position. Shivering against the chill, she quickly donned flannel underwear, a long, fitted corset, and a white long-cloth bustle. White lisle stockings followed and then a plain, white underskirt. She pulled on her robe and hurried out to fill the ewer from the rain barrel, then washed her face and brushed her teeth. Finally, after sweeping her hair into the usual chignon, she put on her black, fitted coat bodice and box-pleated skirt.

"No sense in your staying in here alone, Brutus," she declared. Toting his cage along with her, she made her way to the kitchen to fortify herself with a cup of tea.

That room was nearly as chilly as her bedroom. She quickly threw some pine chips into the stove's firebox and within minutes had a fire started in the cookstove.

While she sat down and ate a slice of bread smeared with homemade apple butter, Sydney continued to rehearse the argument she would present to Michael MacAllister. Satisfied, she cleaned up the kitchen, returned Brutus to her bedroom, then pinned on her hat and left the house. She noticed several women standing in a huddle watching her as she walked the few steps to the office.

Mike MacAllister glanced up casually when she opened the office door. "Good morning, Mr. MacAllister," Sydney offered cheerfully, firing the first volley.

Mike knew he was under siege. "You're wasting your time, Miss Delaney." He picked up a paper from one of the piles on his desk and began to read.

Ignoring his rudeness, Sydney turned her attention to Brandon. "Good morning, Brandon."

The younger man grinned. "G-good morning, ma'am."

Seeing the two brothers together in the bright light of day, Sydney realized how much they resembled one another. Only in a physical sense, of course, she told herself with a scornful glance in the direction of the older brother.

"Mr. MacAllister, we have a serious matter to discuss."

"You're getting on that ship." He didn't even look up.

Turning his back to her, he began to rummage impatiently through a cabinet. Sydney couldn't help but notice how this simple movement caused his plaid shirt to stretch tautly across the broad expanse of his shoulders.

She had to admit that the man did not remind her of Billy Curtis physically. Then she chastised herself for allowing such thoughts to muddy the water. After all, the Billy Curtises of the world came in all shapes and sizes.

"Bran, where's that bill of lading from last week's Seward shipment?" Mike asked, offering a show of gruffness for her benefit.

"I g-gave it t-to you," Brandon replied.

Noticing that such a paper had fallen to the floor, she picked up the docket and discovered the missing bill of lading. "Is this the document you're looking for?"

After a quick backward glance, Mike snatched the shipping list out of her hands. "Ah . . . thanks." He sat down again at his desk.

"You're welcome." Sydney caught Brandon's eye and winked. The young man grinned and returned to his paperwork.

"Mr. MacAllister, I would like to discuss our arrangement," she said politely.

"I have paperwork to finish. I don't have time to argue with you." Mike rose and leaned across the desk. "This is the last time I'm telling you, Delaney. You're leaving on the next ship to Seattle."

Tossing a copy of the contract on the middle of his paper-strewn desk, Sydney leaned over it, meeting him eye to eye. After all, she had made an honest attempt at conciliation—but to no avail. And she had borne insufferable rudeness—but no more.

"And I'm telling you, MacAllister, I have no intention of leaving. According to paragraph two of this contract, 'the Party of the First Part'—which is you, MacAllister—'agrees to pay the Party of the Second Part'—who happens to be me—'not less than fifteen dollars weekly for the performance of said services referred to in paragraph one.' Plus," she added smugly, "an additional bonus of one thousand dollars for remaining a full year from the date of arrival."

Sydney poked a slim finger into his chest, driving home every word of her carefully rehearsed speech. "So, I suggest you mark your calendar, MacAllister, because I'm not leaving for the next three hundred and sixty-five days."

For a breathless moment, his dark gaze blazed angrily into the unflinching jade-green eyes. Michael MacAllister finally broke the stare, rising to his full height of over six feet.

"You know I signed that contract believing Sydney Delaney was a man." Mike thundered.

"And you show me where any reference to gender is mentioned," she voiced triumphantly. "If you intended gender to be a consideration, you should have stated so in the contract."

Mike slammed down a clenched fist on the desk. "Damn it! How many women are named Sydney?" he shouted. "You intentionally deceived me into believing you were a male."

"I did no such thing. This is the second time, sir, you have presumed to impugn my integrity. Furthermore, the last thing on this earth I'd ever claim falsely is to be a male," she retorted, contemptuously. "In truth, MacAllister, it is you who misrepresented the facts, not I. I came here in good faith to honor the contract that I signed *in good faith*. I intend to fulfill my obligation. I expect you to do the same."

With an imperious lift of her chin, she added, "Now will you kindly direct me to wherever you wish me to situate myself?"

The woman had the instincts of a black widow spider devouring its mate, Mike thought tersely. She also had the goddamned legal contract she had tricked him into signing. He prided himself too much on his own integrity not to honor anything he agreed to do—signed or not.

"Go *situate* yourself back at the house, Miss Delaney. We'll discuss this further when I get home tonight."

Sydney's head snapped up in surprise. "I beg your pardon? Home? To whose home are you referring?"

"Our home. Mine and Bran's. You slept there last night." When she didn't budge, he sighed in exasperation. "Miss Delaney, I do have work to do."

Reluctantly, she started to walk away, then turned back to him, her green eyes suffused with bewilderment. "Is there a Mrs. MacAllister?"

His eyes flashed with anger. "Is there a what?"

"Is there a Mrs. MacAllister?" Sydney repeated.

Mike glanced up with annoyance. "Begging your pardon, to whom are you referring?" he asked mockingly. "Me or my brother?"

"Mr. MacAllister, I don't care whether the woman in question is your wife, your brother's wife, or your mother. There are three bedrooms in that house. By whom are they occupied?"

"Our mother is dead; Bran . . . and I . . . are bachelors."

Sydney believed she had observed a momentary flicker of pain in his eyes, but he continued to taunt her. "Regarding your next question: I occupy one bedroom, and Bran occupies one bedroom. And you, Miss Delaney, will occupy one bedroom for the next three hundred and sixty-*four* days." He drew a big *X* through the previous day's date on the calendar.

"I should say not. I have no intention of remaining in a house occupied by two bachelors, sir," she declared, outraged.

Capitulation! The very thing he wanted to hear. Smiling with relief, Mike jumped to his feet. "Good. I'm glad you've finally come to your senses, Miss Delaney. And I'm here to tell you, Alaska is no place for a young lady as defenseless as yourself," he added in a condescending tone.

Sydney hated to be patronized. "Mr. MacAllister, I did not say anything about leaving. I only stated that I have no intention of living in your house." Picking up the contract, she dangled it before him. "Paragraph three, MacAllister. 'Lodging will be provided by the employer . . .' "

"I know what the damn contract says," he grumbled, snatching the document from her hand. "I have provided you with lodging, Miss Delaney." He tossed the contract aside.

"In a household of bachelors," she said, snorting.

"Which would not be a problem to a male. You should have thought of that, *Miss Sydney,* when you *mis . . . led* me."

Casting about for a solution, Sydney ignored the double entendre. "Well, surely there is some other house in this town. All I need is a single room."

"There isn't," he declared. Mike put his feet on the

desk and leaned back with his hands tucked behind his head.

"I find that difficult to believe."

Mike gazed at the ceiling, then looked at her with a grin. "Well, there's always Claire's."

"Now we're getting somewhere," she said, relieved to see he was finally cooperating. "Claire's. Is that some sort of a boarding house?"

"Ah . . . I'd have to say most people stay there when they come to town," Mike replied.

Heartened, she smiled. "Well, see, there's no problem, is there?"

"Of course, I should tell you that most of the people who come to Solitary are men." Mike's devastating smile caught Sydney off guard, and she automatically responded with a smile of her own.

"Mike, you aren't really g-gonna take her th-there, are you?" Brandon asked.

Sydney began to smell a polecat in the pantry. Warily she asked, "What's wrong with the place, Brandon?"

He avoided looking at her. "It's a . . . it's a b-br—"

"Brothel," Mike finished, triumphantly.

"A brothel!"

Mike threw back his head and erupted into laughter.

Outraged, she turned to him. "You are despicable, MacAllister."

"It was only a joke. Where's your sense of humor, Delaney? A boarding house!" His whole body shook with laughter.

Walking over to the other desk, he grabbed Brandon by the shoulder. "Bran, can't you just see our little Miss Prim-and-Proper here quoting her lease agreement while trying to hold off a Russian trapper soused up on vodka?"

Howling uproariously, he pounded on the desk. Soon both men were clutching their sides in convulsive laughter.

Forcing herself not to join in their contagious hilarity,

Sydney rode out the teasing until Mike finally came back and sat down.

" 'The empty vessel makes the greatest sound,' " she quoted in an effort to squelch his muffled chuckles. "And, furthermore, I am obliged to remind you, sir, 'He laughs best that laughs last.' I shall retire to my temporary abode to resolve this dilemma."

She turned and haughtily walked out the door.

Sydney decided not to return to the house right away. Too angry to sit and stew, she decided to take advantage of the sunshine and give her legs a much-needed stretch after the long sea voyage.

Opposite the MacAllister house, a two-story building painted a dark, mustard color stood out garishly against the dingy gray of the other structures. The word *Claire's* was painted in black letters on a glass window. Sydney hurried past the building without venturing a further glance.

The town had no sidewalks or paved roads. Most of the dozen or so clapboard houses were grouped together and appeared to be not much larger than a single room. She noticed the remains of the fall vegetable gardens behind many of the houses.

She passed several people on the road and exchanged a nod and friendly smile with them. Occasionally, a dog tied to a stake in a yard ran the length of its line to bark at the stranger.

At a building marked *Ice House,* she saw a man chopping large chunks of ice. Sydney nodded to a woman on the road toting one of the frozen blocks in a sling made of animal hide.

Blacksmith was painted across the front of a dilapidated barn. "Hello," she said to a man sitting on a stool in front of the barn. He was carving out a piece of wood. He nodded, but said nothing. An Indian woman and two children stood near him, the children huddled against the woman's knees, staring at Sydney.

"Hello," she said and smiled warmly, hoping to get

some response other than a nod of the head. The
woman only nodded, but returned a smile.

"My, that's a lovely tunic you're wearing," Sydney
remarked, admiring the woman's long, red and blue
garment painted with intricate patterns of black and
white.

She was astonished when the woman replied, "Thank
you. Hat pretty." The woman pointed to the rust-colored
felt hat perched on top of Sydney's bright hair. Bound
with a puffing of green grosgrain ribbon, the brim of
the simple and inexpensive bonnet was turned down in
front and raised in back.

"Thank you. Thank you very much," Sydney said,
pleased more by the verbal response than the compliment. "How do you do? I'm Sydney Delaney."

"Me, Hettia. And my husband, Rami," the woman
said, nodding at the man carving the wood.

"It's a pleasure meeting you, Hettia," Sydney replied.
"I'm sure we'll meet again." Smiling, Sydney continued her inspection of the small village.

After making a full circle, she discovered Michael
MacAllister had told the truth; there was no rooming
house in Solitary . . . but there was also no general
store, no bakery, no newspaper vendor, no pharmacy.
No doctor's office, no gaslights, no carriages, no omni-
buses, no train tracks. There wasn't even a stone or
brick building in the whole town. She found no sign
that the twentieth century was approaching.

Nearing the MacAllister house again, she set off a
clamorous barking from a dozen malamutes in a kennel
behind the office. As much as she loved animals, Sydney veered away from the agitated dogs and walked
down the road leading to the dock.

She peeked into the opened door of the large ware-
house that dominated the wharf. Seeing her twelve cartons stacked in the corner, she sighed with relief and
moved on.

As Sydney walked out onto a long wharf built on

sapling pilings, a swirling mist sweeping in from the sea curled around her feet. She tightened her mantle around her. Feeling desolate and uncertain, she stood alone, gazing into the blue waters.

From a distance, Mike glanced down at the wharf as he left the office and saw the lone figure standing on the dock. For a long moment his dark gaze remained fixed on Sydney, then he turned away and walked hurriedly toward the stable.

Chapter 4

Still deep in concentration, Sydney returned to the house, and after brewing herself a pot of tea, she slumped down on a bench at the kitchen table.

What should she do? Surely there must be an answer. She had uprooted her life to come here. What was there for her in Seattle? But one year in Solitary would make all the difference.

" 'Help yourself and Heaven will help you,' " she quoted aloud. "And that's exactly what I'm going to do, Brutus," she announced emphatically, forgetting again that the parrot was in the bedroom. Certainly finding an acceptable living arrangement would take some careful thought.

But the very idea! Sydney expounded, jumping to her feet. *Living under the same roof as two bachelors! And none other than that despot Michael MacAllister along with his sweet but certainly misguided brother.*

By the time she finished the second cup of tea, her anger had abated, replaced by calm determination to resolve the situation. One thing was clear; she hadn't come all the way up to Solitary, Alaska, only to be shipped back like damaged cargo.

Sighing, she rose and walked over to the window, peering out morosely. The building next door loomed up in her view.

For a moment, she stared with resentment at the wooden building. The bleak, square structure seemed to be the manifestation of the heartless attitude of the bull-head who owned it.

Suddenly, like a thunderbolt illuminates a stormy sky, Sydney Delaney was struck by a brilliant solution to her dilemma.

She dashed to her bedroom and grabbed her mantle. "I've got it, Brutus. The answer's been right before my eyes all the time."

"Sydney's right. Sydney's right," the parrot assured her.

Forsaking her bonnet, she dashed out the door and hurried down the road. With soaring spirits, Sydney burst through the door of the MacAllister Alaskan Freight Line, but she stopped in her tracks, somewhat disappointed to find that Mike MacAllister's desk was vacant.

"Brandon, where's your brother?" she asked.

Apparently startled by her entrance, Brandon stammered a quick reply. "Mike's g-gone 'til t-tomorrow."

Sydney's eyes glowed with enthusiasm as she surveyed the room, observing the doors she had previously ignored. "What's behind those two doors?"

"Stockr-rooms," he answered.

She rushed over, yanked open one of the doors, and glanced into the room. Then, after inspecting the other room, she dragged a chair across the floor to Brandon's desk, sat down, and peered imploringly into his eyes. "Brandon, I need your help."

He knew he was in trouble.

"This morning as I glanced out the window, it dawned on me that this building is much larger than the one room I had seen."

When he nodded, she continued. "Well, then, it also occurred to me, there had to be a stockroom. Where else would a freight company store freight?

"Now, as Plato once wrote, 'Necessity is the mother of invention.' And, Brandon," she sighed pitifully, "I have an overwhelming necessity at the moment to create a bedroom." Her eyes beseeched him.

"P-Plato?" he asked, trying to forestall the inevitable.

"Couldn't we convert one of those stockrooms?"

"One used to be a bedroom," he admitted reluctantly. "We slept th-there before we built th-the house."

Ecstatic, Sydney jumped to her feet. "Which room?"

Brandon pointed to the nearest door, then followed Sydney when she rushed over to the room. "There's a fireplace b-behind the crates," he said, entering the room behind her.

"A fireplace!" She was exuberant. "Oh, Brandon, that's more than I could hope for."

"Ah ... maybe, we'd better w-wait until M-Mike gets back," he said uneasily.

"If we do, you know as well as I, he'll pooh-pooh the whole idea. He'd say anything to get me out of Solitary. Oh please, Brandon, let's move these cartons out of here before he gets back."

Brandon knew she was right. Mike had made no secret of his wanting her to leave. He liked Sydney Delaney despite Mike's objections to her, but he certainly did not wish to contradict his brother. And yet, he had never before seen such a violent reaction from Mike toward any woman. Grinning, Brandon suspected Sydney Delaney disturbed his big brother in a way Mike would not care to admit.

Brandon MacAllister deeply loved Mike. He would not betray the love and trust of the man who had raised him. But Brandon MacAllister had spent his life being an observer. Maybe the time had come for Mike to put the tragedy of the past behind him, quit looking after his younger brother, and start his own family.

But it would take a very special woman to entice Mike, and Brandon suspected that Sydney Delaney might work on him like magic.

Brandon nodded to Sydney, picking up one of the cartons. "Mike's not going t-to like this."

So the two conspirators, one doubtful and one determined, set to the business of inventing a bedroom.

"Oh no," Sydney groaned a short time later upon hearing the door open. Fearing Mike had returned in time to thwart their efforts, she turned around to do battle.

The man who entered was tall and boney. His face had high, angular cheekbones and a neatly trimmed moustache and beard. A furry, bearskin cap covered his head, and the ends of his green-and-gold-knitted muffler were draped with panache over his shoulder.

The man cocked an eye and regarded Sydney with avid interest. "Aha! So rumor Pasha hear is being true," he said in a thick Russian accent.

Putting down a heavy trunk, the man crossed the room and stopped before Sydney. "Allow me to introduce, please." He clicked his heels together and with a flourishing bow swept the hat off his head, exposing a bald pate fringed by a thin ring of salt-and-pepper hair.

"Count Pasha Eduardovich Vladimir." He reached for her hand and brushed his lips to the back of it. "At your service, madame."

Brandon offered a quick introduction. "This is M-Miss Delaney, Pasha."

"How do you do, Mr. Vladimir?" she responded, flabbergasted by the unusual man.

"Count," he corrected with a significant lift of a thin brow.

"My apologies, Count Vladimir," Sydney hurriedly complied.

"Now, how is possible Pasha may serve you, madame?" he asked gallantly.

Sydney had no idea whether the man was an employee or a customer. She cast a helpless glance at Brandon, and he came to her rescue.

"Pasha often h-helps us o-out. W-where are Miss Delaney's other c-cartons?"

"Pardon, dere is being too numerous many to carry,

at once." He eyed her boldly. "But to serve a damsel so lovely gives Pasha great pleasure in making numerous more trips, Miss Delaney." His ogle seemed more affectionate than lecherous.

"Gentlemen, I foresee . . . that is . . . I hope for . . . a long and companionable relationship between us, so please do forego the formality and just call me Sydney."

"Then, Sydney 'tvill be so, my little *Красотá.*"

She eyed him with a dubious frown. "*Красотá.* Is that good or bad, Count Vladimir?"

"Is most good, my little beauty."

"And if we call y-you Sydney, I'd think y-you could c-call him Pasha, l-like the rest of us." Brandon gave the Russian a good-natured swat to the shoulder.

The Russian's curiosity was piqued as he glanced around at the cluttered office. "Is appearing in disarray. You haf need of Pasha's services?" he asked. "But I should varn you, Pasha is limited to how much he can carry." He cast Sydney a sorrowful glance. " 'Tis being old var vound in my back. Crimea."

"Oh, I'm so sorry." She paused, then turned to Brandon. "Do we dare tell him what we're up to?"

Pasha raised a long, pointed finger in the air. "Aha! Is being tryst in stockroom, perhaps."

"Nothing l-like that." Brandon blushed. "This c-concerns Mike."

Rolling his eyes, Pasha toyed with the end of his moustache. "Plot she is thickening. Vat you up to, my little *Красотá?*"

"It's just that Mike wants me to leave. And I want to remain," Sydney informed him.

His dark eyes widened with interest. "Aha! Vith every moment melodrama is being more intriguing. Please to continue."

"Well, since he claims that I can't find a room in town, I decided this stockroom could be converted into a bedroom for me."

He nodded in agreement. "Is good."

"Well, Mike may not think so."

"Vhy not? Pasha's good friend Michael is most reasonable fellow," the Russian said.

For a moment Sydney wondered if they were talking about the same man. "Michael MacAllister! Reasonable?"

"Is true. *Nyet?*"

The man must be in the throes of a misguided loyalty! she thought. Nevertheless, she pursued the matter. "Will you help then, Count Vladimir?"

Pasha looked from one pair of anxious eyes to the other, and then he raised his hand to his mouth to tug at his moustache. "Vhy not?" Pasha conceded with a shrug.

"Well, I-I'll warn you, Pasha. M-Mike's not g-gonna l-like it."

Pasha threw open his arms in an all-encompassing embrace. "So he is being mad at Bran and Pasha for little time. Pasha vould defy even Mike for such noble cause."

Sydney's heart swelled near to bursting with gratitude. She had never had a true, male friend. Now she had two. "Just like *The Three Musketeers,*" she sighed ecstatically, her girlish romanticism soaring.

"The three musketeers" slipped through her lips in a soft whisper as she followed the two men into the stockroom.

As the day progressed, the two rooms that once contained haphazard piles of crates underwent a miraculous transformation. One room now held neat queues of cartons arranged alphabetically according to item.

The other room had been converted into a warm and cherry bedroom—a fire crackled on the hearth, a colorful, braided rug covered the floor, a patchwork quilt and pillow sham adorned the bed that Brandon and Pasha had carried over from the house. The framed picture of her parents had been placed on the chiffonier that stood against the wall next to a commode holding the ewer and basin. A painted hurricane lamp glowed warmly on a bedside table that had been pirated from Brandon's room.

Perched in his cage, which now rested on an empty crate covered with a tasseled tablecloth, Brutus continued to extol the virtues of his mistress.

While Pasha and Brandon went to claim her remaining cartons from the shipping shed at the dock, Sydney returned to the house and prepared an evening meal for her hungry helpers.

As a final, thoughtful gesture before saying good night, Brandon and Pasha carried over the round, wooden tub used for baths and placed it in front of her bedroom fireplace. Sydney immediately set water kettles on the hearth to boil.

"Are you sure you won't be scared b-being h-here alone?" Brandon asked. He handed her a key. "This locks th-the front door, and we have a padlock f-for the outside besides. B-But I don't think w-we should use it."

"Heavens, no! Don't lock me in. I'd feel as if I were in prison." For a moment Sydney wondered if she would be scared. Having always lived with her parents or in a rooming house, she was unaccustomed to living in a building alone. "Well, no," she said with a brave smile. "Besides, I have Brutus for company."

Pasha patted her hand. "Tomorrow Pasha vill perzonally put bolt on door, little *Красота.*"

"You both have done so much for me already, I don't know how to thank you." Horrified, she felt the rise of tears. "The two of you must leave before I make a blubbering fool of myself." Impetuously, she kissed the cheek of each ally, waved good-bye, and shut the door.

As Sydney waited for her bathwater to heat, she partly filled the tub with water from the rain barrel, then locked the shutters and the front door. With a sigh of contentment, she returned to her bedroom to await the water kettles. Finally, she sank wearily into a tub filled with the last of the lavender-scented bubbles her landlady had given her the previous Christmas.

It had been an exhausting day, she reflected. Tomorrow she would have to face another confrontation with Michael MacAllister, but tonight, at least, she would enjoy the fruits of a hard day's labor.

Soon the soothing effects of the hot water relaxed her aching body. Slumped deep in the water, Sydney dangled her legs over the edge of the tub, closed her eyes, and rested her neck against the rim, allowing her long hair to hang to the floor.

She lazed contentedly with the fire's warmth toasting her toes while the burning log snapped and popped in a hypnotic lullaby which lulled her to sleep.

Minutes later her eyes opened in alarm and within seconds, she identified the sound that had awakened her—the rapid patter of cushioned paws on the wooden floor in the other room.

Her body seemed paralyzed; she couldn't move except for a glance at the bedroom door, only to see she had left it slightly ajar. Mesmerized, she watched the gap inch wider. A pointed black snout poked through the opening, then a large furry head with glowing yellow eyes appeared.

A nudge of its powerful body opened the door fully, and Sydney found herself staring eye to eye with the large, black and white wolflike animal that had boldly padded into the room.

She was too petrified to scream.

"Lady, I've got to hand it to you. You sure know how to raise a man's . . . spirits . . . after a long day."

Even in her terrified state, Sydney recognized that voice. She glanced up to see Mike MacAllister lounging in the doorway.

Recognizing an even greater danger than the animal, Sydney slumped deeper into the water, but dared not shift too much. "What are you doing here?" she asked, thanking God that the bubbles still covered her.

"Logically, I would ask the same question of you, but the answer is obvious."

The smirk on his face made her squirm. "Mr. MacAllister, Brandon told me you were *not* going to return until tomorrow," she said with all the self-righteousness she could marshal.

"Horse threw a shoe, so I had to turn back. Then when I saw there was no padlock on the door, I figured it might be worth checking on the office."

He leaned back against the door frame and crossed his arms across his chest. "Yep. Delaney, I've gotta admit, it sure was worth checking out."

Sydney could see that her embarrassment and discomfort were adding to his pleasure. She tried to maintain her control. "Would you please leave so I can get out of this tub?"

"Why, Miss Delaney, I was just thinking what an excellent opportunity this would be for us to sit down and continue discussing our contract dispute. We haven't even touched on paragraphs four, five, six, and seven."

"Mr. MacAllister, will you please leave?" she muttered through gritted teeth.

"And another thing, Miss Delaney. I apologize for my earlier accusation." His eyes swept her in a long, lingering perusal from the top of her head to the tips of her bare toes. "From what I can observe, there's no way you could ever claim to be a man."

Her eyes flashed in anger, but before she could reply, Brutus began to stir in his covered cage. With cocked ears, the shaggy animal swung its head toward the sound. Its eyes glowed like topaz crystals, and a low growl emanated from its throat.

"Quiet, Grit," Mike ordered.

"Will you kindly remove that wolf and yourself from my bedroom?" Sydney demanded.

"Grit's a dog," Mike answered pleasantly.

To her increasing horror, the dog began to sniff at her bare toes. "What's he doing?" she asked warily. She was not about to trust the enormous beast.

"Oh, no ... don't do that ... oh, please ... make him stop," she cried when the dog began to lick the bottom of her feet. "I'm ticklish," she confessed.

Unable to bear another second, Sydney reacted out of sheer desperation by pulling her legs back into the tub. However, the jostling displaced the water; Mike caught an appealing flash of a round, milky-white breast before she sank lower into the tub.

"Grit usually doesn't take to strangers. You must taste real good, Delaney," Mike added huskily.

"I fear you're perverted, sir," she said in disgust.

He straightened up, and she hoped he would turn to leave. Her eyes rounded with shock when instead, he stepped further into the room, walked over to the bed, and sat down. Aghast, she watched as he picked up a thin cambric nightgown lying on the quilt.

The voyage from Seattle had exhausted Sydney's limited supply of lingerie, necessitating the use of the lightweight gown she wore during the summer. Tiny pink satin bows woven through a lacy ruffle adorned the low décolletage.

"Nice, Delaney." He dangled the flimsy nightgown from his fingertips. "You expecting company?"

"Of course not!" she snapped, suffused in a hot blush. "A gentlemen wouldn't allude to a lady's unmentionables, much less touch them."

His dark eyes gleamed devilishly, and he grinned. "Well, lady, this is Alaska. There aren't any fancy drawing-room rules up here, and it's for damn sure there aren't any gentlemen."

His grin was irresistible. Despite the bizarre circumstances she could not suppress a smile. "Would you be referring to yourself, MacAllister?"

"The worst of the lot, Delaney." His dark eyes deepened with desire. "So I'd run for cover, if I were you."

She blushed under his intense stare, but could not free her gaze from the lure of his dark eyes. "Thank you for the warning. However, considering the position I find myself in right now, modesty prevents me, sir." He flashed her another grin.

She couldn't believe she was actually having this conversation with the outrageous rogue while sitting stark naked in a bubble bath. The whole thing was utterly inappropriate. Yet, she didn't want the moment to pass.

"And you're mistaken, MacAllister. There are gentlemen in Alaska. This very day I had the pleasure of spending many hours with two such men."

"Oh you did, did you? My brother and who else?" he asked, amused.

"Count Vladimir."

Mike chuckled. "Pasha! How'd you ever get Pash to agree to hard labor? Didn't he explain that 'if the Lord vant him to be beast of burden, he vould be being born vith four legs and a tail'?"

This time Sydney broke into laughter. "He didn't say it, but I rather suspected he was thinking it. Is he really a Russian count?"

"Yeah, I guess so. He lost his family during the Crimean War and came to Alaska to work for the Russian-American Company. When Russia pulled out, Pasha stayed here."

The tepid water and her awkward position had caused her leg to cramp. Against her natural inhibitions, she stretched out the leg to ease the pain, draping it once again over the side of the tub.

"We thought you'd be mad," she said softly.

"No. Gotta give credit where credit is due. You outfoxed me, Delaney," Mike said. "Oh, I'll let Bran and Pasha squirm a bit. And they've got some explaining to do. I'd sure like to know what you said to get them to disobey me."

He picked up the nightgown again and stared down at it. "Of course if you were running around in this damned *unmentionable* or with just that bathtub wrapped around you, I'd probably have done the same thing myself." When his glance swung to her, Sydney once again found herself mesmerized by his dark eyes.

"I . . . I think you better leave. Please, Mr. MacAllister?" Sydney asked, regaining as much poise as one could possibly muster under the circumstances.

Mike stood up and moved to leave, but stopped. Sitting in that tub, she looked so damn enticing, trying to maintain her dignity—and *so damn vulnerable*, he reminded himself. Unable to resist the temptation, he reached out and traced a finger across the bottom of her foot. "Ticklish, huh? Hmmm . . . interesting." Then he lightly squeezed her toe.

Sydney gasped as the shock of his warm touch sent an erotic shudder racing up her spine. Her startled glance swung up at him, and for an interminable moment they stared into one another's eyes.

Then he dropped his hand and continued toward the door.

"You won this round, Delaney. Looks like you've got your bedroom. But a word of warning—no more tricks behind my back. And if you hope to survive, shuck the fancy *unmentionables* for a pair of long underwear." He turned and looked back at her. "And don't take a bath or go to sleep without a loaded gun beside you. You never can tell who or what might drop in uninvited."

Still shaken, she answered throatily, "And what if

I'd had a gun tonight? I could very well have shot you."

"I guess that's a chance I'll have to take, Delaney."

Their eyes met again, then he gave a quick, sharp whistle and Grit jumped up to trail after him.

Chapter 5

The ashes had long cooled on the hearth when Sydney awoke the following morning. Her first thought was of Michael MacAllister—who had also been her very last thought before she went to sleep.

As she lay listening to the patter of rain on the roof, she wondered how she would face him after yesterday. Less then two short days ago they were strangers. Yet, last evening when his dark eyes had looked into hers, they had shared an intimacy greater than she had known with any man.

This intense, new awareness of him frightened as much as thrilled her. Whatever had happened in that single moment?

Shaking aside her daydream, Sydney rose and, after lighting the lamp, dressed hurriedly and tended to her morning toilette.

The office was as dark and cold as her bedroom. Opening the shutters, she looked out on the drab sky and steadily falling rain. She built a fire in the wood stove, and by the time she finished bailing last night's bathwater out of the tub, the office had become warm enough to shed the shawl wrapped around her shoulders.

Neither MacAllister had yet appeared, and her growling stomach soon reminded Sydney that she would need breakfast—or at least a cup of tea. She put on her mantle and dashed the few yards over to the house.

Sydney hoped her guess would be correct; Michael

MacAllister did not appear to be the type of man who would lock himself in at night. She smiled when the door opened.

Moving quietly so as not to disturb the sleeping men, she entered the pantry and began collecting the makings for a pot of tea, intending to brew it back at the office.

"Oh, it's you."

Almost dropping the cup in her hand, she spun around in time to see Mike MacAllister stroll into the kitchen, hastily buttoning a pair of denim Levi's.

He looked all rumpled hair and muscle mean. His wildly tousled hair and the several days' growth of beard darkening his jaw accentuated his dark eyes and stark, rugged appearance. Broad, sinewy shoulders sloped down into powerful biceps and a brawny chest. A patch of dark hair narrowed down a lean stomach into the top of the pants.

Sydney gasped aloud. Not even her father had ever appeared before her in such a state of undress.

Yawning, Mike scratched his whiskered chin. "I thought you were Bran. What are you doing up so early, Delaney?"

"I'm just leaving," she said hastily, turning away to gather the supplies.

"Hope you're making coffee." His voice still had a morning rasp.

"No, it's tea," she quickly replied.

"The coffee's up here." Sydney jumped, startled by his voice at her ear. He had moved so swiftly and silently, she had been unaware of his approach.

She turned as he reached for the tin of coffee beans on the shelf above her head, their bodies bare inches apart. She felt the heated, male essence of him fill the narrow gap between them, stifling her breath. Attempting to retreat, she found herself imprisoned by the wall of shelves pressed to her back.

His disturbing nearness so unnerved her, she could

no longer look into his intense, dark eyes. She lowered her head. "Please release me. Mr. MacAllister."

His warm breath ruffled the tendrils of hair at her ear. "I'm not touching you, Miss Delaney." Mike stared into her frightened green eyes; which shimmered like translucent pools. In a provocative reminder of the previous night, the faint fragrance of lavender drifted up to tease his senses. *God! She smells like a summer garden on a rainy day,* he thought with wonder.

He had to do something with his hands or he'd grab her and kiss her. He gripped the shelf above her head with both hands, boxing her in the cordon of his arms.

Sydney knew she should be running for her life, but her feet felt leaden. She couldn't budge. Swallowing to release her breath, she blurted out nervously, "Sir, I wish you would properly clothe yourself."

She instantly regretted her words. Why had she brought up the subject? Mortified, she saw faint traces of a smile edge the corners of his mouth.

"Something about the way I'm dressed bothers you, Miss Delaney?"

She quickly shifted her glance away from his sensuous lips and cleared her throat. "According to *The Victorian Rules of Drawing Room Decorum,* it is unacceptable for a gentleman to appear without a cravat or shirt in the presence of a lady. The exception, of course, being—" She made the mistake of glancing at him and faltered.

"The exception being what, Miss Delaney?" he asked in a husky whisper.

She gulped and continued. "The exception being in the wearing of beach attire or in the pursuit of an athletic endeavor."

"Hmmm ... would bedroom activity come under the 'pursuit of an athletic endeavor,' Miss Delaney?"

The remark rallied her spunk enough to meet him head on. "You take great pleasure in taunting me, don't you, Mr. MacAllister?"

"Taunting you? On the contrary. You're the one doing the taunting. Do you have any idea what the smell of your perfume is doing to me right now, Delaney?"

Shocked, she made the mistake of glancing at him. His dark gaze devoured her. "I . . . I'm not wearing perfume, Mr. MacAllister."

Her limited experiences with men had not prepared her for a moment like this. Her knees were trembling. She felt dizzy. And he was so close all she would have to do is sway the slightest bit and she would be in his arms.

"Must I remind you that I'm a lady, sir. And I expect to be treated as one." The self-righteous declaration sounded ridiculous even to her ears. But in her disturbed condition, she could only fall back on Victorian platitudes.

Mike lowered his arms and stepped back. His sudden release caught her off guard. Puzzled, she saw his expression change and his grin disappear. At last the game was over.

"You still don't get it, do you, Delaney? There's no drawing room dogma up here. The men are as hard as the country. They drink, smoke, swear, spit, belch, f . . . ah . . . all of it—with or without a damn shirt. And Victorian rules can go straight to hell."

Stunned by his unexpected outburst, she started to object, but he would not be interrupted. He continued in a voice rife with sarcasm. "Well, you wanted the job bad enough to deceive me to get it, *Sydney* Delaney, so don't be shocked when the time comes to pay the piper. And if our habits are too crude for you, then you're in for a mighty long year. But frankly, lady, I don't give you more than six months."

As he walked away, he called over his shoulder. "First order of the day, Delaney. Get a pot of coffee going."

* * *

A pot of coffee was perking on the stove when Brandon entered the office carrying a box of mugs, knives, and food stuffs. Mike followed, toting a small table.

"Good m-morning, we've brought b-breakfast," Brandon greeted her.

"And a good morning to you, such as it is," she welcomed, closing the door behind them to shut out the rain. When Mike glanced her way, she looked him straight in the eye, pretending to be unruffled by his earlier assault.

"Just be glad it's not snow," Mike grumbled as he placed the table in the corner.

"Is that my desk?" Sydney asked.

Grabbing one of the mugs out of the carton, Mike poured a cup of coffee. "For now, it's to hold the food until we can put up a shelf." He tried a few sips of the hot liquid. "Next time make it a little stronger."

"Stronger!" she expounded. "That coffee's strong enough to walk."

"Strong enough to walk to Seattle?" He grinned. But she remained silent, refusing to play his game, so he finished the gibe. "Just another fact of life, Delaney—strong coffee puts hair on the chest." Her baleful glare followed him as he walked into the stockroom.

"How do you like your coffee, Brandon?" she asked as he helped her unpack the box.

"Any way that I don't h-have to m-make it," he said with his usual thoughtfulness.

As she sliced the bread, he glanced toward the stockroom and then ventured a comment in a lowered voice. "I hear you had an uninvited v-visitor last n-night."

Nodding, she whispered, "He wasn't too happy. And this morning he was worse. Was he angry with you?"

"Oh, Mike's j-just all bark and no bite," he replied.

Just then, Mike returned and glanced over at the two in the corner to see Brandon's head bent down to hers. He felt a brief moment of envy as Sydney smiled and handed Brandon a slice of bread. They looked relaxed and comfortable with one another. *Goddammit!* he thought to himself. He hadn't felt comfortable from the first moment he walked in and saw the damn redhead sitting in front of the fireplace.

The rain continued throughout the morning. Sydney glanced despondently out of the window, but her spirits brightened when she saw Pasha dashing toward the office. She opened the door for him.

"Good morning." He greeted them with his usual gregariousness.

Sydney smiled warmly. "Good morning, Pasha. Do you think it will ever stop raining?"

"Just be glad is not snow, my little *Красотá*."

"Yes, I've been reminded of that," Sydney remarked.

Pasha shook the dampness off his hat and returned it to his head. "Michael, guess vat? Pasha haf vonderful news. Valuable gem has fallen into Pasha's hands. Is rare diamond ring."

The announcement immediately caught Sydney's attention, if not Mike's. After a dramatic pause, Pasha reached into his pocket and held up a gleaming jewel between his thumb and finger.

"Pasha, it's beautiful," Sydney exclaimed.

His brows knit together sorrowfully. "True, my little *Красотá*. But, sadly, Pasha must part with his most precious possession."

Mike remained indifferent. "Not interested, Pash."

"But, Michael, we haf here a gem vorth ransom of Tsar. Vere Pasha not in desperate straits, he vould not sell such a treasure."

"Don't know any tsars who need ransoming right now, Pash. But if you're in desperate straits, you can earn a few dollars making a shelf. Delaney needs one for that wall over there."

Sydney did not understand how Michael could remain so indifferent. He hadn't even shown interest in finding out any further details about the ring.

"How much are you asking for it, Pasha?"

He casually flicked a wrist. "A mere . . . fifty dollars."

Sydney couldn't believe her ears. Why, the ring would sell for ten times that much in Seattle. "May I see it?" she asked eagerly.

In her haste to take it from him, the ring slipped through her fingers to the floor. Moving back to retrieve it, Pasha accidently stepped on the gem. Crunched glass grated against the wooden floor.

With a culpable smile toward the three sets of eyes fixed on his shoe, Pasha lifted his foot. The "rare diamond" lay in a crumbled pile of granules on the floor.

"Oh, too bad, Pash," Mike intoned drolly. "Sure hate to see a rare treasure like that end up as a pile of gravel."

From his desk in the corner, Brandon chuckled.

Too late Sydney saw the whole truth. Pasha had tried to swindle them, but Mike and Brandon had not believed him for a moment. Only she had fallen for the story.

Gazing affectionately at the outrageous faker, Sydney joined in the laughter.

Undaunted, Pasha next held up a metal bolt. "Did Pasha Eduardovich Vladimir not promise my *Красота* lock for door?"

Mike leaned back in his chair, tucking his hands behind his head. "What's the lock for, Pash?"

"For the door of our little Sydney. Now she can lock herself in for protection."

"I think you should put one on the outside of her door too. Give's the rest of us the same advantage if we can lock her out for *our* protection," Mike intoned wryly. Under her withering glare, Mike grinned and returned to his paperwork.

"Where'd you find a lock in Solitary, P-P-Pasha?" Brandon quickly asked.

Pasha's triumphant smile preceded his words. "From my dear Claire."

"Claire!" Her voice rose with disdain. "Isn't that the . . . you mean the . . ."

Mike's glower silenced her. "Enough said, Delaney. You don't know Claire, so don't judge her."

Bristling from the sudden attack, Sydney returned to the stockroom. Apparently Michael MacAllister would not tolerate any censure of this precious Claire. Despite the woman's profession, he certainly held this prostitute in high regard. Sydney resented his attitude. Mike criticized *her* every move, perpetually reminded *her* she did not belong in Alaska. But he quickly championed the local whore.

"Evidently, a female's acceptance depends upon the services offered," she mumbled, returning to the task of cataloging the inventory.

Despite Pasha's good intentions, he was unable to find the right size nails or screws to attach the lock. Sydney's disappointment was short-lived when Brandon informed her a shipment of hardware was due to arrive on the next boat from London.

When Pasha prepared to depart, Brandon pulled on his jacket. "Wait for me, I'll come with you. I have to feed the dogs."

Still sensitive over Mike's remark, Sydney remained in the stockroom to avoid him. Finally, after completing the task to her full satisfaction, she approached Mike.

"Mr. MacAllister, will you come to the stockroom? I'll explain what I've done." Wisely, she walked away and he followed out of curiosity.

"All the crates have been arranged alphabetically according to item," she pointed out. "I've attached a card to each crate marking the quantity." Her teeth toyed with her lower lip as she put her hand on the first crate.

"I wasn't certain if you preferred this one to be *A* for ammunition, or *B* for bullets."

"The suspense is killing me, Delaney. What did you decide on?" he remarked drolly, trying unsuccessfully not to grin.

"Ammunition." She moved on to the next box. "Whenever you remove any stock, just deduct the quantity from the attached card. I'll check the cards every week to update my records, that way we'll always know exactly what we have on hand of any given item at any given time," she said proudly.

"Miss Delaney, I can tell you off the top of my head exactly how much I have on hand of *any* given item at *any* given time without referring to *any* cards."

Sydney was resolved not to quarrel with him on the issue. She had worked too hard initiating the change to have it so easily dismissed. "No doubt you can, sir. But that's not true for the rest of us."

"And what if I remove the whole carton?"

"Why then, you just rip off the card and give it to me. I'll know I need to reorder the item."

"And will you know whom to reorder it from?" he asked. He shoved his hands in his pockets and glanced around.

"I hope to soon," she said confidently. "I read about this system in a book, and it is supposed to be very efficient."

Mike shrugged his broad shoulders. "So, you read it in a book," he said, nodding. "Well then, Miss Delaney, who am I to argue with success?"

As he was leaving, Mike stopped to investigate several stacks of cartons in the corner. "What's in these crates? They don't look familiar to me."

"Oh, those are mine," she informed him.

"Twelve crates!"

Sydney nodded. "They contain books."

Mike wasn't sure he heard her correctly. "You shipped twelve crates of books up here?"

"They were my father's."

The significance of the simple statement was evident in her voice. "I see." He returned to his desk.

Trailing after him, she said hopefully, "If you're not satisfied with everything in the arrangement, perhaps you'd like to make a recommendation."

"I have one, Delaney. From what I've observed of your new arrangement, I'd recommend the first item you reorder is more cards to keep up with the flux."

Sydney smiled, despite his sarcasm. "Then you approve of the change?"

"It's fine, Delaney."

"Mr. MacAllister, no one has really explained the operation of your business to me. Perhaps you could spare a few moments to answer a few questions," she said.

"Such as?" he asked, glancing up at her.

"Well, what . . . ah, whom do you deal with?"

He leaned back in his chair and stretched out his legs with his feet on the desk. "Mostly trappers. They trade their furs and dried fish for items like traps . . . ammunition . . . tobacco. And of course the usual necessities like flour, coffee, and salt. The Tlingits trade for the same things except for tobacco. They grow their own." He yawned and closed his eyes.

"This isn't what I expected. You're not really a freight company; you're more of a trading company."

"Yeah, I guess you could say that," Mike agreed, closing his eyes again. "The only freighting we do is when we take the goods to the Indian camps and haul back the furs and fish."

"And then do you export the furs and fish?"

His eyes popped open. "You're not going to let me take this nap, are you?"

"Not until you answer all my questions," she replied, with a return of former verve.

With a show of sufferance, he sat up. "We're not in the export business, Delaney. Once a month an agent from the Hudson Bay Company comes and buys the furs. That's where our money comes from."

"And what about the fish?" she asked.

"Alaskan salmon is popular in Europe and Japan. We deal with a British firm in London and a Japanese firm in Tokyo. Most of the household items that we trade come from Whyte and Son in England; spices and threads from the Orient. The food stuffs from San Francisco and Seattle. When you have time, read through some of the old bills of lading and you can get a better idea of what I'm talking about."

He unlocked a desk drawer and pulled out three large, black check registers. "Do you understand anything about banking, Delaney?"

"A little from a business course I once took. I've never had enough cash to consider banking my own."

"Well, since we deal with several foreign countries, we keep a five thousand dollar deposit with the Bank of England in London, First National Bank of Seattle, and the Bankers Trust in San Francisco. How it works is, when we order supplies, the shipper requests a draft, which the bank guarantees, and we sign the draft when the material is received. With small shipments or incidentals, we write out a check right here. We also have an additional five thousand dollar line of credit with each bank that we can draw upon if we have to."

"Line of credit?" she asked, flabbergasted by this unsuspected wealth.

"That means we can get five thousand dollars on credit if we need it," he said.

"It all sounds quite overwhelming," she said. Nothing she had seen thus far in their office or home indicated assets of this amount.

Mike responded immediately to the casual remark. "If you think you can't handle this, Delaney, I'll understand," he said eagerly. "And I'll pay for your passage back to Seattle."

"On the contrary. I'm relieved. I was afraid I wouldn't have enough work to keep me busy."

"Oh," he said, disheartened. "Well, if you have any questions, just ask Bran. He's got more patience than I have."

Later that day, she turned down Brandon's invitation to join him and Mike for dinner at Claire's. She would starve before frequenting a brothel, even to partake of a meal.

"It's the only p-place in town t-that offers a hot m-meal," Brandon said apologetically in response to her raised brow.

After they departed, she continued reading the bills of lading she had been studying. Before she finished, Brandon returned carrying a tray.

"Claire sent over th-this ven-venison so you would h-have a hot meal," he said, handing her a plate containing meat and boiled potatoes. The tantalizing aroma of the hot food made her aware she hadn't eaten since morning.

Sydney considered that gracelessness betrayed a lack of cultivation, so she graciously accepted the woman's offering, despite her own personal disapproval of the woman's profession. "Please thank her for me, Brandon. Assure . . . ah . . . Miss Claire her thoughtfulness is most appreciated."

After Brandon left, Sydney showed the plate to Brutus. "What thinkest thou, my pet? I've never tasted venison before. Dare I partake of the madam's offering?"

Curiosity about the mysterious woman continued to plague Sydney throughout her meal as she ravenously devoured the food. "Mmmm . . . that venison was ever so tasty, Brutus."

"Sydney's right. Sydney's right," came the immediate response.

"Is that so? How would you know?" she teased lightly.

She washed the plate, locked the door and shutters, and after covering the cage, Sydney retired to begin re-reading her much-worn copy of *The Three Musketeers*.

For the third night in a row, Sydney's thoughts drifted to the image of a pair of dark eyes and broad shoulders before she finally fell asleep.

Near daybreak the following morning, Sydney awoke to the sound of tapping on her bedroom door.

"Miss Delaney, it's Mike MacAllister. May I come in?"

Sitting up in bed, Sydney pulled the quilt up to her chin. "All right, you can come in now."

The sight of Sydney's red hair hanging loosely around her shoulders once again took his breath away. For an instant, he stared, speechless.

"What is it? Is something wrong, Mike?" Mystified by the expression on his face, Sydney didn't notice that she used his first name.

"Bran and I are leaving to deliver some supplies to a Tlingit camp. We'll be gone for two days."

"Yes, I know." She sighed, relieved to hear there was no emergency. "Is there something particular you want done in your absence?" she asked, perplexed by his visit.

"I've written out some items on a sheet of paper. You can make out the orders for them."

"I will, Mike." When he didn't move, she asked, "Is there something else?"

Yes, there was something else, he thought. Something that prevented him from moving—from drawing himself away from the sight of her sitting in that bed.

He started to leave, then turned back, groping for whatever excuse he could think of to stay. "The last time I went away for a day, you turned the stockroom into your bedroom. Hate to think what I'll find when I get back."

"You mean you woke me up at four o'clock in the morning just to say that?" she lamented.

"Well . . . ah . . . I don't want to come back and find lacy curtains at the office windows, Delaney."

"Mr. MacAllister, do you have any other specific instructions?" she asked and then added with a grin, "Or are you, perchance, having difficulty saying good-bye?"

She had touched a sore nerve, and he reacted. "Try getting on that ship back to Seattle, Delaney, and you'll soon see how easily I can say good-bye." He slammed the door on his way out.

Sydney jumped out of bed, pulled on her green flannel robe and raced after him.

"Mike, wait," she cried out, just as he was about to blow out the lamp in the office. Scowling, he put down the lantern and turned to face her.

"Mike, you and Bran take care of yourselves."

Her hair streamed down past her shoulders. She looked so damned small, so vulnerable.

He had never wanted to kiss a woman so badly in his life.

"You, too, Delaney. Stay close to home here and if you need anything, just ask Pasha . . . or Claire. I know how you feel about her, but she's a good friend."

"I will, Mike."

Still he couldn't compel himself to leave—not without the assurance that he would find her here when he returned. In the past few days she had touched an emotion within him that he had believed to be long buried. He knew it must remain buried. That he must convince her to leave Alaska.

But how could he convince her—when he struggled to convince himself?

"Yeah. See ya, Delaney." He hurried out and climbed up on the seat of the wagon. Brandon flicked the reins and, with Grit trotting along beside, the wagon began to roll.

Mike looked back and saw her framed in the doorway. In the dim glow of the lantern, the long hair hanging past her shoulders gleamed a rich auburn.

He forced himself to turn away.

Chapter 6

Sydney simply couldn't go back to sleep. Finally, she gave up trying and decided to get dressed and attack the orders on Mike's desk. She was so absorbed in the task, she ignored the rain that had begun to fall shortly after the men's departure. Half the morning passed before she finished, confident that she now fully understood this particular facet of the business.

Deciding to take advantage of the men's absence to do her laundry, Sydney hurried next door to the house and rooted through the pantry, but the only laundry item the search produced was a yellow bar of naphtha soap.

Preparing to leave, she glanced at the loft, the only place she hadn't checked. When she climbed up to it, her search ended. She found a wooden washing tray, and, to her further delight, a wringer machine with India-rubber rollers and a clothes line. One by one, she hauled each item down the steep ladder and toted them back to the office. She set two heavy kettles on the hearth to boil.

The wooden washing tray consisted of a knee-high stool with a large, attached, square tub. Always having had to do her laundry in a pail, this device was a luxury to her.

Clamping the wringer machine to the side of the tub, Sydney exclaimed with delight, "Gee, Brutus, I had to wring out my clothes by hand in Seattle." Reading the words *Bradford & Co., Manchester, England,* inscribed on the wringer, she glanced in his direction. "I guess there are some benefits in working for a company that does importing."

When the water finally heated to her satisfaction, she poured both kettlefuls into the tub, added the soap and some cool water, then submerged her undergarments. Sydney allowed her mind to drift to thoughts of Michael MacAllister.

Recalling the breathless excitement of those few disturbing moments with him in the pantry, Sydney felt the rise of goose bumps along her arms.

Yet this morning when he left, Mike had appeared to be concerned ... even protective. She found that side of his nature equally provocative.

In truth, she decided, she had never known a man as unpredictable ... or magnetic as Michael MacAllister; he was a puzzle as much as a fascination.

"Well, Brutus, we both know that my experience with men has been limited," she conceded as she sloshed the clothes several times up and down in the water.

"But don't think I'm so naive that I would allow myself to wade into water over my head," she told the parrot.

Shaking her head, she declared confidently, "Oh no, Brutus. Sydney Elizabeth Delaney is much to wise for that. Certainly much wiser than that Alaskan chameleon, Michael MacAllister, who chooses to draw upon his raw sexuality and a dark-eyed stare." Slapping one of the garments against the washboard, she began to scrub furiously.

Then remembering an aphorism of a famous English author, Sydney sighed sadly, " '... but he that thinks himself the wisest, is generally the greatest fool.' "

The seeds of confidence she had planted earlier sifted away like sand through a sieve.

After pressing the wet clothing through the wringer, she carefully strung them on a line in the corner of her bedroom. Picking up the birdcage, she carried it into the office. "There's no reason why you should stay in there alone, Brutus. Come in this room and chat with me."

She had just finished emptying the tub when the door opened and Pasha entered. A wide grin split his face. "So my little *Красотá* is now running freight office," he exclaimed, shaking the moisture off his hat.

"At least, trying to learn *how* to run a freight office," she said.

"Pasha come on such gloomy day to make big smile on face of his *Красотá.*"

"I appreciate your thoughtfulness, Pasha. And I'll be glad to smile when this rain ends so I can get out and become acquainted with the people in the town."

"Pasha hear same from others also being curious to meet *Красотá.*"

His expressive eyes gleamed with excitement. "But little Sydney vill soon meet town people. Saturday is beginning celebration of Founder's Day."

"Founder's Day? Are you saying that a town the size of Solitary actually has a Founder's Day celebration?"

"But of course, little von. People vill come from entire distance around for giving honor to illustrious founder, Hermit Solitary."

Sydney broke into delightful giggles. "Oh, Pasha, can't you ever be serious?"

"But Pasha speak truth, *Красотá,*" he declared with self-righteousness.

She eyed him with skepticism. "You mean there is actually someone named Solitary? I thought . . . I thought . . ." Her giggles resumed. "I thought the town was called Solitary because . . . well because it's . . . so solitary."

"But of course is Solitary. And glorious celebration vill be to your pleasure. Pasha Eduardovich Vladimir is never being vrong about such matters."

"Well, since I'm new to the town, I will look forward to meeting Mr. Hermit Solitary."

"Pasha regret such meeting impossible, *Красота*. So happens, illustrious founder is being no longer among us."

"Oh, he's passed on," she said with a tinge of regret.

Pasha nodded. "But only straight vay to another town." His eyes bulged with innocence. "Hermit vent and founded new town vut he named in honor of his brilliant son, Obscurity."

"Oh, Pasha, you are incorrigible. But I like you," she declared.

Pasha patted her hand. "And Pasha like his little *Красота.*"

At the prospect of the forthcoming celebration, she watched with buoyed spirits as Pasha put up the shelf Mike had ordered.

After he departed, Sydney realized she was hungry. Remembering the well-stocked pantry next door, she made another trip to the house and took the wringer with her.

Climbing back up to the loft to return it, she was about to descend the ladder when she stopped to look around. She saw that the only other items up there were a trunk, a tarnished brass bed covered with a white sheet, and a rolled-up braided rug. Yielding to curiosity, she knelt before the trunk.

As she touched the chest, Sydney suddenly became overwhelmed with a feeling of melancholy. Like the erring Pandora, she raised the lid.

On the very top of the contents, she discovered a framed picture of an aged couple. Beneath it, she found a photograph of three laughing people. Mike was clearly one of them. He had his arm wrapped around the shoulder of a second man who bore a close resemblance to him. The third person in the photograph appeared to be Brandon as a youngster.

She put the picture aside and carefully removed several pieces of boy's clothing that she speculated had once been worn by Brandon.

Her curiosity increased as she next encountered two neatly folded dresses, several petticoats, and a few pieces of feminine undergarments.

From the bottom of the trunk, she cautiously lifted out a soft lace veil and white satin gown trimmed with tulle and lace. Once again, Sydney sensed the shadow of misfortune. A photograph tucked away in the folds of the gown fell to the floor.

She picked up the picture and examined it closely. It was of a bridal couple. Small in stature, the bride was a beautiful young girl with dark hair. She wasn't more than sixteen or seventeen years old, and the glowing blush of love and youth shone through the faded photograph.

Sydney shifted her gaze to the groom. She gasped aloud as she stared in shock at the face of Michael MacAllister.

So he is married—or had been, she reflected, recalling his comment that he was a bachelor.

She felt overcome by guilt—she had no right to pry into his life. Quickly replacing the items in the trunk, Sydney slammed down the lid and gazed intently at the closed chest.

Shamefaced, she felt an overpowering sensation of sorrow for having trespassed on these cherished, tucked-away testimonies of his past. And she sensed that whatever story lay within their folds was one of tragedy.

Sydney continued to gaze numbly at the wooden chest, with no awareness of the tears sliding down her cheeks.

The next morning Sydney felt edgy and short-tempered from her pent-up emotions of the previous day. Seeking an outlet to vent her energy, she climbed back up into the loft and carried down the rug. A vigorous beating of it helped to release some of her tension. As she laid it in front of the fireplace, she wondered how long Mike would allow it to remain there.

A short while later, alerted by Grit's barking, she rushed to the window and watched the men climb down from the wagon. Then, with tired steps, they trudged slowly through the mud toward the office, tracking a muddy trail across the floor as they entered. Sydney crossed her arms over her chest and glared at them.

Brandon took one look at her and gathering up the wet outer clothing he had shed, he called hastily, "I'm l-leaving to take a b-bath," and departed.

Mike was not so easily intimidated. As he sat down to remove his shoes, Sydney's glare remained fixed on him.

"You got a problem, Delaney?" he asked, dropping a muddy boot to the floor.

She wanted to scream, but wisely chose restraint. "Why, no. But couldn't you have removed your boots outside the office?"

"Probably could have." The other boot hit the floor.

"Sydney's right. Sydney's right," Brutus chirped from the corner.

Mike groaned. "What's that bird doing in here, Delaney?"

"Staying warm."

"Ever think of shipping the damn parrot to South America? Plenty warm down there." He pulled off a wet stocking.

"The thought has never entered my mind." She returned to the table that she had converted to a desk.

Mike eyed the cage. "Well, it has mine."

"Sydney's right," Brutus continued to pipe, between pecks at his blue and green plumage.

Mike felt ornery, wet, and tired as hell. "Can't that damned bird say anything else? Sounds to me like you're pretty desperate to get someone to agree with you, Delaney."

"I'm sorry you feel that way, sir." Sydney smiled

smugly. "But if I had thought it was necessary, I would have taught him something more. Right, Brutus?"

"Sydney's right. Sydney's right."

Mike removed his other stocking and threw it at the cage. Brutus immediately hushed his squawking. Smiling with satisfaction, Mike walked over to pick up the wet stocking and for the first time noticed the clean floor.

"Mr. MacAllister, if you intend to divest yourself of any more of your clothing, it shall be my pleasure to retire to my room."

Returning to his desk, Mike leaned back in his favorite position with his hands laced behind the back of his head, his long legs stretched out, and his bare feet propped on the desk. "I appreciate the compliment, Delaney, and I'd expect it would be *my* pleasure to retire to your bedroom too."

"Mr. MacAllister, you are becoming offensive. If I were a man, you wouldn't speak to me in such a manner," she said calmly, trying to hold her temper.

"I won't argue with you on that," he answered sarcastically. He quickly surveyed the neat office. Although pleased with what she had done, he was not about to praise her efforts. "By the way, Delaney, MacAllister Freight does not pay for cleaning services."

She shrugged her shoulders.

Yawning, he closed his eyes. "Was there any important mail?"

"Mail!" she said, puzzled. "From whom? The third house up the street?"

Disgruntled, he opened his eyes. "The mail boat, Delaney. This is Wednesday. The mail boat docks on Wednesdays. Didn't you check it out?"

Sydney was genuinely contrite. She prided herself on her competence. "You didn't say anything about mail. I had no idea it came today."

"You could have asked somebody."

Sydney found that statement unjust. "Whom would I

ask? It has rained practically nonstop since your departure."

Annoyed by her logic, he sat up and reached for his stockings.

Sydney guessed his intention. "I'll go and get the mail, Mr. MacAllister."

"You can't go. The street's a swamp." Mike had not exaggerated. Three days of steady rain had turned the streets into a quagmire.

But Sydney refused to be deterred. "If I were a man, you wouldn't hesitate to send me to get it."

"You're damn right," he grumbled.

Undaunted, she thrust up her chin. "Then it's my duty to go and get the mail."

She saw the irony of the situation. Her former employer had deliberately sent her on errands in foul weather because she was a female, while her new employer refused to do so for the same reason. Well, she was determined to prove herself. Sydney grabbed her shawl and slipped it around her shoulders.

"You're going out dressed like that?"

Ignoring him, she strode gamely out the door.

Bounding from his chair, Mike hurried to the door. "Dammit, Delaney, get back in here." He hadn't meant to goad the stubborn little fool into going out into the mess. When Sydney ignored him, he cursed to himself and snatched up his boots, pulling them on over his bare feet.

The dock was straight down from the office about a block and a half away with only a couple of ramshackle buildings in between.

Overflowing water troughs in front of the scattered buildings forced her to walk down the center of the road. She managed to cover half of the distance to the dock; but the nearer she approached the softer the ground grew underfoot. Clods of mud clung to her shoes and the bottom of her gown was splattered.

Dismayed, she surveyed the remaining distance. The

worst was still to come. Grimy puddles of rain lay in the ruts and potholes that crisscrossed the long stretch of muddy road. Cautiously, Sydney put a foot forward.

She gritted her teeth to keep from squealing as mud oozed over her shoe top. When she took her next step, misfortune befell her. She happened on an unseen hole, and her foot was sucked into the mucky grime.

Losing her balance, Sydney went down on one knee. When she reached out to keep from falling forward, her hands and arms sank into mud up to her elbows.

She wallowed helplessly, trying to regain her balance. Finally managing to get on her feet, she shook her arms and hands in a futile effort to release the clinging mud.

Her shawl slipped off her shoulders, and in turning to retrieve it, she found her foot firmly stuck in the mud. The muck had seeped into the hole and entombed her foot. She wanted to scream.

Maintaining a fragile balance, she wobbled drunkenly until the imprisoned foot slipped free. But her shoe remained wedged in the mud.

Sydney groped in the sludge. Her hand finally found the shoe and she tugged to free it. The effort succeeded in firmly planting her other foot in the muck and once again she could not move.

By this time she was thoroughly disheveled and caked with mud. Suddenly, she felt the touch of a hand, and she looked up hopefully.

Grime dotted her cheeks. The errant strands of hair that had slipped from their knot were stuck in patches to the mud on her face and neck.

Mike grasped her shoulders and smiled at her tenderly.

It was the worst thing he could have done. The fight drained from her.

"Oh, Mike, look at me," she lamented, pathetically.

He was.

Standing ankle deep in the middle of the muddy

road, drenched to the skin and rain dribbling down her face, Michael MacAllister was taking a long look at Sydney Delaney.

And he thought the stubborn, adorable little fool was beautiful.

"It's only mud, Syd," he said gently.

He picked up her fallen shawl and tenderly draped it over her head and shoulders. Then he swung her up into his arms.

Only inches separated their lips, the breath of her shocked gasp a honeyed caress on his cheek. For an interminable moment, their gazes met and exchanged that now-familiar message—wordless, but saying so much.

She slipped her arm around his shoulder.

"Need any help, Mike?" a man called out from nearby.

Mike wrenched his gaze from Sydney to respond to the well-intentioned villager. "No thanks, Rami, we're okay." He carried her back to the office.

Neither one said a word until he put her down in the middle of the office floor.

"Thank you," she murmured, unable to look at him. Holding one shoe, she stood before him, hanging her head like a wayward child. "I should have listened to you."

"I should have stopped you from going."

She raised her eyes and glanced up sheepishly. Mike shook his head. "Delaney, you're a mess."

"You don't look much better, MacAllister."

A faint smile tugged at the corners of her mouth. His lips parted in a trace of a grin. Then they both broke into laughter.

"You'll have to use the public bath to get rid of all the mud on you," Mike advised when their laughter subsided.

"A public bath!" She was aghast at just the thought of sharing a bath with others.

"Delaney, for a dollar you can get a towel, soap, hot water, and the tub's double the size of ours."

"I've never used a public bath before." Leery at the thought, she asked, "Do you . . . are you . . . alone?"

"Of course. There's complete privacy. I'm going over to take one, too. Come on, it's my treat."

Mike saw the indecision on her face. "Miss Delaney, the men and women have separate bathrooms. Do what you want. I'm leaving now."

She thought for a moment, then relented. "Wait. Just give me time to get some clean clothes." Kicking off her other shoe, Sydney quickly found a change of clothing and followed him.

As they entered the door marked by a battered old sign bearing the words Public Bath, the young girl who sat behind the counter glanced up casually. At the sight of Mike, she put aside the book she had been reading. "Hi, Mike."

He grinned broadly. "Hi, Em."

Her young face puckered in a frown. "Oh, Uncle Mike, I told you to call me Emily. I'm getting too old to be called Em anymore."

"Honey, keep scowling like you are, and that pretty face of yours will turn into a prune."

As they talked, Sydney glanced at the book and saw that Emily was reading a copy of *Wuthering Heights*.

"Emily, this is Miss Delaney, my new office assistant."

"Hi. I heard you had come to town."

"It's a pleasure meeting you, Emily." Seeing the curiosity in the blue eyes of the young girl, Sydney added, "I apologize for my appearance. I got stuck in the mud."

"You can be glad it wasn't snow," Emily advised.

Sydney looked at Mike. His expression fell only slightly short of the look of the cat after it swallowed the canary.

Sydney picked up Emily's book. "Are you enjoying your novel?"

"Oh, yes. It's my favorite. This is the third time I've read it."

"It's one of my favorites too." Sydney flipped through the book. The inscription on the inside cover caught her attention. "To Em. Merry Christmas. Love, Mike." Curious, she glanced at Mike. Had he given it to Emily? Did he have the sensitivity to choose a book? Mike MacAllister was an enigma.

Emily's blonde head of curls bobbed appealingly. "Of course, I only learned how to read last year. I'm still not too good at it."

"I'd say you're very good if you've read *Wuthering Heights* three times."

Emily beamed ecstatically. "Do you really think so?" she asked with pride.

"I certainly do," Sydney said kindly. "And if you're interested, I've brought some other books with me. You're welcome to borrow any you'd like."

"Do you have any more by Emily Brontë? So far, she's my favorite author."

"I'm afraid not, dear. *Wuthering Heights* is the only book she wrote." Seeing the girl's sudden disappointment, Sydney quickly added, "But maybe you'd like to read one of her sister's books."

"You ladies can talk books all night, but I want to take a bath," Mike announced. "How about a towel, Emily?"

"Oh, certainly, Mike." Emily got towels and soap for each of them. "The ladies' tub is available, too, Miss Delaney."

"Please call me Sydney."

"Just go right through there," Emily said, pointing to a nearby door. "There's hot water ready. I'll be right in to help you."

The small room had a wood-burning stove positioned

at the foot of a large square tub. In a corner was a sink containing a pump. A long rope hung above the tub.

Sydney tested the water already in the tub and found it to be cold. She felt rather annoyed. She hadn't come here to take a cold bath; *that* she could do in her own room. She was about to leave when Emily entered the room and began to drain water into the tub from a tank behind the stove.

"What is that?" Sydney asked, walking over to investigate the contraption. "I've never seen one before."

"It's just a water back," Emily said. "The tank sets behind the firebox and that's how the water gets heated."

Within minutes the tub was half-filled with hot water. "Mama says we're going to get one of those fancy water heaters that fill and empty the tub automatically," Emily informed her as Sydney helped the girl pump the water to refill the water tank.

Upon finishing the task, Emily added several more pieces of wood to the firebox. "Can't let the fire go out," she said lightly, brushing off her hands.

Emily appeared to linger. "Well, if you need anything else, just pull that cord." She pointed to a long rope hanging over the head of the tub.

"Thank you, Emily. I shall."

As soon as Emily closed the door Sydney shed her muddy clothes and climbed gratefully into the tub. Leaning back, she relaxed, admitting to herself that Mike had been right; using the public bath was a much better idea than hauling pail after pail of water, only to haul it all back out again. Certainly a luxury she could ill-afford, Sydney thought, but for the moment, she would simply enjoy Mike's benevolence.

A light tap sounded on the door. "Sydney, may I come in?"

Apparently taking a bath was one of the most dangerous ventures a person could undertake, Sydney reflected, since no one in Alaska appeared to recognize the concept of modesty. "Yes, Emily, come in," she said.

The young woman entered carrying a small bottle. "I brought you my bottle of soap bubbles if you want to pour some into the tub."

"Well, that's very thoughtful, Emily. I'd love to."

After adding the liquid to the water, Emily once again appeared to linger. "I'll be glad to help you wash your hair, if you'd like," she offered eagerly.

"Thank you, Emily, but I think I can manage to do it myself."

"Oh . . . all right." Obviously disappointed, she slowly started to edge toward the door.

Sydney didn't have the heart to let her go. "Why don't you stay and talk while I bathe?" Emily responded with a wide smile and sat down.

After working the soap into a lather, Sydney covered her face with suds. "Have you always lived in Solitary?" she asked from under her soapy mask.

"Mama says we used to live in San Francisco and didn't come here 'til I was two." Sighing wistfully, Emily added, "So I don't remember living anywhere but Solitary."

"Do your parents own this bathhouse?" Sydney asked.

"Just Mama. I never knew my father. Mama said he left us when I was just a baby."

Sydney paused from rinsing the soapsuds off her face to glance at Emily. Remembering the many cherished hours she had spent with her father, Sydney's heart ached for the young girl.

"How old are you?"

"I'll be seventeen come next June. And when I'm eighteen, if I'm not married, I'm leaving this lonely place."

Sydney's eyes brightened. "Oh, do you have a swain?" she asked, smiling gaily.

"Well, I just might have one in mind," Emily said with a toss of her blonde curls.

The response brought a troubling question to Sydney. "Emily, do you have to attend the men in their baths, too?"

Laughing, Emily raised a hand and covered her mouth. "Heaven's no! Mama would never allow that. She won't let me go near the men's bath when it's being used."

Good for Mama, Sydney silently exclaimed. Recognizing her opportunity to learn more about the town, she pursued her curiosity. "How many families are there in Solitary, Emily?"

"Only about twenty. Mostly all Indians."

"Well, Count Vladimir is Russian," Sydney remarked, soaping her slim leg.

Emily issued a delightful giggle. "Oh, Uncle Pasha."

"Is Pasha actually your uncle?"

"No, I just call him that, like I do with Uncle Mike. They aren't really my uncles."

"And Brandon MacAllister? Do you call Brandon 'Uncle,' too?"

Emily blushed. "Oh, no. Not Brandon." Emily stood up. "Well, I better get back to my work."

As she started to walk away, she turned back and asked shyly, "Sydney, would you mind if I come over and talk to you sometime?"

"I wish you would, Emily."

The two girls exchanged an understanding smile, each aware of a newly discovered and long awaited girlfriend.

After Emily departed, Sydney washed her hair, finished her bath, and gathered her soiled clothing. She would have to soak them all night to get them clean.

When she left the bathroom she saw no sign of Mike, but Emily was back behind the counter absorbed in her novel.

"Good night, Emily."

Emily looked up and smiled. "I'll see you tomorrow."

As Sydney carefully picked her steps back to the office, she smiled, thinking of the three friendships she had formed in the short time she had been here. She still did not know what to make of her relationship with Mike MacAllister, but Sydney decided that coming to Solitary may not have been unwise, after all.

She arrived back at the office and discovered Mike and Brandon had attacked the soup she had prepared earlier for her meal.

"Good soup, Delaney," Mike said, finishing off the last of the liquid. "We should have hired you as cook."

She was so pleased to receive praise from him finally—even a left-handed compliment—that she did not raise a fuss over the loss of her intended supper.

Later, as she tucked her parrot in for the night, Sydney said thoughtfully, "You know, it feels good to have other friends here in Solitary besides my books."

With a flap of his wings, the bird cocked his head and squawked noisily. Whereupon, she hastened to soothe his ruffled feathers. "Oh dear . . . fear not, noble Brutus, thou are my fairest friend of all."

Sydney drifted off to sleep with his words of confirmation echoing in her mind.

Chapter 7

The two days of sunshine that followed gave the town of Solitary a chance to prepare for the celebration honoring its founder.

Much to Sydney's amazement, the deserted streets came alive: children ran and played, dogs romped and barked, and cheerful adults went energetically about their business.

Red, white, and blue bunting had been hung from every one of the buildings in Solitary, with the exception of the privies. American and Russian flags now fluttered from rooftops and the rostrum that Rami had erected in the center of the town.

The transformation of the town seemed astonishing to Sydney, but the tent city that had begun to emerge was even more amazing. Every day, new faces descended on Solitary. Bearded and buckskin-clad trappers rode in with bundles of furs strapped to their horses. Wrapped in colorful blankets and leggings, Tlingit Indians converged on the town, toting a profusion of homemade artifacts. Americans and Europeans had even journeyed from Seward, a hundred miles west, to enjoy the sights and sounds of this final celebration before the winter set in with the boredom of short days and long, cold nights. By Friday evening, over three dozen canvas and skin-covered tents had been squeezed together on the outskirts of the town.

For two days the MacAllister Alaskan Freight Line worked tirelessly to handle the flux of business from the new arrivals. While Mike and Brandon bought furs in exchange for currency, Sydney and Pasha handled the needs of those who wished to stock up on supplies. Near midnight on Friday evening, Sydney fell exhausted into bed.

With the expectation of a young girl preparing for her first date, she arose bright and early Saturday morning and dressed in her only fancy gown, a day dress of purple silk with a double-breasted bodice trimmed in white lace. She brushed out her hair and tied it back with a white ribbon, then, grabbing a shawl, Sydney hurried to the rostrum where Obscurity Solitary was delivering a speech.

From the time of Solitary's founding, Hermit Solitary had always sent his son to officiate in his stead. Since neither father nor son was ever observed in the company of a woman, Obscurity's mother remained a mystery.

However, all agreed that Obscurity Solitary not only resembled his father in image, stature, and mien but—to everyone's distress—Obscurity smelled like his father; the fundamental reason why Hermit's reclusiveness was not a cause for sorrow.

Mike and Brandon moved to Sydney's side as she listened to Obscurity recite Hermit Solitary's life history. "I can't imagine anyone would name a son Hermit," she remarked.

"Yeah, about as strange as naming a daughter Sydney," Mike retorted. She glanced at him in time to catch his wink at Brandon.

"I've heard s-said that his real name is H-Herman," Brandon commented.

Mike nodded. "That's right. People began calling him Hermit because he always wanted to be alone. And the name's stuck."

"Well, you can carry the desire for seclusion to extremes," Sydney chided. "As the English author John Donne said, 'No man is an island.' "

"Seems I recall once reading something about the great wisdom of keeping out of other people's way," Mike remarked.

She met his cynical glance. "I assume you're referring to Haliburton's 'The great secret of life is never to be in the way of others.' I should remind you that just about everything he wrote was humorous or satirical."

Shrugging his broad shoulders, Mike grinned. "His advice still makes good sense to me, Delaney," he said as he walked away.

Sydney watched the tall figure move among the crowd, stopping to chat or laugh. Michael MacAllister was the most exasperating man she had ever known—and the most provocative.

"Hi, Sydney."

She turned to see the smiling face of Emily Montrell. "Good morning. Isn't this exciting?" Sydney glanced casually at the woman standing next to Emily.

Emily's blue eyes glowed with warmth. "Hi, Brandon."

Blushing, he cleared his throat. "Hi, Em."

Expecting Emily to challenge Brandon's use of her girlhood nickname as she had done to Mike, Sydney was surprised when the name slipped past uncontested. She noticed an uneasiness between Brandon and Emily that certainly had not been present between Mike and the girl. Did Brandon dislike Emily? Sydney couldn't imagine Brandon disliking anyone.

Then suddenly a more logical explanation entered her mind that might explain the reason for the tension—Brandon MacAllister was in love with Emily.

Surprised, but rather pleased by this theory, Sydney realized her thoughts must be plainly written on her face. She glanced at the woman at Emily's side. Their eyes met briefly, and although they were strangers, the two women exchanged a knowing glance.

Sydney was quite curious about the woman. Attractive and trim, with an air of dignity and refinement, she wore a brown-plaid, taffeta gown with a modest trim of ecru lace at the neck and wrists. Her head of honey-colored hair had been swept up into a mass of curls and tucked under a beaverskin bonnet adorned with a pheasant feather.

Aware that the woman seemed to be regarding her with the same interest, Sydney took the initiative. "How do you do? I'm Sydney Delaney."

Sydney found the woman's smile gracious and serene, making an already attractive face beautiful. "Kind of thought as much. I'm Claire Montrell, Emily's mother. Been lookin' forward to meetin' you since I heard you came to town."

Stunned and appalled, Sydney's eyes grew round as she stared at the woman in disbelief. This was Claire! Emily's mother was the madam of the town's brothel? Had Claire Montrell just claimed to be Cleopatra, Catherine the Great, or Queen Victoria, Sydney's shock would not have been greater.

"Hi, Bran," Claire said when Sydney continued to stare speechlessly. "Where's Mike?"

"G-guess I'll go and tr-try to find him."

"Wait, Brandon, I'll come with you." Emily turned back to her mother and Sydney. "I'll be right back," she said and hurried after him.

"Looks like that leaves just me and you, Miz Delaney." Claire shifted uncomfortably as Sydney continued to stare at her. "Guess I'll get movin'. It's been a real pleasure finally meetin' you."

Sydney suddenly awakened to her own rudeness. Whatever Claire's profession, the woman had been kind to her. The gesture of sending over a hot meal had been friendly and thoughtful. She could learn a few lessons in gentility from this woman.

As Claire started to walk away, Sydney called out, "Mrs. Montrell, please wait."

Claire turned around, no longer smiling. "It's Miz

Montrell, but everybody around here just calls me Claire."

"I apologize for my rudeness, Claire. And I wish to thank you for your thoughtfulness last week. I enjoyed the meal very much."

Claire nodded. "You're welcome, Miz Delaney. Seemed like the neighborly thing to do."

"I wish you'd call me Sydney."

The corner of Claire's mouth turned up in a smile. "If you don't mind, I'd like to call you Delaney, same as Mike does. Got used to hearin' him say it, and I kind of fancy the sound of it."

Sydney laughed lightly. "Don't tell him, but I do, too. Of course he only calls me that when he's angry with me." She raised a delicate brow. "Which is about ninety percent of the time."

Both women burst into laughter. "Oh, I'd guess you keep that big fellow in a fevered pitch most all of the time."

Surprised, Sydney's eyes gleamed with interest. "Oh, really?" She linked her arm through Claire's, and the two women began to walk together. "Why, what has he said?"

"You'll never hear it from me, Delaney." Claire laughed, patting Sydney's arm.

The two women were soon joined by Emily in the company of Mike and Brandon. They all strolled together among the tents, examining the many items on display. Pouches trimmed with feathers, furry parkas, painted spruce-root hats, jewelry made from the teeth and tusks of animals, and intricately carved totems were just a few of the eye-catching objects laid out on blankets to be sold or traded.

Despite an ancient migration and centuries of interbreeding between the tribes, the black hair and physical features of these Indians still resembled their Mongoloid ancestors who had once crossed the land bridge from Siberia.

"What do you think?" Claire asked hopefully, holding up a pair of earrings carved from walrus tusks.

Sydney nodded in approval. "They're lovely."

Claire bought earrings for herself and Emily. When she decided to pick out some for Lily and Sal, Sydney moved ahead, continuing her exploration. Emily and Brandon stayed behind to examine a painted rattle, and Mike followed Sydney.

After much deliberation, she narrowed her selection to a choice between a pair of embroidered, deerskin mittens and an impractical, but eye-catching purse of woven grass.

Finally, unable to contain his impatience, Mike blurted, "I don't know what the problem is, Delaney. You'll get more use out of the mittens."

"Thank you for helping me to make up my mind," she said peevishly. With that she put aside the mittens and bought the purse.

"I should have guessed you'd do that. You're one obstinate female, Delaney."

"Obstinate enough not to allow you to spoil this day for me, MacAllister," she retorted with a smile.

As they moved on, Mike continued to point out several more garments she should be buying for the winter. Sydney ignored him. It quickly turned into a game between them, and soon they were laughing together.

She glanced up, surprised when she felt the unexpected touch of his hand on her shoulder. "Take a look at that." Chuckling, he pointed to a nearby booth manned by Pasha.

Groaning, she smiled up at Mike. "Oh no! What's he selling now? I hope no more rare diamond rings." They joined the crowd listening to Pasha's sales pitch.

With his usual flair for the dramatic, Pasha held up a pint-sized bottle. "Vhat Pasha haf here, ladies and gentlemen, is being greatest hair restorer known to man."

"Hair restorer!" Sydney exclaimed in dismay. She

looked at the heads of hair surrounding her: heads of thick black hair, whiskered faces and chins, furry hats and vests. Hair seemed as plentiful as grains of sand on a seashore. Certainly, hair restorer was the last thing these people needed.

"Pasha expects to sell hair restorer to these people?" she whispered to Mike.

Mike, trying to keep from laughing out loud, managed a philosophical comment. "That's our Pasha, Delaney." Spying the rest of their missing party, he put a protective arm around her and pushed through the crowd.

"Mike, what are we goin' to do with him?" Claire wailed when they reached her side.

"Where did P-Pasha get hair t-tonic?" Brandon asked.

Claire's blue eyes glowed with amusement. "Hell, you're not goin' to believe this, but he distilled some corn mash and then dumped in half a bottle of Lily's toilet water, hopin' to make it smell pretty. Lily was near to killin' him." Claire patted Sydney's hand. "Lily's one of my girls, honey."

When her colorful description sent them all into laughter, Claire raised a hand to silence them. "You ain't heard the half of it," she continued. "Then the crazy fool decided the brew needed somethin' to give it a fizz, so he dumped in all the baking soda he could find. Well, I don't have to tell ya how well that set with Joseph."

"Who's Joseph?" Sydney whispered aside to Emily.

"Our cook. He's a Tlingit."

" 'Joseph,' doesn't sound very Indian to me."

"A missionary passing through a few years back converted him."

"Oh, I see."

Claire continued with her story. "Well, when he finally escaped Joseph, Pasha poured the concoction into every empty whiskey bottle he could find," she concluded.

Throughout Claire's discourse, Pasha continued an unsuccessful pitch to sell his hair restorer. "*Nyet, nyet,* my friends, do not be going avay so fast. I, Count Pasha Eduardovich Vladimir, vill svear personally to potency of rare concoction."

"Don't you mean 'No-A-Count Pasha,' " one of the jeering trappers in the crowd yelled out. Familiar with Pasha's schemes, he tossed an empty bottle at the booth.

As Pasha ducked to avoid being hit, his hat fell from his head, exposing a bare pate encircled with a thin fringe of hair.

In the shining evidence of the "naked" truth, even the trusting Indians began to laugh and then moved on.

"What are you up to now, Pasha? Nothing that'll get you shot, is it?" Claire asked worriedly, as she approached.

Pasha winked, and his face widened in a sly grin. "Fret not your tender heart, my loving Claire."

Considering that to be good advice, Mike took Claire and Sydney by the arm and led them off. Claire cast a troubled backward glance. "What do you think he'll try next, Mike?"

"Honey, Pasha will never change. You can't keep worrying about him," Mike said gently.

"I can't stop worryin', Mike." Claire managed a weak smile. "I better be gettin' back to my business. I've been gone most of the mornin'."

"Maybe I should go back to the office, too, Mike," Sydney said after Claire's departure.

"The office is closed for the day. Claire's business . . . well . . . this is a busy time for them."

They began to stroll slowly along side by side. "I didn't realize Claire's business included the public bath, too," Sydney remarked at the sight of a long line formed outside the door of the bathhouse.

"She offers it more as a favor to the town." He grinned. "The only time the bathhouse pays for itself is a weekend like this when all the trappers come in for their yearly bath."

"You think highly of Claire, don't you?"

"Next to Bran, she's the best friend I have." This unequivocal declaration startled her.

As if reading her thoughts, Mike's face hardened. "Delaney, the business Claire offers is as necessary to most men as food or water." He paused to stare down at her. "You're a paradox, you know."

Sydney couldn't help wondering if he realized the same was true about himself.

"You can forgive Pasha for conning a man out of his money," Mike said, "but you condemn Claire and her girls for giving a man his money's worth."

"I'm not condemning them, Mike. I like Claire."

"Does that mean you don't look down your nose at her anymore?"

"Just because I like her doesn't mean I condone prostitution."

"Well, even you, Delaney, must know that man has certain needs only a woman can fill."

"Oh, you mean such as being his wife and mother of his children," she said, pretending to misunderstand him.

"You're such a Victorian prude, Delaney. Men don't live by bread alone, you know."

Furrowing her brow, she tapped her chin with a finger. "You know, MacAllister, I bet there's a quote somewhere in there."

As if dismissing the conversation, Mike unexpectedly reached out to tighten the bow in her hair. "Your ribbon's starting to slip."

The move caught her by surprise, and she held her breath until he had finished and dropped his hands. After a breathless hush, she found her voice. "I should have pinned up my hair. It would have been less trouble."

For a lingering moment their gazes locked. Mike finally looked away. "I like it the way it is."

Chapter 8

Later in the day, looking back on that tense moment, Sydney wondered what more might have been said if she and Mike hadn't been joined by Emily and Brandon.

Her mind continued to dwell on the matter throughout the dog trials as she watched Mike put Grit through the obedience commands. On a single word command or whistle from its owner, each competing dog was scored on its speed and absolute obedience, the essential elements for the leader of a dogsled team. Grit won handily over his competition.

"Good dog, Grit," Sydney cooed as she reached out to pet him.

"Don't pet him," Mike ordered. The sharp command made Sydney snatch her hand away, her eyes wide with alarm. "What's wrong?"

"I don't allow anyone to pet him."

"Why not?" she asked confused, remembering her first encounter with Grit. She had seen nothing mean about the animal.

"I have my reasons." Mike gave a short, sharp whistle as he walked away. The dog followed him.

Sydney felt mortified. Mike had dismissed her as if she were an errant child. Had she only imagined that he had a tender side?

When she looked up, Emily and Brandon were watching her sympathetically. She forced a trembling smile to her lips.

"Grit's M-Mike's l-lead dog. It's i-important n-not to p-pamper him," Brandon said, trying to explain Mike's attitude.

"I'm sure Mike didn't mean to sound so nasty, Sydney. But you see, there's so many things that can go wrong. Sometimes in a bad storm, or maybe if there's a crevice or soft ice covered by snow, Mike's life . . . and Brandon's . . . depend on Grit's instinct and his instant response. The other dogs will follow whatever the lead dog does," Emily added.

"Well, I'm certain Michael MacAllister could never be accused of pampering his dog . . . or his office assistant," Sydney said.

She put her hands on her hips and grinned at the pair. "You two can just erase those long faces because I made up my mind that nothing Mr. Michael MacAllister says or does is going to spoil this day for me." With a plucky lift of her chin, she said, "So let's enjoy ourselves."

Arm in arm Sydney and Emily continued to view the sights while Brandon trailed behind them, a silent protector. Eventually, their wandering led them back to Pasha's booth.

They found him hard at work trying to persuade the small crowd assembled before him to buy a bottle of a life-sustaining elixir.

"This rare formula, passed on from mother to firstborn son, is being in Pasha's family for centuries." His expressive brow arched perceptively. "And is tasting so go-o-o-d." He raised the bottle to his lips and took a deep draught of the liquid.

"Is he drinking what I think he is?" Sydney asked, aghast.

"One drink, my friends . . . one drink of vondrous tonic and you too vill feel so good—just like Pasha."

Brandon nodded. "Yeah. And I think he's h-had one drink t-too many already."

Pasha took another deep swallow. "This bottle vill

offer one and all the secret of immortality." With glazed eyes, he leaned groggily across the counter. "Unless, maybe, you are being gobbled up by bear." Throwing up his hands helplessly, he added, "Then Pasha cannot promise."

"I figure one or two more swigs from that pint and it'll be all over," Mike announced, coming up behind them. "Ole Pash can down a bottle of vodka, but he never could hold his whiskey."

"Ain't that the hair tonic you was sellin' this mornin'?" a voice called out from the crowd.

"Vould Pasha drink hair restorer?" he asked, opening his arms in innocence. To prove his sincerity, Pasha took another deep swig of the liquid.

His head lolled from side to side as his words became a measured slur. "One drink . . . one drink . . . and you . . . too . . . vill . . . feel . . . so . . . good . . . like—" He fell forward and slumped across the counter, his long arms dangling over the front.

Sydney clutched a hand to her heart. "Oh, dear God, he's poisoned himself."

"He's passed out, Delaney," Mike drawled.

Stepping forward, Mike began to wave the crowd away. "Okay, folks, that's all for now."

"Let him sleep it off, Mike," a man called out good-naturedly. Laughing, the crowd dispersed.

Pasha opened his eyes as Mike hoisted the Russian over his shoulder. Seeing Sydney's worried frown, Pasha's face split in a wide, congenial grin. "Ah, little *Красотá.*"

Then he emitted a loud burp and passed out once again.

As soon as the sun set, a huge campfire and dozens of lanterns strung from the trees cast the town of Solitary in a golden glow. Despite a prohibition law, which the United States government made no attempt to enforce, whiskey and vodka, and even Pasha's life-

sustaining elixir, materialized from among the celebrants.

A revived Pasha began to strum a balalaika, another
man a fiddle. Soon a concertina and a harmonica
emerged, altogether forming an improvised orchestra.

Sydney couldn't remember when she had enjoyed
herself so much. Throughout the night, she and Emily
were passed from one set of arms to another as the trappers waltzed, shuffled, glided, bounced, skipped, and
sashayed to the music. As she whirled around the floor,
she caught an occasional glance of Mike lounging
against a building, but he made no move to join the
dancers.

The tempo increased. Crossing his arms across his
chest, a young Russian cossack squatted down and proceeded to hop along on alternating feet, kicking out his
legs before him in an amazing exhibition of agility and
balance.

Swept up in the drama of the moment, Pasha cast
aside his balalaika and rushed out to participate. The
two men were quickly joined by two others and with
linked arms the chorus line continued the dance in a
procession, spurred on by the rhythmic claps and ap-
proving hoots of the spectators.

As the evening progressed, the celebrants grew more
boisterous. Sydney sat down next to Claire to take a
much-needed rest. The two women were enjoying
themselves watching Brandon and Emily dancing a
lively polka when a hulking figure walked over to them
and stopped before Sydney.

"You vant dance?" The big man was bearded and
looked to Sydney like he had the girth of a bear.

She glanced up with a smile. "I'm sorry, but I'd just
like to rest for the time being."

"Boris vant dance," the man said belligerently. Grabbing her arm, he pulled her to her feet.

"Please let go of me," Sydney insisted.

Suddenly, Mike seemed to appear from out of nowhere. "The lady said she doesn't want to dance, friend."

Boris had no intention of relinquishing her. "Ve dance." He again tugged at Sydney's arm.

"Mister, take your hands off her." The obdurate command stopped the Russian in his tracks. He released Sydney's arm and turned, his bushy brow knotted in a frown. "Dis your voman?"

"No, and she's not yours either. So keep your goddamn hands off her," Mike declared.

Claire had stood up and reached out a hand to Sydney. "Come over by me, honey." Sydney took her hand, and the two women stepped away.

"Boris think he no like you, Yankee." The Russian curled his hands into fists. "Boris think he teach you good lesson."

"Any time you feel lucky, friend," Mike replied contemptuously.

The scene was attracting a large crowd. Boris swung at Mike, but he easily ducked beneath the blow and delivered a punch to the Russian's jaw. The Russian staggered backwards, then reached into his boot and pulled out a knife.

A murmur swept through the crowd at the sight of the weapon; the fistfight had become a deadly game. Brandon stepped forward to come to his brother's aid.

"Stay out of this, Bran," Mike ordered as he drew a knife from the scabbard at his waist. Crouching, the two men began to circle one another.

Suddenly a man hurried up to the scene. "Boris," he snapped. He stepped between the two men. "We no vant trouble, Yankee," he said to Mike. "Ve go." The Russian turned to Boris. "Ve no vant trouble. You hear vat Lev say?" he said in warning.

The two men traded an angry exchange in Russian, then Boris shook off Lev's hand. With a malevolent glare at Mike, Boris returned the knife to his boot and walked away, shoving aside the people in his path.

The crisis over, the crowd dispersed and returned to their revelry. Shocked by the savagery of the incident, Sydney knew she could not return to her earlier mood. She suddenly felt chilled and tightened her shawl around her shoulders. Mike appeared to have suffered no ill effects from the incident, while she couldn't stop herself from trembling.

She bade a quick good night to the others. "I've had enough celebration for one night."

"I'll walk you back, Delaney," Mike said. Still shaken, she nodded.

Both were silent as they returned to the office. Mike unlocked the door, stepped back and looked at her intently. "Are you okay? You look as pale as a ghost."

"Mike, you might have been killed." A note of desperation had slipped into her voice.

"Hey, relax, Delaney. Everything's fine." He pulled her into his arms. Closing her eyes, she surrendered to the comfort of his arms.

Still trembling, she suddenly felt acutely aware of him—glorying in his nearness, his scent, the power of his arms. She wanted to remain there forever.

"You're trembling, Syd," he said softly.

She stepped out of his arms. "The whole incident has shaken me." Drawing her shawl protectively around her, she leaned back against the solid wall of the building.

In the distance, the sounds of the revelers mellowed to a muted undertone when, exhausted, they sat down to rest. An ex-Confederate soldier softly began to play the haunting melody of a familiar song on a harmonica.

Smiling, Sydney turned her head toward the sound of the music. "Beautiful isn't it? Yet so poignant. The song tells the story of a man saddened by having to leave the woman he loved, a young Indian girl named Shenandoah. I always feel so melancholy when I hear it."

"Homesick, Syd?" he asked with a soft grin.

"No, not really. A beautiful song . . . or poem, will often have that effect on me."

Sighing contentedly, Sydney glanced up at the sky. "These northern lights," she said with reverence. "They're almost too gorgeous to believe."

Mike looked up. Overhead, the sky glowed with a swirling cloud of green, blue, and red. Streaking across the sky, a spiraling bolt of white collided with the spectacular haze and trickled down toward earth in a luminous streamer.

Mike shifted his eyes back to her face when she said, "The aurora borealis. How aptly named. In Roman mythology Aurora was the beautiful goddess of dawn."

Usually her pedantry irritated him, but tonight he took pleasure in listening to the seductive throatiness in her voice. "You remind me of the northern lights, Syd."

Her glance swung to him. Surprised by the unexpected flattery, she accepted his words as the compliment he intended.

"I was disappointed that you never asked me to dance tonight."

"I enjoyed watching you." His voice was a husky caress.

"Was that your only reason?"

"No." She felt her quickened heartbeat when he moved nearer. "Afraid, I guess."

She stood mesmerized as he reached out and toyed with a few strands of her hair. Her breathing became labored as his nearness seemed to rob her of breath. "Afraid of what, Mike?"

"You know, your hair is as soft as silk."

"Afraid of what, Mike?" she repeated.

He shifted his dark gaze to her face. "Afraid that if I ever took you in my arms, I'd never let you go."

Her startled green eyes stared at him. His gaze was steady, unwavering. Just then the nostalgic strains of Stephen Foster's "Jeanie with the Light Brown Hair" carried to the ears of the two people standing in the hushed silence of their emotions.

Wordlessly, he opened his arms and she stepped into them. He pulled her against him and they began to move slowly to the rhythm of the music.

She had never danced like this before. She closed her eyes and basked in sensation. A tantalizing awareness of his masculine nearness. The warmth of his hand holding hers. The feel of his touch at her waist. And the stimulating rhythm of his heartbeat against her ear.

The provocative slide of his hand up her back jolted her back to the present. She stopped dancing and stepped out of his arms. "This is improper," she said, agitated. "We were dancing much too close."

"Would never be a consideration in *The Victorian Rules of Drawing Room Decorum,* right, Delaney?" he mocked.

"Definitely not."

"Well, maybe it's for the best. Good night, Delaney."

"Good night, Mike." She opened the door, and he waited until she closed and locked it, then he walked away.

Sydney's heart fluttered with excitement as thoughts of Mike continued to taunt her. "This has been the most thrilling day of my life, Brutus," she said, undressing for bed.

The parrot had already gone to sleep and didn't blink an eye as she slipped the cover over his cage.

The revelry continued through the night, but undisturbed, Sydney slept on, a smile of contentment gracing her lips.

Chapter 9

By Monday afternoon, the last of the trappers and Indians had left town and business had returned to normal, not only in Solitary, but at the office of the MacAllister Alaskan Freight Line.

Mike had gone to the dock to check in a shipment, Brandon was working at his desk ordering supplies, and Sydney continued to set up a new filing system.

She was happy to put aside the monotonous task when Emily came through the door with a cheerful "Hi."

After a hasty response, Brandon returned to his work and the two girls went into the stockroom to find Emily another novel from Sydney's hoard of boxes.

Following the young girl's departure, Sydney resumed her filing, aware of Brandon's silence. After several hesitant glances in his direction, she decided to act on her suspicion.

"Emily's as nice as she's pretty, don't you think, Brandon?" He nodded, but did not look up. "Don't you like Emily, Brandon?"

His face reddened and his body shifted in agitation. "Of c-c-course, I l-like h-her." His stutter had noticeably intensified.

"Have you ever told her so?" Sydney asked slyly. He quickly shook his head. "Well, why not?"

Suddenly, Brandon flared up in an uncharacteristic display of temper. "Y-y-you k-know w-w-why, s-s-same as I-I-I d-do."

98

Surprised by his strong reaction, she calmly pursued her line of questioning. "I don't think I do, Brandon. Why don't you tell me?"

Brandon threw aside his pencil and lifted his head. She felt a rush of guilt, knowing that her persistence was bringing him pain.

"No g-g-girl c-c-cares a-a-about—" His severe stuttering forced him to break off his sentence.

"Just slow down, Brandon, and take your time," she said gently.

"Y-you k-know what I m-mean." He swallowed, and Sydney could feel his embarrassment as he struggled with manly pride. She tried to put him at ease.

"Do you think because you stutter a girl wouldn't be interested in you?"

When he nodded, she declared emphatically, "Brandon MacAllister, I'm beginning to believe you're as big a fool as your brother. Why, you're one of the nicest men I've ever met. And if I think so, I'm sure other women do too. Especially Emily," she added reassuringly for his benefit.

"You r-really th-think so?"

"Of course. A woman can always tell when another woman has more than a little interest in a particular man. It's really quite obvious."

She dragged her chair over to his desk and leaned toward him. "Let's get down to serious business here, Brandon. How long have you known Emily?"

"Thirteen y-years."

"Well, have you ever ... ah ... kissed her?" He shook his head.

"Hmmm ..." She reflected. "How old are you, Brandon?"

"Twenty-two."

"You're twenty-two, and you've never tried to kiss her? Why not?"

He looked tortured, and Sydney felt tempted to drop

the subject. But she had made him come this far. "I d-don't k-know."

"Do you want to kiss her?" Sydney asked.

His shy grin tore at her heartstrings. "A-All the t-time."

She proceeded slowly. "Well, seems to me . . . if a certain girl likes a certain fella . . . and he feels the same . . . and they've known each other a long time— why, kissing her would be the most natural thing in the whole world."

"I've never . . . ah . . . k-kissed a girl b-before," Brandon said, red with mortification.

"You mean you don't know how?" she asked. He nodded. "But, Brandon . . . you live with a man who . . . I'm sure . . . fancies himself an expert. Why don't you discuss the matter with him?"

"I've n-never told a-anyone but y-you, S-Sydney."

"Hmmm . . ." she repeated. Drumming her fingers on the desk, she pondered the situation for a few moments. Yes, Brandon's quandary definitely called for some drastic action.

She stood up and grabbed his hand, pulling him to his feet. "Well, I haven't had a great deal of experience, but I've certainly read about it often enough." She put his hand on her waist. "Now according to Shakespeare, the kiss has to be hard 'as if he pluck'd up kisses by the roots, That grew upon my lips,' " she quoted with a giggle. She pressed her lips to his.

"Don't you think this has gone far enough?"

Startled by the voice from behind, they both spun around to see Mike standing in the doorway. Brandon dropped his hands and stepped back while Sydney felt as if he had caught them with their hands in the cookie jar. Both began to stutter an explanation.

"It's n-not h-how it looks, M-Mike."

"I-I . . . was just . . . trying to show Brandon how to—how to . . ." She couldn't get the words past the knot in her throat.

"I heard," he said with disgust.

Transfixed, she watched him walk toward her. Forgetting Brandon's problem, she stared into the brown depths of Mike's eyes and knew she was facing a crisis of her own.

"But you're going about it all wrong, Delaney."

He slid his arm around her waist and drew her against him. "Body contact first, Delaney," he murmured in a husky whisper.

His hands glided up to the middle of her back, pressing her even tighter against the hard, muscled length of him. The effect made her light-headed—an exquisite dizziness. His touch, his scent, the strength of his arms, the feel of his body, the husky rasp of his voice all swirled together in her.

He dipped his head, his mouth hovering only inches above hers. "Then, Delaney, when you're just about ready to burst with anticipation—*then* you kiss."

His mouth closed over hers; gentle but firm. She parted her lips in acceptance and from the first second, he proved to be the master, she the novice. And what had begun tenderly, soon deepened. His mouth guided and coached, drawing her response, and passion surged through her as she molded to his body.

When his mouth freed hers, she remained in his arms, breathless and drained of resistance. With an effort she raised her long lashes, her emerald eyes sensuous and shimmering with desire.

Stunned, he stared at her, his own dark eyes suffused with passion. He had not anticipated the intensity of her response. After last night, her fright at being in his arms, he had expected the prim and proper, little scared rabbit to be stiff and cold. Only Bran's presence kept him from reclaiming her mouth—from once again drawing the response that had left him as shaken as she.

Reluctantly, his arms released her. "Now *that*, Delaney, is how to kiss. And you don't learn it from any book." The remark, which he had intended to be flippant, throbbed with huskiness.

Suddenly, Sydney regained her equilibrium. With that came outrage. "How dare you! You, sir, are a lecher and hypocrite with the social amenities of an uncouth barbarian. More to be pitied than condemned. Last night, you dared to challenge a man for an offense far less than the one you just inflicted on me."

She left him without waiting for his reply and sought the sanctuary of her room.

For the first time in his twenty-two years, Brandon MacAllister regarded his brother with disgust. He spoke angrily, unaware his hands balled into fists. "Don't . . . ever . . . do . . . that . . . to her . . . again." He uttered each word slowly and distinctly.

Mike laughed nervously, taken aback by Brandon's fury. "Hey, Bran, I was only—" But before Mike could finish the sentence, Brandon sailed past him out of the office, slamming the door.

"Dammit!" Mike cursed, annoyed with himself. He had only meant for the stupid kiss to be a joke. To teach her a lesson. He had been angry when he had seen her in Bran's arms, willingly offering her lips to him. But how had the damned kiss spun out of control? Swearing, he kicked the chair, sending it crashing against the wall. Then he followed Brandon out the door.

Inside her room, Sydney had heard the argument between Mike and Brandon. She felt responsible. Whatever her quarrel with Mike, she would not allow it to drive a wedge between the two brothers. She must put the incident out of her mind for everyone's sake.

But how could she pretend the kiss never happened when it was the most exciting sensation she had ever known? And knowing this, how could she face Mike every day feeling the way she did? What if he kissed her again? Would she resist? Would she even wish to resist?

In the short time she had been in Solitary she and Mike had shared some tender moments—moments that had caused her to lower her guard. But in his determination to convince her to leave, he would humiliate her as he just had done.

Perhaps she should leave Solitary before he could hurt her any further. For the time being, she could control the confusing emotions she felt for Mike MacAllister—but how long would it be before those same emotions controlled her?

Sydney peeked into the mirror and saw her flushed countenance. Was it from anger or the excitement of the kiss? She was too confused to know. Pouring some water from the ewer into a basin, she wet a cloth and applied it to the back of her neck.

She leaned into the mirror and studied her image intently. Well, nothing had ever come easily in her life. " 'He is the most wretched of men who has never felt adversity,' " she quoted. "Humph," she snorted in contempt, returning to her desk. "Sure would like a chance to find that out for myself, Mr. Shakespeare. And I can't believe that anyone could feel more *wretched* than I do right now."

During the next hour, Sydney spent more time looking out the window for the brothers to return than she did at the files. The sooner they were able to put the matter behind them, the sooner she could get on with the task of playing Cupid. She was determined not to let the scene with Mike discourage her from trying to bring Emily and Brandon together.

"In truth, what has happened here, Brutus? Mike kissed me, that's what. Hah! 'Much ado about nothing,' " she scoffed. Brutus cocked his yellow comb, dropped an eyelid, and regarded her through a single, black eye.

Sydney discovered where Mike and Brandon had disappeared to when Pasha entered the office later that day.

"Boat come from England today so Michael and Brandon are being in varehouse checking shipment. Michael give Pasha bolts to be putting on door of *Красота.*"

"I just need one bolt, Pasha," she said.

He shook his head. "Michael tell Pasha to be putting bolt on inside of front door, too. He vant little *Красота* to be safe ven he is being avay. Michael say Alaska no place for voman being alone."

"Yes, I do believe I've heard Mike say that on more than one occasion." Apparently Michael MacAllister failed to recognize that *he* was the threat, she reflected.

After Pasha departed, Sydney watched from the window and saw Mike and Brandon leave the dock. Laughing, Mike poked Brandon in the arm, and the two brothers continued up the road to Claire's. Relieved to see that they were on speaking terms and apparently heading to eat at Claire's, Sydney decided to hurry over to the house and fix herself a meal.

When she entered, her glance swung to the floor. The rug had not been removed. Sydney thought of how much the house had become familiar to her in the short time she had been in Solitary. But she thought it still could use many more feminine touches.

She clamped the meat chopper to the sink stand and was preparing to grind up a potato and onion when Mike entered the house.

For a long moment he watched her busy activities in the kitchen. He liked watching her move about—in the office, the kitchen—and he wondered what it would be like to see her moving about in his bedroom. Naked—with that glorious mane of red hair hanging past her shoulders.

Good God, he was becoming the lecher she accused him of being.

Frowning, he shoved the image out of his mind. That kind of fantasy had been popping up all too frequently in his thoughts. More reason why she must go back to Seattle, he told himself.

He tossed aside his jacket and walked into the kitchen. "Hi."

"Hello." She didn't turn around and continued peeling an onion.

"Syd, I'm sorry about this afternoon. I . . ." He cleared his throat. "I apologize."

Her back stiffened, but her head remained turned away from him. "I don't understand you, Mike. Sometimes it seems like you're two different people. You can be so nice one moment, and the next . . ."

She shoved the onion into the meat chopper. "Here, let me do that," he said and began to turn the handle. "What are you making?"

"I thought I'd make hash."

"There's some moose meat in the window box."

"Moose meat!" She hesitated. "I've never tasted moose meat before." She shrugged her shoulders. "Oh, well." She got the meat and shoved it into the chopper. "That's it, Mike. Thank you."

After mixing the ingredients, she scraped them into a cast iron skillet on the stove. "Would you like to join me?"

"Thought you'd never ask, lady." He unclamped the food chopper and sat down on a bench at the table.

"What about Brandon?" she asked.

"He's having dinner at Claire's."

The hash began to sizzle in the skillet, and she stirred and turned it over. "Go wash your hands and then we can eat."

"Wash my hands? Delaney, I haven't washed my hands for a meal in thirteen years."

She arched her brows. "Then they must be pretty dirty by now."

Groaning, Mike shoved back the bench and trotted off to his room. By the time he returned, the hash had fried, and they sat down at a table that had been brightly set with stoneware plates and cups.

"Who bakes your bread, Mike?" Sydney asked, popping a bite into her mouth.

"Joseph," he mumbled with a mouthful of hash.

"And where do your vegetables come from?"

"Joseph's vegetable garden in the summer," he mouthed again.

"And your milk and butter?" She raised a hand. "No, wait. Let me guess. Joseph has a cow." He grinned and nodded.

"By the way, thank you for seeing to the locks on both doors."

"Well, after the incident last night with our friend Boris, I thought an extra measure of protection wouldn't hurt, Delaney. Just use it when Bran and I are both gone," he cautioned. "Otherwise, we'll be locked out when you're sleeping."

Moved by the considerate gesture, Sydney glanced up at him. Her warm smile conveyed her appreciation. "Thank you, Mike. Does this mean you've fully accepted the idea of my remaining?"

"No, Delaney. It just means that until I can convince you to leave, I feel responsible for your safety."

"Oh, I see." She could not conceal her disappointment.

"I don't think you do, Syd. Please try to understand, there's nothing personal in my feelings. Alaska is just no place for a woman. I don't want to see you harmed."

"You're not going to change my mind, Mike. I'm staying whether you like it or not." No matter what, they always ended up in the same old argument. She got up from the table and picked up her plate to carry it to the sink. In her haste, she carelessly brushed the stove with her hand. "Ouch," she drew back in pain.

Mike was on his feet and at her side at once. "Let me look at it."

"It's nothing," she snapped.

"Let me see it, Delaney." He reached for her hand.

Sydney's agitation mounted as his dark head bent over her and he gently cupped her hand in his palm to examine the injury. He began to spread a dab of lard on the burn.

"I said it was nothing. Just leave me alone," she cried out, snatching away her arm.

"Dammit, Syd." He grabbed her, swinging her back to face him. Startled, they stared at one another for a breathless second, then his mouth came down on hers. His lips were firm and moist, the bruising pressure of his mouth relayed a hunger that ignited the same craving in her. Sensation replaced any capacity for reasoning as his hot tongue forced her lips apart and probed the hollow of her mouth. In a mindless, instinctive response, she arched against him, feeling the heat of his body through the layers of clothing that separated them.

They broke apart, and she opened her eyes to meet his intense glare. She raised a hand to her bruised lips. Dazed and confused, she stared at him. "Why, Mike?"

"I guess whether I intend to or not, Syd, somehow I always end up hurting you." For a long moment, their gazes remained locked.

"You've been warned, Delaney," he said.

Chapter 10

With Mike gone for the rest of the week, Sydney passed her days by staying busy, but her nights were spent thinking of him. When she did sleep, her dreams were haunted by him, and she'd wake up trembling.

She polished a lovely copper bowl, filled it with pinecones, and placed it on a crocheted doily that she donated from her meager belongings. It added a warm touch to the trestle table in the house.

Mike's absence gave her the chance to continue her effort to bolster Brandon's self-confidence.

"Have you always stuttered, Brandon?"

He shook his head. "Only s-since I was n-nine."

"You know, when I was younger I went through a stage when I stuttered, too."

"You?" he said astonished. "Q-quit joking, Sydney."

"It's true, Brandon. I swear. My father said that I thought too fast and tried too hard . . . that words can't come out unless you give them enough room. He encouraged me to practice by reading very slowly out loud to myself. By doing that, I could *see* where I made mistakes."

Sydney grinned appealingly. "And you know what I discovered? He was right. I only stuttered when I tried to rush or actually wasted time concentrating and worrying about my stutter. Pretty soon, I thought more about the story, and after I had read ten books out loud,

108

I didn't stutter any more." She cocked her head appealingly. "Will you try it, Brandon?"

Brandon regarded her with a dubious frown, but she looked so earnest and sincere, he couldn't say no. "Okay."

She smiled broadly and handed him a copy of *The Last of the Mohicans*. "I know you'll like this story, too. You're a romantic like I am."

Now Sydney turned to the job of bringing Brandon and Emily together alone. But any plan would have to include her at first, so Sydney suggested the three of them go on a picnic.

"Picnic!" Brandon exclaimed.

"Why not? The weather is still warm enough, and we don't have to go far. Then I just may conveniently wander away. You and Emily will have a chance to be alone."

Brandon was unconvinced the plan had any merit. "How f-far away do you w-want to go?"

"Just over the hill near the river. All you need is privacy."

"Yeah . . . but a p-picnic. In October? I'm not s-sure that's a g-good idea."

"Well, if it turns too cold, we'll have an inside one. But remember, you'll never have a better opportunity."

When the time came for them to set off on their picnic, a bright sun overhead promised a picture-perfect fall day. Sydney couldn't believe Brandon wouldn't find Emily just as irresistible. Her blonde hair rivaled the leaves of gold, the hue of her eyes matched the bright blue sky overhead, and the young girl's exuberance was like the refreshing autumn air.

After finding a shaded copse, the fried rabbit and potato salad were no more than half-eaten when Sydney gathered up the dishes and picnic basket. "I'll take these down to the river and wash them," she announced.

"I'll help you," Emily offered.

"That's not necessary. You stay here and talk to Brandon." Sydney grabbed the picnic basket and hurried off.

Having set the stage, Sydney felt sure nature would take its course.

She followed a narrow footpath through a splendid forest of aspen and birch to a spruce-fringed river. Sydney stopped to gape with awe. From the summit of a glacier-capped mountain, the swirling mist of a cataract leaped gloriously into the rushing water below.

To a young woman raised amid the cloying walls of a city, the wonders of Mother Nature filled her with reverence. She sat down on the low riverbank to enjoy the sight, reaching into the picnic basket for a rabbit leg.

When Mike arrived home, he first penned Grit, then unhitched the team. Discovering an empty house and the office padlocked, Mike strolled over to Claire's expecting to find Brandon. The tavern was empty except for the owner.

"Hi, Mike," Claire greeted him affectionately. "You look like you can use a drink."

As she poured him a shot of whiskey, he stretched his arms, flexing his tired shoulder muscles. "I'm getting too old for these trips, Claire. The body just can't take it anymore."

"Hah!" Claire scoffed. "What are you, thirty-four now? If *your* body can't take it, how do you think mine feels?"

"Lily busy?" Mike asked. "She's got great hands." Mike didn't add that shoulders weren't the only thing sore on him. He'd had an ache in his loins since he pulled the damned stupid stunt of kissing Sydney.

"Sorry, Mike. Lily ran off to Seward for the week with some guy she met last weekend." Winking, Claire added, "You oughta have that redhead give you a back rub."

"Delaney?" he scoffed. "I don't think it's in the contract." Mike picked up the glass and downed the whiskey. He closed his eyes, welcoming the wallop to his brain as the liquid entered his stomach.

"Seen Bran around?" He shoved the glass across the counter and Claire refilled it. "No sign of him or Delaney."

"Emily and them went picnickin'."

Mike almost choked on a swallow of whiskey. "Picnicking? Good Lord! At this time of the year?"

"Oh, they weren't going very far. Just over the rise near the river. Emily said they'd be back in a couple hours." She patted his hand. "Hey, they ain't been gone too long. If you hurry, you'd most likely get in on the fried rabbit and potato salad that Joseph packed up for 'em."

"Can't think of anything worse than a picnic. I spend most of my time eating cold meals on the trail. Last thing I want to do is go *picnicking,*" he said in disgust. "That had to be Delaney's idea."

"Come to think of it, you're right." Her laugh was deep, but pleasant.

Mike tossed a coin on the bar. "I'll see you later, Claire."

"Bye, Mike."

The two shots of whiskey had given him a surge of energy. By the time he returned to the house, Mike no longer felt like cooking himself a hot meal—certainly not alone.

What the hell! A piece of fried rabbit would taste good long about now, he thought. Grabbing his rifle, he decided to try to find them. And the quickest way to do that would be to take Grit.

The big malamute had curled up for a nap, but at the sound of Mike's whistle, Grit trotted over to the gate of the pen, and Mike released him.

Cresting the rise, Mike headed toward the worn path leading to the river. After a short distance, he stopped when he spied a bear track in the dirt. Concerned, he raised his head. Bears rarely ventured this close to town.

A few yards farther, however, he encountered Grit, who had stopped to sniff out some droppings on the trail. Squatting down for a closer examination, Mike knew for certain that the fresh spoor had come from a bear. He broke into a run. If Claire had been right about the location, it appeared the bear might very well be attending the picnic, too.

Deciding to give Brandon five minutes more, Sydney reached into the picnic basket and removed the plates, intending to wash them. But she stopped at the sound of rustling behind her. Cautiously, Sydney turned around. When she saw the approaching grizzly, she jumped to her feet, screaming.

"Wait here," Brandon ordered Emily and raced down the path.

Terrified, Sydney tried desperately to remember anything she had read about bears, but could only recall one fact—their fear of noise. Trembling, she frantically began to bang the tin plates together in the hope of scaring off the animal. When the bear continued to advance, she threw the plates at it.

Though falling far short of their mark, the plates landed in the direct path of the bear. The grizzly stopped to sniff the smell that still clung to the dishes, and Sydney began to toss whatever else she could find in the basket. Soon a littered trail of food drew the animal ever closer.

When Brandon reached the site, he stopped suddenly, horrified to see a grizzly within five yards of Sydney. He raised his rifle and took careful aim. When he pulled the trigger, the rifle misfired, jamming the barrel.

"Sydney, get out of there," Brandon shouted. But she

was already backed up to the riverbank and too petrified to move.

In desperation, Brandon drew the knife sheathed at his waist and stepped between Sydney and the grizzly. "Sydney, just begin to back slowly away," he ordered calmly, never taking his eyes off the animal. "Then you and Emily get back to town, quick!"

The bear reared up on hind legs at the intruder in its path. Now towering nine feet, the hulking beast lumbered toward its quarry.

"Get out of here, Sydney," Brandon shouted. With drawn knife, he stood his ground. Still too terrified to move, Sydney stood hers as well.

For the length of a painful heartbeat, Mike froze when he saw the grizzly bearing down on his brother. Then he raised his rifle, but saw that Brandon stood directly between his aim and the bear. He couldn't draw a safe bead without hitting Brandon; so he dashed down the path toward them, firing more than a half dozen shots over the bear's head. Grit too had sighted the grizzly and raced ahead, barking.

Charging past Brandon, Grit leaped at the bear, eluding the lethal claws that could have disemboweled him with a single swipe. Barking and snapping, Grit nipped at the grizzly's haunches while the bear wheeled to defend itself. Lurching on all fours, the startled bear showed surprising speed as it crashed into the brush and down a steep incline. It disappeared into the trees.

When Grit raced to follow, Mike's sharp whistle halted the valiant dog, and he trotted back to the side of his master.

Mike rushed up to Brandon and clasped him by the shoulders. Moisture glinted in his eyes as he studied the face of his younger brother. "You okay?" Brandon nodded, and the two men hugged one another.

When they stepped apart, Mike's glance worriedly swung to Sydney who stood petrified, staring wideeyed as if in shock. "Exactly what happened here?"

"We were—" Brandon suddenly broke off. "Em? Where's Em?"

"Here I am," she cried breathlessly, running up to join them. She had followed Mike when he charged past her. "Oh, Bran, you could have been killed," she sobbed.

"I'm okay. You best see to S-Sydney."

Mike had already started toward her. "It's all over now, Delaney. You're okay, aren't you?"

Sydney wasn't. She felt woozy and began to sway. "I . . . didn't—" Unable to keep her balance, she staggered backward. One foot slipped off the embankment, and for several seconds she tottered on the bank before tumbling into the water. Mike made a dive for her and managed to grab one of her flailing arms.

Sydney began to struggle in the icy water. Only Mike's firm hold on her hand kept her from being swept away by the rushing water. But lying on his stomach, he did not have the leverage to hoist her out of the water.

Brandon rushed over and came to his aid. Between the two of them, they lifted her out of the river and laid her down. "We've got to get these wet clothes off her right away," Mike declared.

"I'll go get the blanket," Emily called. She ran back to their picnic site. Brandon chased after the young girl.

"No . . . don't . . . stop that," Sydney cried when Mike began stripping off her clothes. Despite a bright sun, the air had an autumn chill, and she shivered so much, her teeth were chattering.

"This is no time to argue. You can't stay in those wet clothes."

Sydney slapped helplessly at the hands moving swiftly over her. He released her gown and stripped it off. Her petticoat, shoes, and then stockings followed. Only her underwear remained.

"Dammit, Delaney, you still haven't gotten yourself

some decent underwear," he grumbled when he saw her thin, cotton underpants.

"I haven't had t-time," she managed to gasp. But she couldn't stop shivering. She couldn't remember ever being so cold. Even her fingers and toes felt numb.

"Like it or not, the underwear's going." To her shock he followed through with the threat by grasping the garment and ripping it down the front.

"What are you doing?" she screamed. "Stop that. Stop that at once." She tried to slap aside his hands, but her blows were useless.

Mike quickly stripped off his shirt, clothing her in it. "How dare you? You have no right," she stammered, tearfully.

"I dare because I'm trying to keep you alive, Delaney. Do you understand?" He began rapidly rubbing her feet and hands.

Breathless, Emily and Brandon came running back with the blanket. Mike securely wrapped her, then lifted her into his arms. "Grab her clothes, and let's get back to town."

Even huddled against his warmth, her shivering did not abate until they reached Solitary.

"Dear God, what happened?" Claire exclaimed when the bedraggled group burst through the door of her tavern.

"Mama, Sydney fell into the river after a bear almost attacked Brandon," Emily cried.

"What!" Claire looked grimly at Mike. "Let's get her into a hot bath right away. Em, go get the room ready."

After Emily dashed away, Claire picked up a bottle of whiskey and poured a small measure into a glass. "In the meantime, honey, I want you to drink this."

"I've never tasted whiskey before," Sydney protested.

"You drink it, Delaney, or I pour it down your throat," Mike threatened.

"Now there ain't no call to make threats, Mike,"

Claire scolded. "Honey, this'll help warm you up real fast."

Sydney swallowed the liquid, then gasped for breath. Her throat felt on fire and her eyes watered. While she still struggled to breathe, Mike carried her down a long passageway and through a door, followed by Brandon, Claire, and Grit. To Sydney's amazement, they ended up in the public bathhouse. She had no idea the building connected with the saloon.

Mike shoved through the door into the women's bathroom.

"This is where you boys leave us," Claire announced, closing the door on Brandon and the dog. "And you, Mike, you gonna put Delaney down or are you climbin' in that tub with her?"

Mike blushed, or at least Sydney thought he did. Still feeling the whiskey, she couldn't be certain. Wordlessly, Mike stood Sydney on her feet and hurried from the room.

Chapter 11

After her bath, Claire tucked Sydney into bed and made her drink a cup of hot tea fortified with whiskey. The combination of the earlier excitement and the whiskey had the desired effect on Sydney. She slept undisturbed throughout the night.

Mike was at his desk the following morning. One glance at the solemn figure behind the desk and Sydney knew she was in trouble.

"How are you feeling now?" he asked. His detached tone raised her suspicions even more.

Sydney would have been wise to beg off and return to her room. But his tension unnerved her, and she foolishly admitted to feeling fine.

"That's good," he said coldly. A nerve twitched in his cheek. "Because you're fired, Miss Delaney. I'm paying you off, and fortunately there's a boat due in tomorrow. I want you packed and out of here."

His words stung sharply, as if he had slapped her in the face. Stunned, she tried to protest. "I don't understand."

"No, I didn't expect you would, Miss Delaney."

"Look, Mike, you've got good reason to be angry. And I regret the trouble I caused yesterday. But that could have happened to Emily just as well."

"Emily's a sourdough. She would have known what to do." There was no emotion on his face nor in his voice. Sydney found this icy impassiveness frightening.

"What's a sourdough?" she asked, confused.

117

"An Alaskan, Miss Delaney. She wouldn't have made the mistakes you did."

"Well, I *know* I've read in a book somewhere that a bear is easily frightened away by noise."

"Pity the bear didn't read the same book, Delaney."

"So you're saying the book was incorrect . . . or is it just me, Mike? In your eyes, I'm the one who's always wrong."

His icy control remained steadfast. "First, Miss Delaney, you were confronted by a grizzly. A grizzly is unpredictable, and no bear comes any meaner. It doesn't play according to Hoyle, Marquess of Queensbury, or any *Victorian Rules of Drawing Room Decorum.* Second, the bear smelled food, so a little bit of noise wouldn't scare it off. Third, all you had to do was leave the basket and back away. The bear would have gone toward the scent of the food, not for you."

She saw the nerve twitch in his cheek again. "But no, Miss Delaney, you wouldn't budge. You're too damned stubborn to back down from anything—even a goddamned grizzly bear! You even laid it out a trail leading right to you."

His voice and cold stare never wavered. "Bran still could have gotten the two of you out of there, but you wouldn't listen to him."

He stood up and leaned over his desk. For the first time, the emotion he had kept smothered surfaced in his voice, and she could see the agony in his eyes. "And as a result, you almost got yourself and my brother killed." Aware of his slipping composure, Mike sat down and once again concealed his feelings behind an impassive mask.

"I didn't do it intentionally. I couldn't move. I was too scared to move. I've always had this problem when I'm frightened. Can't you understand what it's like to be so scared you're frozen?"

"I understand more than you can imagine."

"But next time, I'll know what to do."

"There won't be a next time, Miss Delaney. That's what I've been trying to tell you. You dodged the bullet this time. Be thankful."

He shoved a sealed envelope across the desk. "Here's your ticket back to Seattle." He rose to depart, pausing at the door. "Miss Delaney, you're very capable and efficient. I'm sure you won't have a problem finding employment elsewhere." He paused momentarily. "You just don't belong in the territory."

The words were as final as the sound of the closing door.

Stunned for several moments after his departure, Sydney stood motionless. She felt devastated by this unexpected turn of events. Clearly, his mind was set, and she could think of nothing to challenge his decision.

She picked up the envelope. As she pulled out the ticket, a check fell to the floor. Sydney picked it up and stared at a check for one thousand dollars.

The door opened behind her. Brandon entered timidly, and his sympathetic look told her he already knew of Mike's decision. Her eyes were round and luminous—and wracked with pain. "Why does he hate me so much, Brandon?"

"He doesn't h-hate you, Sydney," Brandon said kindly. "He just d-doesn't want to see you g-get hurt."

"By whom? Someone other than himself?" she lashed out. "Why is he so convinced I don't belong here? Other women have survived."

"I guess b-because of J-Jeff and B-Beth."

The faces in the pictures—she knew without asking.

"Beth w-was Mike's w-wife and J-Jeff our b-brother. They b-both d-died the first winter we c-came here." She could tell how deeply the painful memory affected Brandon. And she could easily imagine the effect the same memory had on Mike.

Sydney went over and put a hand on his shoulder. "How long ago was that, Brandon?"

"About th-thirteen years. I was only n-nine at the time."

"And how did they die?"

"Beth f-froze to death."

Sydney closed her eyes. *Oh, dear God!* "And your brother?"

Brandon drew a deep breath and looked up at her. "Jeff got m-mauled by a bear."

Horrified, she slumped down in a chair. "Oh, no," she whispered. The picture had become clear to her. "And yesterday, his other brother came near to meeting the same fate." She hadn't realized she had spoken her thoughts aloud. "No wonder Mike is so bitter toward me. What must have been going through his mind?"

"You can't be b-blamed for what happened y-yesterday, Sydney."

"And while he struggled to save me from freezing, he probably relived the death of his wife as well." She shook her head in shame. "It must have been horrifying for him."

Sydney buried her head in her hands. Mike's reasons for firing her were now crystal clear to Sydney, and this time she had no clever argument. "I've been nothing but a problem to him since I got here. Mike is right. I *really* don't belong."

Miserable and desolate, Brandon sat and shared her heartache, wishing there was something he could do.

Determined not to spend her last day in Solitary languishing in her room, Sydney remained at her desk. She didn't even glance up when Mike returned to the office.

He sat down at his desk and picked up a recommendation she had prepared for expanding the freight line. "Did you put this here, Miss Delaney?"

She glanced up from her desk across the room. "Yes. I intended to discuss it with you later, but since . . . I'll be leaving soon . . . well, I thought I'd put it in writing for you to consider after I leave."

He read it, then glanced over at her. "You're suggesting I set up a trading post in several of the Indian camps?"

She nodded. "Find men from the villages you can depend upon and give them the responsibility of coming here to get the merchandise. Then you and Bran wouldn't have to make those constant trips back and forth."

"We're in the freight business, Miss Delaney. That is the service we offer."

"Yes, at this time. But why not establish a chain of posts or stores in several locations and let them supply one another?"

Brandon, who had been listening to the conversation, put aside his pencil. "It's not a bad i-idea, Mike. If we could g-get a string of posts between h-here and Seward, it w-would make a couple of those inland t-trips easier."

Actually, Mike himself had been formulating a similar plan in his mind for some time in order to eliminate the long trips by wagon and dogsled. But he decided to listen to her whole plan.

"And you could even start offering luxury items as well," Sydney added.

"Such as?"

"Ah ... spices ... tea ... candy ... root beer ... household items. Even women's lingerie," she added intentionally.

"Yeah, there's a big demand for women's lingerie, Delaney." He leaned back in his chair. "And where do I get the men to run these posts?"

"Why not Indians? From what I saw on Founder's Day, they know a great deal about buying and trading." Her eyes lit with a new inspiration. "Why, you could even produce a catalog."

He leaned back with his hands behind his head. "Indians don't read or write, Delaney."

"Well they can count, can't they? That's all that matters."

She saw no reason to continue her argument. Whatever Michael MacAllister decided to do would soon be no concern to her. "It's just a suggestion. I know it creates more paperwork for you and Bran, but at least it would eliminate all those trips you have to make now."

She rose to her feet. "Since it appears there's nothing more I can do here, if you don't mind, I'll go over to the house and make something to eat."

"No ... ah ... that's fine. Go right ahead," Mike said awkwardly.

Overnight the weather had taken a sharp turn. The promise of winter chilled the air, and Sydney tightened her mantle as the blustering wind whirled around her.

Through the window Mike watched her struggle. Unwittingly, a tender smile crossed his mouth when he saw a gust of wind wrench loose the pins anchored at her chignon and her long hair whipped out like a burst of flame.

"You have to admit, S-Sydney's plan has m-merit," Brandon remarked.

Mike returned to his desk. "Yeah, lately I've thought a lot about the same idea. I'm tired of being on the trail all the time. How do you feel about it, Bran? You're affected by this as much as I am."

"I like the idea. And I think you ought to keep S-Sydney around to help i-implement it."

Mike shook his head. "No. She goes. My mind's made up."

"Why are you b-being so damned s-stubborn about th-this?"

"For her own good. She doesn't belong. She's a greenhorn, Bran."

Brandon shoved back his chair and stormed across the room. "D-dammit it, Mike, d-don't I h-have anything to say about r-running this b-business?" He grabbed his coat. "I'm g-going to lunch, boss."

"Bran, wait," Mike called to no avail.

Mike propped his arms on the desk and leaned his head between his hands. "Dammit! Why did the little redhead have to show up and complicate my life?"

"Sydney's right. Sydney's right," Brutus chirped.

Mike glared at the bird. "And train her damned parrot to remind everyone how good she is?"

He grabbed his coat and headed for Claire's.

Pasha, at his usual spot at the end of the bar, greeted Mike with an icy glare. Claire nodded and poured Mike a drink.

"Looks like we can begin getting ready for winter."

Claire bobbed her blonde head. "Yeah, I hate to think about it."

"Pash, what have you been up to? Haven't seen much of you in the last couple days."

"Ha! As if Michael cares," the Russian snorted. Indignant, he rolled his dark eyes in disgust. "Is rumor Pasha hear to being true?"

"And what rumor is that, Pasha?" Knowing full well what was coming, Mike downed the drink.

"You are sending avay our little *Красота?* Vy vould you do such foolish thing, Michael?"

"I'm doing it for her own good."

"Pasha's soul is bleeding." He clutched at his chest. "Better you rip heart right out of Pasha than lef it in broken pieces." He hung his head sorrowfully. "Pasha go back to his room. He does not vish to veep before you."

"Oh, come on, Pash," Mike scoffed. "I'll buy you a drink."

The Russian shook his head. *"Nyet.* A drink vill not vash away Pasha's sorrow. Nor Michael's shame." He walked away in misery.

"Well, I imagine you've got something to say on the subject too," Mike said to Claire after Pasha's departure.

"You're not fooling me, Mike. I know what's behind all this."

"All of a sudden, everyone's an expert on what ails Mike MacAllister," he said bitterly. He tossed down a coin.

"Mike, if you don't want to hear the truth, then don't ask," Claire said as he departed.

Hunching his shoulders against the cold, Mike shoved his hands into his pockets and strode to his house. Emily charged into him as he opened the door.

"Hey, hold on there, honey. Where are you going in such a rush?"

Dabbing at her tears, Emily glared at him. "I'll never forgive you, Uncle Mike. Never." She broke into soul-wrenching sobs and raced away.

"Guess I can forget about running for mayor of this town," he grumbled to himself.

Thinking he would work off some of his frustration, Mike decided to stay outside and chop firewood. Glancing skyward, he realized that they had better haul in some more firewood before the snow started to fly. Tomorrow, if Brandon was talking to him, they'd have to fell a couple of trees.

But for now, he split the firewood. The task of swinging the axe felt good to him, helping him work off his worries. Sweating, he stopped to remove his jacket.

He felt betrayed by the people who should understand the reason behind his actions. Sure they liked Delaney. So did he. Too much. Every moment they were together, he felt more drawn to her. In fact, he could hardly keep his hands off her.

But the obstinate little fool didn't have any idea of the hardships. Or the dangers. She had no understanding of what she would be facing any more than Beth had known. But he couldn't blame Beth. He had been just as naive. Now he knew better. Only the lesson had been a costly one. Well, he wouldn't take on that burden again—*he would not fail again*.

Angrily, he sunk the axe into the stump. "And I don't give a good goddamn if anybody in this godforsaken town ever talks to me again."

The next morning a saddened group had assembled in the office to bid farewell to Sydney. Mike was not among them.

"As soon as I get settled, I'll send you the address where you can ship my books. I appreciate your keeping them until then, Brandon," Sydney said. Her eyes were misty with tears, but she kept up a brave front for his benefit.

"It's no t-trouble, S-Sydney," Bran said. "You take care of yourself."

"And you and Emily go right on reading whichever ones you prefer." She kissed him on the cheek. "And keep practicing the way I told you," she whispered.

"Pasha vill miss his little *Красота.*" The Russian dabbed at his eyes with the ends of his scarf.

"And I you, Pasha." She hugged and kissed him, then stepped back. "My musketeers," she said, smiling through her tears. "I love you both, and I will never forget either of you."

Emily threw her arms around Sydney. "It's not fair. I've waited so long for a friend. I can't bear to lose you."

"We'll always be friends, Emily. And when I said good-bye to your mother earlier, she promised me that whenever I get settled, she'll allow you to come to Seattle for a visit."

Sydney picked up Brutus' wool-covered cage and her valise. "W-why don't you let me carry th-those for you?" Brandon offered.

"No, I'm fine. Besides, I'm too weepy. I'd much rather say good-bye here at the office than at the dock.

Promise me you'll write." She smiled gamely. "And say good-bye to Mike for me," she added in parting.

The three stood huddled together in the doorway, watching her leave. Sydney turned and waved one last time. Sobbing, Emily buried her head on Brandon's shoulder, and he hesitantly put a comforting arm around her.

As Sydney walked down the street with bird and baggage in hand, Mike watched from the window of Claire's. He knew his presence would not have been welcomed, so he had purposely stayed away from the office.

"Well, are you gonna let her go, big guy?" Claire suddenly asked beside him.

"What I'm doing is for her own good, Claire. Why can't you people understand that?"

"We both know better, Mike. A woman has a right to make her own decisions. You don't know what's right for Delaney, but you think you do."

She patted his arm. "We've never tried to fool each other before. So, I'm tellin' you straight out . . . you're makin' a mistake. Don't throw away a future, honey, because of a painful past." Claire returned to her post behind the bar.

For several more minutes Mike watched Sydney. She stood with shoulders squared, clutching the birdcage in one hand and her valise in the other as the wind whipped at her skirt and at the hair that had escaped from beneath her blue tam.

Mike stalked out of the tavern and strode toward the dock. Sydney turned to see him bearing down on her. She felt a momentary stab of pleasure; he wasn't going to let her go without saying good-bye, after all. Then she saw the scowl on his face.

"Okay, Delaney. I can't fight the whole damn town. Just remember, I warned you."

Mike grabbed Brutus' cage in one hand and her valise in the other. "And I want your promise here and now that you won't put one foot out of Solitary without me at your side."

Sydney looked up at him hulking about her. His black hair was wind-tossed, and his brown eyes looked angry. Dark shadows formed hollows beneath his eyes. A frown furrowed his brow and a day's growth of whiskers darkened his jaw.

Her hand fluttered to her chest and she felt her heart throbbing in her breast. She knew this heightened exhilaration had nothing to do with the thrill of an unanticipated victory or a near brush with defeat. The reason behind all her confused feelings and doubts was as clear and overwhelming to her as the tall figure glaring down at her.

For at that moment, Sydney Delaney realized she was falling in love with Michael MacAllister. She brushed aside her tears and smiled up at him. "I promise."

Mike turned around and marched back to the office and—fortunately for Sydney—Brutus said not a word.

Chapter 12

Peace, or at least a temporary truce, had come to the MacAllister Alaskan Freight Line. Some thought was being devoted to the new idea for expansion, but the rest of the time it was business as usual. When the time came for Mike to make a short freight run, he suggested that Sydney accompany him to see an Indian camp for herself. She was ecstatic.

The evening before their departure, Mike tapped on Sydney's door and handed her several articles of clothing. "I want you to wear these. Your clothing is not suitable for the elements. No arguments, Delaney. These garments may not be proper in an English drawing room, my lady, but this is Alaska. We dress for warmth."

Sydney was not about to protest. She certainly wouldn't do anything to ruin the opportunity of being with him. Furthermore, Mike had made a big concession by changing his mind about her leaving, and she intended to make sure he didn't regret that decision.

Despite this resolve, she felt foolish and improperly dressed the following morning when she appeared in the clothing Mike had provided. The plaid flannel shirt and the dark trousers tucked into knee-high mukluks must have once been worn by a teenage Brandon.

While Mike glanced approvingly at her apparel, Sydney took the opportunity to make a similar inspection of him. He looked handsomely rugged and virile in a black-and-red-checkered shirt and a sleeveless deerskin vest. His slightly worn denim pants fit his body to perfection.

"Have you ever handled a rifle or a shotgun, Delaney?" She shook her head. "How about a pistol?"

"No. Neither," she replied, slipping her arms into a light weight caribou parka trimmed with beaver cuffs and collar. There was no doubt that the outdoor garment had been made for a woman. But as to whether the item might be new or used, Sydney could not tell, and she had no intention of prying.

"Time you learned," Mike said.

He strapped on a gun belt and tossed his parka on the wagon behind the seat. "Okay, let's go."

Brandon helped Sydney up and wished them a safe trip as Mike climbed up beside her. As he took the reins, he placed a shotgun at his feet.

"Are we going to war?" she asked facetiously. She smiled to herself, realizing that a mere week ago her remark would have been edged with sarcasm rather than playfulness.

Mike grinned and flicked the reins. "That could depend on you, General." In response to Mike's whistle, Grit rose from sentry duty nearby and trotted next to the wagon.

"Why can't he ride with us? There's plenty of room."

"Can't let him get soft. Be that much harder on him the next time the team has to pull a sled."

"Is that why you keep him penned, too?"

"Yeah. If he got used to the heat of a warm house, he'd lose the edge he needs in frigid weather."

Seeing Mike now through the eyes of blossoming love, Sydney understood how she had misjudged the sound reasoning behind many of his actions—and she was determined to prove to him that he had misjudged her just as much.

"We're headed for a Tlingit camp about twenty-five miles inland," he said once they were on the trail.

"Are those the same Indians who came to the Founder's Day celebration?"

"Some of them, but there were several different Tlingit clans in town that day."

"These Indians aren't hostile, are they? I can remember when my father and I came west our train was attacked by Sioux Indians. That was very frightening."

"You're joking." He glanced at her with a long reflective stare.

"It's the truth. What are you looking at, Michael?" she asked when his fixed look continued.

"I guess I've never pictured you besieged by Indians, Delaney."

"Yeah, well I'm tougher than I look, MacAllister. I've had several harrowing experiences. I survived the big Chicago fire when I was thirteen. I guess the worst disaster though was Billy Curtis."

"Billy Curtis?" he asked, confused.

She glanced askance at him. "My last boss." Shaking his head, Mike expelled a long breath of air.

Laughing, she said, "Well, let's get back to the Indians. Have they always been peaceful?"

"Most of them. The Chilkat Tlingits were the most warlike. They fought a lot with the Russians. But basically the Tlingits get along with Europeans. They sometimes have clan fights, but that's petered out, too, in the last couple decades."

"Are they the only Indians here in Alaska? Back home in the States there must be hundreds of different tribes: Sioux, Apaches, Cheyennes, Arapahos. The list is endless."

"Alaska's a big country, too. There are tribes all over the place. Tsimshians and Haidas. Eyaks along the coast. Three or four divisions of Tlingits, depending on location. More inland. And toward the Canadian border you can find the Athapaskans. Then there are Aleuts in the islands and western part of the territory, and, of course, Eskimos up in the polar region."

"Have you ever been that far north, Mike?"

"Hell, no! Bran and I got as far as the Yukon River once. It was forty degrees below zero. That was cold enough for us."

"Let's see . . . if I remember the shipping list for this trip, you're taking them salt, copper, metal tools . . . and Levi's! Why Levi's?"

"Delaney, these Indians love our clothing."

"And what are you getting in return?"

"Cured fur pelts and dried fish."

"Don't you ever trade for anything except fish and furs?"

"These Indians live primarily by fishing and hunting. And I hate to remind you, Delaney, but Bran and I have done pretty well for ourselves by trading for 'just fish and furs.' Let's take an example of a small, common fur . . . like a marten for instance. We'll buy it for twenty-five shillings—"

"Please keep it in American exchanges so I can follow what you're talking about," she said.

"Well, you'd better learn the monetary exchange quickly. The Hudson Bay Company is English-operated, and that's who we sell the furs to. But I'll make this real simple. Let's say we buy a common fur from a trapper for twenty-five cents. We sell it to the Hudson Bay Company for about thirty-five cents. So we made ten cents, didn't we?"

At her nod, he continued. "Now, that same trapper needs a tin plate, so he buys one from us for the twenty-five cents he just got."

Remembering an order she had just recently written, Sydney popped up, "And we bought the plate for twenty cents."

"Right," Mike nodded. "So we made five cents on the sale of the plate. Add the ten cents from the fur to the five cents from the plate, and what it boils down to is that the trapper traded a fur for a tin plate and we made fifteen cents on the trade."

He flashed a wry grin. "In thirteen years those nickels and dimes add up to a lot of money. And that example was just for a common fur. We make a much greater profit on a rarer fur. You got the picture now, Delaney?"

She nodded. Mike's warm chuckle brought a smile to her face.

They rode on in a companionable silence. Sydney was fascinated by the sights and sounds of the pristine wilderness. After several more miles, she suddenly grabbed his arm. "Look . . . look over there." She pointed to a nearby grove. Amidst the sun-dappled trees stood an animal at least seven feet tall chewing on a willow sapling. "Is that a moose?"

"Yep," Mike said.

Grit issued several challenging barks and despite its awkward appearance, the moose lumbered off, showing a greater speed than the bear's.

"Grit," Mike cautioned when the dog started to follow. Grit immediately returned to trotting beside the wagon.

"My goodness, they're ugly."

Her opinion made him laugh. "Haven't you ever seen a moose before, Delaney?"

"A moose? Well . . . certainly I have. But only in pictures," she admitted. "And they never looked *that* ugly."

Mike regarded her out of the corner of his eyes. Managing to keep a straight face, he said indulgently, "That's a very sharp observation, Delaney." She waited for the other shoe to fall. "Appears all us us critters come out looking darn good—after being lit up and posed rightly by the photographer, that is."

His tongue-in-cheek smile changed to a grimace. "And if you think a moose is ugly, I can't wait 'til you lay eyes on a real, bonafide bull walrus."

The Indian village was situated on the banks of a river in a copse of birch and hemlock. Two tall totem poles stood at the entrance, and over thirty hand-hewn houses were clustered around a huge plank house at the center of the camp.

After the initial greeting to the chief and the village shaman, Mike slipped them each a cigar.

While several young men helped Mike unload the wagon, a young Indian girl graciously volunteered to show Sydney around the camp. Sydney delighted in the assortment of colorful, carved masks and rattles hanging from the doors and walls of the houses.

Sydney drew up in distaste at the sight of drying furs hanging from several dozen rows of ridgepoles. Remembering how much the villagers' existence depended on their fur trade, she still could not help turning away with a measure of sadness.

As she waited for Mike to finish his business, two trappers arrived at the village. To her displeasure, she recognized them as the two Russians involved in the unpleasant incident on Founder's Day. She ignored them and continued to study the intricately carved totem poles.

Fearing another confrontation, Sydney held her breath when the man she remembered as Boris walked up to Mike. "You be trade za fur?" He held up a string of otter pelts.

"I don't trade for sea otters," Mike announced. He turned his back on them and returned to loading furs into the wagon.

"Vy you not trade otter?" the man demanded querulously.

"Because you damn poachers have almost killed off the whole species. Now if you'll excuse me, I've got work to do."

The two men stood with their heads together, mumbling in Russian. Finally, the man approached Mike again. "I gif one skin for two cigar."

Mike turned around impatiently. "I've already told

you, I don't trade for otter. And I don't have any more cigars."

The trapper glanced belligerently toward the two Indians sitting outside of their plank house puffing on the rare treats.

"Vy you haf cigar for Indian, no haf cigar for Lev and Boris?"

Mike glared at them. "Mister, I've got nothing more to say on the subject." He turned to Sydney. "Did you get to see much of the camp?"

"Oh, yes. It's fascinating. And I've seen dozens of artifacts. These Tlingits are gifted artists." She held up a carved wall hanging. "Isn't this lovely?"

"What is it?"

"Just think of it as a bag of salt because that's what it just cost you," she said with a saucy lift of her head.

"Just what are you going to do with that, Delaney?"

"Hang it on your wall," she declared.

He shook his head. "I should have left you in Solitary. If you're ready, we can go. I'm almost finished here, then we'll pull out."

"You got viskey?" the Russian asked, breaking into their conversation.

"Nope. Can't help you out there either," Mike replied as he tied the tarp on the wagon.

The two men walked away still grumbling under their breaths.

"Be right back," Mike said. He returned to the shaman and chief, and the three men disappeared into the big lodge.

Sydney went back to study the totem pole, aware that Boris continued to leer at her. He made a remark to his friend, and the two men broke into raucous laughter.

Stumbling back, Boris stepped on the paw of his sleeping dog, whereupon the yelping animal nipped at the man's ankle.

Cursing profusely in Russian, the trapper drew back his leg and delivered a powerful blow to the dog, kick-

ing it with such force that the poor animal went sprawling for several feet. Yelping with pain, the dog tried to
raise itself on its paws.

His anger not yet fully spent, Boris grabbed a whip
from his pack. Mouthing curses and threats, he struck
the wounded animal over and over, cutting bloody
swatches in its gray fur.

Horrified, Sydney rushed to the injured dog's de-
fense. "Stop that. Stop that at once," she cried. "You're
killing the poor thing." When he raised the whip again,
she grabbed the Russian's arm.

Driven past reasoning by blind rage, the man was determined to teach the dog a lesson. With wild eyes, he
turned the force of his fury on Sydney. "Get avay, you
cyka, or I vip you, too." He shoved her hand aside, and
once again raised his arm to beat the dog.

But the sound of a feral growl stopped him in mid-
motion. Grit stood with raised hackles, his lip curled
back in a snarl. Slowly, the trapper snaked his hand toward the holster on his hip.

Mike appeared in the doorway just in time to see the
Russian's move. "I wouldn't try it. He'll take off your
hand before that pistol can clear the holster," he said
calmly. "Same goes for you, friend," Mike warned
when he saw Lev inch his hand toward his hip.

"If I were in your shoes, right about now I'd just
kind of lower my arms real easy like."

With a final look at Grit, who had not blinked an eye,
the two Russians slowly lowered their arms and backed
away.

In a huddled group, the villagers had watched the
tense scene. They moved over to Sydney who knelt beside the wounded dog, trying to examine its condition.
She gingerly stroked the dog's body and could feel the
broken bones. Its eyes glazed by pain, the dog lay on its
side near death.

True to the Indian reverence for the spirit of all animals, the shaman put on a ceremonial death mask and began an incantation over the fatally stricken dog.

"Down, Grit," Mike ordered, pacifying the vigilant malamute. Mike's dark eyes glowed with loathing and contempt when he turned to the Russian. "It's safe for you to draw that pistol now, Mister. So put your dog out of its misery."

"I no vaste bullet on dog," Boris snarled. He drew a knife from his boot and made a mocking gesture of drawing it across his throat.

"Let's go, Delaney." Mike put a hand on her elbow and lifted Sydney to her feet. He led her to the wagon.

"Hey, Yankee." Sydney glanced back. The Russian waved a bloody hide in the air. "You vant trade for dog hide?" he shouted. Sickened, Sydney covered her ears as the laughter of the two men sounded above the creak of the wagon wheels.

All Sydney's pleasure in the trip was gone. She felt numb. "I should never have brought you out here," Mike said. "In the future, I want you to stay in Solitary."

"Mike, that same man was just as threatening in Solitary. So what difference would that make? It's the man himself. I just don't understand that kind of brutality in anyone."

"I hate to keep harping on this, but I tried to warn you. That's what this land does to people. The land is harsh, Delaney, so the people in it must be just as harsh to survive—survival can make a savage out of even the mildest man."

"I don't believe that. Adversity brings out the best in people, not the worst."

Sydney fell silent again, so Mike saw no reason to belabor the point. After another lengthy silence, she spoke up again.

"Mike, why were you arguing with them about otter

pelts? Was that just an excuse not to do business with them?"

"No. The sea otters are being destroyed faster than they can breed. The poaching gets worse every year. Russia and England are the worst offenders, and the United States government won't do anything about it. For the past five years I've written letters to President Arthur and President Hayes before him. I've tried Senator Benjamin Harrison. Even William Dall and Henry Elliott. They're noted conservationists who came up here when Western Union was laying its cable. I write to anyone who I think can exert some influence in Washington. All I'm asking is for the government to send in a couple of gunboats during the breeding season. Give the sea otters a chance to breed unmolested for a couple years and build up the species again."

Sydney was feeling too numb to be tactful. "That sounds like a pretty noble speech coming from someone who makes a living trading furs," she said cynically.

"Look, Delaney, the mammal and fish population up here is plentiful. But the object is not to kill the females of any species. That way the species isn't threatened. Poachers don't care. If they were interested in playing by the rules . . . they wouldn't be poachers, would they?"

By the time they arrived in Solitary, the only lights in the darkened town came from Claire's house and the freight office window. Brandon had waited up for them. He rose to his feet when the grim-faced pair came through the door.

"Bran, will you take care of Grit and the team?" Mike asked.

"Sure. W-what happened?" He stole a worried glance at Sydney, who sat slumped on a chair.

Mike shook his head. "I'll tell you later." In a silent

signal to Brandon, Mike shifted his glance toward the door. Brandon took the hint and departed.

"You okay, Delaney?" She nodded. Mike tossed his gloves on the desk and pulled off the jacket he had donned against the night's chill. "Why don't you take off that parka?"

"Oh . . . yes, of course," Sydney said. Slowly, she pulled off her gloves and coat.

"Bless you, Bran," Mike murmured upon seeing the coffeepot sitting on the stove. He poured a cup of the hot liquid and came over to her. "Here, you look like you can use this."

"Thanks, Mike, but I don't drink coffee."

He leaned back against the desk, and stretched out his long legs, crossing them in front of him. "Hey, Delaney, don't you know that any sourdough worth his mettle drinks coffee?" he teased gently.

"Her mettle," Sydney corrected with a game smile. His warm grin caused tiny lines to fan from the corners of his eyes and mouth.

How handsome he is, she thought. And irresistible when he uses his charm.

She accepted the cup from him and took several sips of the chicory-flavored brew. "Well, it's wet and hot. I'll say that for it." She set the mug on the desk. Drawing a deep breath, she glanced up at him. "Well . . . I suppose you're waiting for me to say it."

"Say what?" Mike asked. He picked up her cup and took several swallows of the coffee. Then he set it back down before her.

"Say that you're right. That you warned me what to expect from the men here. I can tell that's what is on your mind."

"Delaney, you don't have the faintest idea what's on my mind, right now." For he had just been thinking how vulnerable she looked in her pain. Her eyes were round and luminous. He wanted to take her into his arms and comfort her; to try to convince her there were no bad men ... no bogeyman.

"The act was so senseless and brutal." She shook her head, still wanting not to believe the sight she had witnessed. "So savage ... and uncivilized." Sydney shuddered to shake the image from her mind.

"Civilization requires a woman's touch, Delaney. And unfortunately—the land's too uncivilized for a woman."

She looked up at him with a half smile. "You mean which came first, the chicken or the egg?"

"Guess so. Speaking of food, you hungry, Delaney?"

"No. It's been a long day. I'm more tired than hungry." She stretched and began to rub her neck.

"Your neck hurt?"

"Yes. My shoulders and neck are a little stiff." Throughout the return trip, she had been tense and so sat rigidly. Between her state of discomfort and the wagon's jostling, she knew she would ache worse in the morning. With a desolate sigh, she took another sip of the coffee.

Her pensive gaze followed his lithe movement as he leaned over, picked up the cup, and finished off the coffee. His every motion appeared supple and effortless. "Don't you ever get sore from these trips, Mike?"

"Not the short ones. Guess I've gotten used to them."

"I'll get used to them, too."

There it was, that slight edge of conviction in her voice. She certainly could not be considered a quitter. He liked that about her. "Maybe I can help."

Sydney bolted upright in the chair when Mike shifted behind her and his hands cupped her neck. "What are you doing?" she gasped. Like quicksilver, heat surged through her from the warmth of his touch.

"Just relax, Delaney. You're as taut as a bowstring," he murmured as his fingers began to move with a firm, rhythmic pressure, kneading the tight cords in her neck and shoulders. With slow, steady strokes, his hands manipulated the taut muscles at his fingertips until he felt her tension gradually ease.

"Now lean your head back," he commanded softly. She closed her eyes, and her head lolled back into the cradle of his hand. Now her neck fell vulnerable to the sensitizing stroke of his fingers as he gently massaged it with his free hand.

"Loosen your shirt a little, Delaney."

Lethargically, Sydney released the top two buttons and his hand slid into the shirt. In a langorous slide, he curved his hand around to the back of her neck and worked the muscles.

The touch of his hand on her flesh was exquisite, obliterating all the pain of her tension, all feeling except the magnetic power of his nearness. She opened her eyes, and her gaze met his. His eyes had deepened to the richness of dark brown velvet.

The pressure of his hand at the nape guided her to her feet, and drew her toward him. Cupping her cheek in his free hand, his thumb traced the delicate line of her jaw as her trusting eyes looked into his.

"Such an innocent," he said tenderly. "Don't you see what you've gotten yourself into?"

Tremulously, she smiled. His dark gaze shifted to her mouth. "Please don't tell me I don't belong here, Mike. This is where I *want* to be."

His other hand slid to her cheek and he held her face between his hands. "If you had any sense, you'd get away now, before you get hurt."

"Do you mean away from Alaska . . . or from you, Mike?"

"Oh, Lord, Syd, I wouldn't bet on which is the greater danger," he moaned in a husky rasp. Lowering his head, he claimed her lips.

Having known his touch, she molded her lips easily to the firm shape of his mouth as he breathed new life into the very chamber he had once ravaged.

The warm pressure of his lips demanded a response.

She gave it willingly, surrendering to the delirium that the joining of their lips ignited. And like a fire raging out of control, the heat within her licked at every nerve in her body.

He blazed a trail of kisses to her ear. "You know this is madness, Syd," he whispered tenderly, his breath warm and tantalizing as it hovered above her ear. Then with nuzzling, moist nibbles he retraced the path back to her mouth.

Overwhelmed by his sensual masculinity, she abandoned all defenses. Arching closer into the power of his arms, she felt the strength in the firm, muscled wall of his chest and unyielding length of his long body.

His embrace tightened, pulling her into the solid curve of his hips and his hardened arousal. Feminine instincts over-shadowed virginal restraints, and she leaned into him.

"Oh, God, Syd." He laced his fingers through her hair, and his mouth closed over hers in a deep druglike kiss, his tongue plundering her mouth.

Then he leaned his hips back against the desk and pulled her to him.

In the time it took him to release the buttons of her shirt, her mind found a few lucid seconds. What they were doing was improper. She knew she must stop him. But the exquisite sensations his hands and mouth were creating overwhelmed her sense of propriety. And then his mouth closed over a peak of her breast.

Sensation—hot, arousing, inciting.

"Mike," she gasped, as he continued to lave the turgid peaks. Her pounding heart made her effort to breathe even more difficult.

"Mike, please."

He raised his head. For a few seconds he stared down at the wide-eyed disheveled beauty in her bewilderment. "You really don't want this, do you?"

Still breathless, she gasped, "I don't know. I don't know what I want. I'm afraid."

"Of what? Your own response?" Pain glimmered in his eyes, then he released his hold on her. His hands slid slowly, reluctantly, off her shoulders.

His jolting reminder of her own wantonness quelled all her passion. Engulfed in shame, Sydney denied the cravings of her body and pandered to her conscience, which now heaped accusations of moral laxity on her. How willing she had been to surrender her innocence. What kind of madness had possessed her?

Confused, she still labored for breath. "I . . . I don't understand what came over me, how I could allow you to do that to me." The admission was intended more for her conscience than for him.

Mike had remained silent, waging his own struggle to bring his passion under control. Frustration slid easily into disgust. "Goddammit, Syd, you can't be that naive. You must have learned something from those damn books you read. And I've sure as hell warned you that it's a rough game."

The passionate and beautiful moment had suddenly turned ugly. A heated flush swept through her—her passion had became humiliation. Then her shame gradually shifted to condemnation.

"A game? Is that all it meant to you, Mike? Another one of your jokes to bait Delaney? To test my limits?"

"Of course not," he said. "I didn't plan for this to happen."

He felt like a bastard for letting the situation get out of control. Nervously, he brushed his fingers through his dark hair. "Look, Syd, I . . . ah, feel just as bad as you do about—"

"You have no idea how I'm feeling." She walked to her bedroom and paused in the doorway. "I don't think you're capable of feeling." She closed the door.

"Oh, I'm capable, Delaney," he said softly. "I just wish I wasn't."

He turned when Brandon opened the office door. "What's k-keeping you?"

"I just put Delaney to bed. She's had a bad day," he said.

"What in hell h-happened?" Brandon asked.

Mike put an arm around his brother's shoulder and steered him to the door. "Let's lock up here, and we'll go over to Claire's for a drink. I'll tell you all about it."

Grabbing his parka, Mike paused and took a long look at her bedroom door. Neither a sound nor a glimmer of light came from behind it.

Then he closed the office door behind him.

Chapter 13

Once in the privacy of her bedroom, Sydney struggled with a gamut of emotions. Her feeling of humiliation soon turned to one of loathing for Mike. He was a lecher—the most base of human beings. Once again she had lowered her guard, and he had abused that trust. This time to violate her innocence. And he would be happier if she were out of his life.

When she had exhausted those frustrations, she shifted her anger to herself. Why blame Mike? She was clearly at fault. Where was her moral integrity when he had begun to make love to her? He had never been less than honest with her. He was the one who had principles—she, who lacked character. And he had made it clear how much he wanted her out of his life.

Throughout the night, she vacillated between blaming Mike and herself; but not once did she ever feel shame. She did not regret how close she had come to making love with Mike. Those moments had been exquisite; they were surely too rapturous to rue.

Until the day she had met Mike MacAllister, no man had ever succeeded in making her fall in love. She was a twenty-four-year-old spinster, not by chance—but by choice. At last she had met a man whom she couldn't wait to be with each day, a man whose very touch excited her, a man who not only haunted her dreams but her waking hours as well.

A man who would be happier—if she were out of his life.

Finally, she decided she would have to stop dwelling on the matter. "For 'that way madness lies,' my dear Brutus," she sighed. Forcing a weak smile, she sought an affirmation. "Right?"

"Sydney's right. Sydney's right," he attested as she filled his feeder and water bowl.

So once again Sydney faced a new day with the resolve that she would not allow her personal feelings for Mike to affect her working relationship with him. As sunshine temporarily flooded the office on this waning day of Indian summer, Sydney sallied forth, hiding her true emotions.

She saw no sign of Mike nor Brandon in the office or the house. Next she checked the kennels. The sound of a steady, muffled thudding lured her toward a nearby pine grove.

The two men were hard at the task of stowing up a winter's supply of firewood. Brandon was trimming off the limbs of one of the felled trees. Grit circled him, methodically sniffling out each lopped branch.

"Hi," Brandon said as she approached.

"Good morning. Looks like you're hard at work." Grit trotted over, and to Sydney's relief, she passed the sniff test.

After chatting with Brandon for several moments, she walked over to where Mike was chopping down a tree. He had taken off his shirt, and a film of perspiration glistened on his powerful shoulders and arms.

"Hello, Mike."

He stopped his labor, wiped off his brow with his forearm, and leaned on the long handle of the axe. "Hi."

"Do you mind if I talk to you for a minute?"

"You come to tell me you're quitting, Delaney?" The tendons in his arms stretched as he grasped the heavy tool and raised it. Transfixed, she watched his corded muscles bunch, then ripple across his sweat-slickened shoulders as he swung the axe.

"Mike, I'm taking this load back to the house," Brandon called out. He flicked the reins of the horse harnessed to the skid of lumber. Grit trotted over to Mike.

"I want to talk about last night, Mike."

He sunk the axe into the tree and turned around to face her, wiping his hands on his Levi's. "What about it?" Several strands of his dark hair had tumbled over his forehead. Her fingers itched with the desire to reach up and brush them back into the rest of his thick mane.

"I'm sorry for the unkind things I said to you. I was distraught over the incident at the Tlingit camp. I took it out on you."

He stooped down and picked up his discarded shirt. "Delaney, last night was just the beginning. We both know that. What's between us is like a snowball rolling down the hill. It's gonna get a damn sight bigger before it reaches the bottom. So, get out before it rolls over you."

"I believe we both have the intelligence to work this out."

"Not anymore. What's between our legs is doing our thinking for us now."

She blushed and shifted her eyes. "Please don't resort to crudity, Mike."

Flustered, he threw his hands up in the air. "You just don't get it, do you, Delaney? I'm trying to warn you that if you stay around, we're gonna end up in the same bed. So quit acting like an outraged virgin from one of those damn novels you're always reading."

" 'He conquers who endures,' " she quoted.

"Well, good luck, lady, because whatever happens from now on, I'm through blaming myself. I'll sleep with you—but I won't marry you."

Averting her eyes, Sydney swallowed hard and took a deep breath. "Well, I'll . . . just have to take that risk." She forced herself to meet his dark eyes. "And if what you say is true, then I guess I'll have no one to blame . . . but myself."

He tossed aside his shirt again, and yanked the axe out of the tree. Sydney turned away to go back to the office.

"Hey, Delaney," Mike called out to her. She stopped and looked back. "You want a quote, Delaney. I've got the perfect one. 'Let the games begin.' " He grinned broadly, then resumed his labor.

"Well I've got a better one, MacAllister. 'Forewarned is forearmed,' " she mumbled to herself as she walked away.

The next day Mike left with Rami and his son to hunt fresh game to store for the winter. The weather had taken a drastic turn for the worst when a frigid blast of cold air displaced the warm sunshine they had enjoyed for the past few days.

Even with Mike gone, Sydney found herself thinking about him. The way his eyes crinkled at the corners when he laughed, the feel of his arms around her, the exciting pressure of his lips on her mouth and breasts.

Welcoming the distraction, she looked up with relief when Brandon entered the office and put down several novels on her desk.

"Did you read these aloud to yourself?" she asked.

Grinning, he nodded. "Yeah, and I think they . . . helped."

"Sure sounds like they did. I've detected a great improvement lately. And you know what, Brandon? I noticed you never did stutter at all that time with the bear."

He looked surprised and shook his head. "I didn't know that." He glanced at her thoughtfully. "How does that figure?"

"Probably because you were concentrating on the crisis and not on your stutter."

He pondered what she had said and then shook his head. "Well, I still have the p-problem—"

"There you go, thinking too much about it," she scolded. They both broke into laughter, and replacing the books in their proper cartons, Sydney happily listened to Brandon's enthusiastic comments about the novels.

A short time later Emily came in carrying a book she had just finished. "This must be library day in Solitary," teased Sydney. In truth, she couldn't have been more pleased, for now she had the opportunity to discuss her novels with her friends.

"I hope I can read all those books before you think of leaving Solitary."

"I hope you do too, Emily," Sydney agreed. But her words disguised a selfish motive; she didn't ever want to leave Solitary as long as Mike was there.

She glanced at the calendar. Mike had been making a point of crossing off the days just to irritate her. However, she noticed he hadn't done so all week. "Look at that, Wednesday is Halloween, which means I have been here a month already. I can't believe how the time has gone by. Before you know it, the year will have passed." She sighed wistfully. "And I'm sure Mike can't wait until my contract has expired."

Emily grabbed her hand and squeezed it. "Oh, Sydney, let's not talk about your leaving again. I don't want to think about it." Changing the unpleasant subject, Emily asked, "What's Halloween?"

"You mean you've never celebrated Halloween? What about you, Brandon?" Sydney was astonished.

"I remember we did when we lived in California. But that was a long time ago." Sydney noticed he spoke slowly and managed the whole sentence without stuttering. If Emily heard the difference, she didn't say anything. Sydney winked at him, and he grinned.

"Well how do you celebrate Halloween? Is it like Christmas?" Emily asked.

"Nothing like Christmas," Sydney scoffed lightly. "Christmas is pure light, happiness, and . . . Santa Claus! But Halloween is . . ." Her voice suddenly changed to the cackle of a witch, ". . . the dark of night, ghosts, and . . . Shamhain, the Lord of Death and Evil Spirits."

Emily turned up her pert little nose in revulsion. "Oh, that sounds horrible. And surely nothing to celebrate."

"In Europe it is a religious holiday called 'All Hallow Day' and has been celebrated for centuries. But in America Halloween has become just a holiday for children. They dress up in hilarious costumes and carry jack-o'-lanterns."

"Jack-o'-lanterns? What are they?"

Sydney and Brandon exchanged glances. "This girl needs to be educated, Brandon. I think we should have a Halloween party."

"Sounds like a good idea. But no c-costumes, Sydney."

"Oh, Brandon. Why not? You'd make such a dashing pirate," Sydney remarked.

"No costumes," he repeated emphatically.

"Oh, all right. Have it your way. You sound just like your brother." She rubbed her hands together with pleasure. "Well, the first thing we need is pumpkins."

Brandon shook his head. "You might as well forget it. There aren't any pumpkins in Solitary." He turned away and returned to his desk.

Sydney could not be so easily discouraged. Deep in thought, the two girls sat with their heads together until Pasha came through the door. "Vell! Vat you two little darlinks being thinking so hard? Making so much commotion Pasha hear noise outside."

"Oh, Uncle Pasha," Emily scoffed.

"Is true, my little darlink. Vould Pasha lie?"

"Yes," came the simultaneous reply from all three of the young people.

"Th-the girls are planning a Halloween party," Brandon explained.

"Halloween party?"

At the sight of his confusion, Sydney said, "To celebrate All Hallow Eve."

Pasha clutched his face between his hands, his eyes round with mock fright. "Aye-e-e! You mean night of ghosties and goblins and things vat are going poof in the night."

"Oh no! You know about it, too, Uncle Pasha?" Emily wailed. "I've never heard of Halloween before."

"Of course *not,* my darlink. Is because you are always being in Solitary."

"Our biggest problem is where we will get pumpkins to carve for jack-o'-lanterns," Sydney reflected, still deep in thought. "We could use gourds, or even turnips like the ancient Romans."

"Haf no fear, my little *Красота.* Pasha vill be thinking of vay to make jack-o'-lantern." He broke into a wide grin. "Yes, Halloween party is being enormously, fantastic idea. Pasha likes."

"Will someone please tell me, what are jack-o'-lanterns?" Emily demanded.

"You hollow out a p-pumpkin, carve a face on it, and stick a candle inside," Brandon said.

"Ah, but a jack-o'-lantern has the power to ward off the evil spirits," Sydney added. "That's the whole purpose."

Emily was enthralled. "Oh, this sounds like it's going to be fun."

"So Pasha vill go find pumpkin."

"And what do you want me to do?" Emily asked, eagerly.

"We've got apples. How about some popcorn?"

"I'll go ask Mama. She'll help us." Emily ran out after Pasha.

Sydney spent the next two days determining the bank balances. Apparently, like the inventory, Mike carried a running total in his head. She could not find any evidence that he ever attempted to reconcile anything. Fortunately, he did save all the paperwork connected with the business. "Even though he just shoved it into a drawer," she grumbled as she continued to delve into the old records.

By the time Mike returned on Wednesday, Sydney had entered and verified the past ten years' records. He cast a quick eye on her work and looked at her, unimpressed. "What good does that do, Delaney?" He leaned back in his chair and propped his feet on the desk. "Old figures are ancient history."

"Well, if you ever have to look up any past amount, the record is there. Right?" she cajoled.

"Sydney's right. Sydney's right," Brutus piped, following the proclamation with several whistles.

Irritated, Mike's glance swung to the cage. "Someday that bird is going to end up as a toothpick for Grit."

"Aha!" she said profoundly.

He glanced at her with an impatient look of suspicion. "And just what does 'aha' mean, Delaney?"

" 'When a man is wrong and won't admit it, he always gets angry,' MacAllister," she quoted. "Your friend Haliburton," she added smugly. With a groan, he leaned back and closed his eyes.

"Deny the obvious if you can. But as I recall, you reacted the same way over the new inventory arrangement . . . and the filing system. Now the checkbook. Your record's unblemished, MacAllister."

"Well, in the future, you can write the checks, Delaney."

"I intend to," she said, emphatically. "I don't want all my hard work to go for naught." She smiled, not in victory over his capitulation, but from the sheer pleasure of hearing him inadvertently link her presence to his future.

"Now, if you hurry, you'll just have time to freshen up for the party."

He raised a brow and opened one eye. "Party?"

Her eyes flashed with mischief. "At your house."

He shifted upright. "What kind of party?"

"Halloween. Everything's ready."

"Halloween!" he groaned. "Who in hell celebrates Halloween?"

"That's just it, Mike. We may be up here in the middle of nowhere, but that's no reason why we can't have fun. If you can celebrate a day honoring Hermit Solitary, why not Halloween?"

"This had to be your idea, Delaney."

"Yes. And we expect to have a wonderful time."

"And I expect to go to bed. So have *fun.*"

The door opened and they both turned their heads to see a man standing in the doorway. Sydney reacted immediately. Smiling, she rose to her feet.

"Colonel Kherkov! What a surprise." She hurried over and offered her hand to the Russian diplomat whom she hadn't seen since her arrival in Solitary.

"Miss Delaney, vat a pleasure to see you again." Kherkov kissed her hand.

"Oh, Colonel, how good it is to see you. I've thought about you so often in the past month."

"And I you, my little Sydney. Has Alaska lived up to your expectations?"

"Oh, yes," she enthused. "Everything here is so fascinating." Remembering Mike's presence, she added quickly, "You know Michael MacAllister."

Kherkov nodded. "Yes, of course. Mr. MacAllister." He gave a slight nod in Mike's direction.

"Kherkov," Mike responded with an equally indifferent shrug. Sydney uneasily sensed the men's dislike for one another.

"And will you be staying long in Solitary?" she asked, mystified by the coolness between the two men.

"No, my dear. Ve have only docked long enough to make a minor repair. The captain expects to set sail shortly. So I took this opportunity in the hope of seeing you before we depart."

Mike watched with resentment. The two appeared very friendly. Too friendly for his liking. He and Yuri Kherkov had bucked heads many times on an explosive issue concerning the Alaskan waters—the almost total annihilation of the sea otters.

"No doubt you and your crew are hell bent to hurry off to poach in American waters, Kherkov," he said scornfully.

"You presume too much, Mr. MacAllister. And I might ask, vhat of you Americans? You poached these vaters ven this territory belonged to Russia."

"Yeah, but thanks to you Russians, the sea otters are practically extinct. Only senseless butchers would destroy the females."

"Mr. MacAllister, there are several foreign governments that fish these vaters. Russia is but one. Ve are no more guilty than the British or Canadians."

Kherkov's distinguished face curled with scorn. "Vy are you condemning my countrymen alone?"

"You don't think they deserve to be condemned, Kherkov?"

"Fishing is their livelihood, Mr. MacAllister."

"Livelihood? Killing off a species?"

"You sanctimonious Americans. Vat have you got to say of how you kill your buffalo? And for sport! Buffalo Bill!" he snorted in contempt.

Sydney listened, aghast. Yuri sounded vitriolic. The diplomat had previously appeared so composed.

"I don't like that either. But my concern is for what's happening right here and now." Mike moved to the door. "How much do you get out of it, Kherkov? Or do you want me to believe it's all for Mother Russia? You politicians stink worse than dead fish." He glanced at Sydney. "Be careful, Delaney, some of his odor could rub off on you."

"I know that the poaching of the sea otters is a very

sensitive issue with him, Yuri," Sydney said after Mike's angry departure.

"As much as I admire idealism, my dear Sydney, such noble sentiments have their time and place."

A short while later, in response to several warning toots of the ship's horn, Yuri said good-bye and hurried back to the dock, leaving a somewhat befuddled Sydney behind.

She rushed over to the house and joined Brandon. A kettle of fish chowder bubbled on the hearth.

"Is Mike going to join us for the party?" she asked as she stirred the hearty dish she had prepared for the occasion.

"He wasn't going to until he smelled the ch-chowder. That changed his mind." Brandon grinned. "He's cleaning up now."

When Brandon opened the door in response to a steady rapping, Pasha proudly carried in two large gourds. "No pumpkins, *Красота,* but Pasha bring jack-o'-lanterns."

"Oh, Pasha, they're perfect. Did you do these fabulous carvings?" she exclaimed as she studied the grotesque faces carved on the gourds.

"No, *Красота,* Pasha is not so good with carving."

"Did Rami carve them?" Brandon asked. At Pasha's nod, Brandon explained, "Rami is one of the villagers."

"Is he the same person who did the carvings on my chest of drawers, by any chance?" Sydney asked, remembering the intricate designs she admired on the piece of furniture.

Brandon nodded. "You should see some of his other work."

"Oh, I would love to," she said excitedly.

"All right, when do we eat?" Mike asked, joining them. He looked refreshed after a shave and a change of clothing.

"As soon as Emily gets here." Sydney set out plates and flatware. "Some of us will have to hold the bowls in our laps and sit on the floor. There aren't enough benches to sit around the table."

"Well Brandon and I don't usually throw parties," Mike responded with an edge of sarcasm, "so there's enough *benches* for me and him." He glanced purposely around him. "I'm glad to see you didn't invite your Russian friend to this ... ah ... party."

Once again Brandon hurried to open the door when Emily called out from the other side. Her face glowed with excitement as she entered carrying a basket containing several loaves of freshly baked bread. "Happy Halloween," she greeted. "Or whatever I'm supposed to say for the occasion."

"Let me help you with that, Em," Brandon said. He took the basket out of her hands.

"Joseph sent this over for the party. We invited my mother, but she's busy at home and decided not to join us."

"Okay, we can eat now," Sydney informed the hungry crowd. "But first, Mike, will you carry over that pot of chowder? And, Brandon, you light the candles and put out all the lamps. Pasha, you light the jack-o'-lanterns." The men jumped to obey her commands.

"Oh, look!" Emily squealed with delight. The two jack-o'-lanterns glowed eerily in the dimly lit room as Pasha placed one on each end of the hearth. The scene finally set to her liking, Sydney began to ladle the chowder.

With a bowl of the savory dish in hand, Emily sat down on the floor near the hearth. And when Brandon and Pasha soon joined her, Mike chuckled warmly, "See, Delaney, now we have enough benches." He pulled one out for Sydney and sat down on the other.

"You make this?" he asked after finishing his second bowl of the savory fish soup, thick with onions, potatoes, and corn.

"Yes." She waited for his verdict.

"It could use more salt," he complained, refilling his bowl.

Exasperated, she blurted out, "Are you ever going to give me credit for doing something right?"

"I'm willing to give credit where credit is due," he said with a grin. "And I'll admit there is something you do right well."

"Oh, really, Michael?" She leaned across the table. "What's that?"

"You're a great kisser, Delaney."

She turned beet red. "Oh, Michael!" she said through gritted teeth. Sydney rose to her feet. "Well, the way you're devouring that saltless chowder, be careful you don't choke on a fish bone." Picking up her spoon and bowl, she moved over and sat down on the floor before the fireplace.

After they ate their fill, Sydney and Brandon brought out a small washtub of water with several apples floating on the surface. "All right, who's going to be the first to bob for an apple?" she asked.

"Not me. I just shaved," Mike quipped.

"What do you have to do?" Emily asked, innocently.

"The object is to pick up an apple in your teeth without using your hands," Sydney explained.

"Hah! Is not difficult, Pasha think."

"Vell, hah! Then let's see Pasha do it," Sydney teased.

The Russian knelt before the tub and bent his long, lanky torso over the water.

"Keep those hands behind your back, Pasha," Mike joshed as Pasha tried to catch the stem of an apple in his teeth. The elusive piece of fruit bobbed away. He tried for another, but met with the same result.

After several more unsuccessful attempts, he raised his head. With water dripping from the ends of his beard and moustache, he shook his head vigorously like a drenched dog.

"*Nyet*. Is not possible. Pasha is now thinking these

are not being apples but little red fishes. He is giving up." He rose to his feet, and Mike tossed a towel at him to wipe off his face.

"Emily, now you and Brandon try it together," Sydney suggested. "Have a race to see who wins."

The young couple got down on their knees with the tub between them. Cheered on by the spectators, the two attempted to grab an apple with their teeth. Finally, Brandon snatched one in his jaws, just as Emily raised her head. Their cheeks brushed together. Shocked, Brandon dropped the apple from his mouth and stared into her equally startled eyes, only inches from his own.

With a demure smile, Emily lowered her gaze. "I guess you win, Brandon." She stood up.

"Here, my little dove, let Pasha help," the Russian said, patting the moisture off her nose and cheeks.

As Sydney handed Brandon a towel, she arched her brows with an I-couldn't-have-planned-it-better-myself smile on her.

"Now you and Sydney try it, Uncle Mike," Emily said.

"Not me. I'm too old to bob for apples. That's for children, and I only play big boy games," Mike remarked.

"You afraid I'll beat you, MacAllister?" Sydney challenged.

"At which game, Delaney?" he asked with a smirk.

At the sight of her disgusted grimace, he bragged, "Listen, Delaney, I could be in and out of that tub before you even lower your head."

Her green eyes gleamed. "I'll accept your bet."

The two adversaries knelt at the tub. "Watch closely, folks," Mike boasted. "Hey, Bran, you've got a second hand on your watch. Time me."

Brandon raised his hand as a starting signal. "Okay. Ready. Set. Go."

As Mike lowered his head to swoop down on an apple, Sydney shoved his head into the water. Sputtering, he raised his head with water running down his forehead and cheeks.

"Five seconds, Mike," Brandon said, laughing.

Wide-eyed with innocence, Sydney handed him a towel. "Gee, Mike, you were right. You were in and out of the tub before I even lowered my head."

"Lady, I hope you're thirsty, 'cause you're about to have a drink."

He leaned across the tub and grabbed her by the shoulders. "Oh no!" Sydney squealed. As she dodged to avoid him the tub fell off the bench.

The others jumped aside to avoid getting wet as water sloshed in all directions. Grinning, Mike reached out a helping hand to Sydney.

Trying not to laugh, she put her hand in his. "I ought to pull you right back down."

Pasha scratched his head and eyed the two with his large, expressive eyes. "Pasha is thinking Michael is right. Perhaps Pasha's dear friends are being too old for children's games."

The party came to a momentary halt as Emily and Brandon dashed off to get Sydney some dry clothes. Meanwhile Pasha and Sydney wiped up the wet floor while Mike changed his pants and shirt.

A quarter of an hour later, the small group settled down before the fireplace. "Well, are you finally going to explain to me what Halloween is all about?" Emily asked.

As they sipped warm cider—Mike opting for hot coffee instead—Sydney related the traditions of Halloween.

"Long before the birth of Christ, this night was the eve of a religious festival for Saman, or Samhain, and some even called him Shamhain—the Lord of Death, who appeared on the eve of the Celtic New Year, November first."

She stopped to look around the small group. Seeing she had everyone's attention, including Mike's, Sydney continued her tale. "On that night, the Druids, who were the priests of the Celts, commanded their people to extinguish all of their household fires and candles, ordering them to light a big bonfire where they sacrificed animals ... and even humans ... to celebrate this festival."

"Oh, ick!" Emily exclaimed, turning up her nose.

"Then after the sacrifices, everyone relit their fires from the bonfire—a ritual supposedly offering them good luck and prosperity for the coming year."

"So vat does that haf to be doing vith jack-o'-lanterns, *Красота?*" Pasha asked.

"Well, using jack-o'-lanterns is a superstition going back to the ancient Romans and their Feast of Pompona. They believed they could protect themselves from evil spirits by lighting hollowed-out gourds or even turnips. And after the Roman invasion, the traditions from the Celtic and the Roman festivals merged together."

Taking time for a refreshing sip from her cup of cider, Sydney went on. "The traditions continued into the Middle Ages along with the belief that on this night evil spirits and damned souls searched for victims. The jack-o'-lantern prevented one of these demons from possessing your body."

"But how did it come to be called Halloween?" Brandon asked.

"With the spread of Christianity, the holiday came to be called All Hallow Day to honor any saints who didn't have their own feast day. And the evening before, Halloween."

"But why costumes?" he questioned.

"I bet I can guess," Mike interjected. "Just to confuse all those evil spirits."

"That's right. So they wouldn't be able to tell the living from the demons."

"Well, I think the practice of warding off evil spirits should have been buried with the ancient Romans,"

Mike announced, getting up and pouring himself another cup of coffee.

"I think it's kind of fun," Emily said. "I wished we had dressed up in costumes."

"Yes, but I have another idea I am sure you will all enjoy," Sydney announced. "Let's finish the evening by reading Washington Irving's 'Legend of Sleepy Hollow.' "

"Sleepy hollow? Sounds like a very good idea. Think I'll go to bed," Mike quipped.

"Oh, don't break up the party, Uncle Mike. We're all having such a good time."

"The good time could be coming to an abrupt end."

Sydney glared at him. "It's an enjoyable story, Michael, and most appropriate for Halloween. Why don't you be the one to read it?"

"I'll forsake the pleasure," he said dryly.

"What about you, Brandon?" she asked.

"I'd rather l-listen to you, Sydney," he declined.

"Vy don't you get on vith it, *Кpacoтá*. Michael, be closing your mouth vith another cup of coffee," Pasha said.

Sydney reached for her book and began reading the beautifully expressive tale concerning the mysterious disappearance of the unfortunate schoolmaster, Ichabod Crane.

Brandon stretched out on the floor with his hands under his head and an enthralled Emily sat with crossed legs, absorbing every word. Pasha shifted to a nearby chair, and with cup in hand, Mike sat down on the floor with his back against a nearby wall.

Sydney's pleasant voice glided over Irving's lyrical alliteration.

". . . and listen to their marvellous tales of ghosts and goblins, and haunted fields, and haunted brooks, and haunted bridges, and haunted houses, and particularly of the headless horseman, or Galloping Hessian of the Hollow, as they sometimes called him."

As Sydney continued with the story, Mike watched more than he listened. After getting wet, Sydney had released her hair. It now hung below her shoulders, gleaming like auburn satin in the glow from the fire. He stared, fascinated, whenever a gleam of copper rippled down a long strand.

Feeling his eyes upon her, Sydney glanced up at him. For a fleeting moment their gazes locked. A barely perceptible smile graced Sydney's lips, then she shifted her eyes back to the page.

Outside, dark clouds drifted across the starless sky of the crisp October night. A blustery wind, rustling through the trees, swooped and hurled the falling leaves as playfully as a child tossing a ball in the air.

Deep shadows in the darkened corners of the room stretched out ever nearer to the small group huddled before the fireplace. The eerie moan of the wind whistled down the chimney, puffing at the fire on the hearth and flickering the flames of the jack-o'-lanterns.

Nearing the climax of the story, Sydney's voice deepened dramatically. Emily leaned forward, fearful of missing a single word.

Suddenly a low, blood-chilling groan sounded from nearby. Sydney glanced up from her page; the words froze in her throat. In the dim glow from the fireplace she saw a white ghostly figure floating down from the ceiling above.

Emily turned to see what had caused the looks of horror on Sydney's face. She screamed and flung herself toward Brandon. His arms closed around her protectively as he turned to see what was wrong.

Mike leaped to his feet, then drew up abruptly and started to laugh. Just then the "specter" slipped near the lowest rung of the loft ladder and came crashing to the floor.

With a wild and frenzied thrashing, a plaintive, muffled voice called out from under the twisted sheet. "Vill someone please to be helping Pasha out from under sheet before he is being strangled?"

Later, after a laugh all around, Pasha and Emily departed, while Mike walked a contented Sydney back to the office. He unlocked the door and lit a lantern, setting it down on his desk.

"You had a good time, didn't you, Mike?" she asked hopefully.

He smiled and her heart jumped a beat. "I had a great time, Delaney."

He reached out and ran his knuckle along her cheek. "You be sure and slip the bolt on this door. We don't want any of those evil spirits to get you."

He waited outside until he heard the bolt slide into place.

Chapter 14

Startled, Sydney awoke when the tremor shook the building. Still in a stupor, she got out of bed and stumbled across the darkened room to check on the persistent squawking of Brutus. Outside, every dog in the village appeared to have set up a howling.

The second shock wave caught her midway between her bed and the birdcage. At first she thought she must be dizzy, but then she became aware of the ewer rattling in the basin and saw her parents' picture fall off the chest. When the floor beneath her seemed to heave, Sydney screamed as she lost her balance and slammed into the foot of the bed just as the table lamp crashed to the floor. Her screams merged with Brutus' screech, and she clung to a leg of the bed.

The ten seconds of the tremor seemed to last an eternity and then the shaking ceased. Dazed, Sydney reached up and felt blood coming from a gash on her forehead. Sticky, warm, and wet—she was not dreaming.

Groggy from the blow to her head, Sydney used the bedpost to pull herself up. Light filtered into the room from beneath the crack of the door—which didn't make sense, since at this time of year the sun didn't rise until late in the morning. She staggered toward the door. Her fingers groped to release the bolt but it wouldn't budge. The quake had sprung the door jamb, and the bolt was stuck. But in the darkened room, she could not see the damage to the wood and continued to struggle help-lessly to release the jammed bolt.

Then she smelled the smoke.

Instinct warned her of the danger and cleared her foggy mind. The light under her door was from fire! She was trapped in the windowless room of a burning building. Terrified, she began to pound on the door and shout for help.

The first tremor woke Mike. He had experienced quakes before, but each one made him feel just as help-less as the one before. He was about to arise when the second shock, longer and more severe, hit. He waited until it passed, then jumped to his feet and pulled on his clothes. His first concern was for Sydney. Alone in the office, she would be petrified.

Brandon had dressed just as hurriedly, and without checking the damage in their house, the two men grabbed their parkas and headed for the office.

People were already moving about on the street. Lighted lamps appeared from all directions. "Every-thing okay by you?" Mike yelled to Claire as he dashed to the office.

"We're all fine," she called out.

When he saw the black smoke streaming from under the office door, he felt his stomach constrict. He had not anticipated a fire. His fear intensified when he saw the flickering glow through the window. The office door was locked.

The two men threw their shoulders against the door, but to no avail. "It's that damned bolt. We'll need an axe," Mike shouted to Brandon.

As Brandon dashed back to the house, he passed sev-eral of the townsmen hurrying over with buckets. Pasha was the first to reach the building.

"Give me that bucket," Mike shouted. He swung the pail and broke the window.

Mike drew back as a cloud of black smoke gushed

through the window, then he climbed into the burning building, succeeded in releasing the bolt and, after several thrusts from his shoulder, broke down the door.

Outside, men and women alike had already formed a bucket brigade to the water trough; Indians, prostitutes, children, Russians, Americans—no distinction of nationality, class, or color a consideration at this time of crisis.

In the smoke-filled room, the fire had been centered in the area of Mike's desk and had not spread to the rooms on the opposite wall.

His eyes and throat stung as Mike rushed to Sydney's door. As expected, he found it locked. "Delaney, can you hear me?" he shouted.

"Mike! Oh, Mike!" she sobbed in relief. "I can't open the door. The lock's jammed."

"Well, get away from it. I'm gonna break it down."

He threw the force of his shoulder against the door. The frame splintered, but did not release. Once again he threw his weight at the heavy panel, gritting his teeth from the shock of the pain to his already bruised shoulder.

Just then Brandon arrived and motioned him aside. "Mike, let me." He swung an axe into the wooden door. After a couple more swings of the sharp tool, and several firm kicks from Mike, they broke through.

Tears streaked Sydney's face from the smoke that had filtered under the door. As she flung her arms around Mike's neck, he swooped her into his arms. Frantically, she cried out, "Brutus. Don't forget Brutus." Snatching up the birdcage, Brandon hurried after them.

Once outside, Claire and Emily ran to them at once. Brandon handed the birdcage to Emily and dashed back to the fire. Claire started removing her fur jacket to wrap it around Sydney, but Mike carried her to the house with Claire close on his heels. Emily followed right behind, toting the birdcage.

"Are you okay, Syd?" Mike asked worriedly. "Looks like you've got a bad cut on the head."

"I'm fine now," she said. Her eyes deepened with concern. "Did Brutus survive the smoke?"

"It'd take more than a little smoke to stuff that old bird. Can't you hear him?" Mike asked, still not releasing his hold on her. Sydney cocked her head to listen as Emily lifted the cage. Sure enough, Brutus' complaining squawk sounded from under the cover.

Weeping with relief, Sydney buried her head against Mike's chest and his arms tightened around her. He held her closely for a few seconds until he felt her trembling cease, then he settled her in a chair.

"Claire, will you take care of that cut on her head?" Mike asked. "I've got to get back to the fire."

The gray clouds of early morning were flushed with a carmine glow by the time Mike and Brandon, accompanied by Pasha, returned to the house. Claire handed Mike a cup of coffee as soon as he shed his parka. "Lose much, Mike?" she asked.

"About half the building." He took several sips of the hot brew and his brow arched in surprise.

"I put a little kick in it," she said with a slight smile, glancing at a nearby bottle of whiskey.

"Thanks, honey," Mike said gratefully. "Any damage here?"

"Couple of dishes fell off the shelf. That's all I could see. You were lucky," Claire teased.

"Oh, sure," he said grinning, "real lucky." He tousled her hair, then stretched out the long length of his body, reclining on the floor before the fireplace. "I guess nothing else in town was damaged."

Curled up on the chair in Emily's warm robe and slippers, Sydney observed the camaraderie between Mike and Claire. They were both so comfortable with each other, she envied them their closeness. For a moment she felt jealous of Claire, and her feminine curiosity made her wonder what had happened between them to form that friendship.

As soon as Brandon and Pasha plopped down at the table, Emily hurried to pour each of them a cup of coffee. "Pasha is thinking he vould like to be kicked like Michael."

"What, Uncle Pasha?" Emily asked, dumbfounded.

"He wants a shot in his coffee, honey," Claire said. She poured some whiskey into Pasha's cup. "Remember, this isn't vodka." She held up the open bottle. "What about you, Bran?"

Grinning, Brandon warned, "Just make it enough to kill the coffee taste." Claire winked and poured some whiskey into his cup.

"Well, I don't know about the rest of you, but I've had enough excitement for one day." Setting aside the bottle, Claire reached out a hand to Emily. "What do you say we go back to bed, sweetheart?"

Emily took her hand. "Good idea, Mama. If you need anything else to wear, Sydney, just ask."

"Thanks for everything you've done, including patching up my head," Sydney said, hugging Claire.

"It was just a small cut. Didn't even need a stitch."

As Sydney and Emily parted, the younger girl said gravely, "I'm so glad you weren't seriously hurt, Sydney. I'll see you later."

Gulping down his remaining coffee, Pasha jumped to his feet. "Vait for Pasha, my darlinks. He come, too." Shoving back the bench, he dashed after them, slipped an arm around their shoulders, and the three made their way back to the tavern.

Their departure motivated Brandon. He stood up and stretched. "I'm going to get out of these dirty clothes. They're full of soot." He disappeared through the door of the extension.

"You ready for another cup of coffee, Mike?" Sydney asked when they were alone.

"Yeah." He raised up enough to lean on his elbow, then suddenly winced with pain.

"What's wrong?"

"My shoulder. I hurt it earlier. It's stiffening up on me." Removing his shirt, he tossed it aside and began to flex the injured shoulder.

"Do you have any unguent?" Sydney asked.

"There should be a tin on a shelf in the kitchen." Lying back, he closed his eyes.

After a hurried search, she found the tin of salve and knelt down beside him. "Your shoulder's all bruised, Mike." She gently began to spread the salve over his knotted muscles.

At her touch, his flesh tensed and became rigid under her fingertips. Sydney drew back her hand. "Am I hurting you?"

"No, you're not hurting me," he said.

Her fingers slid across the muscular brawn of his shoulder as she rubbed the lotion into him. The tantalizing feel of his corded muscles created a burning heat that spread languidly through her body. She quivered, thinking of their shared intimacy and the feel of his hands gliding across her flesh. The memory was too provocative. "How did the fire start?" she asked, trying to divert her mind.

It took Mike a brief moment to realize she meant the fire in the office—not the one blazing in his loins. "Apparently, the lantern fell over on my desk and set the papers on fire."

"I can't imagine why I left that lantern burning," she said. "Oh, Mike, I'm so sorry to have been so careless." Each stroke had become a caress. "Turn over and I'll do the other side." Her voice was a throaty caress.

"I'm the one at fault. I put the lantern on the desk," he said, turning on his back. "I should have hung it up."

Neither gave much attention to what the other was

saying, for the physical attraction between them had built to a level too compelling to ignore.

He reached up and cupped the back of her neck, slowly drawing her head down to his. His lips possessed hers, sending an exquisite sensation spiraling through her. Moaning, she slipped her arms around his neck and he pressed her down to the floor. His mouth grew bolder, and he thrust his tongue between her lips.

"God, Syd, I've spent a lot of nights thinking about this moment."

The whispered admission lowered her resistance. She closed her eyes and he pressed a kiss to her soot-colored lashes. His mouth returned to hers, drawing out her breath as his tongue explored the honeyed chamber. Passion blazed through her out of control.

She lay down languorously. He accepted the invitation, nibbling a path down the slender column of her neck. She allowed him to part her robe.

Ice and fire—the shock of cool air on her breasts as he slipped the gown off her shoulders and then the fiery heat of his mouth closing around a taut peak.

She lunged to action, arching her back for greater closeness under the moist, provocative pressure of his mouth. Her breasts swelled, the buds hardening to peaks. He drew one into his mouth. She gasped for breath when he suckled the hardened nub.

She writhed beneath his touch, her nerves leaping to meet the sweeping exploration of his hand.

"Oh, Mike," she whispered in breathless gasps as his hand slid lower. Through the thin flannel of her gown, she felt the heat of his palm close over her most intimate chamber. He began to slowly massage it.

"Oh, God. Oh dear God," she moaned. Her incessant pleas for him to stop fueled the fire of his passion.

"No stopping this time, Syd," he murmured. His mouth returned to her thrusting breasts and his tongue laved and toyed as the rhythm of his caressing hand increased.

He lifted his head and once again claimed her lips. His tongue drove into her mouth. With bold and possessive sweeps, he drove her passion skyward, and she gave a shuddering response, spinning helplessly out of control. For several seconds, she lost all sense of reasoning or restraint, until she suddenly became aware of the loss of his heated touch. She opened her eyes.

Mike had sat up as the thump of Brandon's footsteps sounded in the hallway. Stunned, she stared at him. He pulled up her gown and tied her robe, then quickly raised her up to a sitting position.

"I'm sorry, Syd. I forgot he was here." Then he released her, and Brandon entered the room. "Thanks. My shoulder feels better already," Mike said coolly to Sydney. He pulled on his shirt.

"What's wrong with your shoulder?" Brandon asked.

"I bruised it trying to break down the doors. Delaney put some unguent on it."

The mention of her name propelled Sydney to action. "I guess I'd better make us some breakfast." As she rose to her feet and moved to the kitchen, she wondered how much longer her body could bear these exquisite moments with Mike—before that snowball rolled over her.

She went through the motions of preparing oatmeal and slicing bread. When Brandon went back to his room, Mike immediately approached her. "No apologies, Syd," he said softly.

Sydney turned and faced him, candidly meeting his troubled gaze. "I'm not asking for any, Mike. You were right. Why try to pretend that nothing exists between us? You better go wash up. Breakfast is almost ready."

Mike eyed her suspiciously. She looked too confident, too self-assured when she should be showing either anger or distress. He thought he'd test the waters again. "So you're admitting I was right."

With a cocksure smile, she turned her head to look over her shoulder at him. "Oh, there's something between us, Mike. But maybe it's not what you think. Maybe it's love, Mike."

He chuckled warmly, his teeth flashing white in his tan face. "Delaney, my brain may be between my legs, but my heart's not. ' 'Tis one thing to be tempted, Another thing to fall.' "

Shocked, she stared at him. "Shakespeare from the tongue of Michael MacAllister?"

"Not much else to do up here on these long, freezing nights except go to bed and read," he replied. He popped a piece of bread into his mouth. "But I'll be honest with you, Delaney. There *is* something that scares me about our relationship."

"What's that?" she asked. She glanced up expectantly, then turned away and stirred the oatmeal.

"I'm beginning to recite those goddamned quotations back to you." He grabbed a hunk of the bread and headed for his bedroom.

A short time later a desolate trio stood in the middle of the office and surveyed the damage. Mike's desk and chair, as well as part of the wall, were ruined. The ceilings and walls were black from smoke, two doors had been destroyed, and the floor at one end of the building was crushed.

"Well, considering we were hit twice by the quake, it could have been worse," Mike said, sounding more certain than he felt.

"How often do you have earthquakes here in Alaska?" Sydney asked.

"We get more than our share. But so far, we've been lucky. This is the worse damage we've ever had." Mike regarded her intently. "Another reason for getting back on that boat and heading home, Delaney." Left unspoken was a reminder of their earlier conversation and his awareness of the pressing need for her to get as far away from him as quickly as she could.

She cast him a challenging look. "Not on your life, MacAllister." She moved away to check her bedroom.

Other than part of the floor and a broken lamp, Sydney found no damage to anything in her room that a good scrubbing would not set right. She next inspected her books. The cartons in the stockroom had sustained only smoke damage. She hoped that a few days in the fresh air would help.

"Well, all things considered, I guess I got off pretty well. Brutus is unharmed, and my father's books weren't damaged."

"Yeah, but now you have to move back into the house with Bran and me." He paused for effect.

"Oh, dear. I hadn't thought of that."

Putting her hands on her hips, she declared, "Well, 'you can't make an omelet without breaking eggs.' So the job's not going to get done by just looking at it, now is it?"

They set to work.

After scrubbing down the bedroom furniture, Mike and Brandon carried it back to the house while Sydney washed and aired out the bedding. Fortunately, the day was sunny enough to dry the wash, and by nightfall, she was entrenched again in a bedroom, this time under the MacAllisters' roof.

Later that evening as they all sat down together for an evening meal, the nightmare of the earthquake and fire still remained an unpleasant memory for Sydney.

"I don't understand why this house wasn't damaged since it's so close to the office," said Sydney.

"The quake was mild with scattered damage, Delaney. At least, it's nothing that can't be rebuilt. The fireplace in your room wasn't structurally damaged, so there's no problem there, thank goodness."

"You know how we always t-talked about connecting the house and office. Now would be a good time," Brandon added.

"That's a good idea, Bran. Let's hope we can get

Rami and his son to help. They're both good carpenters."

As Mike and Bran began to draw out their plans for rebuilding, Sydney washed the dishes. They still had their heads together when she said goodnight.

The two men glanced up. "Oh, good night, Delaney," said Mike, seeming to have forgotten she was still there. "And sleep in tomorrow morning. There's nothing much you can do until the office is rebuilt." Mike returned his attention to the papers on the table.

Chapter 15

Exhaustion had taken its toll. Sydney did sleep in the next morning and she had expected the men to do the same. She awoke, instead, to an empty house.

After dressing, she hurried to the kitchen and saw the activity outside. The debris had already been hauled away and fresh lumber was stacked ready to be used.

Throughout the day, the ring of hammers sounded in the air as half a dozen of the villagers assisted in the task of rebuilding the office.

That night, long after Mike and Brandon retired, Sydney remained before the fireplace. Basking in the glow of contentment and the fire's warmth, she had no idea that a tall figure was standing in the door of the hallway, watching her.

"What's on your mind, Delaney?" Mike asked, moving over to sit down beside her. A lock of his dark hair had fallen over his forehead, making him look unaccountably vulnerable.

She smiled at him. "I thought you were asleep, Mike."

"I should be. Bran and I are going out on a run as soon as we can load up after the ship docks tomorrow."

"Can I go with you, Mike? There's not too much I can do here while the office is being rebuilt."

"Ah, Syd, it's a long, uncomfortable trip. And we'll be staying in the village overnight."

"I don't mind the inconvenience, Mike. Truly I don't."

"Well, I suppose Bran could stay and supervise the building. We do have to cut a door in the kitchen wall to hook up the passageway, so maybe that wouldn't be a bad idea." He grinned wryly at her. "The noise and mess would probably drive you crazy."

"You mean, I can go?" she asked excitedly.

"Yeah, I guess so."

"Oh, Mike, thank you." She flung her arms around his neck and kissed him spontaneously.

Within seconds, the pressure of the playful kiss increased as his arms encircled her, drawing her closer against him. His tongue slipped between her parted lips and began to seek and explore.

The force of his embrace pressed her to the floor and as their kisses intensified, he parted her robe. Cupping her rounded breast, he raised his head, a devilish look gleaming in his eyes. "You're a handful, Delaney, you know that?" he teased lovingly, continuing to caress her breasts. Then he dipped his head to nibble at her neck.

"Mike, I haven't recovered yet from last night. I need time to think," she whispered. "So if you don't mind, I'm going to bed."

Lifting his head, he seemed to devour her with his dark gaze. "I would think a smart gal like you can do two things at one time."

"What do you mean?" she asked, confused.

"Do your thinking *and* this at the same time." With that he traced her parted lips with his tongue.

Inundated with sensation, she whispered breathlessly, "It's not easy to think about something else while you're kissing me."

His dark brown eyes never wavered from her trusting gaze as he opened the buttons at the neckline of her gown. Slipping it off her shoulders, he bared her breasts to his roving glance. His fingertips brushed the peaks of her breasts, sending erotic shocks throughout her body. She closed her eyes, and a groan of rapture slipped past her lips.

Grasping her under the arms, he lifted her up as he rose to his feet, bringing her breasts to his mouth. His teeth tugged at a turgid peak, sending exquisite sensation to the core of her. Her fingers curled around his corded biceps, which held her suspended as he continued to gorge hungrily at her breasts.

"Mike," she pleaded as he lowered her trembling legs to the floor.

His warm chuckle stroked her. "No quarter, Delaney. Remember?"

"And I made it clear to you yesterday that I don't expect any. But remember, this can be a double-edged sword."

He tucked a hand under her chin, tenderly lifting her head to meet his gaze. "You don't have to tell me that. Right now I ache because I want you so much."

He grasped her shoulders, and his dark gaze locked with her green one. For a long moment he battled between kissing her and shaking her mindless. Slowly, he released her. "Get to bed, Delaney, if you expect to leave with me in the morning." He departed hurriedly.

The next day, dressed in the furry parka and mukluks Mike had given her, Sydney left with Mike for a Tlingit camp farther inland than their previous trip. Of course the ever-vigilant Grit trotted along beside the wagon.

They stopped for lunch, and after finishing the light meal she had packed, Mike drew the Colt from the holster on his hip. "Delaney, I think it's time you had your first shooting lesson."

Her nose turned up in distaste. "Do I have to, Mike? I couldn't bear to kill anything."

"The time may come when knowing how to fire a weapon could mean the difference between life or death," he cautioned. Emptying the chamber, he handed her the Colt. "It's not a toy, so don't ever treat it as one."

"Mike, I don't even want to hold a gun, much less play with it," she replied.

He ignored her obvious distaste for the subject. Spinning the chamber, he explained. "As you can see, this is a breech-loading revolver, and the chamber holds six cartridges. Once you cock the hammer, the chamber will automatically revolve when you squeeze the trigger."

"Breech loading?" She had been lost from the start.

"As opposed to muzzle loading, Delaney. That's not difficult to understand, is it?"

"No, now that you've explained it. And what is the hammer, and how do you cock it?"

"See this metal head? It looks like the head of a hammer. Now watch," he said. "Press it back with your thumb until you feel it lock. Then by pulling the trigger, the firing mechanism will be activated." He handed her the pistol. "Try it a couple times."

Sydney awkwardly went through the motions until she finally succeeded in cocking the gun with one hand.

Mike then picked up the bullets he had emptied from the chamber. "Now, you load the gun by sliding a cartridge into each of the empty chambers. It's important to know exactly how many bullets you have left. You just spin the chamber to check it out."

After having her go through this maneuver several times, he pointed to a nearby tree. "Okay, the pistol's loaded. Now aim at that tree and see if you can hit it."

"You're crazy, MacAllister." Raising the weapon, she squinted through one eye and took careful aim.

When she missed the target by a good six feet, Grit set up a howl that seemed to echo for miles. Indignant, she lowered her arm. "Is he laughing at me?"

"No, but the horses are," Mike said with a grin. "Grit's just warning everything within ten miles to run for cover."

"This was your idea, MacAllister," she mumbled, disgruntled.

"You have to relax, Delaney. Your problem is that you don't understand the animal kingdom. You're too used to that damn parrot agreeing with everything you say."

Moving behind Sydney, he put his arms around her and lifted her arm. "Now hold your arm steady and point the pistol directly at the target." His hands closed around her raised hand as he helped her to take aim.

"Now steady," he cautioned. Her cheek pressed against his when he stooped to help steady her hand. She could feel the firmness of his jaw. "That's it; now just gently squeeze the trigger," he said softly.

"I think this is just an excuse for you to put your arms around me," she said lightly.

Mike jerked in surprise and the bullet missed its mark.

"Delaney, you're hopeless. I think the lesson is over for now."

Gingerly removing the weapon out of her hand, he uncocked the hammer and returned the gun to its holster. "When we get back, I'm going to give you a pistol. I'm sure that after a few more lessons you should be able to shoot well enough to defend yourself."

"Oh really! Won't that put you in jeopardy?"

He ignored the innuendo. "Let's go."

They reached the Indian camp shortly before nightfall. As Sydney watched Mike and several of the young men unload the wagon, a young woman shyly approached her.

Sydney wasted no time introducing herself. "Hello, my name is Sydney."

"And I am Taitana."

Marveling at the young beauty, Sydney felt like an old woman. The girl couldn't have been more than sixteen years old. She had jet-colored hair and black eyes, and she glowed with an exuberance that enhanced her vibrant, youthful loveliness.

"Are you the wife of Michael?" Taitana asked.

I wish I were, Sydney thought woefully, but she managed a smile. "No, I'm his office assistant."

Sydney's curious glance fell on a wizened woman standing nearby, who was watching them intently with hostile, dark eyes. An abalone-shell ring dangled from the nose of her gaunt and haggard face. Long tangled hair, which appeared to Sydney as if it hadn't seen soap and water for years, hung down to the old woman's hips.

Wrapped around her shoulders was a beautiful gray and blue woven blanket, lavishly ornamented with strands of white fringe. Matching leggings and an apron that fell past her knees added to her extraordinary, eye-catching garb.

"We are pleased for you to share our house tonight," Taitana said graciously. Sydney couldn't have been more delighted at the prospect.

Taitana led her to a plank house. Upon entering, they stepped into a large room that opened onto several individual family units. The artistic talents of the people were obvious, judging by the clan crests and emblems painted or carved on the walls and posts.

"Oh my, who is the talented artist?" Sydney enthused as she studied a particular wall of paintings in Taitana's private unit.

"My brother," Taitana said proudly.

She pointed to several symbols that appeared to be bird tracks. "We are of the Raven Clan. The crest of my mother's family is the Salmon," she added, explaining the many fish heads painted on the walls. Sydney was amazed to see how these symbols and patterns had been sculpted into a variety of wooden spoons, baskets, masks, and trays.

"I will miss these beautiful things when my husband and I begin our own house after the birth of our child."

"And when will that be, Taitana?"

The girl's joyous smile glowed with pleasure. "The

child I carry is expected during the first moon after the winter solstice."

"I'm so happy for you," Sydney exclaimed, calculating that the girl must be referring to the month of January. She thought of how wonderful it must be to be carrying the child of the man you love. Her mind drifted. What if she were carrying Mike's child, Sydney thought wistfully.

As Sydney's glance swept the room, she gasped in surprise to see the old woman standing in the doorway. Regaining her composure, Sydney offered a smile.

The woman did not return the greeting. Instead, she marched toward her, and Sydney tried not to cringe when the woman reached out a dirty hand with long fingernails to examine several strands of Sydney's red hair.

"You paint?" she asked.

"Paint?" Puzzled, Sydney replied, "You mean my hair?" Shook her head. "No, I don't paint my hair." Without another word, the woman departed.

Despite an intuitive revulsion to the old woman, Sydney tried to maintain a gracious smile. "Is she your mother, Taitana?"

"No, that is Tanya, our village shaman."

Sydney's eyes widened in surprise. "Your village has a female shaman? I thought shamans were always male."

"No, that is not true of all our villages. Tanya has great powers. But she is very old and clings to the old customs."

The conflict of changing societies, Sydney thought. "How did you learn to speak English so fluently, Taitana?"

"From Father Jacob. He lived in our village for a year."

"You mean a priest? Surely Tanya objected," Sydney said. She couldn't imagine the old crone accepting a Christian holy man on her doorstep.

"Yes. Father Jacob converted several of our people to your Christian beliefs. They have left our village. That is why Tanya is distrustful of the white man. Michael is the only one she welcomes into the village."

A short time later they were joined by Mike and Taitana's husband, Alexi. The man appeared to be only a few years older than his wife. Their feelings for one another were evident in the exchanges of loving looks between them.

Later, Taitana introduced Sydney to the rest of the household, which consisted of her parents and her three married brothers. Sydney was greeted with warmth and friendliness by all.

That night Sydney and Mike lay side by side on a furry pallet on the floor. The presence of the young married couple on their own pallet across the room prevented Mike from making any advances toward Sydney. But this restraint only made each of them more aware of the other.

"I like these people, Mike," Sydney whispered to him, breaking the hushed tension in which they lay.

Amazed at how well she accepted and adapted to the varied nationalities and mores of these natives Alaskans, he took her hand and squeezed it. "And they like you, Delaney."

They finally slept with Mike still holding her hand.

The next morning as they prepared to leave the village, Taitana and Alexi approached her. The young man carried a white, woolly wolf cub.

"Alexi found this cub. We want you to have it," Taitana said.

Sydney was thrilled. "Oh, how adorable." She turned pleading eyes to Mike. "Can I keep it, Mike?"

"Not as a house pet, Delaney. You know the rules."

Sydney put down the cub to give Taitana a good-bye kiss and hug. The wolf scampered over to Grit and began to sniff out the larger animal despite Grit's warning growl.

"Look, isn't that sad? The poor little thing is looking for its mother or father," Sydney exclaimed.

"I think we'd better keep these two separated for awhile," Mike suggested. Bending down, he picked up the cub and put it in the wagon bed.

On the ride home Sydney cuddled the little cub in her arms. "What do you think I should name him, Mike?"

"Oh, you'll be thinking of a few choice names to call him right soon, if you keep holding him on your lap. Remember, Delaney, he's not housebroken."

"Mike, you're a steadfast realist. But I'm not giving up until I make a true romantic of you." She lifted up the tiny wolf and rubbed her cheek against its soft fur. "I think I'll call him Caesar."

"Caesar?" Amused, Mike looked askance at the small ball of fur.

She nodded emphatically. "Yep. Caesar. 'Veni, vidi, vici.' I came, I saw, I conquered." She smiled joyfully. "The name suits him perfectly, don't you think so?"

"Remains to be seen," Mike said drolly.

She looked at him in mock dismay, turning down the corners of her mouth. But before she could answer, Mike set forth a new rule. "Just don't go getting any ideas about finding Caesar a Cleopatra."

"You have the soul of a skeptic, MacAllister." Taking a hand and feeling the muscle in his arm, she quoted with dramatic flourish, " 'Alas! While the body stands so broad and brawny, must the soul lie blinded, dwarfed, stupefied, almost annihilated?' What a pity. Right, Caesar?" she asked, lifting up the cub to look into his alert yellow eyes.

"If that damn wolf starts yelping 'Sydney's right,' I'm tossing him off this wagon."

"Don't pay any heed to him, Caesar. It's just his 'wit larded with malice,' as Shakespeare would say," she declared.

"One more quotation, Delaney, and I pitch you off

along with that wolf—who's about to pee all over you,"
he warned, eying the animal's extended penis.

"Oh no!" Sydney screamed. Galvanized to action,
she managed a timely disposal of the cub over the side
of the wagon.

That night when they reached Solitary, Sydney ob-
tained Brandon's assurance that he would provide a
comfortable and warm pen for Caesar. Exhausted but
content, Sydney went to bed and immediately fell
asleep.

The following morning, a knock at the door drew her
away from the kitchen window where she had been
watching the progress of the construction.

Looking utterly dejected, Emily entered the room.
Sitting down, she propped her elbows on the table and
cupped her pert face into her hands. "Sydney, what am
I going to do?"

"About what, Emily?" Sydney asked, troubled by her
friend's woeful attitude. "What's happened?"

"It's Bran. Something's got to be done about him."

"Brandon? Whatever did he do?" Sydney was
shocked by the complaint. She couldn't believe Brandon would have done anything to offend Emily.

"It's not what he did, Sydney; it's what he's not
doing," she wailed.

Shoving back her chair, Emily walked over to the
window. "Look at him. Isn't he handsome?" She stared
adoringly at Brandon, who was busy hammering nails
on the roof next door.

Sydney joined her at the window. "He certainly is."
But her eyes rested on his older brother who was hard
at work raising a wall of the building.

Sighing, Emily returned to the table. "Sometimes I
feel that if he doesn't kiss me soon, I'm going to burst."

"Brandon?" Sydney asked, sitting down at the table.

"Yes. I think I've loved him my whole life. And if he
thinks I'm going to sit around Solitary waiting for him

to tell me that he loves me, he has another thing coming. When I'm eighteen, I'm leaving. That'll show him."

Her confession was too good to be true; Emily really did care as much about Brandon as he did about her. Sydney beamed with delight. The pieces were beginning to fall into place, but it appeared that the situation called for a little more effort on her part.

"This can only be resolved over a cup of tea. Would you like one, Emily?" Sydney asked as she put the kettle on the stove.

"None for me, thank you," Emily replied, burying her chin in her hands. "Oh, I'm sorry to be so nasty, Sydney. But that's what unrequited love will do to a person."

"Sounds like you've been reading *Wuthering Heights* again," Sydney remarked with a knowing smile.

Emily glanced up, confused. "What?" Then she returned to her woeful lament. "You've got to help me, Sydney. Tell me, what can I do to make Bran notice me?"

Sydney found herself in a quandry. She could not break Brandon's confidence by telling Emily of his love for her. And now, she would have to get Brandon and Emily to admit their true feelings to each other, not just to her.

"Have you told Brandon how you feel about him?"

"Of course not," Emily said. "I'd be too embarrassed. Why, what if he laughed at me? I'd be devastated."

"Emily," Sydney said kindly, "if you really love Brandon, then you know he would never laugh at you."

"No, he would just turn red and start stuttering."

"You're probably right, but I also think he would be honest with you."

"Do you really think so, Sydney?"

"Yes. But this is going to take further thought," Sydney said. Throughout the morning as she baked biscuits and fried moose steaks in gravy, her mind continued to dwell on the matter, but she could not come up with a solution.

Chapter 16

"Why, this week is Thanksgiving," Sydney remarked as she hung the calendar back on the wall, adding the final touches to the office. Between the cold, the snow, and only a few hours of daylight to work with, construction of the building had slowed. The restoration of the office had been completed, and they were now nearing the finish of the passageway linking the office to the house.

Adding to the loneliness of the long hours of darkness, Mike and Brandon had spent most of November delivering supplies to the more remote Tlingit camps before the severe cold and snow of winter. Although Mike's many absences gave her the opportunity to think about her relationship with him, Sydney had too many lonely hours of missing him. And the few scattered days he was home, Mike worked himself to exhaustion and fell into bed.

"How do you celebrate Thanksgiving Day here in Solitary?" she asked him, her spirits considerably buoyed by his presence in the office as much as by the fact that the final nail had just been driven into the passageway.

Mike cast a long-suffering look in her direction. "We don't."

"How can you not celebrate such an important American holiday? Why, we celebrated Halloween, didn't we? Thanksgiving Day is certainly more important than Halloween."

"Delaney, if you remember, I was opposed to celebrating Halloween, so don't try to use that strategy on me."

"Why don't you hear her out, Mike?" Brandon said. "What did you want to do, Sydney?"

Since the thought had just occurred to her, she really had no overall plan. Her imagination quickly scurried for ideas. "Well, for a start, we could act out the first Thanksgiving with the Indians bringing food to the feast."

"What feast, Delaney?" Mike asked.

"A Thanksgiving feast, of course. That's the main idea. Anyone in town who wished to attend would be welcome, and we could all sit down together. Wouldn't that be wonderful?" She looked at Brandon, hoping for his support. His expression definitely was not encouraging.

"Why, we could have turkey, and dressing, and potatoes . . . and all those things that go with a Thanksgiving meal."

"There's no turkey, Sydney," Brandon said in response to her hopeful look.

"Maybe Rami could carve one out of a gourd," Mike interjected.

Sydney ignored his sarcasm. "Well, we could substitute any fowl for a turkey. Right?" she asked eagerly.

"Hey, Bran, I think Delaney's on to something here," Mike suddenly agreed. "We could always roast that damned parrot of hers."

In response to Sydney's withering glance, Mike smiled and leaned back in his favorite position, propping his feet on his desk. "Yep, Delaney, sad but true. No pumpkins for Halloween, no turkeys for Thanksgiving, and in case you get any ideas, I'll prepare you in advance—no Santa Claus."

"I don't see anything wrong with her idea, Mike," Brandon relented.

Laughing, Mike shrugged a pair of broad shoulders.

"Oh, I don't care. Go ahead and have your Thanksgiving celebration if you want," Mike agreed. "I just like to tease Delaney."

"Oh, thank you, Mike," she cried joyously. Hurrying to the door, she grabbed her mantle off the peg.

"Don't tell me you're running off to start the *feast* already?" he quipped.

" 'The affair cries-haste, And speed must answer it.' I'll be back shortly."

Sydney dashed out and Mike shook his head. "Bran, do you realize we have a whirlwind right under our roof?"

"Yeah, and don't think I haven't noticed how much you like it," his younger brother replied with a grin.

Sydney made short work of convincing Claire and Emily of the idea. The three sat down and put their heads together, then sent Pasha on the mission of approaching each house in the village with the word.

"Pasha and I will tend to roundin' up the food. We'll push all the tables together in the bar here and still have plenty of room," Claire said.

"Now, I think for entertainment," Sydney pondered, "we should put on a pageant commemorating the first Thanksgiving Day. I'll write the script." With her usual enthusiasm, she turned to Claire. "And think, we have actual Indians right here in Solitary. They just need to dress up as the Indians."

"Honey, they *are* Indians," Claire remarked with a motherly pat to Sydney's hand.

"I mean dressed like the Pilgrim Indians in the picture I have in one of my books. They were wearing feathers and leggings."

"Well, all you can do is try," Claire replied. "But this time of year, you're gonna be hard-pressed to get them out of their fur parkas."

"Yes, I think you're right," Sydney agreed. "I shall have to abandon that idea."

Suddenly, the solution for the problem of Emily and Brandon popped into her mind. "I know, we can put on a short enactment of 'The Courtship of Miles Standish.' Emily and Brandon will make a great Priscilla and John Alden," she said, deep in reflection.

"Priscilla and John Alden? Who were they?" Emily asked.

"As soon as you read the poem, you'll understand," Sydney replied, raising her brows meaningfully.

The gesture did not go unheeded by Claire. "What are you up to, Delaney?" she asked suspiciously.

Sydney winked. "Just trying to open the eyes of a certain young man here in Solitary."

"Well, I hope you don't open a can of worms, instead." Claire frowned. "Mike don't take too well to connivin'."

"Trust me, Claire, this has nothing to do with Mike MacAllister. Furthermore, why is everyone in this town intimidated by that man?"

"He keeps the town alive."

Just as Claire made the statement, Sal walked by in a feathered peignoir. "Gee, I thought it was Lily and me who keep the town alive," the blonde prostitute said in passing. Laughing, the three ladies returned to planning the celebration.

Sydney began to chew on her lip. "I have one more big decision."

"What's that?" Emily asked.

"Who's going to play Miles Standish?"

"Who was Miles Standish?"

"He was the town's big hero," Sydney said.

"Well, that can only be Mike," Emily declared.

"Mike in a play?" Claire snorted. "Good luck, Delaney! You're gonna need it."

Sydney nodded slowly. "I'm afraid you're right. I can just hear his objections. Convincing him is going to take some careful thought." She sighed deeply. "Well, come with me, Emily, and I'll get you the poem to read."

Shaking her head, Claire smiled as she watched the two girls walk off arm in arm. "Mike may keep the town alive, Delaney, but it sure has been hoppin' since you got here."

Sydney couldn't keep her mind on business while Emily read the Longfellow poem. She tried not to appear too impatient, but she knew that Mike and Brandon would be back at any minute.

Emily finally closed the book of poetry and handed it back to Sydney. "It's very lovely, but kind of sad, too. At first I didn't like him."

Sydney's spirits drooped. "Well, I can't believe you don't see the comparison. But if you don't like the poem, we can forget about the play. I just thought Brandon would make a perfect John Alden."

"John Alden! I'm talking about that Miles Standish. At first he did nothing but strut around looking at his weapons and thinking about what a great soldier he was. But he seemed kind of pathetic at the end."

"Yeah, kind of reminds me of Mike," Sydney said, sighing.

"Uncle Mike! I should say not. Why, Uncle Mike is nothing like him at all," Emily declared. "Mike is kind and thoughtful, and he ... ah ... certainly wouldn't expect someone to do his talking for him. Or run off and start killing Indians at the blink of an eye."

"Well, it's only for the play. Anyway, don't worry about Mike. The main object here is to get Brandon to confess his love for you, Emily, just like Priscilla got John Alden to do. That's the point of it all. Are you game, or aren't you?"

"Of course, I'm game," Emily said, excitedly. "I'm game for anything that will get Brandon to notice me."

"Well, after I persuade Brandon to play John Alden, the problem will be to convince Mike to play Miles Standish. I have to give this some serious thought."

"Well, as Mama said, you're never going to get Uncle Mike to agree."

"Agree to what?" Mike asked, coming through the door. "What are you concocting now, Delaney?"

"I'll see you later," Emily said, quickly grabbing her coat.

"What are you doing with that pistol?" Sydney asked, glancing at the gun he carried.

"Delaney, didn't I tell you to keep this in your room? I found it in the kitchen. You're always forgetting it. And I've warned you not to leave a gun lying around. Next week, I'll try to find time to take you out for target practice again."

"Mike, you know how I feel about guns. And my shooting hasn't improved despite your lessons. So you *mind* the guns and I'll *mind* the books," she announced.

"That's just what I'm doing," he declared. Glancing around hurriedly, he entered her bedroom and put the pistol in the drawer of the nightstand next to her bed. "Now, let's go and have lunch."

Once seated at the table, Sydney took a deep breath. She began hesitantly. "Ah . . . Mike, I don't suppose you'd do me a big favor?"

He eyed her warily. "What?"

There was no turning back. Bravely, she jumped into the water. "Emily and I were just reading the poem 'The Courtship of Miles Standish,' and we thought how fitting a play it would be to commemorate Thanksgiving. The Pilgrims' first winter in Plymouth and all that." She smiled sweetly. "Don't you agree?"

He smiled and shook his head. "No." Turning away from her, she regarded his profile, his strong lean jaw and hawklike nose. He looked remote, determined.

Well, she had suspected it wouldn't be easy. "Mike, I'll eliminate all the small talk and get right to the point."

"Yes, why don't you do that, Delaney?" he replied, amused.

"What would it take to get you to play Miles Standish in the Thanksgiving pageant?"

He threw back his head in laughter. "Delaney, that's funny. That is really funny."

She cringed, gritting her teeth as he chuckled. "You won't even have to deliver half a dozen lines."

Smiling, he leaned across the table and patted her cheek. "You are so right, honey."

Deep in thought, she sat drumming her fingers on the table while he finished his lunch. Mike finally asked, "Nervous, Delaney?"

"I don't suppose there's anything I can say or do to persuade you to reconsider? What if I arranged for Miles Standish not to have to speak any lines?"

"Then you've got your man." Her face broke into a smile, until he added, "Pasha."

Pasha. The mention of his name brought a thought to her mind and her glance shifted to the deck of cards lying on the table. "Are you a gambling man, Mike?"

"Enough to bet a hundred to one that I'm not playing Miles Standish in your pageant, Delaney."

"Enough to take your chance in a game of Red Dog?"

Pasha had been teaching her the card game, and although it involved more luck than skill, at this point Sydney felt she had nothing to lose.

He eyed her skeptically. "You fancy yourself an expert in Red Dog now, Delaney?"

"No, I don't fancy myself as any expert. I'm just desperate enough to gamble. 'The wish is father of the deed' as they say."

"Okay, Delaney, I'll take you up on that gamble. And if I win, you have to promise we won't have to hear any of those damn quotes for a month."

"Agreed."

"*And* I get a kiss."

She regarded him dubiously. "Just a little one."

"We'll see. Should I deal?" Mike asked, confidently.

Sydney picked up the deck of cards. "Since I suggested the hand, I'll deal it." After shuffling the cards, she dealt five to each of them. Then she placed the stock in the center of the table.

Mike picked up his hand and organized the cards: nine and ten of spades, the queen of diamonds, the king of clubs, and the ace of hearts. Nothing but a higher card in a respective suit could beat him. The odds were in his favor since, out of the forty-two left in the stockpile, the possibility of only seven cards remained to top his—the four top spades, the king and ace of diamonds, or the ace of clubs.

"I'll beat it," he told her.

Sydney turned over the top card on the pile—the jack of clubs. Grinning, Mike laid down his king of clubs. 'You lose, Delaney. Looks like my action speaks louder than your words. At least for a month anyway."

Sydney gathered up the cards. So she had gambled and lost. Well, somehow she would just have to put on the play without a Miles Standish.

"Aren't you forgetting something, Delaney?" Mike asked, a wicked twinkle in his eye as he stalked her around the table and pressed her up against the hard edge.

She gave a squeak of surprise as he swooped down and captured her mouth in a possessive kiss that went on and on. At last, just when she began to feel light-headed with desire, Mike reluctantly released her.

"That was not a little kiss," she accused him.

"Just taking advantage of an opportunity," he replied with a wink and a chuckle, striding out the door.

After Mike left, Sydney cornered Brandon when he came into the house, and she made an appeal to him to play John Alden. She met with another negative response. "Why don't you just read this poem you're talking about, Sydney? Forget acting it out."

She attempted the same approach she had tried on Mike. "I promise you won't actually have to say more than half a dozen lines, and it would be something different for the people in the town," she said soulfully. "I didn't expect Mike to cooperate, but I expected more of you."

"Oh, Sydney, I can't get up in front of a bunch of people and talk. I won't be able to get the words out."

"Sure you will. Just think how much it will mean to me . . . and to Emily. . . ."

Tenderhearted, Brandon simply could not withstand her look of dejection. "Well, write out what you want me to say. But make sure it's not more than six lines."

She hugged and kissed his cheek. "Oh, thank you, Brandon. And you won't regret it, I promise you."

"Just make certain . . . no costumes, Sydney," he added in a final warning.

"I swear," she avowed. Sydney immediately set to work writing a condensed version of the Longfellow poem.

Two days later on the evening of the holiday, the whole town turned out for the celebration. Every household had contributed to the feast, and all were now seated at two long rows of tables offering a generous assortment of roasted ptarmigans, rabbit stew, baked trout, golden squash, succotash, and mashed potatoes. Several dozen pies, made from apples or dried peaches, had been set along the bar waiting to be sliced.

The room quieted and all bowed their heads as Joseph led them in a Christian grace. Then one of the Indians rose to conduct the gathering in a reverent Tlingit prayer of thanks to the animals, fish, and fowl that had allowed themselves to be caught in order to feed all of the assembled crowd.

Finally, the moment came for the presentation of the play. Sydney had elected to give a condensed narration of the Longfellow poem, rather than a reading of it.

She told the audience about the brave and courageous warrior, Miles Standish. With a withering glance at

Mike, she informed them that he could not be among them that night.

Then she introduced them to John Alden, the handsome and youngest man who had arrived on the Mayflower. When Brandon stepped up, the audience broke into applause. He waved self-consciously.

Sydney continued the narration, relating how Miles Standish made a confession to John Alden in which Miles expressed his desire to marry the lovely maiden Priscilla. But although fearless in battle, Miles lacked the courage to ask the young girl to wed him. So instead, he asked John, his trusted friend, to go in his stead and speak for him. Alas, poor Miles did not know that the young man himself was desperately in love with the fair young damsel whom he considered "the May-flower of Plymouth."

Emily then made her entrance. Beguiling, with her blonde curls and bright-blue eyes, she lowered her head demurely and bowed to the audience amid a chorus of applause . . . and whistles from Mike.

Brandon then recited the simple lines Sydney had given him containing the message that Miles Standish wished to wed the fair Priscilla.

Having been carefully coached by Sydney, Emily faced him with stalwart intent, looking Brandon directly in the eye.

"If I am not worth the wooing, I surely am not worth the winning! . . . When one is truly in love, one not only says it, but shows it."

Then abandoning any further measure of modesty, instead of quoting, "Speak for yourself, John," Emily put her hands on her hips, and deliberately changed the line to suit her own purpose. "So when are you going to speak for yourself, *Brandon MacAllister?*" she declared.

Utterly flabbergasted, Brandon blurted out his deepest feeling. "I do love you, Em." The sentence slipped from the startled young man.

"Then when are you going to show me?" Emily asked, even bolder.

Brandon became uncharacteristically oblivious to the audience. He took Emily in his arms and kissed her.

Although Sydney had not even dreamed, much less rehearsed, this delightful development in the performance, the two young lovers spontaneously managed to carry on without her coaching.

The audience was so busy clapping and cheering that the play came to an abrupt end. Many of those present had lived in the town for years and had watched the two young people grow up. Lily and Sal were on their feet. Whistling and clapping, they led the applause as Emily ran into the outstretched arms of her joyous mother.

Only Michael MacAllister was not among the celebrants. Unnoticed by the merrymakers he remained seated. Sydney's glance sought his, and she looked into his angry glare.

Returning to the table, she took her seat beside him. "Aren't you happy for them, Mike?"

"Let's go, Delaney. I want to talk to you," he said curtly.

He slipped her mantle around her shoulders, and they left unobserved. With a firm arm on her elbow, Mike marched her to the office.

"What's this all about now, Mike?" she asked as soon as they entered.

"Up until tonight, Delaney, I thought you were harmless. I see now how dangerous you are. You deliberately instigated this whole thing, didn't you? You set Bran up."

"Mike, I don't understand what is so disturbing to you. Brandon and Emily are in love with each other.

Why aren't you happy for them tonight? Everyone else is."

"Are they in love, Delaney, or was that dumb play just another of your crazy excuses to manipulate Bran? If they are truly in love, couldn't you just let nature take its course? But no. You had to add that Delaney touch to hurry it up."

"Are you jealous, Mike? Is that the problem?" she accused.

He grasped her shoulders firmly. "Look, try to scramble my mind all you want, but keep out of Bran's. I don't enjoy seeing him manipulated."

"By any one other than yourself, that is," she lashed back.

He released her and walked over to his desk. Standing silently, he grasped the edge of the desk. She stared at the broad shoulders that now appeared so unapproachable. Nevertheless, she went over and put a hand on his back.

"Mike, I love Brandon. I'd never intentionally do anything to hurt him," she said softly.

Anger still gleamed in his eyes as he turned to her. "Maybe not intentionally. Look, Delaney, I appreciate what you've done for Bran . . . especially about his stuttering. I should have thanked you sooner. But damn it, woman, you're always charging in and taking over without worrying about the outcome. Your coming to Alaska in the first place . . . and now the situation between us . . . are good examples. Everyone's not like you, Delaney. Bran's a nice guy who tries to please everyone. But he's sensitive. Years ago he . . . well, he took the death of our brother pretty bad. It took many years for him to get over seeing Jeff die the way he did."

"You mean mauled by the bear?" Mike looked surprised that she knew. "Bran told me, Mike."

"He's never discussed Jeff's death with anyone. Not me . . . not even Claire."

"Then it's time the two of you did."

"We'll make that decision, not you. Stay out of our lives, Delaney. Bran's as well as mine." He shoved past her, vanishing into the passageway.

A night's sleep did not appear to have much effect on Mike. He was still tense and depressed the following morning as he entered the kennel where he found Brandon feeding the dogs.

Brandon glanced at him curiously. "What's wrong, Mike?" he asked, seeing his brother's worried frown.

"Oh, forget it. It's none of my business."

Frowning, Brandon straightened up. Normally, Mike was not one to shy away from speaking his mind. "What's none of your business?"

"You and Em."

"Yeah?" Brandon questioned, waiting for him to continue.

"Do you really love her?"

"Of course I do. What the hell are you getting at?" A defensive tone had crept into his voice.

"Dammit, you know what I mean. Are you *in love* with her, or is this something Delaney's convinced you to believe?"

Brandon could not understand such a ridiculous suspicion. "You know, Mike, you're a damn fool when it comes to women. Tell me something. Why are you always trying to find fault with Sydney? And do you really think she had to *convince* me of how much I love Em? Christ, I've loved Em as long as I can remember."

Startled by the truth, Mike looked at his brother as though he was seeing him for the first time.

"All Sydney did is give me the confidence to tell Em how I feel," Brandon continued. "And that's exactly what I did. Before God and the whole damn town."

He tossed down the rest of the fish and headed for the gate. "Why don't you get your own head straight before you try to understand other people's?"

"Bran, wait." Brandon halted and turned impatiently. "I'm sorry, Bran. I've just never thought about you falling in love," Mike said solemnly. "I figured that teaching you how to shoot, giving you your first slug of whiskey, and . . . paying for your first visit to Claire's were enough to satisfy a growing man. I guess I was judging your needs by my own."

Remorse gleamed in his dark eyes. "I should have figured out how you felt about Em a long time ago. Should have made you feel free to talk about it with me." With a grim frown, he added, "That and a whole lot more."

Seeing Mike's distress, Brandon's anger quickly cooled. "Never mind, Mike. It doesn't matter."

"Yes it does, little brother," Mike said sadly, and he looked at Brandon for a long thoughtful moment before he continued. "But Delaney understood you from the beginning, didn't she? She even helped you cure your stutter. That's something I should have tried to do. I guess because of Jeff, I dwelled on the cause of your stutter instead of how to cure it. I failed you there, too."

Brandon went over and clasped his brother's shoulder. "Mike, you've never failed me. You're the best brother a man could ask for. Nothing or nobody could ever change my thinking on that."

Brandon continued with his earnest declaration. "And what makes you think you only taught me how to shoot and drink?"

He paused and shook his head. "All those years of hanging around you, I sorta picked up a couple of dumb ideas like integrity . . . and fair play. Just a couple more things you didn't notice, I suppose."

He grinned, trying to ease the tension. "But I've leaned on you long enough. I'm a man now, Mike, and it's long past time I start acting like one. What say we both get on with our lives?"

"Hope you're not telling me you plan to leave Solitary, Bran."

Brandon's grin broadened, and he lightly punched Mike in the shoulder. "Hell no, big brother. I'm telling you that that was the longest and last speech you'll ever hear from me. But the MacAllister brothers have a freight line to run. I think it wouldn't be a bad idea if you'd start a family of your own, too."

Mike shook his head. "Hey, you know what *I think* on that particular subject. But every man's entitled to make his own mistakes." Grinning, he grabbed Brandon in a bear hug. "So you do what will make you happy, little brother."

For a long moment the brothers held their embrace and then, in typical male fashion, substituted slaps on the back for the tears they would have liked to shed. Grinning, they pulled apart.

Brandon hunched down and picked up Sydney's little cub. Digging into the pocket of his jacket, he pulled out a slice of dried meat. "Poor little guy." He put down the cub, and Caesar began to chew on the scrap of meat. "Caesar's not too popular with the dogs." The two men exchanged a meaningful glance. After tossing the wolf cub another scrap, Brandon and Mike left the kennel.

Chapter 17

That night Brandon and Emily stood in the darkened doorway of the bathhouse. Still unable to believe he had finally confessed his love for her, she snuggled in his arms.

"I think I've loved you since the day you trailed around after me when you were nothing more than a mass of white curls, big blue eyes, and two skinny legs."

"Is that how I look to you now?" she asked, somewhat abashed.

"Well, you've kind of rounded out in all the right places," he teased.

At first, Brandon had felt awkward confessing his love to Emily, but when his beloved Em reciprocated, his confidence increased with each moment they were together. He slid easily into the attentive role he had wanted to play for so many years.

"Well, I've always loved you, Brandon Mac-Allister. Even when I was a child I kept telling Mama I would marry no one but you. She would just smile and continue to brush my hair. But I think she knew too."

He kissed her and she slipped her arms around his neck, leaning closer into the solid wall of his body. When they broke apart, she looked up at him worriedly.

"After we say good night, you won't go and visit Lily or Sal, will you?"

His warm chuckle caused her to smile. "No, sweetheart, I have no intention of visiting Lily and Sal again." Sighing with contentment, Emily leaned her cheek against his chest, and he continued in mock seriousness, "So, under the circumstances, I think we should get married as soon as possible."

She raised her head and smiled up at him. "Is that a marriage proposal?"

"The only one you'll ever get," he declared.

Her mouth puckered into a kissable pout. "How can you be so sure?"

Brandon did not ignore the temptation. He lowered his head and claimed her lips in a lengthy kiss. "Because we've loved each other from the beginning and we'll love each other to the end."

After another quick kiss he turned her toward the door. "I think it's best for all concerned if you get inside now. Good night, Em."

In a happy daze she entered the building and absentmindedly headed down the connecting passageway toward her room. Then she abruptly changed direction and stepped back outside. With an adoring smile, she watched Brandon stride down the street to his house. She was about to go back inside when she saw a glow shining from the office window.

Despite the late hour, Emily felt too excited to go to bed, so she decided to dash over and tell Sydney the good news. As she hurried down the street, she failed to notice the two men who had been watching her and Brandon for some time. One nudged the other in the ribs, and they followed.

Reaching the office, Emily tapped lightly on the door. "Sydney, it's Emily."

Sydney slipped the bolt and opened the door. "Emily! What in the world are you doing out at this late hour? I've been waiting for Mike and Pasha to get back."

Grabbing Sydney's hands, Emily gushed excitedly, "Oh, Sydney, you won't believe it. You simply won't."

"Believe what?"

"Bran asked me to marry him."

Sydney pretended surprise. "Marry you! The man has been too shy to hold your hand. Now you're telling me he asked you to marry him? You're right. I don't believe it."

"Oh, neither can I. I haven't even had time to tell Mama yet." Emily's eyes sparkled with tears. Hastily, she pulled off her coat, then hugged Sydney. "But I've got you to thank, Sydney, more than anyone."

Smiling into her friend's glowing face, Sydney said gently, "No, Emily. Brandon has loved you for many years. That, Fate had decreed, not I."

She pivoted when the door opened, expecting to see Mike and Pasha. Instead, two men stepped into the room. In the clearer light, she recognized Boris and Lev, the two Russian trappers. A shudder of revulsion raced down her spine.

"I'm sorry, we're not open for business at this hour," she informed them. "You'll have to come back in the morning."

"Ve not vant trade. You go," Boris growled. His salacious smirk fell on Emily. "Ve vant dat yellow hair *cyka.*"

Appalled, Sydney gaped at the two men. "I don't know what you're talking about, but I want you both out of here at once."

"Ve go, after ve haf voman."

Sydney put up a show of bravado, hoping a strong refusal might persuade the men to leave. "You're in the wrong building. You should go to Claire's if that's what you want. But get out of here."

"Claire?" His dark eyes blackened with malice. "She

make Boris and Lev go avay. Our money same as others. So ve haf yellow hair *cyka* here."

"You're mistaken. Emily isn't one of Claire's girls."

Emily had stood petrified, listening to the conversation. She screamed when Boris suddenly lashed out with a vicious backhand across Sydney's face that sent her slamming into a wall.

"No lie to Boris. Ve see her at whorehouse. She *cyka* ... bitch, just like others." Dazed, Sydney slumped to the floor as the room spun around her.

The two men converged on Emily. Boris grabbed her, clamping a huge hand over her mouth, and lifted her off her feet in a viselike grip that cut off her breath. She pounded and clawed at his face, desperately trying to free herself. Lev wrenched her hands away from Boris and the two men easily overpowered the struggling girl, forcing her to the floor.

Lev stretched her arms above her head and pinned them to the floor with his knees. He held down her shoulders with his hands while Boris straddled her.

"You no scream," Boris snarled, striking her repeatedly across the face.

Emily's cries turned to sobs. "No. Please, don't," she whimpered in a pitiful plea. The Russians laughed, deriving added pleasure from the frightened girl's terror.

"Hey, ve pay you good." Gleaming with lustful anticipation, Lev snickered to his companion. "If she is good to Boris and Lev."

Boris ran his hands down the curves of her body and with a lascivious smirk nodded to his companion. "Da. Little yellow hair *cyka* feels good." As she cringed beneath his touch, the Russian's eyes gleamed. She squirmed to get free. "Is good. Boris like little *cyka* to viggle like fish. Soon little fish vill viggle on Boris' pole."

As soon as Sydney's head stopped spinning, she rushed over and jumped on his back, trying to pull him off Emily. But her effort was useless. With an angry roar, the brute swung an arm the size of a hog's hock, and sent her sprawling across the floor.

"Ve take dat red-hair bitch, too," he snarled to Lev.

Sydney looked about helplessly for something to use as a weapon. Then she remembered the gun Mike had given her. She crawled into her bedroom.

Her hands shook as she retrieved the pistol from her bedside table. "Check the chamber, cock the hammer," she murmured brokenly, going through the exercise Mike had taught her as the sounds of the struggle in the next room drove her into a panic.

"You move. Lev vant, too." Lev pushed Boris aside and grunted, ripping open Emily's bodice. He pawed her breasts. Then lowering his head, he put his slobbering mouth over hers.

Emily twisted her head, trying to free her mouth. The brute viciously squeezed her nipples. She parted her lips to scream and he drove his tongue into her mouth. Hysterical, Emily writhed and twisted beneath his assault, her struggles only adding to the excitement of the brutal perverts.

Lev stood up and moved a little away. He opened his pants, filling his hand with his engorged phallus. His eyes glittered like a feral animal's as he stood looking down into the face of the horrified young girl. "Lev varn you, *cyka,*" he snarled malevolently. "You bite and he cut out your tongue."

Salivating, Boris shoved up Emily's skirt and pulled her legs apart.

Sydney stumbled back into the room. Trembling, she clutched the gun with both hands and pulled the trigger just as Boris started to lower his body over Emily's.

The shot lifted the hat right off Lev's head. He clutched at his head, and shocked, both men looked up to see Sydney pointing a smoking pistol at them.

The amazed expression on Sydney's face registered

as much disbelief as theirs. She had been aiming for the ceiling.

"Get away from her or my next shot will be right between your eyes," she warned in a bluster of feigned courage. Her knees shook and her heart pounded. Nevertheless, she had murder in her eye. Having made believers of them with her first shot, the two men scampered away from Emily.

"What's going on?" Brandon asked, bursting through the passage door.

When Sydney swung her attention to him, Lev shoved her into Brandon, knocking them both off balance. The two Russians scampered out of the office, disappearing into the darkness.

"Were they trying to rob you?" Brandon asked as he and Sydney untangled themselves. Then he heard Emily's sobs. Glancing over, he saw Emily huddled on the floor, clutching together the front of her torn bodice.

Brandon rushed over to her, kneeling beside her. Emily flung herself into his arms, burying her head against his chest as his arms closed protectively around her. His grave glance swung over to Sydney. "What happened?"

"Emily was attacked by those men." She knelt down beside the sobbing girl.

"Attacked? You mean they raped her?" Brandon asked grimly. His arms tightened around the woman he loved.

"No, the shot I fired scared them away in time."

When half a dozen villagers rushed to the office, Sydney stopped them at the door. "Thank you. Everything's fine here. No problem," she said.

Just then a harried-looking Claire burst through the door. "What happened? Who fired the shot?" Seeing Emily on the floor in Brandon's arms, she cried out in alarm. "Em. Dear God, did something happen to Em?" Claire reached for her daughter, and Brandon reluctantly gave up his hold on Emily.

Claire embraced Emily and held the girl to her breast, patting her head and rocking her as if she were still an infant. "What happened, honey? Tell Mama what happened."

"Why don't we all go back to the house. I'll tell you the whole story there," Sydney said. She squeezed Emily's hand, then got to her feet.

Brandon took Emily's arm and helped her up. He cuddled her to his side and led her toward the passageway. Distraught, Claire followed behind.

Preparing to lock the office door, Sydney shrieked when two figures entered. "What in hell's going on?" Mike asked. "Looks like the whole town's awake. What are you celebrating this time, Delaney? Fourth of July?"

Then he saw the pistol dangling limply at Sydney's side. Gently easing the gun away, he uncocked it. His dark gaze swept her face, observing her disheveled hair and the bruise on her cheek. His gaze shifted to her green eyes. For a lengthy moment, he stared deeply into her unwavering eyes. Raising his hand, he tenderly caressed her bruised cheek. His brow furrowed. "I want to know exactly what happened here," he said grimly.

Surveying the somber group, Pasha shook his head and slapped a hand to his cheek. "Aye-yi-yi. Pasha is thinking that Michael vill not be liking so good vat he hears."

By the time Sydney finished telling her story, Mike wasn't the only person to be upset in the room. Claire dabbed at her eyes as a sad-eyed Pasha patted her hand. Mike stood in silence, his back to them, kicking at a log on the hearth.

Brandon sat on the floor before the fireplace. The quiet man sat with Emily nestled in his embrace. Only a twitching muscle in his cheek betrayed his anger.

Exhausted from terror, Emily had been lulled into a

merciful sleep by the effects of a hot cup of tea and the sanctuary of Brandon's arms.

"The whole thing happened so fast. It couldn't have taken more than five minutes," Sydney remarked.

"Thank God you had the pistol," Claire said. "I knew those two were bad news the moment they stepped into my place. But if I hadn't kicked them out, maybe they wouldn't have hurt my . . ." Sobbing, she buried her face in her hands.

Pasha put his arm around her. "Is not your blame, sveetheart. They are being most evil men."

"You're sure they were the same two trappers we met in the Tlingit village?" Mike asked, turning around and breaking his silence for the first time. His eyes seemed as cold and black as marble.

"Yes, I'm sure. I have no doubt about that. They even called themselves by name several times." She shuddered. "Lev and Boris."

"Which one held down Em?" Brandon asked, glancing at the face of the sleeping girl in his arms.

"The one called Lev held her arms and shoulders. Boris held her legs." Sydney quickly turned away. The scene was too vivid in her memory.

She felt Mike's hands on her shoulders. "And which one smacked you around, Syd?"

"Boris. I think he slapped Emily a couple times too," she answered listlessly.

Glancing at each other, the two brothers exchanged a wordless message. "When do you want to leave?" Mike asked.

"Now," Brandon said. Mike nodded and left the room. "Claire, will you take Em?"

Claire went over and sat down on the floor. Brandon laid Emily's head in her lap. "I love her, Claire."

Claire's eyes filled again with tears. "I know you do, honey. And you be careful," she said.

Mike returned and tossed a rifle to Brandon. "You sure your rifle's in good working order?"

"Yeah, Rami repaired the firing pin. That's what caused it to misfire last month."

Pasha stood up. "Pasha get rifle and go vith Michael and Bran," the Russian said.

"Pasha, I was hoping you'd stay and give Delaney a hand with the business while we're gone. Keep an eye on the gals."

Claire reached out a hand to him. "Yes, Pasha, stay here. We all need you."

He glanced at the sleeping girl. "Pasha stay and keep eye on his little darlinks."

Sydney felt sickened as she listened to the talk. "What . . . are you planning to do?" she asked as the men loaded their rifles with shells.

"Can't you guess? They're going after the bastards," Claire said. She turned tortured eyes to the grim-faced brothers. "Listen to me, you two. Be careful out there. And keep your eyes open for an ambush."

The grief of her daughter's frightening experience was foremost in Claire's mind. Now concern for these two young men she loved added to her heartache. "I ain't gonna close a eye 'til you're back."

"This is a marshal's job. Can't you get legal help from him?" Sydney asked.

"Hell, by the time a marshal showed up here, the trail would be colder than the tundra in January," Mike scoffed. "We handle our own problems, Delaney."

Sydney followed Mike when he left the room. She tapped lightly on his bedroom door, then entered without waiting for a reply. He was in the process of changing his shirt.

"How long do you think this . . . manhunt will take?"

He shrugged. "Can't say. But they shouldn't be that far ahead of us." He finished buttoning his shirt. Her breast constricted when he strapped on his gun belt.

"How do you expect to find them? No one knows which way they headed."

Mike picked up Boris' hat, which he had retrieved from the office floor. "Grit will find them with this. That's why we can't let the trail get cold." He studied the bullet hole in the cap. "Delaney, I'm impressed. How'd you ever make a shot like this? Have you been practicing in my absence?"

She smiled and dropped her eyes. "Not really. I was aiming for the ceiling." He laughed in spite of the grave situation.

"Hey, you're improving. Probably missed it by only three or four feet. And the ceiling's a pretty small target."

Distressed, she looked up at him. "Mike, please don't joke at a time like this. What do you intend to do if you find them?"

"That all depends on what they do."

"Mike, I don't think I can bear knowing you're setting out with the intention of killing them. Please promise me you won't do that?" she pleaded.

Mike ran his knuckles along her injured jaw. "Syd, we deal out justice in our own way up here. That's something you're going to have to accept . . . if you're planning on sticking around here."

He cupped her cheeks between his hands, his smile spreading to his eyes. "While I'm gone, try to stay out of trouble for a change, Delaney."

For an interminable moment, he gazed into her sorrowful eyes, luminous from unshed tears. Then he gave her a deep, intense kiss that left her shaken when they separated.

The pewter-colored sky of another dawnless day cast the earth in a dusky somberness. With the prospects of daylight still hours away, the two riders followed Grit out of Solitary. Standing huddled in the doorway with their arms linked around one another's waists, the three women who loved them watched the brothers ride away.

With the hat Boris had worn as his lead, Grit had no problem tracking the scent. The MacAllisters caught up with the Russians that evening just after the two fleeing malefactors had finished their evening meal.

As soon as Mike rode into their camp, the Russians started to reach for their rifles, but Grit's low, deadly growl stopped them. Dismounting, Brandon picked up the weapons, pumped the shells out of the chambers, then tossed the guns to Mike.

"Now the knives, boys. Slow and easy," Mike warned with his rifle pointed at them. They unsheathed the blades strapped to their waists. "Just toss them into that fire there," Mike said. With murderous glares, the two scoundrels threw the blades into the campfire.

"Now the ones in the boots, fellas," Mike said pleasantly. "Remember, no unexpected moves."

Each man drew out the dagger strapped inside his boot. After a nod from Mike toward the fire, they tossed their knives into the flames.

Mike lowered his rifle and returned it to the scabbard on his saddle. Then resting an arm on the saddle horn, he casually leaned forward. "Seems you boys left town in such a hurry the other night, some unfinished business got left behind. We feel real bad about that. Makes Solitary sound like a real unfriendly place to visit."

"Which one of you is Boris?" Brandon demanded.

Smirking, the Russian stepped forward. "Boris break you in haf."

What the larger man had not anticipated was Brandon's strength. Brandon had spent the last thirteen years loading and unloading heavy freight boxes.

Lighter and faster on his feet, he easily ducked beneath the punch the Russian threw and lashed out with a blow to the bigger man's solar plexus. His next blow cracked one of the man's ribs. Clutching his stomach, Boris doubled over, gasping for breath.

"Come on, you sonnabitch," Brandon shouted. "Let's see you break me in half. Or did you think I'd be a pushover like the sixteen-year-old girl you tried to rape?"

Before the Russian could regain his breath, Brandon delivered an uppercut to the man's chin. Boris' head snapped back, and he fell to the ground. Leaping on him, Brandon began to pummel the man's face with one blow after another until Boris' face ran red with blood from the smashed nose and broken flesh.

"Bran, that's enough," Mike shouted. He leaped off his horse and tried to pull his brother off the man.

"Let me alone, I'm not through," Brandon yelled. In his determination for revenge, he appeared deranged. "Sydney said it took five minutes. I'm gonna show this bastard what five minutes of hell is like."

"For God's sake, Bran, if you keep that up you're gonna kill him." Mike yanked his brother off the man, then shoved Boris over so the Russian wouldn't choke on his own blood.

"Come on, little brother, get back on your horse," he said gently.

Lev chose that moment to make an unwise comment to Mike. "Ve no hurt your woman. Vy you care vhat ve do to that yellow hair *cyka?*"

Mike's punch sent the big man staggering backwards. Blood ran from his mouth as he spit out a tooth.

Swinging into his saddle, Mike paused to look back at the two men. Lev lifted his head, wiping his face on the sleeve of his shirt. "You lef us here vit no veapon? How ve defend ourself?" asked Lev.

"What the hell, a couple of big men like you shouldn't have any problem," Mike scoffed. "The two of you managed to overpower a defenseless girl with just your bare hands."

His tone changed to a lethal warning. "You'll find your rifles a couple miles down the trail. If you ever come near Solitary again, we'll hang you."

They wheeled their horses and rode away.

Chapter 18

After pricking her finger for the tenth time, Sydney cast aside the piece of needlepoint she had been stitching off and on for the past five years. "Never could stand the darn thing anyway," she grumbled aloud. "Why should I bother with it now?" She knew very well why she should bother with the piece, since she intended to give it to Brandon and Emily as a wedding gift.

She began to pace the floor, crossing her arms across her chest. The long wait had made her edgy and ill-natured. "Two days, Brutus. They've been gone two days." The parrot watched her silently.

When the door opened, she glanced up hopefully. "Oh hi, Pasha," she said in a despondent greeting to the Russian.

"Vy Sydney be giving Pasha such a long face? She no like Pasha anymore?"

"Oh, Pasha, I'm sorry. Of course I like you. I had hoped you were Mike and Brandon, that's all."

"That's all!" he exclaimed, rolling his expressive eyes. "If Sydney vants Pasha to be Michael and Brandon, is being extremely big foots to be filling in the shoes."

Sydney smiled, despite her gloom. "I believe the expression is that you would have 'big shoes to fill.' "

"Dat vat Pasha say. He already has big foots."

Realizing the conversation was becoming too complicated to cope with in her present mood, Sydney shook

214

her head and changed the subject. "Pasha, how is Emily today?"

"The little darlink is being most sad because she is missing her sveetheart. Is most vorried like you, little *Красотá*. Pasha is thinking that Sydney is missing sveetheart, too."

"I don't have a sweetheart, Pasha, except Brutus there and Caesar, of course," she said, sighing deeply. "And for your information, Count Pasha Eduardovich Vladimir, I am deeply concerned for the safety of Mike and Brandon."

The Russian shook his head. "Pasha tell Sydney vhat he tell his darlinks Claire and Emily. Is not to vorry. Michael and Brandon vill soon be coming back. Is being Lev and Boris who haf much vorry. But Pasha is thinking already too late for dat." He curled his lip and made a cutting motion across his throat.

Sydney buried her head in her hand. "Oh, good grief. Get out of here, Pasha. You're making matters worse."

Reaching into the pocket of his coat, he pulled out a folded piece of paper. "Sydney, Pasha is hafing map to gold mine he trade for at Indian village."

"A treasure map!" she said aghast. "What did you trade for it?"

His eyes brightened with cunning as he held up a bony finger. "Aha! Pasha made unusually best deal in whole Alaska. Trade vatch for map."

"You mean your watch that actually worked, or one of those worthless watches with the broken hands you were trying to sell?"

He appeared offended that she would impugn his integrity. "Vud Pasha trade vorthless vatch for valuable treasure map?"

"You mean you actually traded your good watch?" She shook her head in disbelief. "Pasha, whatever is going to become of you?"

He looked around cautiously, then put up a hand to

shield his mouth and whispered sotto voce. "Sydney vant to buy treasure map?"

She glanced askance, softening her voice to match his. "Why are you whispering? There's no one here except you and me."

Viewing her with a narrowed eye, he continued to whisper. "Pasha can tell Sydney no understand importance of secret. Cannot be too careful vhen valuable map is concerned. So vat you say? *Красота* vant to buy treasure map?"

"Pasha, you must be dim-witted if you think I would ever waste my hard-earned money on any ridiculous, fly-by-night, pipe dream like a treasure map."

"Is *nyet?*" he asked with a baffled frown.

"Is definitely *nyet,*" she declared with an assertive toss of her red head.

With an affable shrug, he accepted her refusal good-naturedly and wrapped his muffler around his throat. "Vell, Pasha go now to feed dogs."

Sydney jumped up and grabbed her parka. "I'll go with you and see how Caesar's doing."

Once back at the kennel, she noticed Caesar was still penned by himself. Upon asking Pasha, he only shrugged. "Bran say other dogs no like little cub. He smell like volf."

"He is a wolf," she said sadly. Looking at the lonely little thing only depressed Sydney more.

As they returned to the house, she saw that the arrival of a Japanese freighter had stirred up a lot of activity in town. Especially at Claire's, she thought wryly, seeing the sailors streaming up to the brothel.

"Oh look, Pasha, a Japanese freighter. We have some supplies ordered. I'd better get busy."

"Pasha come vith Sydney."

She hurried back to the office and found that Mike had ordered tea and rice from the Shito Maru Company in Yokohama. "Pasha, how often do ships arrive here from Japan?" she asked.

Pasha held up two bony fingers. "Ship from Orient be coming two times a year on vay to Juneau. Is closer for Nipponese to sail to Alaska dan be going to San Francisco. Many ships come fish in Bering Sea, but dey no be coming to Solitary."

"What do they go to Juneau for?"

"Nipponese need much pine and hemlock vood."

Sydney had seen many Japanese freighters in Seattle, so the ship from the Orient was no novelty to her. But she welcomed the distraction because it took her mind off Mike and Brandon.

The sun set early in the afternoon, and the dismal gloom of the dreary twilight returned. Unable to concentrate on reading, Sydney resumed her needlepoint in front of the fireplace.

She had just retired for the long night when she heard the thud of footsteps in the passageway. With a lightened heart, she unlocked her door and peered out to see Mike and Brandon. The weary brothers slumped down at their desks.

"Oh, thank God you're back," she said.

Mike yawned and leaned back in his chair with his hands laced behind his head. "Hi, Delaney. What's new?"

"What's new?" She threw up her hands in frustration. "What's new? Is that all you've got to say? I've been worried sick for the past two days and when you finally show up, you ask me 'what's new?' "

He didn't even open his eyes. "I'm sorry I asked."

"How's Em, Sydney?" Brandon asked worriedly.

Her tone became gentle and she smiled at him. "She's fine, Brandon. Missing you, of course."

"Yeah, I can't wait to see her, but it's too late to bother her now."

"If you think that, you've got as much romance in your blood as your brother."

Mike groaned. "Keep me out of this discussion, will you, Delaney?"

"You don't think she'd mind if I wake her?"

"Brandon, I *know* she would be thrilled," Sydney assured him. Casting a reproving glance at Mike, she declared, "Women are relieved to know as soon as possible when the men they love are safe."

"Thanks." Brandon kissed her on the cheek and bolted down the passageway.

Sydney turned back to find that Mike had shifted his feet to his desk and was now stretched out in his favorite position, almost asleep.

"Good night. Be sure and put out the lantern when you leave." She stormed back into her room, slamming the door behind her.

Fuming, she pulled off her robe, blew out the lamp, and climbed into bed, now thoroughly convinced that Michael MacAllister was the most exasperating man on God's green earth.

For two days I've worried myself sick. Two whole days. Forty-eight hours. And all he has to say is, "What's new?"

After several solid punches to her pillow, she settled back in bed, further persuaded that no woman, with even a minute fragment of intelligence, had any need for a man in her life.

The door opened and she sat up. Her breath caught in her throat. The flickering light from the office lantern cast the tall figure in shadows. He hooked his thumbs into the waistband of his pants and lounged lazily against the frame of the door, naked except for the faded Levi's that hugged his hips and long legs.

"Mad at me, Delaney?"

The male essence of him seduced her. Temptation beckoned, and she felt a rise of panic in her breast.

"It's a long walk back to the house, and that bed sure looks tempting," he said lightly.

"I suggest you get started on that long walk." Lying

back down, she turned over with her back to the door. "Good night, MacAllister." She tucked a hand under her pillow and closed her eyes.

Then she suddenly felt his weight on the bed. "What are you doing?" she said, sitting up with a jolt.

"Thought I'd go to bed. Haven't slept in a couple of nights."

"Not *my* bed," she declared.

"Ah, come on, Delaney. Don't be like that. Your bed's all warmed up. You wouldn't turn me out to face a cold one, would you?"

"I certainly would." She brushed aside the quilt, relieved to see he was still wearing woolen drawers. "Michael MacAllister, get out of here this minute."

"What if I told you I was too tired to move?"

"Well then, I'll help you." She pressed her foot against him and started to shove. Mike grabbed her ankle, and she tried to pull free from his grasp. "Let go of my foot."

"Seems I remember something about you being ticklish," he said.

She rounded her eyes in alarm. "Oh no! You wouldn't."

"Wouldn't I?" With that, he sat up and started to tickle the bottom of her foot.

"Mike, stop it," she giggled. Squealing with uncontrollable laughter, she thrashed and struggled to break his hold. Her shrieks were joined by his as they rolled entwined.

When the struggle ended, she lay on top of him. He closed his arms around her and hugged her more tightly against him.

"God, you feel good, Syd," he murmured as his palms cupped the firm cheeks of her derriere. He turned his face to her neck, breathing deeply. "And you smell so damn good, too," he murmured in a husky whisper.

The heat of his body filtered through the fabric of her gown and seemed to fuse her rounded softness to the hard, muscular length of him. For a long moment they lay in this snug cocoon as his hands continued their slow sweep of her spine.

"So damn ... good," he mumbled. She raised her head when his voice faded.

Mike had fallen asleep.

The following morning while she was eating breakfast, Mike padded sheepishly into the house. Sydney glanced up casually. "Well I hope you passed a pleasant night, MacAllister?"

"Best sleep I had in a couple of months, Delaney. It must have been the company I was keeping. Where's the coffee?"

"I didn't make any. I wasn't certain how long you intended to remain in bed. And I certainly wasn't going to stay to find out."

Smirking, he leaned boldly over the table. "Delaney, did I miss anything ... ah ... exciting last night?"

Sydney picked up her teacup and walked to the door. "You probably did. But I'm confident I didn't."

Later when Mike entered the office, he continued to keep quiet about his encounter with the two Russians. And Sydney was determined not to ask him. Instead, she hoped Mike would find a reason to leave the room so she could coax the story out of Brandon.

But as soon as the office opened, Claire rushed in. "Well what happened?" she demanded.

Sydney sat gritting her teeth, listening while Mike willingly told Claire the whole story of the fight with the Russians. Not one quip passed his lips while he talked to her.

"Well, I've got something *new* to tell you," Claire said when he'd finished. Her message proved to be serious. "While you were gone, a Japanese ship docked here, and the captain told me they saw some Russian ships poaching the sea otters."

"Damn!" Mike swore. He leapt to his feet and began to pace the floor. "I've written to everyone I can think of to try to get the navy involved. I don't know what more I can do."

"Why don't you go to Seattle, Mike? Maybe if you talk to somebody in person you can get some results," Claire suggested.

"I don't have that kind of time, Claire." Returning to his desk, he glanced at the calendar. "Of course, I'll never have a better time than this. And there's a ship from Seward due to stop here today that's bound for the States."

Sydney looked up in surprise when Brandon said, "Why don't we all go? I think it would do Em a world of good to get her away from this place for awhile. We could be there and back before Christmas."

"If we all go, who's going to take care of the office?"

"Pasha can look after things for you, Mike," Claire said. "I can't leave my place, but with Delaney along as a chaperone for Emily, I don't see anything wrong with it."

As much as Sydney found the idea to her liking, she shook her head. "I can't afford to go, so I'll be here to run the office."

"Heavens, Delaney, I don't expect you to be spendin' your own money. I'll pay for you."

"Of course not. I wouldn't consider taking your money, Claire."

Claire turned to Sydney with a sad smile and reached for her hand. "But you'd be doing me a big favor, Delaney. Sure wish I could be there with Em to help her pick out her weddin' gown. But as long as I can't, it would make me feel a lot better to know you will be, Delaney."

"Hey, this isn't a pleasure trip," Mike declared. "I'm only staying for as long as it takes to settle my business."

"Well, while you attend to business the girls can go shoppin' for Em's weddin' dress," Claire said. "Darn sight better than orderin' it through that Montgomery Ward catalog that she and Delaney've been pagin' through."

"Sounds like a lot of wasted expense for the short time we'll be there," Mike argued.

"Wasted expense!" Claire put her hands on her hips. "We're talking about my daughter's wedding, Mike MacAllister."

"What do you say, Mike?" Brandon asked.

Grinning at the huddle of expectant stares, he said, "I think we'd better start packing."

Sydney swung her glance toward the sound of fluttering from the corner. "Oh, my! I've forgotten about Brutus. What will I do with him."

Claire and Brandon exchanged meaningful glances, then said concurrently, "Pasha."

"I'll go tell Em," Brandon said.

"I'll come with you to help her," Claire said excitedly.

Sydney was still slightly overwhelmed by the sudden turn of events. "Well, this is unexpected," she declared when the others had departed. "I mustn't forget to give Pasha some last-minute instructions about Brutus."

"Gee, I feel bad the bird's not coming along." Mike said. "What a disappointment."

"Just cover your ears, Brutus, and don't listen to what he's saying," she cooed. "As you've already noticed, he's not a very nice person. Right?"

"Sydney's right. Sydney's right," Brutus screeched, hopping along his perch. An added two whistles seemed to echo the sentiment.

"Hmmm ... maybe if I cut a notch in the piece of wood he's perched on, that damn bird might just fall and break his neck."

"You have a very nasty mind, MacAllister. I imagine

you and those two perverted Russians must have sat down and compared notes before you parted company."

Mike grimaced and raised his hands. "Okay, I surrender." He got up, came over to her desk, and stuck out his hand.

"What?" she asked.

"Listen, as long as we're all going to Seattle, let's not you and I spoil the trip for Emily and Bran. Let's call a truce. What do you say?" he asked with an infectious grin.

Slipping her hand into his, Sydney returned the smile. "Agreed. No spatting until we return."

"You want to seal it with a kiss, Delaney?"

"Considering how you've already warned me about the 'no commitment' clause attached to your kisses, I trust that a handshake would be more binding, MacAllister. Wouldn't you say?"

"Right as usual," he agreed.

"Sydney's right. Sydney's right," Brutus chirped.

Sydney glanced up at Mike with a self-satisfied smile.

Mike shook his head. "Keeping this truce is going to be harder than I thought."

Chapter 19

When Sydney stepped off the boat in Seattle, she was suddenly struck by a case of homesickness.

In the past months, she had not realized how much she had missed the sights and sounds of the familiar city: the rows of houses and buildings, the cobbled streets, the carriages, the gas lights, the bakery carts, the church steeples—*and the people.*

Wherever she looked, she saw white-clad milkmen, uniformed policemen, businessmen in top hats, or elegantly groomed ladies out for a promenade. Shawl-covered housewives scurried to the market. Sailors on shore leave clustered in small circles. Children laughed and shouted, tossing balls or chasing after one another.

She felt energized from the hustle and bustle of the crowds around her. She closed her eyes and listened to the sound of civilization.

While Sydney basked in the joy of nostalgia, Emily stared with the awe of a child taking a first glimpse through a candy window. Too many delights! Her limited trips to Seward had never prepared her for the sights of Seattle.

As they rode in a carriage to the hotel, Emily stroked the leather carriage seat as if it were velvet—whenever she wasn't gawking at some fascinating scene out of the window. She was constantly tugging at Brandon's sleeve to point out a lovely house, a brightly decorated storefront, or ice skaters in a park.

Once settled in their hotel rooms, the four companions planned their schedule for the day.

Sydney and Emily decided to go on a shopping spree during the time that Mike and Brandon met with the territorial governor. Then they agreed to meet back at the hotel to have dinner together.

As the men prepared to leave the two women on their own, Brandon and Emily drifted into the brothers' room for a private good-bye. Mike stopped to give Sydney a parting warning. "Just stay out of trouble while we're gone, Delaney."

"Are you forgetting we're in my milieu now?" She fluttered her lashes coquettishly. "Matter of fact, Mr. Neanderthal Man, if you feel too much out of your *element*, I'll be more than glad to offer my services."

"Neanderthal Man. Hmmm . . ." he reflected. "Got something to do with a caveman, right?" As he advanced on her, she backed away until she found herself pressed against the wall. Before she could dart away, Mike's arms imprisoned her on each side.

Laughing, she tried to shove him back. "I was only joking," she started to say, but his mouth closed over hers, halting any further attempt at speech.

The kiss began with a light pressure, and her lips molded to his. Then he slipped his tongue past her lips and in a slow, heated exploration began to probe and toy. He drew a breath, and then the pressure of his lips increased as their passion intensified. He began to stroke her mouth with his tongue, sending heated shocks of sensation throughout her, making her senses soar to dizzying heights. Slipping her arms around his neck, she leaned into his strong body. His arm circled her waist, drawing her closer.

Their bulky clothing prevented much contact, so he slid his hands inside her coat. The fabric of her gown offered little protection under the fiery touch of his hands sweeping over her curves. She groaned rapturously into his mouth until breathlessness forced them to separate.

Sagging against him, she rested her cheek against his chest. For several moments, Mike held her in the curve of his arms. Then he slipped a finger under her chin and tilted up her head. As their eyes met, his face curved into the grin she so adored.

"You see, Delaney, I'm never out of my element."

He kissed the tip of her nose. Then he stepped back from her.

Sydney stood immobile. Mike stopped at the door and looked back. "But I'm sure not gonna turn down that offer for your services." With a wicked wink, he disappeared.

After his departure, she remained motionless. Her racing mind pondered his parting words: were they a threat or a promise?

Claire had given each of the girls more money than Sydney had ever seen before, accompanied by firm instructions to spare no expense in the purchases of finery for Emily's wedding and trousseau. With vehement insistence, Claire had reminded them to be sure to include a bridal attendant's gown for Sydney.

And as final parting words to Sydney, Claire had said, "I'm countin' on your good taste and judgment, Delaney. I want my little girl's weddin' to be the finest ever. If you run out of money, just ask Mike for some. I can always give it back to him when he gets home."

With their purses full of currency, and Claire's words echoing in their heads, the girls headed for the bridal shop. A sign embellished with flourishing calligraphy was tucked tidily into a corner of the window:

MADAME FLORINDA'S BRIDAL BOUTIQUE
For The Lady of Ultimate Style.

Silk or satin, aigrette or bow?
Only Madame Flo will know.

Madame Florinda turned out to be a short, bustling woman who exhausted every person in her presence. Her mind seemed to race ahead at a frantic pace.

With one look at Emily, the couturiere ruled out the use of white, which she felt would not enhance Emily's pale loveliness. After much discussion, the three women all agreed upon the ivory-colored satin gown with tiny seed pearls encrusted in small embroidered lace florets. Scattered florets were to be duplicated on the bridal veil as well.

For herself, Sydney chose a gown of green brocade along with a dyed ostrich plume tipped with brown.

With unrestrained delight, the two girls chose a pale-blue gown for the mother of the bride, plus an aigrette of blue and green peacock feathers that they felt would look stunning in Claire's blonde hair.

Madame Florinda would not consider allowing the two women to leave without matching satin shoes and undergarments; and finally, after choosing several peignoirs and additional pieces of lingerie, the monumental task had been completed.

Darkness had descended on the city by the time the girls returned to the hotel. A worried Mike and Brandon had been on the verge of setting out to hunt for them.

The two couples ate a quiet meal at the hotel and planned to celebrate Brandon and Emily's engagement in fine style on the following evening.

"Maybe they'll make a decision sooner than you think, Mike," Sydney said the following morning at breakfast.

Mike shrugged. "See what happens when you deal with bureaucrats, Delaney? The territorial governor said we'd be informed of their decision at a later date. By the time the government makes up its mind to send the navy to investigate, there won't be any otters alive."

"Well, you've done your best, Mike," Sydney said.

"So ... what's on the agenda for today? Unfortunately, we have to leave tomorrow," Mike said.

"Em and I are going to buy a wedding ring," Brandon piped up cheerfully.

"I have some personal business I want to attend to," Sydney replied.

"Oh," Mike said. He wondered what personal business she had in mind. Perhaps the return to Seattle had helped to remind her of what she had given up to go to Solitary ... or maybe there was an old beau in the picture? "Well, I guess I'll just browse around and look at the city."

"Why don't you come with us?" Brandon suggested.

"No thanks," Mike said. "I've got a couple of things I want to do anyway."

Sydney did not notice Mike perusing the newspaper stand in the lobby when she left the hotel. Tightening her mantle around her against the sharp bite of the wind, she hurried down the street.

Mike had no intention of following her. Whatever her personal business, it was her own private affair. Even so, he tucked his hands into the pockets of his parka and just happened to leave the hotel right after her and take the same route.

What the heck! As long as he was out seeing the city, what did it matter which direction he took?

After about ten minutes, her route led them to an older section of the city. His curiosity increased with every step. Wherever could she be going?

Then he guessed her destination even before she passed through the wrought-iron gates.

Now that he had come this far, Mike saw no reason to turn back. For several moments he stood at the fence, then he opened the gate and walked over to where Sydney knelt at the grave of her father.

"You followed me," she said, surprised when she looked up and saw him.

"I hadn't intended to when I started out. It just ended up that way."

Whatever Mike's faults, Sydney knew that lying wasn't one of them. "I would have asked you to come, but I didn't think you would be interested."

"Why didn't you take a carriage, Syd?" he asked gently, seeing how the wind had stung her cheeks.

"Why waste money on a carriage when I can walk? 'A penny saved, is a penny earned,'" she reminded him.

"Well, while you're ... ah ... visiting with your father, I'm going to find a carriage. I'll be back."

After Mike hurried away, Sydney's gaze lowered to the gravestone. "You see, Father? Is it any wonder why I'm falling in love with him?"

Mike and Sydney spent the rest of the day shopping. Sydney bought several skeins of yarn, and she helped Mike select gifts for the forthcoming wedding and Christmas holiday.

That evening when they joined Mike and Brandon in the lobby, the two girls caught the eye of more than one man. And many a lady's lingering glance fell on the tall, dark-haired brothers.

They dined in an elegant restaurant and toasted the engaged couple. Sydney couldn't remember ever having had such a wonderful time. Everything about the evening was exciting.

As they prepared to leave a man who was hurriedly rushing into the restaurant collided with Sydney.

"Why, Mr. Curtis," Sydney exclaimed, recognizing the acne-covered face of her former employer.

"Well, Miss Delaney," Billy Curtis said, "I heard you had left Seattle for a position in Alaska, I believe."

"That's right," Sydney replied. She looked uneasily toward the others who were waiting for her.

Curtis smiled smugly. "So, you're back. The job get too ... hot ... for you, Miss Delaney?" Snickering, he asked, "What happened? Your employer ask you to shovel snow?"

Mike stepped over and took Sydney's arm. "Are you ready to leave, Sydney?"

"Yes, of course. Forgive me for not introducing you. Mr. Curtis, this is Michael MacAllister, my employer. We're here in Seattle on business."

Curtis observed Mike's possessive hand on her arm and his face curved into an insulting smirk. "Yes, I'm sure you are."

The smirk did not set well with Mike. "Curtis, in Alaska we have mosquitos that are bigger than you, but just as annoying." Mike's smile was threatening. "Know what we do with them?"

Billy blanched. "N-no. Not at a-all."

"We simply squash them between our fingers and watch them drop." Mike settled Sydney's mantle around her shoulders. "Now, perhaps you haven't noticed, but you're delaying our departure. I suggest you apologize to the lady for almost knocking her off her feet. We'd like to be on our way."

Curtis was trembling so hard, he could barely get out the words. "Of-of course. I-I apologize for my clum-clumsiness, Miss Delaney."

"Ever try reading aloud to yourself, Curtis? You'd be amazed what it could do for your stutter," Brandon threw out as a parting gibe to the little man.

Billy Curtis vanished as hastily as he had appeared.

The foursome left the restaurant laughing. Once outside, they discovered that a light snow had begun to fall. Brandon and Emily decided to walk to the park and watch the ice skaters.

"How about a carriage ride in the moonlight?" Mike suggested. "We don't have such opportunities in Solitary."

"Oh, I'd love one," Sydney exclaimed.

Mike whistled for a carriage. "Once around the park, cabbie, then back to the hotel."

"Gotcha, Capt'n," the carriage driver said cheerily.

After tucking the blanket around their legs, Mike slipped his arm around Sydney's shoulders. Cuddling against him, she listened contentedly to the clip-clop of the horse's hooves on the cobbled street.

"I can't believe you actually worked for that guy," Mike remarked. "I'm surprised you lasted even one day."

Her saucy grin warned him of what was coming. "Why not? I've managed to last longer than that with you, haven't I?"

"How is it I always manage to open the door so you can walk right in with those remarks? I'm not that bad, Delaney."

"Ah, 'would some power the giftie gie us, To see ourselves as others see us,' MacAllister."

He put a finger under her chin and lifted her face to meet his worried frown. "Lord, Delaney, I'm sorry if I've been so hard to work for."

Her beauty was as luminous and serene as the night surrounding them. Her face glowed with exhilaration. Fluffy flakes of snow feathered her hair and dusted the tips of her long lashes.

"You're not, Mike. I enjoy working for you. You couldn't be a Billy Curtis even if you tried. You're too secure in your manhood. You've got nothing to prove. That's the difference between you and him."

"You know, Delaney, you can be irritating at times, but you make damn good sense." He hugged her tighter.

"Mike, this has been the best day of my life. I've had a wonderful time."

"So have I, Delaney. Can't think of a better one myself."

"Do you still think I was wrong for interfering in Brandon's life?"

"No. I know now I was wrong. I should have realized long before this how much those two loved each other."

"Then maybe you'll admit you've been wrong about me, too."

Mike looked into her hopeful gaze. "Syd, seeing you today at the cemetery and tonight with Curtis reminded me that your life hasn't been all sunshine. You're a courageous young woman. But try to understand . . . I can't change what's deep inside of me. I wish I could. You have become very precious to me, and I don't want to hurt you."

Tears of love glimmered in the green depths of her eyes. "You'd never hurt me, Mike. My instincts tell me that much."

"Maybe not intentionally, Syd." Lowering his head, he kissed her.

The two became lost in the magic of their own making as the carriage quietly rolled along, muffled by the fallen snow.

Chapter 20

❧

On the return voyage to Solitary, they discovered the snow that had lightly dusted Seattle had fallen on Alaska as well. For as far as the eye could see, the countryside had been transformed into a white, pristine wilderness. The spectacular beauty left Sydney breathless. She spent every free moment at the ship's railing.

Once in Solitary, the days passed swiftly as preparations for the wedding continued. On the day the boat arrived with the shipment from Madame Florinda's, the women couldn't wait to open the boxes.

The couturiere proved why her expertise was worth every penny she charged; the dresses fit perfectly and had been crafted by an expert's hand. Claire was thrilled with the selection the girls had made for her, but her excitement quickly turned to tears at the sight of Emily in her wedding gown and veil.

With an understanding hug, Sydney put an arm around the sentimental woman. "It seems like just yesterday she was a babe in my arms, Delaney," Claire said. "Now look at her, all grown and ready to become a wife."

"But aren't you happy knowing she's marrying as fine a man as Brandon, Claire?"

Claire smiled at Sydney through her tears. "Delaney, I've loved Bran like my own son. I've watched those two grow up together. They were inseparable from the moment he and Mike came to Solitary. Em was only two years old then. Brandon was nine. A shy, wet-nosed little kid who still needed a mother. Em has always loved him. And my mother's instinct told me that Bran loved her too."

Claire dabbed at her eyes, recalling a bygone day. "Oh, it's been so beautiful to watch through the years. Bran always looked after her. Made sure she was safe. And now I know he'll keep on doin' it."

"And where was Mike while all this was going on, Claire?"

Claire dried her eyes. "Mike's story isn't so nice. But maybe you can give it a happy ending, Delaney." She patted Sydney's hand and walked over to hug Emily.

Sydney reflected silently on Claire's words. Would she ever know any more than bits and pieces about Mike's past?

As the ship pulled into the bay carrying the preacher from Seward, Captain Reid repeatedly tooted the horn in celebration. The sound was like the joyous peal of church bells to the residents of Solitary awaiting the wedding celebration.

They hurried from their homes to the passageway of the MacAllister house. With his scarf flying and Lily and Sal on either arm, Pasha rushed over to join the spectators. Even Yuri Kherkov was in attendance.

The bride and her mother were sequestered in Sydney's bedroom. The groom and the best man were anxiously pacing the floor of their home.

Since Solitary did not have a church, the wedding was to be held in the long passageway connecting the house and the office. All crates had been removed, and the walls of the corridor had been decorated with spruce and large satin bows.

By the time the preacher and Captain Reid disembarked and arrived on the scene, the wedding guests lined the walls of the passageway behind the long streamers of ribbon that cordoned off a narrow aisle for the bride.

The preacher, the groom, and the best man took their positions at the end of the long hallway. When all was to his satisfaction, an excited, wild-eyed Pasha hastened back down the passageway to Sydney's room.

The mother of the bride led off the procession. With tears of happiness, Claire entered the passageway on the arm of Joseph. Mike winked at her when she took her place beside him.

Then his gaze shifted to Sydney, and he held his breath.

The décolletage of her gown exposed the creamy curve of her breasts and shoulders to his hungry gaze. Her hair had been pulled to the top of her head and thick curls hung past her nape to grace her shoulders. The wispy ends of a plume tucked into her hair fluttered with an airy delicacy as she moved down the aisle.

He wrenched his gaze away from her to look at Emily, who followed on the arm of a proud Pasha.

In her satin gown with its flowing train sweeping behind her, Emily looked like a storybook princess. An ethereal smile glorified her loveliness as her blue eyes met the worshipful gaze of the man who adored her.

And as the young couple vowed to continue their love through eternity, Sydney shifted her gaze and met Mike's dark stare.

Once the ceremony ended, the celebration moved to Claire's. With only five hours of daylight, nightfall came swiftly. Following Claire's instructions, Mike had brought back four cases of champagne from Seattle, and accompanied by countless toasts to the bride and groom, the music and dancing soon became as lively as it had been on Founder's Day.

The bubbly wine lightened everyone's spirits except Sydney's. She couldn't help but feel depressed watching the bride and groom. She loved Brandon and Emily dearly and didn't begrudge them one moment of happiness. But the wedding ceremony had made her achingly aware of how much she now yearned for the same commitment from Mike.

For a brief moment, she let down her guard and allowed her feelings to show. Pasha pulled her over to the bar beside Yuri Kherkov.

"Vhy is my little *Kpacorá* being looking so sad?"

"Yes, Sydney, have some of this caviar that I brought vith me from Russia," Yuri said. He spread some of the appetizer on an unleavened cracker. "There is no better."

"I've never eaten caviar before," Sydney replied. "I'm not certain I care for any."

"My dear Sydney. If you've never eaten it before, how can you possibly know vether or not you vill like it?"

She accepted the cracker he gave her. Cautiously nibbling, she chewed several times. "Well, it's okay, but I'm sure I could exist without it." She laughed as she swallowed.

"Is not being just good, *Kpacorá*. Is being excellent," Pasha said, heaping a spoonful of the caviar on a cracker and popping it into his mouth.

"Well, I'll have another, but just a very little piece," she cautioned.

Pasha winked at Yuri. "You see, Colonel Kherkov. Our little *Kpacorá* is being true Russian at heart."

Mike watched from a nearby table. Much to his consternation, Pasha and Yuri insisted that Sydney sample a drink of vodka to perk up her spirits.

"But I don't like the taste of alcohol. *That* I know for certain," she declared.

"How can Sydney not be hafing one drink on such vondrous occasion?" Pasha insisted. "Is not vedding vithout vodka," he urged.

"Very well, I'll try a few sips, but that is all," she declared, accepting the glass Yuri held out to her.

"You vill like it, my little Sydney," Yuri assured her. Sydney tried a few sips of the liquor. "Well, it's okay. I can't say it has very much taste at all." She finished the drink to smiles of approval from Pasha and Yuri.

"See? Vat Pasha say is being true, *Красота́.*"

When Yuri poured her another small drink, Mike walked over to the bar. "I don't think Delaney should have another drink, Pasha. She's not used to alcohol."

"Michael, vud Pasha let his little *Красота́* be drinking too much vodka?"

"Perhaps I am confused," Yuri interjected. "I thought you vere Miss Delaney's employer, MacAllister, not her father."

Mike turned to him with an icy glare. "I'd say that role would fall better into your age group, Kherkov."

Sydney resented the insult to Yuri as much as she did Mike's attitude toward her. He refused to make a commitment to her, yet he presumed he had a right to control her life.

"Really, Mike. I think you owe Colonel Kherkov an apology. And I also believe I'm old enough to know what I'm doing." Her eyes flashed defiantly. "There is nothing wrong in toasting the wedding of Mr. and Mrs. Brandon MacAllister with a small glass of vodka." She raised the glass and drank the liquor.

"Okay, Delaney. I guess you are *old enough* to know what you're doing." He walked away and plopped down in a seat next to Claire.

Drinking a glass of champagne, and already having had one too many, Claire leaned over and smiled at Mike. "Hey, big fella, I don't allow such long faces at my daughter's weddin'. Lily," she called out to the passing girl, "get this guy out on the floor for a dance."

"Come on, Mike," Lily said, taking his hand and pulling him to his feet. "I always enjoy dancin' with you." Her brow arched suggestively. " 'Course, I ain't talkin' about no dance floor, am I?"

"Lily, you're shameless." Mike laughed, but allowed

her to lead him to the dancers. Soon he was enjoying himself along with the other celebrants.

His levity had not gone unnoticed by Sydney. Watching Mike having a good time with the prostitute only made her more aware of the intimacy he had shared with the woman. Her second drink of vodka had made her reckless.

"Hey, Pasha, why don't you teach me that Russian dance?" she asked.

"Is not good time now. Pasha is thinking Sydney is not being dressed so rightly to learn. But come, *Красота,* ve dance anyvay."

"You come, too, Yuri," Sydney said, grabbing the arm of the older man.

With Sydney in the middle, the three people linked themselves together side by side, crossing arms at the back of each other's waist. They began to move with rhythmic hops and dips.

Giggling, Sydney counted out the beat. "One, two, three, kick. One, two, three, dip."

"Hey, that looks like fun," Lily declared. "Let's join them."

"You go ahead," Mike said. "I'll sit and watch."

Lily attached herself to Yuri, and the four people continued moving along. Soon the bride and groom were lured into the line, and the dance floor cleared to make room for the long string of people who joined the dancers.

"One, two, three, kick. One, two, three, dip," Sydney called out gaily, and the crowd joined the chant.

Claire clapped along to the music as Mike sat silently, never once diverting his stare from Sydney. The sound of her laughter and the appealing sight of the curls bouncing on her shoulders brought a tender smile to his mouth.

Bright with excitement and the effects of the vodka, Sydney's eyes glowed and her cheeks flushed. She looked up into Yuri's face as the music increased in tempo.

Mike's smile disappeared, replaced by a grim frown.

When the dance came to an end, Yuri lifted her off her feet and swung her around.

"Vas most exhausting, but most enjoyable," Pasha declared, throwing his arms around the shoulders of the pair.

"And most thirst-provoking," Sydney added. Yuri poured more vodka into her glass and handed it to her.

"Must dance vith my darlink Claire," Pasha announced and rushed off to claim her. Sydney smiled as she saw him draw the protesting woman onto the dance floor.

"Your spirits appear much lighter now, my little Sydney," Yuri said.

"Oh, they are, Yuri." She turned to him with a smile, and then her face fell into a frown. "Why are you swaying back and forth, Yuri?" She blinked several times and groped for the bar. "Oh, my, the whole room is spinning. Are we having another earthquake?"

"Perhaps some fresh air vould help," Yuri suggested.

"Yes, I think so."

"I'll get your coat."

Sydney leaned heavily against the bar, trying to maintain her balance. The spinning images and sounds merged together, becoming a whirling kaleidoscope. She felt him slip her mantle over her shoulders, and then with a firm grasp on her elbow, he led her to the door.

Which is as far as Yuri got before Mike stopped him. "Just where the hell do you think you're taking her, Kherkov?" Mike demanded.

"Miss Delaney is in need of some fresh air. I vas assisting her outside."

Mike's black glare bore into the Russian. "Maybe if you hadn't poured all that vodka into her, it wouldn't be necessary." He took Sydney's arm. "I'll take care of her."

Yuri released his hold. "As you vish, Mr. MacAllister." He returned to the bar.

Once outside, Mike lifted her into his arms. Even in her inebriated state, Sydney recognized the feel of the arms holding her. Sighing, she closed her eyes and leaned her head against his chest.

"How are you feeling, Delaney?" he asked.

Through her mind's groggy muddle, she responded to the deep, familiar voice and cuddled against him. "Better. At least the room and the music aren't spinning around anymore."

"I would hope not, Delaney. There is no room and no music. We're outside now."

Her eyelids felt too heavy to raise. "I'll have to take your word for it," Sydney slurred.

"Too bad you didn't take *my word* about the vodka," he remarked.

"Please don't yell at me, Mike."

"I'm not yelling, Delaney," he said, smiling despite his annoyance.

After reaching her room, he removed her mantle, laid her on the bed, and then lit the lamp. Eying him, Brutus began to hop along his perch. "Sydney's right. Sydney's right."

"Sydney's tight," Mike corrected. "Intoxicated. As in, drunk as a skunk." He picked up the neatly folded cage cover nearby. "And you, I don't need. Good night," he declared, slipping the cover over the cage.

Sitting down on the edge of the bed, Mike began to undress Sydney. He raised her to a sitting position and removed the plume and pins from her hair, combing his fingers through the red tresses until they tumbled to her shoulders. Then laying her back down, he slipped the dress off her shoulders and pulled it down past her hips.

Sydney opened her eyes. "What are you doing to me, Mike?"

"I'm taking off your clothes," he announced, trying to sound as detached as possible. Her shoes and hose came next.

"Oh, are you going to make love to me?" she asked with a vivacious smile. She sat up and slipped her arms around his neck.

Disentangling her arms, he laid her back. "No, Delaney. I'm putting you to bed so you can sleep it off. Which is a damn sight more honorable than what that Russian gentleman friend of yours had in mind." After he pulled off her petticoat, only the scanty underwear remained. He found her nightgown and pulled it over her head. She was already asleep when he tucked her under the covers.

She sat up hurriedly. "I don't want to go to sleep." Suddenly her eyes widened with distress. "Mike! I don't feel so good."

"Which is exactly why you need to lie down now, Delaney. No more popping up and down. Just lie quietly and think about pleasant things."

"Just go away and let me die," she groaned.

Ignoring her, Mike tucked her under the covers, then sponged off her face with a cool cloth and laid another one across her brow. Minutes later, she fell asleep.

To ward off the chill, he built a fire and the room soon warmed. Picking up one of her hands that lay listlessly on the quilt, he held it in the warmth of his own. With a loving gaze, Mike studied her face—the face that had become so dear to him.

Yes, he was in love with her. Although he could not admit the truth to her, he could no longer deny it to himself. And his soul cried out for her as much as his body did.

The rest of the night passed peacefully for Sydney. Drifting in and out of sleep, Mike maintained a vigil in a chair at her bedside. At daylight, he slipped quietly out of the room.

* * *

Brutus' squawking awoke her. Sydney opened her eyes, then quickly grabbed her head, cringing under the punishing blows inside her head.

Gradually, she sat up and looked around, realizing she was in her own bedroom—with no recollection of how she had gotten there. Clutching her throbbing head between her hands, she tried to remember. Her last memory was of standing at the bar with Yuri.

She slipped two slim legs over the side of the bed, then slowly rose to her feet. She could not remember a time when she had felt so miserable.

Frantic to stop Brutus' screeching, she staggered over to the cage and yanked off the cover. "Don't suppose you care to tell me what happened last night?"

"Sydney's right," he squawked. The sound sent a shock wave to her brain and a shiver down her spine.

Continuing to tremble, Sydney thought the fire must have gone out until she discovered she was wearing only a thin nightgown. Snatching her robe off a wall peg, she quickly donned it and shoved her feet into slippers.

When Sydney opened her bedroom door, she stopped at the sight of Mike sitting at his desk. Shielding her eyes against the light shining through the window, she walked over to the stove and put on a kettle for tea.

"Feeling a little under the weather this morning, Delaney?" he asked. He began to toss around a piece of paper he had crumpled into a ball.

"I don't want to talk about it," She *did* remember his warning her not to drink the vodka.

"I've heard tell that the morning after, you're supposed to take a bite from the dog that bit you," he said, continuing to toss the paper ball into the air. "I'll be glad to run over to Claire's and get you more vodka."

Her stomach churned at the thought. "I'm quite aware of what's wrong with me, Mike. I have read about the effects of over-imbibing."

"Reading about a hangover is not quite the same as experiencing one, is it, Delaney?"

In her present condition, his smugness was unbearable. "Will you stop tossing that damn paper up and down?" Clutching her head, she took several deep breaths to regain her composure. Then with Herculean strength, she raised her head, which she knew for certain was too heavy for the frail neck that supported it.

"If you don't mind, Mr. MacAllister, I would like to be excused from my responsibilities today. Of course I will expect you to deduct the lost time from my weekly wages. But I am feeling indisposed and would like to spend the rest of the day in my room."

"Gee, Bran and Emily are doing the same thing. Sure hope it's nothing catching."

Picking up the teapot, Sydney gave him a scornful look just before closing the door to her room.

"Course, I could have caught it from you in your room last night," Mike called after her, chuckling.

She opened the door immediately and popped her head back through the crack. "What do you mean, last night?" She had held out hope that Claire might have put her to bed. Still holding the teapot, she rushed over to his desk. "Are you the one who brought me back here last night?"

"Yep."

"Did you put me to bed?"

"Yep."

"And undressed me?"

"Yep."

She snatched the ball out of the air and flung it to the floor. "Did you . . ." She swallowed. ". . . ah . . . spend the night with me?"

"Yep."

"And did we . . . ah . . . do anything out of the ordinary?"

"Well, you *did* ask me to make love to you, Delaney," he responded defensively.

Her suspicions roved riotously through her muddled head. "You wouldn't ... not while I was ... no ... you'd never ..."

She cut off her stammering when his expression changed to a look of remorse. "Nothing personal, Delaney, but I've had a lot better times than the one I spent with you last night."

For a lengthy moment she struggled with her doubts. Finally, she raised her head. "I don't believe one word you're saying Michael MacAllister. You're making up the whole thing." She strode to her room and, with no consideration for her throbbing head, she slammed the door.

Chapter 21

When Mike tapped on her door several hours later, Sydney had dressed and already felt better. "Delaney, may I talk to you for a moment?"

She opened the door to the sight of his grim look. Pasha, right behind Mike, cast her a sorrowful look.

"What is it, Mike?"

"I'm afraid I've something to tell you that you're not going to like."

"Pasha go. Vill vait in stable." The Russian rushed away as if the hounds of hell were yapping at his heels.

Resigned, Mike shook his head and simply said, "I have to get rid of Caesar."

Aghast, she was on the verge of tears. "Get rid of him? You mean he's been hurt? What happened?"

"I mean, we'll have to turn him loose. For his own good."

"Turn him loose? But he's just a puppy. What will become of him? Please, Mike. Don't do this," she pleaded.

"The dogs won't accept him. We've tried time and time again. He repeatedly annoys Grit. Won't leave him alone. Today Grit nipped at him. Next time, it could be worse."

"So keep them separated."

Mike didn't feel any better about what had to be done than she did, and her pleading only added to his guilt. "That's ridiculous, Delaney. I can't do that. They're sled dogs. Grit is the undisputed leader."

"Grit. Is he the only dog you care about? That puppy trusts us. How can you just turn him loose in the wilds to fend for himself? Why, he'll be an easy prey for any animal."

"He'll find a pack, and they'll adopt him. Wolves are very protective of their young."

"And what if he doesn't?" she asked, tears streaking her cheeks.

"He's a wolf cub, Delaney, not a puppy. Get that straight in your head," he said angrily. "So he's born with better instincts for survival than a human being. Certainly better than yours anyway, if last night was any example."

"So that's what this is all about. You're doing this just to get even with me for my friendship with Yuri."

She might just as well have slapped his face. For a few seconds he stared in shock. "Believe whatever you want to believe. I've got nothing more to say."

When he turned to leave, she grabbed his arm. "Well then, I'll go with you."

"Damn it, Delaney, you're not going to change my mind. So why make this harder on yourself?"

"May I go with you?" she repeated, unwavering.

"If you're ready by the time I hitch the team."

The blanket of snow did not require a sled. Pasha had the team hitched up and ready to leave when they reached the barn.

" 'Et tu, Bruté?,' " she accused Pasha after he climbed up on the wagon to accompany them. The glum trio left Solitary, and as they drove past the kennel, Grit charged up to the fence, howling persistently in protest at being left behind.

Unable to bear the thought of sitting between the two men who had betrayed her, Sydney climbed into the bed and cuddled Caesar in her lap.

Occasionally Mike and Pasha spoke softly to each other, but neither made any attempt to converse with her. Sydney was grateful because she doubted if she could have responded. Her heart felt near to breaking and her chest constricted from the effort of restraining her tears.

After about two hours, Mike stopped the wagon to examine some spoor on the trail. Sydney closed her eyes and said a prayer, clutching Caesar to her breast.

Nodding to Pasha, Mike climbed back up on the wagon, then flipped the reins, and the wagon rolled on. After several more miles he stopped again, climbed down, and examined the trail.

"What's he doing?" she asked, finally breaking her silence.

"Michael is checking trail for volf spoor. Dat is volf vay to mark own territory. He be sure to lef little cub vere other volfes vill find him. Michael is good man. Sydney is being most vrong to think else."

Mike returned to the wagon. Wordlessly, he walked back and reached up for the cub. As Sydney lifted him, Caesar licked away the salty tears that streaked her cheeks. She handed him to Mike.

While Mike carried Caesar away, Pasha turned the wagon around. When Mike returned, he climbed up, took the reins and they moved off.

Sydney looked back as Caesar came bouncing out of the woods. For several yards the cub chased behind them, then exhausted, he stopped and with his little head cocked, watched perplexed as the wagon rolled away.

Burying her head in her hands, Sydney muffled her sobs.

The trip back passed in silence. The short day had turned into night by the time they arrived home. Pasha lingered just long enough to give Sydney a hug.

"Sometimes, little *Красота*, being big man is most hard. Dat is vy, must be big man to begin vith."

"It's been a long day, Pasha. I'll try to decipher that tomorrow," she said listlessly, and returned to her room.

Shortly thereafter, a light tap sounded on her door. "Sydney, it's Emily. May I come in?"

Sydney opened the door, and the two girls embraced. "I'm so sorry, Sydney."

Sydney stepped away and forced a weak smile. "You mean marriage is that bad?" she teased half-heartedly.

Puzzled at first, Emily smiled, shaking her head. "Oh my, no." She blushed and turned serious again. "I'm talking about Caesar, of course. We all know how attached you were to him."

Sydney turned away and busied herself at the fire. "Well, I hope he'll be all right." She turned back, smiling. "Now tell me, how do you like married life?"

"You mean, how do I like having Bran make love to me?" Emily giggled. "Oh, Sydney, it's wonderful. *He's* so wonderful. And I'm so happy. It's not fair for me to be so happy when I know how badly you're feeling," she added wistfully.

"Don't even give that a thought," Sydney said.

"Well, I've held dinner . . . waiting for you and Mike to get back." She took Sydney's hand. "Bran and I wish to share with you the first meal that I, Mrs. Emily Elizabeth MacAllister, have cooked as a wedded woman."

"Oh, I just think Brandon's afraid to try it out alone," Sydney teased. With their arms linked, the two girls walked down the passageway.

Sydney was not surprised to see that Mike had been invited, too. Why wouldn't she expect to see him? He lived there. But unlike the fun and laughter the foursome had shared in Seattle, this meal was tense and uncomfortable. Emily and Bran had to carry the brunt of the conversation. All four people were relieved when the meal ended.

As Emily washed the dishes, Sydney dried them. The younger girl glanced over at her. "Don't think so unkindly of Mike, Sydney. He was only trying to keep Caesar alive."

Sydney sighed deeply. "Emily, I've heard this from

Mike, from Pasha, and now you. How do you think he's helping Caesar by turning him loose in the wilds? I just don't understand that kind of reasoning."

"Sydney, given the chance one of the dogs would eventually have torn the cub apart. They just wouldn't accept him. That happens sometimes. A couple years ago, Mike was given two wolf cubs. The dogs accepted one of them, and killed the other. It's one of those crazy things that no one can really explain. Maybe dogs are like people. You can love the Mikes and Brans on sight, and hate the Levs and Borises."

"Pretty much wisdom for a soon-to-be seventeen-year-old to be toting around," Sydney said.

"I just want you to try to see that Mike gave Caesar the best chance he could. And besides, Caesar is a wolf."

"Oh, Mike reminded me of that fact," Sydney said bitterly. "Several times, as a matter of fact."

"But you don't understand what we mean by that. The Indians believe every animal has a spirit, just like a human being. And a wolf's spirit? Well it's not meant to be penned. A wolf must be free to run wild. *That* is their spirit. Deny them freedom, and you've destroyed their soul."

Blushing, Emily lowered her head. "Listen to me . . . explaining something to you. I'll never know as much as you do, Sydney, if I live to be a hundred."

Sydney stood abashed, too embarrassed to admit how pathetically inadequate her book learning was compared to this young girl's wisdom.

She didn't turn when Mike walked over. "Thanks for the dinner, Emily. It was delicious."

Emily pointed to the blanket and pillow he carried. "What are you doing with those?"

"I thought I'd sleep in Rami's stable for a couple of nights. I just thought you and Bran could use a couple of days to yourselves."

"Hey, Mike, this is your home, too," said Brandon as

he joined them. "Em might feel that she's driving you out."

"Hey, I'm just sleeping in the stable for a couple of nights. I'm not moving out. I'll see you in the morning."

"Well at least sleep in the office, Mike. It will be a lot warmer than a stable," Sydney said.

"I might disturb you, Delaney."

"It's no bother, Mike."

Mike put down his blankets and pillow. "Well, I'll give you a chance to bed down."

After helping to finish the dishes, Sydney made her departure. Walking down the passageway still adorned with satin ribbons and bows, she found it hard to believe that the wedding had taken place only yesterday.

As she lay in the darkness, she heard Mike enter the office and shuffle around for a few minutes. Then there was silence.

Sleep, as usual, eluded her as it usually did after an argument with Mike. Her bitterness had already turned to guilt. Accusing Mike of getting rid of her pup because he was jealous of Yuri. How childish. How utterly stupid. Why did she always misjudge his actions and motives? Challenge his decisions?

Pasha had tried to tell her that it took a man of strength to make difficult decisions. And Mike was such a man. He lived by a code that young and old trusted and understood—everyone but herself, that is.

Sydney knew she had to tell him she was sorry. And as the night stretched on, she realized she would not be able to fall asleep unless she told him *now*.

Slipping on her robe, she unlocked her bedroom door.

"Mike, where are you?" Sydney half-whispered.

"I'm over here." Sydney turned toward the sound of his voice and could distinguish his outline in the corner of the room. "What do you want, Delaney?"

His tone sounded cold and impersonal. She felt her

courage falter. "I want to apologize for what I said to you today."

"So what will you accuse me of next, Delaney? Pulling off frogs' legs or wings off butterflies?"

"I know I was wrong. I guess I try to think the worst of you because I . . ." She hesitated, feeling foolish about continuing when the air was charged with his hostility.

"Because why?" he asked.

"Because . . ." *How can I admit to him that I love him, when I'm afraid to admit it to myself?* "Because I guess my pride, or something like that, makes me strike out at you."

His silence made it more difficult, but she was determined to finish. "You were right about Caesar. I know I acted like a child, Mike. I guess I just let my emotions do my thinking for me or I never would have made such a ridiculous accusation. I'm very sorry for being so unfair to you."

For a long moment she hesitated. "But you know as well as I, those things I said to you really had nothing to do with Caesar." She paused and took a deep breath. "The argument was about us, Mike. This feeling between us. It's getting worse every day. But you warned me, didn't you? You were right about that, too."

He remained silent, and she moved to the door of her bedroom.

"Delaney." She stopped without turning around.

"Nothing happened between us last night."

She closed her eyes and smiled. "I know, Mike. You've got too much character to take advantage of a woman. And too much respect for life to use a puppy . . . I mean cub . . . as an instrument of revenge." She stepped into her bedroom and closed the door.

For a long moment after she left, Mike sat unmoving. He wanted her so badly he ached. He raised his hands and stared woodenly at his wet palms. Then rising, he opened the door and stepped outside.

He shoved his hands into his pants pockets and drew a deep breath. Cold air stabbed at his lungs. Crisp and dry. It exhilarated him. He glanced up at the sky. This evening, the swirling phenomenon above painted an azure patina on the crusted snow and ice crystals coating the trees.

His head quickly swerved toward the sea when the sharp crack of splintering ice on a distant glacier shattered the night like a rifle blast.

God, how he loved this land.

Daily, men came to Alaska, lured by the glitter of gold, a promise of richness, the hope of a new beginning. But these were not the enticements that had beckoned to him.

Her untamed, unrestrained wildness had seduced his soul.

How could he explain to Syd the peace that a wilderness brings to a man—when everyday he warned her of the savagery of those same wilds?

He couldn't make any promises to Syd until he was able to answer these questions himself. But what of the ache in his loins?

Chapter 22

Wearing a pleased smile, Sydney left Rami's house and hurried down the street to the office. She clutched a crudely wrapped package concealed under her mantle. With Christmas two days away, she now had only the small embroidered sampler to finish and her Christmas list would be complete.

She waved to Mike and Brandon who were adding on a bathroom at the rear of the house. After experiencing the luxury of a private, marble bathtub in Seattle, Mike had ordered a water heater and a bathtub. Of course he claimed it was for the convenience of Emily and Sydney. He had assured them that by New Year's Day they would be able to take a hot bath, right in their own house. His announcement brought a big smile to Emily, who was accustomed to the easy access of her mother's bathhouse.

Sydney hastened into the office, removed her mantle, and quickly boxed the present she had so zealously concealed. After adding the gift to the pile of other presents in her bedroom, she returned to the office and was absorbed in writing checks when Mike and Brandon came in a short time later.

"If you two don't go out soon and get a Christmas tree, Emily and I will do it ourselves," she declared.

She did not see Mike wink at Brandon. "Christmas tree? Who said anything about a Christmas tree?"

Mike scratched his chin. "I suppose we could go out and try to find a yule log. What do you think, Bran?"

"Gosh, Mike, I'm kind of tired. Thought I'd go to bed early tonight."

"Christmas won't be Christmas without any tree," Sydney started to quote from *Little Women*. Then she brought her hand to her mouth in dismay. "No, that's not right. Jo said, 'Christmas won't be Christmas without any presents.' "

In a dramatic display of histrionics, Mike leaned against the wall for support. "Good Lord! Did you hear that, Bran? Delaney almost misquoted."

"Well, the quote would make just as much sense if it was about a tree," she rebutted. "And I always had a Christmas tree, even when I lived alone."

Mike threw her a disgusted glance. "Delaney, I think this is just another one of these holiday celebrations you're hell-bent on organizing. You're not going to get me all wrapped up in sentimental drivel."

Her mouth opened in astonishment. "Sentimental drivel!" Slipping her hands on her hips, she scolded, "MacAllister, I can't believe that even a dispassionate person like yourself would not feel some kind of sentiment at Christmas."

Mocking her, Mike put his hands on his hips. "Oh, yeah, lady. Well just hang up some mistletoe and you'll see how *unimpassioned* I am."

"Is that so? What would you know about mistletoe when you don't seem to celebrate *anything?*"

Mischief gleamed in his eyes. "Come to think of it, why wait for mistletoe?" He advanced toward her desk.

She had seen that look in his eyes before. Squealing, she raced around the corner of the desk. "Stay away from me, Mike." She dodged him, keeping the desk between them as he tried to grab her. Playfully, Mike lunged across the desk and missed her.

"Let's get going and find a tree," Brandon said. "Otherwise, I'm leaving you two to your games and I'll go find Emily."

"All right, grab the axe. Guess we can't get out of it," Mike grumbled.

"And when you get back, we'll eat. Then we'll all decorate the tree," Sydney said excitedly.

"Can't wait," Mike said drolly. He picked up his rifle. "But we never decorate the tree until Christmas Eve."

She looked at him, chagrined. Once again, she had presumed too much. "So you do celebrate Christmas?" she asked sheepishly.

"Yes, of course we do, Sydney," said Brandon. "Mike just likes to tease you. Why am I beginning to feel like the old man in this group?"

"Well, I wasn't teasing about that mistletoe, Delaney. So when I get through choppin' up the forest, look out," Mike warned.

As soon as they disappeared from sight, Sydney hurried back into her room and grabbed her embroidery. She would work on it for another half an hour, then go and help Emily with the evening meal.

The two men returned an hour later toting a huge pine tree. They pounded the trunk to a cross bar and stood the pine on end. The tree, its branches hanging thickly, filled a corner of the room, sending out the familiar Christmas scent of fresh pine.

After dinner, though Sydney's fingers itched to get at the tree, she helped Emily with the dishes and then returned to her room. Tucking herself in bed for the night, she worked on the sampler.

The following day, the air was charged with anticipation—at least for Sydney and Emily. Mike and Brandon appeared unaffected as they resumed construction on the bathroom addition. Mike was determined to complete it that day.

Later in the afternoon, they were joined by Claire. The three women laughed and chatted as they worked on the special meal and preparations for that evening. While a tasty plum pudding bubbled on the hearth, they painted pinecones, cut streamers of satin ribbon, and strung popcorn on a string.

By late afternoon, all was in readiness. As two plump ptarmigans roasted on the spit, the men, accompanied by Claire, headed for Claire's bathhouse to clean up. Sydney returned to her room.

She heated a flat iron, then shaped and pressed the sampler. A smile tugged at the corners of her mouth as she carefully wrapped it. Later, dressed in her purple gown, with a bright white bow holding back her hair, Sydney gathered up the pile of brightly covered packages and walked down the passageway.

Mike heard her coming and opened the kitchen door. His arms enclosed her, then he pointed to the sprig of mistletoe hanging over the archway.

"Merry Christmas, Delaney," he murmured as he bent to kiss her. The touch of his lips heightened her excitement, and she reacted spontaneously.

"Okay, move on, big brother." Brandon shoved Mike aside. "Merry Christmas, Sydney. And thanks for making *this* Christmas very special for Em and me." He kissed and hugged her.

An impatient Pasha would no longer be denied. "Vhat is being taking so long? Pasha is most anxious to be giving his little *Kpacorá* most big kiss." Sydney found herself enveloped in a bear hug that almost squeezed the breath out of her. She felt certain that only the presents in her arms prevented her from sustaining crushed ribs.

Once freed from Pasha's grasp, Sydney had a chance to look around. A cozy warmth pervaded the large room, along with the aroma of the roasting fowl and the fragrance of fresh pine from the tree and the boughs that decorated the walls. Tall bay candlesticks flanked a silver wassail bowl resting on a bed of pine boughs bedecked with red bows.

As Sydney added her presents to those already under

the tree, Mike walked over and playfully swung her off her feet.

"Look, everyone, don't you think Delaney looks colorful enough to hang on the tree as a decoration?"

Emily's eyes glowed with love. "Only as an angel at the top."

Laughing, the two girls hugged one another. "I'd say you look like the angel, Emily. Not I."

Always the diplomat, Brandon put an arm around each of them. "And I'd say you both look like angels."

"I feared this party would get carried away with sentimental drivel. Now I'm convinced," Mike declared.

"Keep it up, MacAllister, and we'll hang *you* on that tree." Sydney winked at Brandon and Emily. "By your neck, that is."

Grinning, Mike threw up his hands. "Peace on earth, goodwill to men, Delaney." He dug into a box and pulled out one of the candleholders. "But okay, as long as we've ruled out using Delaney, let's get this poor naked tree decorated."

Smiling, Pasha and Claire sat back with their spiced cider. They watched Mike and Brandon place the candleholders on the tree while Sydney and Emily hung satin bows and painted pinecones. The four people were always getting into one another's way, which only added to the pleasure of the occasion. Mike and Bran added the final touch by draping popcorn garlands from branch to branch.

When the task was completed and the candles lit, they all stepped back with a chorus of "oohs and ahs" to admire the sparkling tree.

Mike handed Sydney a cup of cider. "Looks real good, Delaney."

"I think so, too," she said with enthusiasm.

Brandon and Emily sat down before the fireplace and slowly sipped their cups of cider, continually stealing pleased glances at their handiwork.

"Our first Christmas tree," Emily murmured, smiling lovingly into her husband's face.

"Good heavens, Em, you and Bran have celebrated Christmas together for thirteen years," Claire said.

"I know, but this is our first Christmas together as husband and wife."

Slipping an arm around her shoulders, Brandon assured her, "The first of many, sweetheart."

The moment abounded with too much sentimentality for the emotional Pasha. Dabbing at his eyes, he said, "Is most beautiful. Pasha is thinking he soon vill be veeping."

"If this evening gets any more syrupy, Michael is thinking he soon vill be veeping, too," Mike announced. "So I want an honest answer; does Delaney have any plans to read a story or poem?" He looked at her suspiciously.

"No, I haven't, Michael MacAllister. But we could sing Christmas carols."

He took her hand and pulled her toward the kitchen. "I've got a better idea, Delaney. Let's eat and then make another pass at that mistletoe."

The food was succulent, and after eating their fill, they all settled down before the fireplace. Sydney stole a glance at Mike as he sat with his back against the wall, gazing broodingly into the flames.

What an enigma, she thought. He was all male. In his arms she had known unexpected, overwhelming pleasure. The warmth of his touch. The excitement of his kiss. Yet how often had she also felt the sting of his harshness? His maddening stubbornness? The bite of his wrath? And then, like tonight, the playful little boy in him would come out to remind her of how much she loved him.

Of course, am I so different from him? she thought. Shifting her gaze to the Christmas tree, her excitement glowed like that of a little girl and the lines of a poem came to her mind.

"Backward, turn backward, O Time, in your flight,
Make me a child again, just for tonight!"

"What?" Mike asked. Sydney hadn't realized she had
spoken the words aloud.

"Oh, I was just commenting on how much Christmas
makes children of us all," she said hastily.

Jumping to his feet, Pasha rushed to the tree. "Pasha
is thinking is time for presents to being open. Is big
moment ve all haf been vaiting for to come.

Mike shifted nearer to Sydney. "Is this when you've
planned for Santa Claus to come down that chimney?"
he teased. She smiled with pleasure, but did not reply.
The little boy had returned.

"First gift to be gifing is from Pasha." He pulled out
several packages from under the tree and handed one to
Sydney. "Is being for you, my little *Красота*. And von
for each of my darlinks," he added, following suit with
Claire and Emily. "And my good friends, Michael and
Brandon."

Spreading his arms, he rolled his eyes expressively.
"Now be opening presents for Pasha to see how happy
he is making you."

Sydney eagerly opened the gift to discover a pair of
doeskin gloves with fox cuffs. "Oh, Pasha, they're
beautiful." She slipped her hand into one. "And they fit
perfectly. Thank you. I love them."

Claire and Emily each received gloves identical to
Sydney's. As all three of the ladies hugged and kissed
him, he smiled with pleasure. "Is part Pasha like most."

Mike and Brandon were the recipients of new leather
sheaths for their knives.

"This is great, Pasha, but don't expect a kiss," Mike
said. The Russian did, however, get a slap on the back
from both brothers.

"Did you make all these gifts yourself, Pasha?" Sydney asked. "They're so lovely."

Nodding, Pasha beamed with pleasure. "Is nothing."

Then, like an eager child, Pasha sat down on the floor before the fireplace and opened his gifts from the others: a knife from Mike, a pair of mukluks from Brandon and Emily, and a wool sweater from Claire. The last gift was a new scarf that Sydney had knitted.

Sydney's gift from Claire was a carved cameo from a walrus tusk, and the older woman delighted in the knitted shawl that Sydney gave to her.

Opening her presents from Brandon and Emily, Sydney discovered a beaded purse from Emily and a box of scented gift soap from Brandon.

Emily's eyes glistened with tears at the sight of the bound copy of "The Courtship of Miles Standish." Sydney said gently, "I thought it would always hold a special meaning for you."

"It always will," Emily said, hugging the book to her breast.

"And this one is for you," Sydney said, handing Brandon her treasured copy of *The Three Musketeers*. She reached out and squeezed his hand. "My dear musketeer."

"You'll have to open this one next, Delaney," Mike said. He pulled out a huge, brightly wrapped box.

"Oh, my! I can't imagine what's in a box this size." Her eyes flashed with childlike excitement. "But I'm glad I get to open it." Ripping at the paper, she lifted out an elegant parrot cage crafted with engraved brass bands, tinned wires, and a zinc bottom. The perch was made of an expensive lignum vitae.

"It's from all of us," Emily informed her. "When we saw it in the catalog, we couldn't resist it."

"It's lovely." Sydney was thrilled to realize they had thought of Brutus.

"Hey, wait a minute." Laughing, she looked up with a dubious frown. "Are you trying to convince me that Michael MacAllister actually donated money toward a gift for Brutus?"

"It was his idea, honey," Claire said.

"Well, this wasn't what I had in mind for him," Mike said. "But they don't sell nooses for parrots."

"Well, as long as you thought of Brutus, I'm please to tell you, he thought of you, too." She reached for a package. "This gift is from Brutus to Mike."

Eyeing her skeptically, Mike untied the paper and held up the gift for all to see. Embroidered in neat little stitches, the colorful sampler depicted a blue and green parrot and proudly displayed the infamous message, "Sydney's right."

"I'll hang this on the wall in my bedroom as a reminder to me the first thing in the morning and last thing at night," he said good-naturedly.

"From me to you," he said, handing her another box.

Opening the package, Sydney pulled out a one-piece suit of wool underwear. When she realized that what she held was an undergarment, she blushed and quickly shoved the garment back into the box.

"Well, I figured I'd have to buy it for her," Mike explained to the laughing crowd. "She wouldn't do it for herself."

"Ah . . . Mike," Brandon said tongue-in-cheek, "mind telling us how you know Delaney doesn't already wear long underwear?"

This time it was Mike's turn to flush red. "Well, listen to my little brother, the old married man," he remarked, stalling for an answer. "Ah . . . I remembered Delaney wasn't wearing long underwear the day of the bear attack."

"Quick thinking, Mike," Brandon gibed.

Sydney took little pleasure in the moment's humor. "Thank you, Mike. And now I would appreciate it if you two gentlemen would refrain from any further discussion of my undergarments."

"And this is for you, too." Mike handed her a tiny box.

"Gee, I got the biggest box and the smallest one."

She laughed gaily as she pulled off the string. The tiny box had a jeweler's inscription. She removed the lid and her eyes widened in surprise as she lifted out a small gold whistle on a chain.

Mike took it from her and slipped it over her head. "I thought if you had an emergency, for instance with a bear or unruly Russian trappers, you could just blow the whistle. Someone would be sure to hear you." At her dubious look, he added, "It's solid gold, Delaney, so you'll never have to take it off. That way you'll always have it with you."

"Well, thank you again, Mike. It's very thoughtful . . . and practical. Both of your gifts are very practical," she said, hoping she sounded gracious. The lack of sentimentality in the selections was disappointing to the romantic side of her nature, but she appreciated them just the same.

"Now open my gift to you." She handed him the last remaining present under the tree.

Removing the paper, Mike stared amazed at a framed portrait of Grit. "I had Rami paint him," she said, nervous about his reaction.

Rami's talented and discerning eye had caught the proud stance and intelligent look of the malamute. "Ah, Delaney, this is great," he said, moved by her thoughtful gesture. "I don't know why I never thought to have it done myself." He proudly passed the portrait around for the others to inspect.

"It's a perfect likeness," Claire said, handing the portrait back to Mike. She yawned, covering her mouth with her hand. "It's gettin' late," she said regretfully. "I'm afraid it's time for this old girl to call it a day."

"Okay, honey. Leave your gifts here, and I'll bring them over in the morning," Mike said, pulling her to her feet.

"Pasha vill come vith you, darlink," he said. As if she were a tiny child, he put her feet into her boots and wrapped her fur cape snugly around her shoulders.

With a tweak to her nose, he added, "Pasha not vant his precious Claire to being cold."

Shaking her head with affectionate indulgence, Claire prepared to leave. "Remember, all of you, dinner's at noon tomorrow."

"Merry Christmas, and thank you for the lovely brooch," Sydney told her as she kissed her good-bye.

She turned to Pasha. "Merry Christmas, Pasha, and thank you again for the gloves."

"And Pasha is thanking his little *Красота* for gift of beautiful scarf."

Then with a grave frown, he pulled Mike aside. "Michael, Pasha haf question of most importance to be asking." He opened his jacket, flashed a paper, then quickly rebuttoned the coat. "You see?" he whispered covertly, casually tugging at the ends of his moustache as his glance shifted around the room.

"Yeah ... I saw a sheet of paper of some kind."

"Michael vant to buy valuable treasure map?"

Mike grimaced. "Good night, Pasha." Putting a firm hand on the Russian's shoulder, he steered him to the door. "And Merry Christmas."

While Emily and Brandon said their good nights at the door, Mike returned to the kitchen where Sydney had begun washing the dishes.

Grinning, he picked up a towel when she handed him a wet cup. "Gotta admit it, Delaney, you do manage to make every holiday special."

"Must be all that sentimental drivel," she teased. "But this evening has been fun, hasn't it? I can't remember such an enjoyable Christmas Eve since ... well, since before my mother died."

"How old were you when she died?" he asked.

"I was eight." Her head remained lowered at her task.

"And your father?"

"Ten years later."

"No other relatives?" Mike inquired.

Glancing up for the first time, she smiled gamely. "No. Just Brutus and me."

"You carry a lot of sorrow around, don't you, Delaney?" he said, sympathy gleaming in his eyes.

"Doesn't everyone? 'Believe me, every man has his secret sorrows, which the world knows not.' At least according to Longfellow," she said.

"I think Mr. Longfellow could be right," Mike agreed, deep in reflection.

With all four of the young people pitching in, the house was soon restored to order. Seeing Sydney gather up an armful of her gifts, Mike volunteered to carry them back to her room.

"That's not necessary. I can get the cage tomorrow."

Mike waited at the kitchen door and watched her walk through the passageway until she disappeared through the office door.

Once in the privacy of her bedroom, Sydney put aside her boxes and began to remove her gown. Glancing down at the tiny gold whistle that dangled from around her neck, she picked up the object and fondled it. Made of solid gold, the small whistle most certainly must have been costly to craft. And Mike had given it to her. Which, in truth, was all that mattered to Sydney.

After removing the rest of her clothes, she was about to pull on her nightdress when her eyes fell on the box that contained Mike's other gift—the suit of underwear. Impetuously, she reached for it and slipped her legs into the garment.

The underwear cleaved to the contour of her body like a kidskin glove to a hand.

Pivoting before the mirror, she tried to get a closer look at the fit, but the dresser mirror gave her only a limited view. From what she could see, the tightly knitted raiment stretched across her breasts, cushioning their rounded fullness. The dark circles of her aureoles were clearly outlined with their tips protruding against the snug material.

Sydney was about to give up any further inspection when a noise caught her attention. Pausing to listen more closely, she thought she heard a sound like a sharp yelp of an animal.

Dismissing the thought as ridiculous, Sydney was about to unbutton the underwear when she heard the noise again. This time, closer. So close, she swore the sound came from right outside her door.

Curiosity got the better of her. Sydney opened the door slightly and cautiously peeked through the crack. Yipping up at her from inside a box, a tiny four-legged ball of white fur stood wagging its tail furiously. Two yellow button-eyes plaintively stared up at her.

She sucked in her breath, then the air gushed out of her in a rush of delight. Bending over, she lifted the little pup into her arms. "Hey, little guy, where'd you come from?" she cooed.

"I brought him." Mike stepped out of the shadows.

In her confusion, Sydney had forgotten she was wearing only the underwear. However, Mike was very much aware of the sensual sight before him.

The skintight garment revealed to him every curve, every crevice of her body, just as if she were naked. His gaze traced the voluptuous outline past the swell of her breasts to her waist, down the plain of her stomach, then over the smooth curve of her hips to the valley at the junction of her legs. He paused at that juncture. The vortex of his desire.

Cuddling the puppy to her breast, Sydney looked up laughing. Seeing his raw passion, she became shockingly aware of her state of undress. Flustered, she put down the dog and rushed into her room, returning a moment later in her robe.

Sydney picked up the puppy again and stammered an apology. "I'm sorry, Mike, I was trying on the suit to see if it fit."

"It fits," he said hoarsely. Missing was the usual levity she had grown to expect from him at these embarrassing moments.

The tension between them flashed like lightning. "So . . . ah . . . who does this little fellow belong to?"

"You. That's my other Christmas gift to you."

Her amazed look swung back to him. "Me? You mean to keep? Right here in the office?"

Mike nodded. "Grit fathered him." He walked over and began to scratch the puppy behind its ears. "This little guy was the runt of the litter."

Deeply moved by the gift, Sydney could barely speak. And now Mike's nearness made her even more breathless. "And what did you name him?" she managed to ask.

"I thought you'd want to do that, Syd."

Her eyes misted over with tears as she looked up at him. "Then I'll just have to call this little guy Runt for now," she murmured softly.

For an interminable minute, their gazes remained locked. Then Mike took the puppy out of her hands and returned it to the box.

Mesmerized, her gaze was unwavering as he stared into her trusting green eyes. "Darn. I didn't bring the mistletoe with me."

"Are you asking if you may kiss me?" she asked in a hushed whisper.

"I guess I am. But I should warn you that the way I feel right now, I know damn well it's not going to stop with a kiss."

She slipped her arms around his neck. "Mike, I've come to realize that as long as it begins with a kiss and ends with a kiss—that's all that matters. Whatever happens between . . . well, I guess you would know more about what to expect than me."

His hands gripped her waist, drawing her to him. "And you trust me?"

"With my love, Mike."

He stepped away, reaching up and releasing her

arms, which were clasped around his neck. "Let's keep any talk of love out of this."

"If I didn't love you, how could you think I'd let you make love to me?" She turned and walked into her bedroom.

He followed on her heels. "Dammit, Syd! I thought we agreed. No commitment."

"We agreed to no commitment on your part. But I'd never agree to any such terms for myself. Besides, what difference does it matter now? I can't change how I feel."

Throwing up his hands in frustration, Mike grumbled, "I've never had such an asinine conversation with a woman before making love to her. I'm surprised you haven't quoted one of your many gems of wisdom."

"I don't have a quote, MacAllister," she said, bristling. "Just a word of advice. You better go back and find that mistletoe because it looks like you're going to need it."

"Don't you wish, Delaney." Infuriated, he stormed out the door, tripping over the box containing a sleeping Runt, and ended up sprawled on his stomach. Sydney leaned against the door frame, suppressing a smile as he picked himself up.

"Merry Christmas," she called out, smothering her laughter.

"Yeah, same to you," he snarled as he stomped off.

Suddenly struck by a notion, Sydney pulled out the whistle he had given her and blew on it. Mike pivoted in surprise. "What did you do that for?"

"Just trying it out," she said. She picked up the box with the now yelping puppy and carried it into her room.

Brandon was in the kitchen when Mike stormed through the door from the passageway. After one look at the black rage on Mike's face, Brandon guessed what had transpired between the volatile pair.

"You and Sydney just have a fight?"

"That woman ... that woman is the most exasperating, mind-boggling female I've ever known," Mike ranted. He waved an arm in the air, jabbing a finger in the direction of her room. "From the moment that crazy redhead walked through the door, I knew she had the instincts of a black widow."

"Ah ... Mike, when was the last time you made a visit to Claire's?" Brandon asked calmly.

"What? Visit to Claire's?" When he was suddenly struck by the implication, his eyes bulged in disbelief. "What are you trying to imply? You think I'm in need of a woman? That mixed-up redhead drives me to the brink of distraction, and you think it's my fault? Boy, has she got *you* buffaloed, *little brother.*" Mike slammed out of the house and headed for the barn.

Grinning, Brandon quietly slipped into the bedroom so as not to disturb Emily in the event she was sleeping. However, he found her sitting up in bed. Her blue eyes were round and alert as her blonde curls bobbed up and down in a nod.

"Yep. Definitely in need of a woman," she said. Then the two broke into laughter.

Flopping down in the bed beside her, he pulled her into his arms. "While I, on the other hand, don't have to worry about that kind of problem."

"Not as long as I'm around," Em whispered and started to unbutton his shirt.

Chapter 23

As if the restless night he spent was not trial enough to tax his Christmas spirit, Mike's bad mood lingered into the next day when he entered Claire's and spied Yuri Kherkov. The Russian was bending attentively over Sydney.

Being the last guest to arrive, Mike sat back and watched in brooding silence as Sydney gave Lily and Sal each a bottle of toilet water and Joseph a box of cigars. Then they all sat down together to share the Christmas meal.

Disturbed by Mike's reserved attitude, Sydney leaned over when they finished eating and whispered, "Mike, you still aren't angry about last night, are you?"

"Of course not, Delaney. I'm just not happy about breaking bread at the same table as your boyfriend over there." He cast a black glare toward where Yuri sat engrossed in a conversation with Lily.

"Mike, I have no romantic interest in Yuri Kherkov. And he has none in me. We're just good friends."

"Glad you feel that way, Delaney, 'cause Lily might have succeeded in jumping your claim."

Sydney glanced over to see what he meant. The dark-haired woman whispered something into the Russian's ear, then rose to her feet and moved to the stairway. She stopped long enough to look back with a seductive smile at Yuri, then climbed the stairs.

"I think Lily and the colonel are about to have dessert."

"Must you indulge in depraved conversation even on Christmas Day?" she complained.

Mike chuckled with amusement. "Kinda looks like you just landed out in the cold, Delaney."

"You mean like you did last night?" she retorted. Rising to her feet, she threw down her napkin. "You know, Mike, you sound like a spiteful, jealous little boy."

Convinced more than ever that Mike did not understand her relationship with Yuri, Sydney walked away in disgust. She did not care about Yuri Kherkov's love life, but hers was a disaster—thanks to the bullheaded, stubborn fool she had just left.

"Sydney." She turned her head, and Yuri motioned her over to the bar. "I vish to give you this small token in honor of the occasion." To her chagrin, he reached for a box he had set aside and handed it to her.

With a contrite smile, she stammered, "I'm so sorry, Yuri. I didn't know you were joining us today, or I would have brought you a gift as well."

"Is of no importance, my little Sydney."

"I've never received so many Christmas gifts." Her eyes sparkled with excitement as she opened a large hat box.

"Yuri, it's stunning," she exclaimed, glowing with pleasure as she lifted out a tall, dark fur hat fashioned in the style worn by hussar cavalrymen.

"A pity it vill conceal such beautiful hair as yours, my dear, but I am certain the hat vill also be a source of varmth."

A border of golden fox fluffed against her forehead and nape as she tried on the hat. "It's so elegant. Oh, thank you so much, Yuri." Kissing his cheek, she said regretfully, "But I feel bad that I haven't a Christmas gift to give you."

"Your kiss and pleasure is gift enough, my dear Sydney. Now, I regret I have a pressing engagement, so I vill say good-bye."

"Good-bye, Yuri. And thank you again."

Sydney rushed over to the table where the others sat observing the scene. "Look at the lovely gift Yuri gave me."

Emily managed a weak smile. "Yes, it's very lovely, Sydney."

"Looks great on you, Delaney," Claire remarked. "I'd better go check to see if Joseph needs any help." She left hastily with Pasha at her heels.

Deliberately attempting to goad Mike, Sydney preened before him. "Don't you think Yuri's gift is lovely, Mike?"

He shoved back his chair and stalked out the door.

Startled by his reaction, she glanced at Emily and Brandon. She could tell by their long faces that both seemed embarrassed and ill at ease.

"I don't think Mike should spoil the day for everyone with his churlishness," she declared, removing the hat and returning it to the box.

"I don't think he's being churlish," Brandon asserted. "I thought you understood how deeply Mike feels about the issue." He rose to his feet. "I'll see you back at the house, Em."

On the verge of tears, Sydney stared dumbfounded. "I don't understand. What is he talking about? What issue?" Suddenly the truth dawned on her. She felt a knot form in her stomach. "This hat is made of otter pelts, isn't it?" Emily nodded.

Sydney sank into a chair. Propping her elbow on the table, she buried her head in her hand. "I didn't know. . . . Most of this fur all looks the same to me and I was so excited, I never thought about what kind of fur it was."

Emily came over to put an arm around her. "I know that, Sydney. And once they think more about it, the guys will realize that too. But Yuri knew. He did it on purpose just to annoy Mike. And Mike probably thought you were playing along with it."

Kissing Sydney's cheek, she gave her a final sisterly pat on the shoulder. "Well, I'd better go. I've still got some packing to do before Bran and I leave tomorrow."

Sydney had lost all taste for further celebration. She, too, returned to her room. Runt scampered to greet her as soon as she opened the door. Desolately, Sydney picked up the puppy and hugged him to her breast. "I've really hurt him," she mumbled.

"Sydney's right," Brutus piped, hopping along the perch of his elegant new cage.

"Not this time, I'm afraid," she lamented. Then burying her face in the puppy's fur, she burst into tears.

The next day, Sydney maintained a false gaiety as she said good-bye to Emily and Brandon, who were leaving for San Francisco on their honeymoon. They would be gone for the next two months. Claire and Pasha had joined them on the wharf, but there was no sign of Mike.

Before departing, Brandon put his arm around her shoulders. "Sydney, I'm sorry about yesterday. I should have realized you couldn't tell one kind of fur from another."

"I hope Mike realizes that, too," she said with a distressed glance.

"Of course he does. You know Mike. He gets mad easily, but he gets over it just as fast. By the time he returns, he'll have forgotten the whole incident."

She glanced at him in surprise. "Returns? From where?"

Brandon looked startled. "Seward. Didn't he tell you he was going to Seward?"

"No, not a word." She felt her chest constrict. "He left without even saying good-bye."

The ship's horn sounded several times. Contrite, Brandon exclaimed, "Oh, damn. I thought you two would kiss and make up before he left. He said something about making arrangements for setting up an office there."

Sydney felt devastated. "He never mentioned a word to me. When did he make these plans?"

But just then, the ship's horn sounded two more times. "Come on, Bran, we've got to go," Emily exclaimed, tugging at his sleeve. She threw her arms around Claire for a final embrace. "See you all in a couple of months."

Hating to leave Sydney after unleashing such news, Brandon lagged behind. "God, Sydney, I'm sorry." When the horn sounded again, he offered a helpless glance. "I've got to go." Following Emily up the gangplank, he turned a remorseful look back to Sydney. "I'm sorry."

"Don't worry about it. Just have a good time," Sydney called out. Smiling cheerfully, she waved good-bye. From their vantage point at the railing, the honeymooners waved back to the well-wishers on the dock as the ship pulled away.

"Just have a good time," Sydney called out again in a pitiful attempt at jollity.

Walking back from the pier, Claire linked her arm through Sydney's. "Why don't you join us for dinner tonight?"

"Ve could haf game of Red Dog," Pasha agreed.

Sydney knew she wouldn't be good company for anyone. "Not tonight. I've had enough celebrating. I'm looking forward to a few days of peace and quiet."

"Well, if you need anything, honey, just call out," Claire said with a light wave.

Once in the privacy of the office, Sydney abandoned the cheerful façade she had maintained for the benefit of Claire and Pasha.

She sat down at her desk to reflect on Mike's actions. Surely, he wasn't angry with her over the incident with Yuri. She knew Mike well enough by now to know that even though he had a quick temper, given a few minutes of rational thinking afterwards, he always reached a fair conclusion.

So why would he leave without so much as a good-bye?

The question continued to plague her throughout the day and evening as she cleaned up after Runt and put down fresh newspapers.

That night Sydney decided to try out the newly-installed bathtub for the first time. Shortly after lighting a fire in the water heater, she filled the tub with hot water by just turning a spigot.

"Bless you, Mike." She sighed. After luxuriating in the water, she was delighted when all she had to do was merely pull a plug in the tub and copper piping discharged the wastewater into an outside barrel.

The next day, Sydney decided that with everyone gone, she would clean the office and passageway. Tying back her hair, she took broom in hand and began with the passageway. She tore down the ribbons and bows that had been put up for the wedding and carefully packed them all away in the event Emily and Brandon wanted to keep them as a memento.

Soon the sixty-foot-long corridor was spic-and-span, ready for Mike and Bran to return the crates that had been removed for the wedding.

She next attacked her own room. Moving the bed to sweep beneath it, she discovered scattered paper scraps. Upon closer examination, she recognized Mike's heavy-handed scrawl.

All at once the mystery of his unexpected departure became clear to her. Apparently, while she had been asleep, Mike had slipped a message under her door. Runt must have discovered it, carried the letter under the bed, and proceeded to rip it into pieces.

"Not fair, Runt," she scolded. "Do you have any idea how I've been fretting when all the time the answer's been right under my bed? Naughty pup," she scolded.

She quickly gathered up every scrap and hurried out

into the office. Impatiently brushing aside the papers on her desk, she cleared away a large area and laid out the torn scraps.

"Why did you choose this time to write a two-page letter, Michael?" she grumbled. After half a day, interrupted only by short walks for Runt and several cups of tea, she pasted together the tiny scraps, allowing for the pieces Runt had chewed up and swallowed.

Then she carefully turned over each patchwork sheet and read the backside of both pages.

According to the letter, an unexpected opportunity had arisen for Mike to accompany Rami and his son to Seward. Mike thought since Brandon and Emily would be gone, for her sake as much as for his, that it would be a good time for him to leave as well. He expected to return sometime within the next two weeks and informed her that she was not to worry since there were no scheduled shipments. The latter information she considered to be superfluous, since she was the one who made up the shipping schedules.

"And will you listen to this, boys," she said. Two quizzical heads snapped to attention while she read from the letter. " 'And, Delaney, if you expect that puppy to continue residing in the office, I suggest you use this opportunity to get him fully housebroken before my return.' "

A portion of the page had been chewed off, and part of the bold signature scrawled across the bottom of the page was missing. Only the letters *M E* remained.

"ME," she expounded, intentionally reading the two separated letters together. "That sums up his attitude perfectly. Good thing he wasn't named **GOD**frey or **CHRIST**opher, because with your help, Runt, I might have mistaken this letter for a holy edict."

Sighing, she smiled. "Well, I suppose it's better than nothing," she told her two animal friends. "At least now I know why he left in such a hurry." She cradled her face in her hands. "And, Lord knows, I sure miss him."

Sydney managed to keep herself occupied the rest of the week. On New Year's Eve, she agreed to join the revelers gathered at Claire's to welcome in the new year of 1883. However, with the situation so uncertain between herself and Mike, Sydney could not capture the gaiety the occasion normally warranted.

"New Year's Eve. I've never celebrated this night," Sydney said to Claire. "What's so special about the eve of a new year? Besides, everybody can't agree on when that is anyway. There're so darn many calendars. The Julian . . . then the Gregorian. The Hebrews have their own. The Chinese have theirs. . . ."

Her lips turned up in a pout as she stared belligerently at the crowd. "Seems people just look for an excuse to have a party."

Claire suppressed a smile and patted Sydney's hand. "Pity Mike isn't here to hear you say that, Delaney."

"Mike!" Sydney grumbled. "I wonder whom he's celebrating *New Year's Eve* with?"

Once again the corners of Claire's mouth twitched with amusement. "I've been thinkin' about Emily and Bran. I wonder where they are this night. They'd still be on the ship."

Pasha rushed over and kissed a cheek of each of them. "Happy New Year, my darlinks."

"Happy New Year, honey," Claire said, and Pasha hurried back to the bar.

"Are you in love with Pasha, Claire?"

"Of course I love him . . . but we're not lovers, honey, if that's what you're thinkin'. I guess I've just kind of fallen into the habit of lookin' out for him." She leaned over and smiled. "And he does take a heap of lookin' after, Delaney."

"Have you ever been in love, Claire?" Sydney asked.

Claire's face sobered. "Just once."

Forlorn, Sydney asked, "How can you be sure that you love a man, Claire?"

"Heck, honey. You're askin' the wrong person. I'm sure no authority." Her mind drifted off to a memory of a bygone day. "I guess when being with that fella matters more to ya than all the proper things you were ever taught."

"You mean like *The Victorian Rules of Drawing Room Decorum,*" Sydney reflected.

"Victorian what?" Claire asked, shaking aside her memory.

"It doesn't matter." Sydney stood up to leave. "I thought of a much more appealing way to welcome the new year. I'm going to take a hot bath." She kissed Claire on the cheek. "Happy New Year, Claire."

"The same to you, Delaney." Her warm gaze followed Sydney.

Mike arrived back in Solitary about an hour before midnight. After penning Grit, he noticed a light in the office, but when he went to the door, it was bolted.

He hurried to the house. A lamp glowed in the kitchen, but there was no sign of Sydney, so Mike headed down the corridor to the office.

Her bedroom was empty except for Runt and Brutus. "Where in hell are you, Delaney?" he grumbled impatiently. Then he figured there was only one other place she could be. He went back to the house, and headed for Claire's.

"Happy New Year, Mike," said Claire, giving him a friendly kiss. "Glad to see you home in one piece."

"Same to you, honey. Have you seen Delaney?"

"She was here until about an hour ago. Said she was going back and soaking in the tub."

Mike snapped his fingers. "Of course! The bathroom! It's so new, I forgot all about it."

He waved and hurried out the door.

* * *

Dressed in her robe and nightgown, Sydney stepped out of the bathroom and drew up startled at seeing a figure in the hallway. She stifled her scream when she recognized it.

"Mike!" Her hand fluttered to her chest. "You scared the life out of me."

"I'm sorry. I was just about to knock."

She laughed nervously. "That probably would have scared me just as much."

His gaze shifted to a single bead of water remaining on her forehead. Nervously, she brushed it aside. He walked toward her, and she backed up to the bathroom door.

"You're overdressed, Delaney."

Confused, she glanced down at her robe. "Overdressed?"

He lifted her into his arms and carried her into his bedroom, kicking the door shut behind him. Her legs trembled when he set her on her feet and slipped the robe off her shoulders.

"Mike, stop that." She shoved away his hands. "We have too much to talk about."

"Talk? About what?" he asked as he pulled out pins to release her hair.

"You left almost a week ago without even saying good-bye. Now you show up and expect me to fall willingly into your arms. So why don't you begin by telling me what you were doing, or asking me how my week went?"

"If your week went anything like mine, that's the last thing I want to talk about," he murmured as he slipped the gown off her shoulders.

The gown dropped in a heap around her ankles, baring her nakedness to his hungry inspection. His gaze came to rest on the gold whistle cushioned between her breasts.

The faint traces of a smile softened his expression.

Her gasp was barely audible when his knuckles brushed her breasts as he lifted the whistle in his fingers.

"Damn you, Mike!" Shrugging out of his grasp, she picked up her robe and quickly pulled it on. "What makes you think you have the privilege of treating me as if . . . as if I work at Claire's?"

Nervously, she threaded her fingers through her hair. "This is awkward for me, Mike. How do you expect me to keep my dignity dressed in just a . . . damn whistle."

"I've seen you naked before."

"You were trying to keep me from freezing at the time. This is different."

She picked up her gown and started to open the door. He shoved it shut again and she found herself penned between the door and his body, his outstretched arms at either side of her head.

His warm breath grazed her ear. "Would it help to tell you that I think you've got a beautiful body, Syd? A perfect body." She closed her eyes and reveled in the thrill of his nearness, the sound of his voice.

"And would it help to tell you that since I saw you in that damned underwear, I haven't been able to think of anything else. That I wasted a trip to Seward because I couldn't think of anything except getting back to you."

Her hope of resisting his seduction crumbled with his words. Her grasp on the gown weakened and it fell to the floor in a forgotten heap.

She turned. They were only inches apart, so close she could feel the heat of his body. "I think it would help if you kissed me, Mike."

"Thought you'd never ask," he said in a husky whisper as he slipped his hands under the curtain of her hair. Cupping the nape of her neck, he pulled her into his arms.

Unleashing the hunger and passion he had struggled with for weeks, he devoured her with his kiss. She met the thrust of his tongue with her own.

"Mike." His name passed her lips as a sigh, and she threw back her head to allow his mouth to roam down her throat.

"You taste as good as you smell, Syd," he murmured against her flesh, trailing kisses to her breasts as he slid the robe off her shoulders.

Once again she was naked. And once again his hands and mouth feasted on that nakedness.

He picked her up as she moaned his name. The solidness of the bed helped her to muster her senses. She opened her eyes and saw that Mike was on the bed removing his boots and socks. Rising, he stripped off his shirt.

Her modesty deserted her under his worshipful gaze. Her slumberous green eyes invited him; her heaving breasts enticed him. Unconsciously, she slipped her tongue between parted lips that felt parched from passion, moistening them.

Standing beside the bed, he stared down at her as if giving her one final chance to change her mind. "Syd, I'm not going to enter you. I won't take the risk of making you pregnant. Do you understand what that means?"

"Not completely, but I don't care. Whatever you're trying to tell me, I trust you, Mike. I want you to go on."

He removed the rest of his clothing and for several seconds she stared awestruck at the beautiful symmetry of his male body—even more powerful in its nakedness. She had to touch him, to taste him. Smiling with desire, she raised outstretched arms to him.

Her arms curled around his neck as the hard, muscular length of him settled against the soft curves of her body. For an endless moment his mouth moved on hers, exploring and probing the warm chamber while his hands roved her nakedness in provocative sweeps.

The feel of his arousal pressing against her ignited a new and uncontrollable response throughout her body, and she returned his caresses, allowing her hands and fingertips to roam and examine the muscular brawn of his body.

Nibbling a trail to her breasts, he stopped to tease the hardened nubs, then he continued to trace kisses downward, his tongue a hot flame licking at her flesh. When he parted her legs, instinctively her body tensed and she clamped a hand over her mouth to smother her shocked outcry.

He felt her become suddenly rigid and so raised his head. Seeing the stunned and frightened look in her eyes, his expression softened. "You said you would trust me."

"I do, Mike." She felt a swell of tears and closed her eyes, trying to will her body to relax.

He lowered his head and covered the sensitive mound with his mouth.

At the first touch, liquid fire streaked through her, licking at her—a tongue of flame. She writhed beneath the exquisite sensation, hot blood drumming in her head and ears as the tempo of her pulse raced wildly out of control. With the fear of blacking out at any second, she wove her hands into his dark hair and clung to him as a buttress to maintain her consciousness. But she only succeeded in increasing the divine sensation, and for several, mindless seconds she tottered on the brink of passing out as her body quivered with contractions.

Slowly she floated back to wakefulness and could distinguish the pounding in her ears as the sound of her own heartbeat. Only then did she open her eyes.

"Mike," she whispered in awe.

He smiled down at her, tucking a few strands of hair behind her ear. "I'm waiting." At her puzzled stare, he offered a puckish grin. "For the quote. I would expect nothing less than Shakespeare."

She sighed deeply. "I can't think of any quote at the moment."

"Hallelujah!"

She gloried in the sound of his warm chuckle. Then she lowered her eyes. "Mike, I must appear very stupid and naive to you, but I've never been with a man before, much less know that . . ."

"That there's more than one way to be intimate?"

Blushing, she lowered her eyes. Mike gathered her into his arms and kissed her. "There's no shame in it, Syd. And you're a sensuous woman. Warm and responsive."

They shared a long kiss. His arousal pressed against her stomach. Startled, she jerked away as if burned.

Mike chuckled. "As you can see, it's difficult for a man to keep his . . . feelings to himself at a time like this." His eyes deepened with desire. "Touch me, Syd."

Shocked, her startled glance met his. "You mean . . . ?" He nodded.

Her hand trembled as she reached out and closed her fingers around him. Hard and hot, the organ throbbed with energy. The feel of its urgency straining against her hand drove her to greater boldness. She glided her thumb to the tip of it.

She gasped with pleasure. It felt like velvet. Amazed, she swung her glance to him and smiled. With a smothered moan he pulled her into his arms, covering her face and eyes with rapid kisses.

"Taste me, Syd. As I tasted you," he rasped.

She slid her mouth down his chest. Her tongue tasted the fine film of perspiration that coated the powerful brawn. She continued to press kisses down the flat plane of his stomach. Hesitating, she lifted her head when she reached his extended organ.

"Taste me, Syd. Taste me," he groaned. He tangled his hands in her hair, pressing her to his throbbing need. Her mouth closed around him.

"Oh, God, Syd! Yes! Yes!" He rasped erotic messages of guidance and approval as she brought him to ecstasy.

* * *

Later, she lay contentedly with her head on his chest. "God, Syd, you're a remarkable woman." His hand idly swept her spine. "Such an innocent . . . such a trusting innocent."

She raised her head and smiled into his eyes. His finger began to toy with her bottom lip. "Too much woman for any man." He tried to make the remark sound light, but an underlying huskiness lay in the tone.

The sound of the clock tolling the hour intruded. Shots and shouts of celebration sounded from outside. Glowing with delight, she raised her head. "Oh, listen, Mike. It's midnight. Happy New Year, my love."

His hands curled around her neck, and he gently drew her down to him. "Happy New Year, Syd," he murmured in a husky whisper before he reclaimed her lips.

Chapter 24

Sydney awoke with a smile of contentment and a languorous stretch. Then she sat up abruptly upon discovering she was alone. Rising, she donned her gown and robe, then padded barefoot across the floor.

As soon as she stepped into the hallway, she could smell the coffee brewing and knew that Mike would be nearby. Then she heard splashing from the bathroom.

To put the moment to good use, she hurried back to her room. The previous night's unexpected turn of events had resulted in Brutus spending the night in an uncovered cage and Runt curled up next to his box, rather than in it.

Sydney made no apology to either of them.

After dressing and attending to her morning toilette, she returned to the house. The din of splashing and an off-tone baritone sounded from the bathroom. Smiling, she poured coffee into a mug and carried it down the hall. She gave a quick tap of the door. "Are you decent?"

"No, so come on in," Mike said.

She entered and smiled to see him in the tub, his long legs bent at the knees. "Good morning and Happy New Year. I thought you probably could use this."

"Good morning and Happy New Year," he echoed. "And I certainly can." He took the cup and sniffed it, closing his eyes as the aroma permeated his senses. "You're a saint, Delaney." After several sips, he leaned back in contentment. Then with a side glance, he added, "But I see you're overdressed again."

Sydney couldn't help blushing. "M-i-i-ke," she groaned.

He chuckled and shook his head. "Women! I'll never understand the species. The moment the sun comes up they become virtuous saints, but turn them loose in the dark and they're wildcats. And I've got the scars to prove it." He shifted to show her several streaks on his shoulders.

"Oh, Mike, did I do that?" she asked, horrified. "Why didn't you stop me?"

"I'm the one who suffers in silence," he gibed, putting aside the empty cup.

"Oh, really? Well, if that's true, then all those groans I heard last night couldn't have come from you." She tapped her finger on her chin. "Hmmm ... could be someone else was in the bed."

"You were making all the noise. Sounded like you were celebrating New Year's."

Her eyes danced devilishly. "I think we both were."

"Well, I do have to say, Delaney, your holiday celebrations are improving." He arched a roguish brow. "What say you take off all those clothes you've piled on yourself and hop into this tub with me?"

"As scandalously sinful as that may sound, right now a cup of hot tea seems more inviting." She ducked to avoid the wet sponge he threw, and she hastened from the room.

After eating breakfast, they sat down in front of the fireplace. He began to kiss her lazily, then he took her hand and placed it over his arousal. She felt the throbbing heat of it through his pants. "Undress me, Syd," he said huskily.

She rounded her eyes with shock. "Mike, it's the middle of the day. There's sunlight streaming through the window."

"I know," he said. Passion swirled in the depths of his dark eyes as he began to unbutton her bodice. He felt the satisfaction of a teacher when Sydney performed his lessons from the night before to perfection. Nevertheless, he looked forward to the day when their lovemaking would be consummated, when his passionate teachings could reach fruition. Meanwhile, he would bide his time, relishing this moment with her in his arms in front of a fireplace while bright sunlight streamed through the window.

As they walked Runt later that day, Pasha came rushing out to join them. "Is mozt happy day for first day of happy new year," he exclaimed. *"Nyet?"*

Sydney drew a deep breath of the crisp, invigorating air. "Yes, it certainly is, Pasha."

"Say, Pasha, I've been thinking how this would be a good time to make the winter run to the Tlingit village at Beaver Dam. I had planned to wait until Bran gets back, but what the hell, weather's good now. Who knows what it'll be like next week? Rami's agreed to come along with his sled and team, but we could always use another musher."

Pasha shrugged his shoulders. "Vy not? Ven you vant to go, Michael?"

"How about early tomorrow morning? We can't hang around waiting for daylight or we won't get to the camp by nightfall."

"Is agreed," Pasha said.

"Good. I'll load up the sleds today. All we'll have to do is hitch the teams in the morning."

"How long will you be gone, Mike?" Sydney asked that evening as they played Red Dog.

"No more than three or four days, I hope. You've been to the camp."

"You mean Taitana's camp?"

"Yeah, that's the one."

"Mike, can I go with you to the Indian camp?"

"No way, Delaney." He shuffled the cards and dealt them.

"Taitana's baby is due this month. I'd love to see her."

"No, Delaney," he said firmly.

"Why? You took me there before."

"Well, it's out of the question now." Mike glanced up impatiently. "You betting or passing?"

Sydney had long since lost her interest in the game. "Mike, I've learned there's always a good reason for your decisions, but why won't you let me go with you now, when you did before?"

He took a deep breath. She knew Mike was not used to explaining his decisions to anyone, and the effort did not come easily. "You went in a horse and wagon, but it's a damn sight different in a dogsled. It was warmer then. Now it's January, the coldest month of the year. And we're headed inland, so it'll be much colder than here. When I took you before, there was still plenty of game available. Now it's gone, so there are a lot of hungry predators prowling around looking for food. The hungrier they get, the more chances they take. Explanation enough, Delaney?" he asked, irritably.

"You mean you think it's too dangerous?"

"I don't think it, Delaney. I know it."

"Mike, if I'm ever going to be of any use to you, you've got to let me take the same chances as a man. If you aren't concerned about Pasha's or Rami's safety, why are you concerned about mine?"

He threw down his cards. "Because you owe me some gambling debts. It's payoff time."

"One more hand. If I win, I go. If I lose, I'll drop the subject."

"Syd," he said firmly, beginning to lose his patience. "I've already told you it is too dangerous. I'm not going to risk your life on the turn of a card." He started to walk away. "I'm going to bed. You coming . . . or not?"

Once Sydney set her mind on an idea, it was hard for her to shake the thought. She sat down before the fire and stared into the flames. The longer she sat, the more difficult it became to swallow her pride and take that first step toward his bedroom.

She lost track of time, unaware she had been sitting there for over half an hour. She rose to tend Runt, but her mind remained on Mike and his trip.

"Must mean a lot to you, Delaney." His presence caught her by surprise. Barefoot and dressed only in Levi's, he leaned casually against a wall. "Enough to welch on a bet?" As light as Mike tried to make his tone, he was concerned about her thoughts, and there was no laughter in his eyes.

"Of course not, Mike. I was just going to check on Runt, but I'm coming back for a good-night kiss."

His somber face broke into a grin. "I'll walk back with you." He snaked an arm around her shoulders, and she slipped her arm around his waist as they walked down the passageway.

Mike watched in silence while Sydney tucked Runt into his box for the night and covered Brutus' cage. "Ah, the responsibilities of motherhood," he teased. "What are you going to do with those two while you're gone?"

She jerked up her head in surprise. "Gone where?"

"Thought you said you wanted to come with me."

Knowing Mike's mercurial nature, Sydney didn't want to raise her hopes too high. "Sal is crazy about Runt. Said she'd watch him for me anytime," she said casually.

"Well, what about Mr. Obnoxious in the cage over there? Don't try to convince me people are breaking down the doors to take care of him."

"Oh, Brutus just needs someone to give him food and water once a day. Claire would do that, I know." She glanced at him cautiously, still uncertain of his sincerity. "But you said you didn't want me to go. That the trip was too dangerous."

"Well, maybe I exaggerated a little. There will be three men with rifles and two teams of dogs."

She walked toward him slowly, her eyes deepening with warmth. "You know, MacAllister, you make it awfully hard for a woman not to love you," she murmured, slipping her arms around his neck.

Mike looped his own arms around the back of her waist, drawing her nearer. "Yeah, well don't read too much into it, Delaney. I just thought I'd protect my interests by keeping an eye on you. You're liable to skip town without paying off your losses."

She smiled seductively and moved her hands down to his belt. "I always pay my debts."

Claire had arisen to see them off. After she had promised that she would guard Brutus and Runt with her life, Sydney gave her instructions on the care and feeding of the cherished pair. Then Sydney joined the men.

Her presence necessitated a last-minute change in the arrangements. Since Rami's lighter sled had a seat and would be more comfortable for Sydney to ride, the men switched sleds. They harnessed a nine-dog team to Mike's heavier, sideless sledge and a seven-dog team led by Grit to the lighter load on Rami's sled.

Sydney watched with fascination as each dog was harnessed. Mike then checked the lashings on the sledge. Satisfied the cargo and tarp were securely bound, he turned his attention to Sydney.

"Right now it's ten degrees below zero, Delaney. Once the sun comes up, it'll warm up for a couple hours. But until then, keep yourself bundled up." He checked her hooded tunic and boots, gave her mittens a final inspection, then lifted her into the small seat and covered her with a warm blanket.

A box of food and a pair of snowshoes were the last

items to be lashed to the sled. Then he handed her his rifle sheathed in a scabbard and a box of shells.

"Keep this handy in the seat with you."

Pasha was already perched on the sledge and Rami on the runners. Mike went over to them. Talking in low tones, the three men put their heads together for a last-minute consultation.

Sydney couldn't hear the discussion over the noise of the yapping dogs, but she shared their impatience to be underway. Her body trembled with excitement when Mike returned, braced himself on the runners, and took a firm hold on the handlebars.

He gave a loud, shrill whistle and the team quieted. The air became charged with expectancy as the dogs strained at their harnesses, waiting for the command.

With Mike's shout of "Hi," they leaped ahead, and the sled moved forward, gliding as smoothly as a skater on ice.

With Grit in the lead, the sled skimmed across the surface of the frozen snow. "How fast are we going?" Sydney asked.

"I'd guess about fifteen miles an hour." Mike glanced behind him to make sure the sledge was following. "I don't want to get too far ahead of them."

When the wind and cold began to sting her cheeks, Sydney pulled off her mitten long enough to cover her face with the wolf skin flap attached to her hood. Now only her eyes were exposed to the cold.

No movement of bird or animal appeared to disturb the giant snow-clad spruce forest that lined their passage as the sled sailed across a snow speckled with wind-tossed waves of frosted whitecaps. An occasional animal print or dropping in the snow gave evidence of life, but there was no sign of human footfall on the pristine wilderness.

At midday when they stopped to rest the dogs, the men built a small campfire and put on a pot of coffee.

Sydney remained snuggled in the warmth of the bear-skin while they talked among themselves.

As Sydney chewed on the salty piece of dried venison Mike had given her, his sudden outburst of laughter caused her to shift her gaze to him. His teeth flashed against his dark skin, tanned by sun and wind. Oblivious of the cold, he shoved off the hood of his parka, and his dark hair lay rumpled on his forehead.

Sydney's adoring gaze swept his rugged features: high Celtic cheekbones, firm, sensuous lips, the acquiline nose, and the strong chin with a day's growth of stubble. He was so handsome, her feminine heart ached as she looked at him. And he appeared so at peace—so in harmony with his environment. He was comfortable with this cold land.

Finishing the salty meat, Sydney climbed out of her warm haven to quench her thirst. Remembering the childish pleasure of eating snow, she reached down, picked up a small handful, and raised it to her mouth.

Mike's hand on her arm halted the motion. "Don't do that, Delaney."

"Why not? I'm thirsty. And I often ate snow as a child."

"Don't do it here. Snow is too cold on the mouth and lips. Always melt it first. And when you're thirsty, drink hot liquid, not cold." He handed her his coffee mug. "Here, sip some of this coffee."

"I don't like coffee," she said adamantly.

"Then I'll melt some snow and you can drink that."

She stifled a smile, but her eyes danced with impishness. "I don't like hot water either unless . . . unless it's flavored with tea."

"Drink the coffee, Delaney," he ordered, handing her the cup. "My orders." He pulled up the hood of his parka.

"Yes, sir. The gospel according to capital M E." Her eyes sparkled with merriment as she took a few sips of the hot brew, then handed it back to him.

"Capital M E? I don't get it," Mike said, perplexed as he tied his hood.

"Oh, just a shared joke between me and a couple of my friends."

He eyed her suspiciously, knowing by the devilry in her eyes that her answer wasn't very innocent. "You know, Delaney, given the chance, you could probably drive a man out of his mind. Get in the sled," he groaned. Finishing the coffee, Mike walked back to the fire.

Snowflakes began to fall gently, deceptively mild in their silent descent—fluffy white dots dusting the furry parkas and clinging to eyelashes.

The sledge, following about thirty yards behind the sled, suddenly hit a huge snow-covered ground hole that threw it off balance. Top heavy with freight, the big conveyance fishtailed, then tipped on its side. Fortunately, Pasha rolled clear and was not injured.

The two men shouted to alert Mike. Looking back, he saw the problem with the sledge and halted his team.

Mike put his hands to his mouth. "Need any help?" he shouted.

"Is being no problem," Pasha hollered and waved for him to keep moving.

But Mike waited to make certain the sledge had not been damaged. In the few minutes it took Pasha and Rami to get the loaded sledge upright again, the intensity of the snowfall had increased. By the time they signaled Mike to move on, both of the motionless sleds were covered by a blanket of snow.

Casting a worried glance at the turbulent sky, Mike shouted, "Hi," and once again the sled shot forward.

Suddenly, without warning, a howling wind swept down from the mountains, driving the snow with unrelenting force. Mike glanced back and could barely make out the dim outline of the sledge still following about a hundred feet behind him. The bawling wind deafened him to Pasha's shout to Rami.

"Rami, stop! Freight is no being balanced."

Rami stopped the team. Snow smacked against the sledge in swirling drifts as the two men struggled to tighten several lashings that had come loose. Finally satisfied the load was firmly secured, they continued on, unable to see more than a few feet ahead.

Glancing behind, Mike could not see anything except a swirling wall of snow. He pulled up again and peered through the flurry for some sign of the approaching sledge.

Within minutes, the sled had become drifted in, and still the other conveyance had not appeared. Fearing the sledge had broken down, Mike decided to check it out.

"They must be in trouble. I'm going to backtrack," he shouted to Sydney. Not able to distinguish all of his words, she merely nodded and ducked her head under her protective cover.

"Gee," Mike shouted to the dogs. Sensitive to every summons from his master, Grit veered to the right while the rest of the team followed automatically. Mike repeated the order until the sled had made a 180-degree turn. But the blustering wind had already destroyed their tracks, so he depended upon Grit's sense of direction as much as his own.

Mike backtracked for several hundred feet. Unable to find the sledge, he guessed what might have happened. Somehow, they had passed each other. With visibility restricted to only a few feet, he didn't know if he was even on the track. A few yards to one side or another could throw him entirely off course, and he would miss the village by miles.

So once again he halted the team.

When he bent over her, Sydney peeked out from under the snow-laden bearskin. "There's no sense in trying to go on. I'm going to find some cover, and we'll pull up until this storm passes."

Uncertain how long that might be, he knew he had to get her to shelter.

The terrain was not unfamiliar to Mike. He had once lived in the general area and knew the region well. Depending on his sense of direction rather than sight, he headed for what he hoped would be a timberline to the west. And if he was right, he knew there would be an abandoned cabin in that vicinity. If he guessed wrong, the sled would have to shelter them from the blizzard.

His judgment had not failed. Reaching the timberline, the trees provided something of a buffer from the swirling snow, and he managed to use his compass to get his bearings. Another hour passed before he succeeded in reaching the cabin.

Relieved at the prospect of shelter, Sydney prepared to jump out and rush into the cabin. "Stay in the sled until I check it out," he ordered, reaching for his rifle.

Sydney waited anxiously as he disappeared inside. Within minutes, Mike returned.

"All clear." He lifted her out of the seat. "Grab that bearskin, we're gonna need it," he told her.

"Well, all the comforts of home," she remarked looking about when he set her on her feet inside. The tiny room contained only a fireplace, a bunk, and a loft. The ladder leading to the loft was missing.

"Damn sight better sitting out this storm in here than outside. Wonder how Rami and Pasha are doing."

"Will they be okay, Mike?" she asked worriedly.

"Should be. They can take care of themselves. They'll probably pull up, same as we did. They can make themselves a pretty good shelter by just unloading and making a lean-to out of the sledge and cartons. Bran and I did that once." He glanced around casually. "We lived in this cabin the first winter we came to Alaska."

"You mean you built it?"

He nodded. "Yeah, me and my brothers."

Whatever thoughts were going through his mind remained hidden behind an enigmatic expression. "I've got to go out and take care of the dogs. I'll try to find some wood for a fire, then I'll bring in the food and packs. You stay put until I get back."

After several moments, Sydney realized she had to relieve herself. She looked around hopefully for a slop pot, but knew she wouldn't find one. Having no other choice, she stepped outside.

She saw no sign of Mike in the limited visibility. The snow continued to swirl and drift furiously, so Sydney decided she would swallow her modesty and wait for his return.

After several more moments, the wait became impossible and she ventured outside, heading for the closest clump of trees.

In the blink of an eye, the fury of the storm intensified. The snow swirled around her head from all directions, pelting at her face and eyes.

As she glanced up toward the low-hanging clouds, she suddenly had no sense of direction. Cabin . . . trees . . . earth . . . sky . . . vanished—melded together into a milky fury.

Had she suddenly gone blind? she asked herself frantically. No, not blind. Blindness was black, not white.

Not knowing if she walked or floated, ran or crawled, she groped for the stability of a tree or the ground, any foundation to cling to until wakefulness released her from the throes of the nightmare.

Spinning, she stumbled in circles—wondering if each step was carrying her farther away from the refuge she sought so desperately.

She cried out for Mike, but her voice was swallowed by the howling wind. In a frenzied panic she began to swing her arms wildly, batting at the opaque cloud that enveloped her.

She waged the valiant but useless struggle until her courage drained with her strength. Then, panic-stricken, she began to suck in air more rapidly than her lungs could release it.

In an effort to breathe, she clutched at her throat, tearing away the clothing that bound her. And in the frantic motion, the chain around her neck tangled in her fingers.

Her instinct for self-preservation overcame her hysteria. With consciousness fading rapidly, she sensed the charm could be her instrument of deliverance. As a drowning man grasps the hand reaching out to him, the tiny talisman became the solid buttress to which she clung.

She blew on the whistle, exhaling much of the amassed air trapped in her lungs. However, the release came too late to avert an overpowering dizziness.

With no sense of right or left, up or down, she slumped to her knees, her only impression being the diffused opalescence that she could not see beyond.

She continued to blow on the whistle until she slipped into oblivion.

Returning to the cabin and discovering Sydney gone, Mike dropped his armload of wood. Grabbing the rifle that had been slung over his shoulder, he raced outside.

"Syd," he shouted at the top of his voice. But the wind tossed the sound back at him. With only a few feet of visibility, he had no idea where to begin looking for her.

The team of huskies, curled up in balls with their heads and paws tucked beneath them, did not stir from their rest as he continued to shout.

Mike's hopes brightened when he saw Grit lift his head. The dog stood up, his yellow-eyed stare fixed on some nearby trees as he listened with cocked ears. Mike couldn't hear anything except the roaring wind. He waited, expecting Sydney to emerge from the trees. When she didn't, his grasp tightened on the rifle.

Grit barked at whatever sound was disturbing him,

and Mike hurried over to release him. The dog's stance remained alert. "What do you hear, boy? Is it Syd?" he asked. "Let's go."

Grit bounded into the trees, and Mike followed on the run.

The malamute led him to where Sydney lay in a crumpled heap, the gold whistle still between her lips.

For several seconds, with a horrified feeling of déjà vu, Mike stared strickened at the unconscious figure in the snow. Then he took action. He picked up Sydney and carried her back to the cabin. Laying her on the wooden bunk, he pressed his head to her chest and felt her heartbeat. He quickly removed her wet outer clothing and stripped her. He was heartened to see that she was wearing the protective underwear he had given her for Christmas. This time he gave no thought to sensuality as he frantically worked to warm her body.

Divesting himself of his own outer garments, he removed his shirt, still warm from his body heat, and put it on her. Then he vigorously shook out the bearskin to rid it of all snow and covered her. Reversing both parkas, he piled them on top of her as well.

"Come on, Syd, stay with me," he pleaded as he furiously rubbed her hands and feet. A frantic desperation drove his actions. "Stay with me, honey. Please," he pleaded.

Sydney's head lolled to the side as she began to stir. "That's it. Come on. Come on," he beseeched. His firm hands massaged her body to stimulate the circulation.

Long lashes fluttered on her cheeks as she was slowly drawn back to consciousness. She raised her eyelids.

Her green eyes were the most beautiful sight he had ever seen. "Hi, honey," he said, unaware of the emotion in his voice.

"Mike?" she questioned faintly. "What happened?"

"Lie still," he warned. "I'll be right back. I'm just

going to the sled." He snatched his parka off the bunk and dashed out of the cabin.

When he returned minutes later, she had already slipped back to unconsciousness. He produced a flask from his pack. Slipping an arm around her, he sat her up and lightly slapped her cheeks several times to revive her. Dazed and weak, she responded enough to swallow the few sips of brandy he forced past her lips.

Then, laying her back down, Mike covered her securely and hurried over to the fireplace. There were not enough dry logs to fuel a blazing fire throughout the night, so he built a low fire to offer enough heat to keep the chill out of the cabin.

He went back to the bunk and checked her fingers and toes, relieved to see no evidence of frostbite. But her pale and lethargic condition worried him, since he didn't know how long she had been exposed. And the mystery of why she had wandered so far from the cabin nagged at him.

Mike dug through Sydney's pack and found a pair of clean socks. Once again he rubbed her feet, then put the stockings on her.

Sydney opened her eyes. Her expression appeared more alert to him, but her color remained waxen. "How are you feeling, honey?"

"What's wrong with me? I can't see you, Mike." Panic rose in her voice. "I'm cold, Mike. I'm so cold." Her body shook, and her teeth chattered.

He made her take several sips of the brandy. "Drink all you can, Syd." When he tried to get more down her throat, she flailed widely at the flask, attempting to shove away the distasteful liquid. "The brandy will help warm you," he insisted, unrelenting. The effort drained her of strength, and she soon slipped off to sleep again.

Her shivering would not cease. Despite the added stimulation from the brandy and fire, her hands and feet remained cold. Mike took several deep swallows of the brandy, then stripped off Sydney's underwear and then his own clothing and he climbed under the bearskin and gathered her into his arms.

Nestling her into the curve of his body, he draped his arms and legs around her like a protective mantle. When a sob slipped past her lips, he pressed even closer. "You're not going to leave me, honey, do you hear? I won't let you. I won't fail you." Moisture glinted in his eyes as he drew her closer and kissed the top of her head. "I love you, sweetheart."

He fused his naked warmth to her.

Chapter 25

The howling wind lulled Mike into slumber, and he awoke with no idea of how long he'd been asleep. But since the ashes were still glowing, he figured not more than a couple of hours had passed. The cabin was cold and dark except for the few dying embers on the hearth.

He was relieved to see that faint patches of color had returned to Sydney's cheeks. He lifted the blanket and watched the even rise and fall of her chest. The crisis had passed.

For a long moment he studied her face, so calm in slumber, and relived the horror and despair he had known when he found her lying in the snow. He had come so close to losing her.

Mike rested his head on his arm. Deep in thought, he stared at the embers. Then he sensed something different. The silence. The wind no longer howled through the trees or whistled through the loose logs of the cabin.

Naked, he padded across the floor to the fireplace, stirred up the embers, and added another log to the fire. He had no idea of the time, but what did it matter? They weren't going anywhere until he was sure Syd had fully recovered.

The floor was cold, and so he pulled on his Levi's and dug through his pack for socks. The growl in his stomach reminded Mike that he was hungry. Food he could do without—coffee never. He grabbed a parka and went outside long enough to scoop snow into the coffee pot.

Mike discovered he had not been mistaken about the storm. While he had slept, the blizzard had blown over, and a quick glance at the dogs revealed that they were still curled up, almost buried under an insulating snowdrift.

As he waited for the coffee to perk, he shed his pants and climbed back beneath the bearskin to keep warm. The incident with Sydney had stirred up many memories. Glancing around the cabin, he shifted his gaze to the loft. The tanned lines of his countenance were set like granite.

This cabin held no nostalgia for him—only painful memories.

After drinking several cups of hot coffee, he returned to bed a final time and pulled Sydney back into the snug cocoon of his body.

Sydney awoke to warmth. She could see again. Rejoicing, she rolled over and discovered the source of the warmth—Mike. The memory of the previous night came flooding back to her. Tears welled in her eyes as she remembered the fright of her close brush with death. Were it not for Mike, she would simply not be here. *Mike.* Tucking her hands under her cheek, she lay gazing adoringly at the face of this man whom she loved so dearly.

Mike opened his eyes and looked into her face, smiling. "How are you feeling, Syd?"

"I feel as good as new." Then her expression sobered. "How will I ever thank you, Mike?"

He shifted to his back and pulled her to his side. "You gave me a scare last night."

"So it *did* happen. I had hoped the whole thing was just a nightmare."

"Just what happened out there last night, Syd?" he asked solemnly. "And why'd you leave the cabin?"

"Well . . . I went out to the trees to relieve myself . . . and . . . suddenly I went blind. The cabin . . . trees . . . everything disappeared."

"No horizon. No boundaries," he said.

"Yes. That's it exactly. So you know what I'm talking about," she replied, relieved.

Mike nodded. "Yeah, I've heard of it happening to others up here. Comes on when there's nothing but driving snow. I guess it's something like a mirage in the desert—only the opposite of what you'd want to see. At least that's how other people have explained it to me."

"I'm glad it's over." She cuddled closer to him. Slipping an arm across his stomach, she laid her cheek against his chest. "I was so frightened, Mike." Her voice quavered as she whispered against the matted hair on his chest.

He lifted her face between his hands and gazed intently into her eyes. "So was I, Syd." He kissed her tenderly, reverently. He curved a protective arm around her and drew her even nearer, his hand lingering idly to sweep her hip and derriere. "I love you, Syd."

He felt her smile against his chest. "I love you, too, Mike."

"But this doesn't mean I've changed my mind about your leaving. Last night convinced me more than ever that this territory is no place for a woman."

He had confessed his love, which was half the battle, she thought. That knowledge was enough for now. Last night's near brush with death was still a vivid fright. She needed time to recover. And knowing Mike loved her was the best medicine to help that healing. Time heals all wounds, she thought with contentment.

She pressed a kiss to his chest. "Well, I'm fine now, Mike. Thanks to you."

He turned and leaned on his elbow. He picked up the golden whistle glittering between the ivory mounds of her breasts. "And this whistle."

For a long moment his fingers toyed with the trinket.

With methodical care he replaced the whistle. As he did, his thumb accidentally brushed one of her nipples. The buds on her breasts stiffened.

Mike grinned. "Great reflexes, Delaney."

Lowering his head, he skimmed his tongue across the hardened crowns. A tremor rippled down her spine in response. "Yep, looks like there's been no permanent damage."

Sydney's eyes matched the mischief gleaming in his. "How can you be so certain with such a cursory examination, Doctor MacAllister?"

"A point well made, Miss Delaney." His brow arched and he reached out and thumbed the stiffened peak. "Or should I say, a well-made point?"

He laced his fingers through her silken hair and lowered his head in a deliberately slow descent. His appreciation of her nakedness excited her. She parted her lips in anticipation, then felt the arousing pressure of his mouth. His tongue moved in a sensuous, provocative exploration, and erotic sensation licked through her body.

Raising his head, his hooded stare consumed her as his finger traced the curve of her lips, then her cheek. She responded with a shudder.

"What are you thinking, Mike? What thoughts lie behind those guarded eyes?" Desire throbbed in her voice.

"I'm thinking how much I want to taste you. Devour you," he said in a husky voice as intoxicating as an aphrodisiac.

"Then taste me, Mike. Feast on me. Gorge on me. Because that's what I want you to do."

He slipped his hands beneath her back and lifted her torso slightly. Her head fell back when he curved her pliant body like a bow and raised her upthrust breasts to meet his plundering mouth. His tongue teased the peaks, moving from one to the other, bringing her sensual torture. Liquid fire flashed through her, and her back arched in writhing spasms as he continued to suckle her voraciously.

Releasing her, for a brief moment he gazed into her green eyes that were so suffused with passion, they glimmered like emeralds. A trace of a smile tugged at the corners of his mouth. "That was the appetizer. Now it's time for the main course. You sure you want to stay for dinner?"

"I wouldn't miss it."

He slid down lower on the bunk as his tongue returned to the exquisite torture of her breasts. "Bend your legs, Syd," he murmured. She did as he asked.

As his mouth feasted at the heaving mounds of her breasts, he parted her legs and his fingers lightly grazed a course up the inside of each thigh to the hub of her passion. She cried out, and abandoned all thought to sensuality.

Groaning and sobbing his name, she writhed and strained beneath the relentless pursuit of his mouth and hands that sought and found every sensitive nerve, every throbbing pulse, every aching, vulnerable spot of her body.

She swirled in hedonistic ecstasy when his tongue licked a moist trail down the lean, silken plane of her stomach as his fingers probed the opening at the vee of her legs. Raising his head, he parted the lips and covered her sex with his mouth. His tongue speared the opening and climactic tremors again swept her spine.

When he released her, she stretched out her legs. Her throbbing chest ached from her effort to breathe. Lying down beside her, Mike gathered her in his arms and drew her to his side, clamping a long, muscular leg over hers.

They lay side by side until her breathing returned to normal. Then propped on an elbow, she leaned over him and pressed a passionate kiss to his mouth.

Long strands of red hair dropped in a curtain on his naked chest. Gliding her body over his, she stretched out on top of him. He slipped his hands under the thick mane of her hair and cupped her nape.

"Mike, I want more," she whispered, nipping at his ear. Her tongue licked the shell, then traced the outline before dipping into its center.

"God, you're an insatiable wench. What am I going to do with you?" He tangled his fingers in her thick strands of hair and pulled up her head, crushing her mouth in a long, bruising kiss.

His loins were on fire. He attacked her face, pressing quick, hot kisses to her lips, eyes, and cheeks.

Raising her shoulders, she shifted her legs and straddled him. Her moist center pressed against the side of his hardened arousal. "Don't do that, Syd," he cried.

But the warning came too late. The feel of his hot, hard organ stimulated her. The stricken gleam that leapt to his eyes aroused her further.

"Mike, when I said I wanted more, I meant more of you. I want to feel you in me." To ease her ache, she instinctively began to rub her warmth against his pulsating organ.

The movement was his undoing. His blood surged in response. He pulled her forward, his erection cradled between her legs. He sucked in his breath. Her bare breasts pressed into the wall of his naked chest in the continued assault on his senses.

Hot blood pounded in his brain, his ears, his loins. He no longer had control. The restraint he had guarded so zealously snapped, and he became driven by a lust that demanded assuagement.

He rolled her over on her back. Parting her legs, he drove into her and pierced the thin tissue that veiled her virginity.

She welcomed the momentary stab of pain, and her fingers dug into the stretched, taut muscles of his shoulders as she stifled her outcry against his neck.

Her slickened chamber stretched around the large,

pulsating hardness that had filled her, and when his movements intensified, she cried out in ecstasy.

Driven by a lust for release, he pumped faster and faster until his body shuddered in a sublime implosion, and he spilled his seed into her.

Mike slumped across her, and Sydney slipped her arms around his neck, hugging the dark head to her breast. A fine film of perspiration dotted his lip when he finally raised his head, and his tortured gaze met the innocence of love glowing in her eyes.

"I'm sorry, Syd. I know I hurt you."

"Did I complain?" Her eyes sparkled with merriment. "Besides, as John Dryden once said, 'Long pains, with use of bearing, are half eased.' "

He peered at her. "Just what in hell does that mean?"

Sydney turned on her side, propping her head on her arm. She smiled contentedly as she gazed at him. Her hand idly caressed the hair on his chest. "A free translation would be, the more often and longer you have to bear it, the less the pain becomes." She leaned over and put a light kiss on his lips. "I'm ready, any time you are."

Shaking his head in disbelief, he gave a chuckle. "Delaney, you're outrageous. You have absolutely no shame."

"Not where making love to you is concerned," she said with open-eyed candor. "I never suspected such ecstasy could be possible."

He couldn't resist the temptation she presented and began to gently stroke her swollen mouth with his tongue. A long, contented sigh slipped past her lips. She closed her eyes, opening herself to his touch.

This time there was no driving urgency. He caressed her slowly, taking the time to savor as well as taste. Her flesh awakened wherever he touched. When he finally eased into her, thrusting inside her again, her arms slipped around his neck in the glory of the fulfillment of this love.

* * *

Later, Sydney pulled on her long underwear and sat on the bearskin on the floor. She ate a piece of the venison pemmican, washing down the meat with an occasional sip from Mike's coffee mug.

When she finished, she dug through her pack and found her brush. Sitting on the bearskin with her legs tucked under her, she brushed her hair.

Amused, Mike watched her as she moved around nonchalantly, with no sign of self-consciousness. Grinning, he finally asked, "Whatever happened to that modest woman who wouldn't even consider sleeping under the same roof with two bachelors much less step into a brothel?"

"She met you, MacAllister," Sydney said, trying to sound carefree. "And fell in love."

"And it has to stop before it goes any further. What if you get pregnant?"

She glanced up, stunned. "Are you so insistent I leave that you wouldn't reconsider under those circumstances?"

"My God, Syd, that would only intensify my determination for you to leave." She looked at him, perplexed.

He continued slowly, trying to explain. "I admit . . . that . . . somewhere along the way, you've touched me, Syd. You stir up certain emotions. But that scares the hell out of me. And I won't make a commitment to you . . . or to anyone."

"What kind of emotions do you mean, Mike?" she asked hopefully.

"There's no way to explain how I felt when I saw you lying there in the snow last night. I don't think I could have handled losing you. But last night also resurrected . . . memories . . . that I try not to think about."

She rose and walked over to him. "Memories of your wife and brother?"

His jaw hardened. He started to turn his head, and

she caught his chin, turning his face back to hers. "Mike, don't you think the time has come when you should tell me about it?"

"I suppose I owe you that much." Slumping down on the edge of the bunk, he sat staring into space. Intuition told her not to press the matter. He began to speak in a low voice.

"I guess the best place to start is with the Civil War. My folks had a small horse ranch in northern California. When the war broke out, my older brother, Jeff, was eighteen, so he enlisted in the army and went east. A couple years later my dad broke his neck trying to bust a bronco. That left my mother alone to try to run the ranch and raise us two kids. Ma just wasn't cut out for ranching. She had been a schoolteacher when she married my dad, and with Jeff gone, well, she had no heart to keep the ranch going. So she sold it and we moved to Sacramento. With all the wagon trains coming in from the east, she found a teaching job."

Sydney smiled at the coincidence—both his mother and her father had been teachers. She wondered why Mike had not mentioned that before.

"But after the freedom and space of living on a ranch, even a small one like we had, I hated city life." Sydney nodded, remembering how she had sensed that Mike could never be happy in a city.

"Jeff didn't get back home until '67, about the time the United States bought Alaska. I was almost sixteen then, and all I could think about was this wide open country. That a man could ride for days and not see anybody. I made up my mind—I'd come here to live some day."

"And is this where you met your wife?"

"Beth lived next door to us in Sacramento." A faraway look crept into his eyes, and his voice began to trail off. "Beth was kind of like Em. Hair the color of honey . . . and big blue eyes. Full of romantic ideas. She was only sixteen.

"She put up a big fuss when I told her where I was going and begged me to marry her. Well, marriage was the farthest thing from my mind at that time, but I promised her that after I got settled in Alaska, I'd come back for her. But she didn't want to wait. Kept begging me to marry her and take her along."

His face hardened. "I should have stuck to my guns. If I had, she'd be alive today."

Sydney sat down beside him and took his hand. "Mike, I believe in destiny. Our death is decreed from the day we're born."

"Believe what *you* want, Delaney. But don't expect me to swallow any of that mumbo jumbo," he said bitterly. "Life is nothing but a big gamble. The luck of the draw." His jaw hardened. "And Beth and Jeff were losers 'cause they gambled on me."

Frowning, she put her hand on his chin and turned his face to her. "Why do you blame yourself?"

"Because I was the one who insisted we come here." There was raw pain in his eyes. In his nervousness, he got up and began to pace the floor.

"But, Mike, you just told me that Beth begged you to bring her."

"Sure, because she was a wide-eyed romantic who didn't know what she was getting into." He started to turn away, then paused and looked back at Sydney. "Something like you, Syd."

Sydney rose and walked over to her pile of clothing. "Now I understand why you refused to bring love into our relationship. In truth, you've never gotten over your love for your wife," she said as she dressed.

"I never loved Beth."

The stark confession took her by surprise. She pivoted and stared at him in astonishment. "But you married her!"

He plopped down again on the edge of the bunk. "I married Beth because she told me she was carrying my child."

Stifling a gasp, Sydney returned to the bunk. She sat down and reached for his hand. Her eyes glistened with unshed tears when she spoke. "I'm so sorry, Mike. I never knew you lost a child, too."

"There was no child. Never had been. Beth admitted after we were married that she had lied. She just wanted her own way. She often lied to suit her purpose." His eyes glimmered like ice.

Mike lay back on the bunk and tucked his hands under his head. "Beth hated Alaska from the moment we arrived. And she reminded all of us of that fact every day. Our first winter, Jeff and I were running beaver traps. We all lived together in this cabin. She and I slept in the loft, Jeff and Bran in this bunk. Bran was only nine years old at the time, still trying to handle the grief of Ma's death."

This revelation was a twist she had never anticipated. She climbed on the bunk and sat cross-legged beside him. "Mike, I can see these memories are painful. I don't need to know the rest."

"It's just as well I tell the whole story so you'll understand."

She lay down beside him, and Mike continued. "Beth complained about everything. The cold. The snow. The crowded cabin. She begged me to take her back to California. Finally, I agreed I would take her back as soon as the snow melted. But that wasn't soon enough for Beth. She wanted to get out of here right away. When I refused, she started to work on Jeff's sympathies."

Sydney saw the torment in his eyes, and she wanted to stop him just to alleviate his pain. But she sensed it was critical for her to know the whole story if they were ever to have a future together.

"Jeff was a big, good-natured guy with a heart of gold." He paused, shaking his head. "Lord knows what she said to him, but she convinced him to take her to Solitary, and she would take a boat home from there. When I returned one morning from checking traps, they were all gone. He had taken Bran along and left a note telling me what he was doing. So I followed and caught up with them about halfway to Solitary. Jeff and I argued about it a bit, but since we were already halfway there, I agreed to go on to town."

He drew a long shuddering breath. "We were greenhorns and had a lot to learn about the wilds. Didn't know then how to read signs. We stumbled on a pack of wolves who had flushed a bear out of hibernation. The wolves turned on us, and the wounded bear took off. I told Beth to stay put, but while we were fighting off the wolves, she panicked and ran into the open. Jeff saw her go, and he took off after her. I was shooting as fast as my rifle would fire to keep the wolves from them and Bran, too. Finally what was left of the pack scampered off in the opposite direction."

His face had become drawn with emotion. "Mike, why don't you stop?" she said gently, stroking his forehead "You can tell me some other time."

He shook his head. "You've heard it up to now, you might as well hear the rest. I wasn't with him so I can't say for sure what happened, but you don't have to be a genius to figure it out. The bear had doubled back, and Jeff must have run right into him . . . too close to even use his rifle . . . and the bear was wounded and mad."

Mike threaded his fingers through his hair, pausing momentarily to retain his self-control. "God, sometimes I wake up hearing his screams. That's what led us to him. His leg had already been chewed off. The bear was half-dead and dragging Jeff back to his den. I finished off the bear but it was too late to save Jeff."

Tears streaked Sydney's cheek when Mike lifted his head. "And what about Beth?" she asked softly. She didn't know if she was helping or hurting, but she wanted to divert his mind from the picture of his brother's grisly death.

"Daylight was gone . . . Bran was sobbing his heart out. But I didn't dare leave the kid alone with Jeff's body in case the wolves came back. So he had to come with me while I searched for her through the night. We finally found her the next morning. She had frozen to death ... her tears were still on her cheeks."

With eyes wracked with pain, he suddenly sat up and grasped her shoulders. His fingers cut into her flesh. "She might have been spoiled, and vain, and manipulative. But she was only sixteen years old. She didn't deserve to die."

Sydney felt numb. She wished there was some way she could take on his misery. "Mike, I can't tell you how sorry I am."

He released her and rose to his feet. "It's all in the past, Delaney. Thirteen years ago. As I told you, last night kind of brought it all back."

She expected him to drop the subject and was surprised when he continued. "I didn't want to bury the two of them out here. Thought some animal would burrow down to them. So I wrapped up the bodies and kept on going to Solitary."

Still numb, Sydney sat staring down at her hands in her lap. "Is that when you met Claire?"

His thoughts appeared to have drifted again, and she waited silently. "Oh ... Claire? Yeah. She's the one who got Bran and me through it.

"Claire had lived in Solitary for a couple of years. The bastard she came with took off and left her with a two-year-old. Solitary was always a good stopover for trappers. That was before she had Lily and Sal. So she worked the customers herself.

"But she always had time for holding Bran in her arms when the kid would wake up crying, or talking me through the bad nights. Yeah. Bran and I would never have made it ... if it hadn't been for Claire."

A thought crossed Sydney's mind that she had not considered before. Throughout the whole tragedy, Mike would have been only eighteen years old. Almost a child himself.

Cautiously, she broached a subject that had piqued her curiosity since coming to Solitary. "It's easy to understand why you and Bran are so devoted to her. Were you and she ever more than just—"

He jerked up his head. His eyes glinted with resentment. "You mean did we ever sleep together? Sure, Delaney, plenty of times. When I'd wake up screaming, she'd climb into bed with me and hold me in her arms with my head on her breast. But did we ever have sex? No. It would never have occurred to either of us." Sydney colored with embarrassment at the raw honesty in his reply.

"I gotta tell you about Claire, Delaney—she keeps her business separate from her personal life. She has her customers . . . and her family and friends. No one *ever* crosses the boundary." Mike's tone softened. "I wish Jeff could have known her. They were so much alike. They would have been good together. Kind of like Bran and Em."

His mood had changed entirely. He was no longer the man who had made love to her earlier. The memories of those glorious moments appeared to have been already forgotten—replaced by painful memories of the past that would always be with him.

He put on his parka. "I'm going out to take care of the dogs and pack up the sled. We'd better be getting out of here."

Chapter 26

A fter their long winter night's sleep, the dogs were as frisky as puppies to be underway. The storm had completely stopped, though the sky was still dark.

"How long will it take us to get to the Tlingit village?" Sydney asked, once Mike had her tucked securely into the seat of the sled.

"I'd guess about four hours. The going's tougher in this drifted snow. But it's getting toward mid-morning. There will be more light soon."

Mike halted the dogs for a rest two hours later. The sky had lightened considerably, and the rising sun was shining dully behind a dispersing cloud cover. As he cleaned away the snow from between the dogs' toes, he lifted his head at the sound of a distant howl. Sydney heard it, too. "Is that the wind?"

He shook his head. "No. Wolves," he replied when the mournful wailing continued.

She cast a wary glance around her, conscious of how alone the two of them were in the remote wilderness. "Are they after us, Mike?"

"Wolves rarely attack human beings unless the animals have been provoked or are starving. And the winter hasn't been that severe. They know we're here, and they're letting us know. In all probability, they'll trail us for a few miles, then veer off."

Nonetheless, Sydney found little comfort in his words when Mike reached for his rifle and hooked it onto the handlebars.

After another quarter of an hour, he stopped the sled and shaded his eyes, peering toward a distant ridge. Mike immediately spotted the wolves stalking the sled. Trotting along in a straight line, they followed in one another's tracks where the going was easier—the higher, windblown ridges less laden with snow. His stomach knotted when he counted fourteen of them. The unusually large pack would be aggressive and not inclined to back off easily.

Mike knew that once the wolves reached the trees, the pack would split and come at the sled from all directions.

He slashed the lashings and shoved the tarp-covered freight cartons off the sled. Guessing the reason behind his actions, Sydney watched in silence. "You're going to try and outrun them, aren't you?"

"Yeah," he said grimly. "But it's not easy to outrun a wolf. They're the definitive predator, Delaney. No animal up here can touch them. They can run nonstop as fast as twenty-five miles an hour for over a mile. And they can maintain a steady pace and cover forty miles in eight hours."

"How many of them are following us?"

"Enough," he said succinctly. Not wishing to frighten her further, he said calmly, "Our best bet is to find a good spot where we can make a stand to drive them away."

He climbed back onto the runners. "But it's sure not gonna be in these trees," he mumbled to himself. "Hi," he shouted, and the team moved on.

Deep mounds of snow slowed the progress of the huskies, forcing them to plunge through deep drifts. When the howling resumed, this time much nearer and louder, Mike knew the wolves had entered the timberline, and the pack had split. With only one rifle with which to defend themselves, he had hoped to find a spot that would protect their back and sides. But that now appeared to be impossible.

He spied a stand of birch. Two trees arched side by side. Their spindly, leafless boughs were twisted together, strangling the life out of one another. Their bent, misshapened trunks almost touched the ground to form a gnarled bower. A fallen hemlock laid across the entrance of the decaying alcove.

It was an inadequate barrier, but the only one.

Mike led the team into the shelter and plugged the gap with the sled. Responding to his sharp command, the dogs lay down, their heads erect and ears perked.

Mike offered a solemn warning to Sydney as she climbed out of the seat. "When the attack comes, it will be hard not to panic. But remember, they're after the dogs, not us. So whatever you do, Syd, don't run or they'll go after you. And you won't have a chance in the open."

She nodded, forcing a weak smile. "You know I can't move a muscle when I'm scared anyway." The fright in her eyes belied her tone.

A high shrill sounded from the trees to the right. Startled, she swung her head to the responding howl from the opposite side. Then the clamor resounded from all directions. Her eyes grew round with increased alarm. "They're all around us, Mike."

He grasped her shoulders and stared down at her. For the first time she saw a sign of desperation in his dark eyes. "Remember, Syd. Don't run. Stay with me. Whatever happens, stay with me."

"When we get out of here, I'm going to hold you to that request, MacAllister," she said gamely.

He gave her chin a light tap with his finger. "Just keep that chin up, Delaney, and stay down."

Mike released Grit and ordered the big malamute to lie down. Then, checking his rifle to make sure the weapon was fully loaded, he pulled out the Colt and laid it between him and Sydney.

"Sure wish you'd have taken that target practice a little more seriously."

"Not half as much as I do, Mike," she said regretfully. Then, spying several gray and black shapes darting back and forth among the trees, she could not stop from crying out. "Mike! They're in those trees."

Suddenly, two barking wolves dashed out of the trees and raced toward them. A shot brought down one of them, and the other quickly turned and sprinted back into the forest cover.

Mike kept up a steady barrage of rifle fire to try to drive them away. It appeared he had succeeded until the harness snapped on one of the dogs. The animal leaped the barricade and raced out barking.

Several of the wolves darted out of the trees and leaped on the dog, their huge paws dragging it down.

"Grit!" Mike shouted, but the warning shout came too late to prevent the malamute from dashing to the aid of the other dog. Mike fired as near as he dared, but the thrashing animals made it impossible for him to get in a sure shot.

The other huskies set up a chorus of barking and yapping; straining at the harnesses that fettered them. "I've got to cut them loose," Mike shouted.

The moment he slashed the lashings, the remainder of the dogs raced at the wolves. Instantly, other howling animals bolted out of the trees and joined the fray.

Crouching, Sydney buried her head in her hands. She wanted to scream. Surely the horrendous carnage was a nightmare from hell!

Feral snarls ... blood-spattered snow ... fallen shapes. The incessant blast of the rifle. The acrid smell of gunsmoke.

Dogs and wolves leaping ... ripping. Gray fur ... black fur ... canine fangs ... streaked and bloodied.

She wanted to cover her ears and run until absolute silence freed her from the savagery.

Sydney raised her head at the sound of loud thrashing behind her. Turning, she saw two wolves about to crash through the brittle limbs and boughs of the birch.

A huge paw clawed through the barrier, then a snarling head with bared fangs and fierce yellow eyes, driven wild with the frenzy of attack, poked through the broken branches.

Instinct forced her trembling hand toward the pistol, and her fingers closed around the cold metal. Her hand shook so violently, she steadied it with her other as she aimed and pulled the trigger. With a yelp of pain, the animal fell away and the other wolf darted back into the trees.

Meanwhile, Mike was on his feet, firing whenever he had a sure target. Two of the wolves charged him and his shot brought down one of the barking animals. The click of his rifle's empty chamber galvanized him to desperate action. Clutching the barrel of the rifle, he swung it like a club to drive back the other one. The jaws of the snarling beast clamped onto the rifle stock, but a powerful kick from Mike sent the animal sprawling. The wolf rolled over, then limped into the trees.

The attack ended as quickly as it had begun. Scurrying away, the remaining wolves disappeared into the trees. Mike reloaded his rifle and climbed over the tree trunk.

When her trembling eased, Sydney stood up. "Are they gone?" she asked in wary relief. Mike nodded.

Then, after a moment's delay, she took in the absolute silence. Her voice rose in alarm. "Mike! Where are the dogs? Where's Grit?"

But Mike was already bending over the big malamute.

Grit whined softly and tried to raise his head when Mike touched him. Sydney knelt beside them. "How badly is he hurt?"

Mike shook his head. "He's alive . . . but he's bleeding badly." He started to pack the dog's wounds in snow. "Maybe this will slow the bleeding."

"I'll check the others."

She started to get up, but he grabbed her arm to stop her. "Don't, Syd. I've already checked."

She stared at him in disbelief. "No ... it can't be." Tears streaked her cheeks. "Not all of them." She shook her head in denial. "You're wrong, Mike. They can't all be dead."

She struggled to shrug off his hand, but his grasp held firmly. "Syd, it's no use." He shook her slightly to ward off her mounting hysteria. "Syd, listen to me. You've held up until now. Don't break down on me. I need your help with Grit. Maybe we can save him if we can get to the village."

Sydney closed her eyes and took a deep breath. "What do you want me to do?"

"First, we have to get out of here. The smell of this blood is going to attract more predators."

He walked away before she could ask how he intended to leave. "Get in, Delaney," he ordered after freeing the sled from the wedge.

Reluctantly, she climbed in. Grit whimpered when Mike picked him up and placed the dog on her lap. "Keep him warm, but we'll have to keep snow on his wounds."

Then Mike put on snowshoes, wrapped the reins under his arms, and harnessed himself to the sled.

They stopped several times for Mike to rest and put fresh snow on Grit. Three hours later, they finally arrived at the village. Pasha and Rami were just preparing to leave with a search party to find them.

One look and the two men could guess what had happened. Grit was still breathing when the grim-faced trio carried the wounded dog inside the main lodge.

"He made it this far. Will he live?" Sydney asked a short time later after Grit's wounds had been treated and bound.

"I don't know. He's lost a lot of blood," Mike said somberly.

The two sat down to an anxious vigil.

When Pasha and Rami returned after taking care of the sled, Mike began to describe the wolf attack. Not wanting to relive the experience, Sydney decided it would be a good time to visit Taitana.

As she neared the young woman's house, Sydney saw Alexi sitting in front of the lodge. "Alexi, how are you?" The young man nodded but appeared in a deep gloom. "I've come to see Taitana. Is she home?"

"Taitana have baby now," Alexi said.

"You mean she's in labor?" Sydney asked excitedly.

"Taitana birthing much time," he said, clearly distressed.

Sydney put a hand on his arm. "May I go in and see her, Alexi?"

"Tanya say no one come in. Evil spirit enter body."

"Evil spirit!" Sydney wouldn't tolerate any such argument. She shoved past him.

As soon as she entered the lodge, Sydney felt a sense of foreboding. The main room was quiet, deserted except for one woman stirring a pot over the fire. She gave Sydney a cursory glance then returned to her task.

Sydney entered Taitana's dark and smokey room, lit only by the dim light from a single candle, and found the young woman lying on a blanket on the floor.

The sachem, Tanya, sat cross-legged in a dark corner, and Sydney saw the source of the smoke: a small, round crucible glowing with ashes on the floor before the old woman.

With closed eyes, she was mumbling an incantation. In a trancelike state, she dropped a powdered substance on the coals, sending another stream of smoke into the air.

Sydney moved quietly to the side of the young girl. Taitana's eyes were closed and her dark hair lay dank with perspiration. Drawn and pale, her face testified to her long, painful labor.

When her body was seized with a spasm, Taitana

groaned and opened her eyes. Sydney gasped with shock at the dull look in her once alert, dark eyes.

Seeing Sydney, Taitana tried to smile. "It pleases me to see my friend." She barely had strength to speak.

Sydney knelt beside the suffering girl and clasped her hand. "I wish there were something I could do to make you more comfortable," she said gently.

Another spasm gripped Taitana, and she squeezed Sydney's hand. Taitana's forehead was damp with perspiration. Sydney looked around helplessly for a cloth or sponge with which to wipe off the suffering girl's brow, but to no avail. There wasn't a sign of anything to relieve the poor girl's agony.

"Is there something I can get you, Taitana?" Sydney asked.

"Water. I would like a drink of water," she whispered.

"I'll be right back."

She hurried out to the other room. "Water. Do you have some water?" She made a gesture of drinking in the event the old woman didn't understand English.

The woman nodded toward an urn in the corner. Sydney ladled water into a cup, and seeing a cloth nearby, she moistened the material and returned to the room.

Lifting Taitana's head, Sydney was able to get a few sips of water down the girl's throat. Then after rinsing Taitana's face with the cool cloth, Sydney dabbed some water on her parched lips.

Seized by another contraction, Taitana clutched Sydney's arm, moaning in agony. Sydney tenderly stroked her head. "You'll forget all this pain when you hold your baby in your arms, Taitana."

"I think I will never know that pleasure." Her eyes glazed under the pain of another contraction. "Alexi. I want Alexi," she mumbled weakly.

Suddenly, a bony hand grasped Sydney's shoulder and yanked her away from Taitana. "You go. Out. Out,"

Tanya ordered. "White woman bad medicine for Tlingit."

Sydney recoiled from the filthy woman's touch. "Why don't you help her? Surely there's some kind of powder you can give her to ease her pain."

The old hag's glance darted to the cup of water on the floor. "No drink. Must drive evil spirits from body." Her eyes glittered with malevolence as she pointed a bony finger at Sydney. "You bad medicine."

Appalled, Sydney felt revulsion at the sight of the woman's dirty hands and nails. "You're the bad medicine here. How do you expect her to breath in this smokey air?"

"Out. You go!" Tanya ordered, waving a hand toward the door.

"I'm going. But just to get help," Sydney announced.

Once outside, Sydney confronted Alexi and told him Taitana was calling for him. The saddened youth shook his head. "Tanya say to wait."

"Good Lord! Your poor wife is in there alone with just that crazy old woman. Where is Taitana's family?"

He pointed to a nearby lodge. "They are praying for their daughter and sister. Tanya say everyone must stay out."

Sydney hurried over to the other lodge. She remembered many of the people from her previous visit, but no one responded to her pleas to help Taitana.

"But your daughter is dying," Sydney said to Taitana's mother.

The woman shook her head. "Tanya say we stay here until she drive away evil spirit in daughter's body. Then baby born."

"By that time Taitana will be dead," Sydney said angrily.

Seeing the situation was hopeless, Sydney hurried back to the lodge where she had left Mike.

"How is he?" she asked when she saw Mike sitting

near the dog. Taitana's condition had made her forget about the wounded Grit.

"No change. But he's still breathing. That's a hopeful sign at least."

"Mike, I need your help." Sydney quickly related the details concerning Taitana. "What can we do? She needs better attention than witchery from that old hag. Why, the woman is filthy! She shouldn't even touch an ill person."

"Syd, we can't do anything. You must stay out of this. You can't interfere in the beliefs and customs of these people."

"What are you saying? I should just stand by and let Taitana die? She's been in labor for two days, Mike. Two days! She's so weak, she's going to die before the baby is even born."

Mike frowned and rose to his feet. "Tanya's the doctor here, Delaney." He went outside.

She slumped down on the floor and rested her head on her raised knees. Tears welled from frustration. Surely something could be done to save her friend.

Pasha came over and patted her shoulder. "Vat Michael say is being true, little *Красотá*. Is matter for Indian, not Sydney."

Mike returned a short time later and sat down next to her. "I've talked to a few of the villagers. They know Taitana is dying, Syd, but it's too late to get a shaman from another village. They think it's a good omen that we came here with Grit in his condition. The Indians feel that if the dying dog's spirit enters Taitana's body, the baby will inherit Grit's courage and nobility."

"Witchcraft! That's all it is. We're all supposed to sit around and do nothing, waiting for Grit and Taitana to die?" Her voice choked with anger. "What makes them think the baby won't die with the mother?" She jumped to her feet. "Well, I'm not as patient as you. I won't sit idly by and watch it happen."

Mike was on his feet at once. He grabbed her arm

and halted her before she got as far as the door. "Like hell you won't!" Mike declared. "You stay out of this, or I'll have Pasha and Rami take you back to Solitary *now*. You cannot interfere in this matter."

She glared up at him. "You interfered quickly enough when Lev and Boris were killing a dog, but you won't interfere to save a young woman and her unborn child. I don't understand you, Mike. I guess I never will."

She found herself in his grasp, bearing the full force of his anger. "From the first day you came, I've told you this country is no place for a woman, Delaney. The conditions are primitive . . . violent. The men are uncivilized . . . the Indians superstitious. And there are no doctors to offer medical skills. Now maybe you'll believe me."

He released her and sat down. "Taitana's life is in Tanya's hands," he said, resigned.

Sydney went back to Taitana's lodge, but this time Alexi blocked her entrance. "Tanya say no," he said sadly. Shaken and heartbroken, Sydney had no recourse but to return to the lodge.

The sixteen-year-old woman's ordeal ended during the night when she died after giving birth to a healthy daughter.

Upon hearing the news the following morning, Sydney sat stunned, unable to cry. Mike came over and knelt beside her. "I'm sorry, Syd. You've got to believe there was nothing you could do . . . any of us could do . . . to change what happened."

"Well, at least you can say you were right again, Mike," she lashed out bitterly.

She saw the wounded look in his eyes and knew she was blaming Mike for something over which he had no control. But by condoning these beliefs, he accepted them, as far as she was concerned.

"Believe what you want to believe, Syd." Mike walked away and returned to Grit.

* * *

Mike and Sydney remained in the village waiting for Grit's wounds to heal. The dog appeared to be gradually recovering, but the tension between Mike and Sydney did not lessen. They spoke politely to one another, but despite the intimacy they had shared, the events of the last couple of days had raised a barrier between them.

Pasha had become a Pied Piper to the children. They crowded around the jovial man, who entertained them for hours on end.

Despite her grief, Sydney could not help smiling as she listened to the children's laughter one morning as he tried to confuse them with three shells and a small round bead.

He held up the red bead between his thumb and finger. "Now, you be vatching closely to see vat Pasha is being about to do."

He lifted one of the shells and slipped the bead under it. "Vatch how Pasha's hand is being faster zen eyes of you, my little lemmings."

Waving his long hands, he chanted, "Come, hokum and the pokus." Quickly shifting around the shells, he declared mysteriously, "Now tell Pasha vich shell is being vere little red bead is hiding?"

One of the youngsters immediately pointed to the middle shell. Pasha lifted up the nutshell to reveal the bead. "Aha! So you vin! How you be doing dat so good? Pasha be thinking dis little lemming played game before." He dug into his pocket and gave the youngster a piece of candy.

"Now vich von vant to being next?" He motioned to a little girl nearby. Burying her chin in her chest, the shy little girl stepped forward.

"Hokum and the pokus," Pasha chanted, sliding around the shells. "Vat your guess, little dark eyes?"

Giggling, the little girl pointed to a shell. Pasha lifted the shell, once again revealing the bead. Throwing his hands in the air, he clutched his head. "How you be doing dat?" He produced another piece of candy. "A sveet for a sveet, my little darlink."

He continued the game until each of the children had succeeded in winning a piece of the candy. "Pasha is broke. No more candy. Off with you little mices," he shouted in mock dismay, shooing them away.

"Pasha, I think you're supposed to palm the bead or something like that, aren't you?" Sydney asked when the children had departed.

"Is true." Pasha winked at her. "But dat vay little lemmings no vin sveet from Pasha."

Sydney reached out and clasped his hand. "You're not always the fool you'd like us to believe, are you, Pasha?"

"It vould be impossible." He laughed and cast a sagacious eye as he squeezed her hand. "Everyvon, sometimes, is not being vat ve seem. *Nyet?*"

Three days later, the family of Taitana's father arrived, and the potlatch for the young departed girl was celebrated.

"Is being most sacred ceremony," Pasha explained to Sydney. "Honor dead is time for gifing many gifts."

Tanya made it clear she did not want Sydney present at the potlatch. However, the villagers and kin of Taitana paid the older woman no mind and gave their permission for Sydney to attend.

Mike tried to prepare her for the celebration that would follow. "These Indians do not fear death. They see it as a chosen honor, Delaney. The beginning of a great journey, an occasion for celebration, not mourning. . . . A time for feasting and the giving of gifts," he explained.

"Well, I don't see how that differs so greatly from our Christian beliefs," Sydney challenged. "We believe that death is a beginning. It is the people left behind who must bear the grief. What about those who loved Taitana? Look at Alexi; he certainly doesn't look like he's celebrating."

She pointed to a bereaved Alexi whose expression bore the pain of a broken heart. Sydney's soul ached for him as she recalled the love she had witnessed between the young couple.

"And what about the baby? Now she must grow up without a mother. That's really something to celebrate," she scoffed.

"Syd, Alexi will find a new wife, and that woman will love and accept the child as her own. And she *will* love that child. All children among these people grow up feeling cherished." Frustrated by her unwillingness to understand, he walked away from her—and the rift continued to widen between them.

Alexi began the ceremony by singeing his hair to reflect his loss while the rest of the clan sang songs in memory of Taitana and other deceased relatives.

Taitana's body was then brought forward and placed on the burial bier. Sydney watched with tear-filled eyes as the grandfather of the dead girl raised a lit torch.

After the body had been cremated, the ashes were placed in an urn and carried to the top of a totem, then dumped into the hollow pole.

Then the feasting and celebration began. Everything belonging to Alexi and Taitana was given to members of the family who had come to participate in the ceremony. Except for one item.

Sydney felt the rise of tears when Alexi stopped before her and handed her a pair of Taitana's beaded moccasins. A firm hand clamped on her shoulder to lend her more strength. She discovered Mike had returned to her side.

Sydney opened her hands and accepted the gift. "Thank you, Alexi, I shall always cherish them," she murmured, moved by this considerate gesture.

Then the festivity continued, becoming a celebration of the birth of the child. And as Sydney mourned the passing of her young friend, she gradually drew comfort from the message of hope in the promise of the child's new life.

The following day, Sydney remained in the village and watched over Grit while the three men and several of the Indians went to retrieve the freight Mike had dumped.

To Sydney's relief, early the following morning, they lashed the sled onto the sledge for the return home. The three men alternated driving, and Sydney sat with Grit, still swathed in bandages but able to raise his head.

On the return to Solitary, Sydney was a far different woman from the enthusiastic and wide-eyed innocent who had begun the trip. Desolate, she wanted nothing more than to be left alone.

Chapter 27

That evening Sydney's room became a sanctuary for her. She wanted to huddle inside it and never leave. During the past few days, she had experienced an entire range of emotions: panic in the throes of near death, ecstasy in Mike's arms, horror during the wolf attack, grief over the death of Taitana. She felt completely drained of strength and will.

The crackle and pop of the fire on the hearth along with the company of her beloved pets—the flutter of Brutus in his cage, the patter of Runt's feet—these, and these only, were the sights and sounds from which she drew comfort. She sat in her bed with the quilt pulled up to her neck as she watched and listened.

Later that evening, Mike tapped lightly on her bedroom door. "Syd."

Wearily, she rose to her feet and pulled on her robe. "What do you want, Mike?" she asked, opening the door wide enough to make eye contact with him.

"Are you okay? You disappeared so quickly when we got back, we've all been concerned about you."

"I'm fine. Just tired."

"You haven't had anything to eat," he said.

"I'm not hungry, Mike. I appreciate your concern, but if you don't mind, I'd just like to go back to bed."

"Are you sure you're feeling all right?" he asked, alarmed. "It wouldn't hurt to have something hot in your stomach. You've lived mostly on cold rations for over a week. What do you say to me running over to Claire's and bringing you back a hot meal?"

"I'm not hungry. Really, Mike. I appreciate your thoughtfulness." She started to close the door.

"Syd, are you sure you don't want to talk?"

She smiled and shook her head. "I'm sure I will later but not at this time, Mike. I just want to go to bed and rest. I'm tired."

"Well, I have a couple of things to do in the office. I hope I won't disturb you."

"No, go right ahead. You won't disturb me. If you have any work for me, just leave it on my desk, and I'll do it first thing in the morning."

He nodded. "Good night, Syd."

"Good night, Mike." Sydney closed the door and leaned against it. Her eyes filled with tears. Why had she gone on that accursed trip? If only she had stayed home.

The next morning Sydney observed that the restless night she'd spent had only succeed in deepening the black circles under her eyes. She was already at her desk checking a shipping schedule when Mike joined her in the office.

His greeting added to her depression. "You look like hell, Delaney," he grumbled. "Obviously you aren't feeling well."

"Thank you for the compliment," she said crisply. "And I'm fine." She returned to her shipping schedule. "How is Grit doing this morning?"

"He's up and around."

"Not jumping around, I hope. Just because his wounds are healing doesn't mean he's well. He lost a lot of blood. His body needs times to restore that loss."

"Next week by this time, he'll be back to his full strength," Mike remarked, sounding like a proud parent.

Sydney cast a guarded glance at Runt, snoozing on the floor at the base of Brutus' cage. Not raising her head, she tried to sound nonchalant. "I suppose you'll need Runt."

Mike glanced up from the paper in his hands. "For what?"

"Well, I know you've lost most of your dogs."

"That's right. But I need another team *now,* Delaney. I can hardly wait until Runt's old enough to pull a sled." He threw aside the paper and stood up. "That's why I've decided to go to Seward. Last time I was there, I saw a fellow trying to sell his team. I'm going to find out if it's still available. A lot of work goes into the making of a good sled dog. It would be a big help if I were lucky enough to get a trained team."

Sydney felt a little of the weight lift from her shoulders. "I can't tell you how relieved I am. I don't know what I'd do if I had to give up Runt."

Hearing his name, the puppy scampered over and jumped at her skirt. "Okay. I'll take you out," she cooed.

"I'll take him. I need a walk," Mike said. He grabbed his parka and opened the door. Runt raced outside with Mike following before Sydney could voice a protest.

As she watched them stroll away, a troubling thought entered her mind. Before the unfortunate trip, they had often walked the puppy together. But this time it hadn't even occurred to Mike to ask her. *What's happening to us, Mike?*

Returning to her desk, she sat down and buried her head in her hands. She knew her actions were widening the gap between them; but, somehow, she couldn't find the words to close it. Anytime they had quarreled in the past, the argument was usually forgotten by the next morning. But this time . . . *this time they had not quarreled,* she realized with a startling revelation. But she felt confident she would be over her depression by the time he returned from Seward.

Against her will, she was drawn back to the window. She watched Mike's tall figure walking toward the wharf. Runt trotted along at his feet, sniffing at the snow. Soon the puppy's black snout had turned to white.

Her gaze returned to Mike. The wind ruffled his dark hair as he formed a snowball and tossed it into the air. Runt leaped at the ball, and Mike's teeth flashed in a grin as he laughed at the romping puppy.

With an aching heart, Sydney watched the pair until they moved beyond her vision.

Later that afternoon Sydney walked down to the dock with Mike as he prepared to board the mail boat bound for Seward. They acted like a pair of awkward strangers when they said good-bye.

"While I'm in Seward, I'll make contact with John Gaines. He will be operating the office in Seward. When Bran gets back, the three of us will go to Seward and set everything up."

"That's a good idea, Mike. I'll look forward to meeting him." The ship's horn sounded. She started to turn away.

Mike pulled her into his arms. "Hey, Delaney. Isn't this the part in those novels you read where 'he' kisses 'she' good-bye?"

She closed her eyes and allowed his warm lips to remind her of how much she loved him.

"Well, I admit that maybe I have been acting like a fool since my return," Sydney conceded to her two faithful companions that evening. "And I intend to try to put the whole, unpleasant memory out of my mind. It won't be easy, but I can do it," she said with a lift of her chin. "I've learned to put other tragedies behind me. Of course, I've never had the sky fall on me like it did this last time," she reflected.

"Sydney's right," Brutus assured her, and Runt seconded the motion with a wagging tail.

Sydney spent the time during Mike's absence going

over past vouchers to determine what would have to be ordered in the spring. With the additional storage space available, she realized that a considerable amount of shipping charges could be saved by consolidating shipments.

The task kept her occupied and also helped to keep her mind off Mike. For whatever their differences or misunderstandings, Mike's absence left a void in her life and an ache in her heart; his presence made the difference between living life—or merely existing.

Her spirits brightened when Mike returned after a week's absence. Just the sight of his tall figure moving around the dock as the dogs were unloaded set her heart racing—and her passion rocketing. They had been apart too long. And her need called for action, not words.

Pins flew in all directions as she hurriedly shook out her hair and raced to her bedroom. She ran a quick brush through the thick strands, then pinched her cheeks to add color to a face that already bore the blush of anticipation.

Her fingers flew to the row of buttons on her high-necked bodice. She had nothing to wear in its stead. Then she dismissed the fleeting fear when she thought of Mike's ease at dispatching obstinate buttons. She could always sew them back on later.

At the sound of the office door opening, she had no further time for such trivial worries. She rushed out of her room. The smile died on her lips.

Darn! If it weren't for bad luck, I wouldn't have any luck at all, she thought in disappointment at the sight of Yuri Kherkov. The last thing she wanted at the moment was to have Mike set off by another confrontation with Yuri.

But her fears materialized. Before she could politely dispose of Yuri, Mike arrived.

With one look at the Russian, Mike's face shifted

into a frown. "I might have known you'd show up about now, Kherkov."

"Hello, Mike," Sydney offered with a welcoming smile.

"Hi." He tossed his keys on his desk and walked to the passageway without a backward glance. She blushed in embarrassment at his curt greeting.

"I stopped for only a moment to say hello, my dear Sydney. I hope you have been vell."

Sydney found it impossible to be her usual friendly self with Yuri after he had given her the hat made of otter fur at Christmas. Taking a deep breath, she explained how she felt to him, and the tension eased somewhat when he apologized with what seemed to be heart-felt sincerity. They parted on cordial terms, though Sydney knew she would never completely trust him.

Yuri left, and Mike was in the process of preparing a pot of coffee when Sydney entered the kitchen. "How did your trip go?" she asked, hoping to ease this renewed tension between them.

"Okay," he responded, gruffly.

"Did you get your team?" He nodded.

"What about Mr. Gaines? Did you have a chance to meet with him?"

"Yeah. He's all set."

Any thought of seduction went up in the smoke of her anger.

"Dammit, Mike. Just once it would be a pleasant relief to have you come back and show a little courtesy toward me."

He slammed down the coffeepot. "And just once I'd like to come back and not find that goddamn Russian sniffing around you like you're a bitch in heat."

"Must you resort to crudity? And that is a ridiculous accusation. Yuri's interest in me is purely platonic. He's a friend, nothing more. And, of course, it's not the same between us since he gave me that fur hat. Once I found out it was made from sea otters, I realized he did it to aggravate you. But he hurt me, too, and I've explained that to him. He's apologized, and we're still friends. You have to learn to get along with people, Mike, even when you disagree with them."

"You always learn the hard way, don't you, Delaney? This fight between Kherkov and me has been going on for ten years. You may think you've settled your differences with him, but at this very moment that bastard's probably got a couple of ships less than thirty miles from here harvesting otter pelts. Come on. Grit needs a workout, and I've got six dogs that need a good run. Change your clothes and we'll go for a little ride. Maybe when you see it for yourself, you'll find out just how *much* of a gentleman your *good friend* Yuri really is."

Within minutes the sled was skimming across the frozen snow. As she felt the crisp, fresh air on her face, Sydney realized she had needed the outing as much as the dogs.

After a couple of hours, Mike pulled up the team on a bluff overlooking the sea. She saw two trawlers flying the Russian flag bobbing on the water below.

Sydney felt a steady, rhythmic pounding like the thump of a tom-tom. Frowning, she cocked her head to listen. "What is that thumping sound?" she asked.

"Why don't you see for yourself?" He led her to the rim of the bluff. Then, horrified, she traced the source of the disturbing sound.

Far below on the rocks hugging the cliff, she saw hundreds of the small sea otters stretched out sunning themselves. Like a precision troupe, sailors carrying huge cudgels quickly moved among them, bashing the animals senseless. They were followed by other men who immediately skinned the animals and stuffed the pelts into bags.

The mothers, who would not leave their slower-moving pups, fell victim to the blows along with the young. And those otters who were quick enough to make it into the water were instantly snagged by the nets of the trawlers.

The air soon rang with the mournful cacophony: the shouts of sailors, wails of the mothers crying to their dying pups—and the steady crack of wood striking flesh.

Sickened beyond thought, Sydney turned away.

"Have you seen enough?" Mike asked.

She nodded. "Please take me back, Mike."

He grasped her arm and turned her toward the sled. Suddenly two hulking figures blocked their path. Terrified, Sydney stared at them—the sinister faces of the two depraved Russians, Lev and Boris.

Each held a pistol trained on Mike. "Drop rifle or ve shoot your voman," Lev ordered. Mike had no choice but to comply. He threw aside his rifle.

"Now Yankee get vat he got coming." Without a sign of compunction, Lev pulled the trigger.

Mike slumped to his knee, clutching at his leg. Lev's second shot knocked the other leg out from under Mike.

Sydney screamed and rushed to aid Mike, but Boris shoved her aside and swung his rifle, striking Mike on the side of the head. He fell to the ground, and the two men began to render vicious kicks on his fallen body.

"Stop it! Stop it, you're killing him!" she screamed. She crawled over and grabbed the legs of the nearest scoundrel. Her efforts met with a backhanded slap that sent her sprawling face first into the snow.

They yanked Mike to his feet, and as Boris held him upright, Lev pummelled Mike's face and ribs.

Suddenly a bullet kicked up the snow at their feet. The two men glanced up in surprise only to face a gun pointing at them from the hand of Yuri Kherkov. The Russian colonel barked a sharp command. Releasing Mike, he slumped to the ground, and they tossed aside their weapons.

As the three men began to argue in Russian, Sydney crawled over to Mike. Unconscious, his breath sounded raspy, and he was bleeding from his nose, his mouth, and a wound on his forehead. Both pants legs were saturated with blood from the gunshot wounds.

She looked up desperately at Kherkov. "He needs medical attention at once. He's lost a lot of blood, and I think his ribs are broken."

Yuri yanked off a white silk scarf from around his neck. "Bind legs vith this."

Sydney pulled Mike's knife out of his boot. Her hands trembled as she cut off hunks of the silk material and folded the pieces into compresses. Then she quickly tied the thick wads over the wounds with the remaining strips of scarf.

Yuri issued another order and backed it up with a wave of the pistol in his hand. Mouthing curses and casting murderous glares, the scurrilous pair lifted Mike and threw him into the seat of the sled. Sydney quickly moved to adjust Mike more comfortably and firmly tuck the bearskin around his unconscious body.

"You must leave, Sydney," Yuri said.

"Aren't you coming?" she asked, surprised.

"No. I vill be all right. These men vill not harm me."

"I've never . . . driven a sled before," she stammered, feeling a rising panic.

They heard the sound of voices approaching, and Kherkov waved a hand to hasten her. "If you vish to save his life, you must go now. Your safety I can guarantee but not that of MacAllister. He has made many enemies among my people."

Only scant minutes remained of precious daylight. Sydney knew she would be alone in the darkness of the vast wilderness with no idea how to control the sled or keep it on the traces. She would have to trust Grit's training and intelligence to get them through.

"Hi," she shouted, remembering Mike's command. The sled shot forward.

Mike's weight at the rear helped to maintain a firm balance. As the team dashed across the ice-crusted snow, she occasionally glanced at the yellow, glowing eyes of an animal lurking in the dark shadows lining the trail. Never knowing what might spring from the cover of the trees, her mind raced with imagined fears; primary among them—the image of the feral yellow eyes and bared fangs of a snarling wolf pack.

But the fear that Mike would die before she could get help for him was foremost. At the sound of a sudden bark from the trees to her right, she jolted reflexively, throwing the sled off balance. For several seconds the sled tottered, threatening to tip to its side. She gripped the handlebars and leaned away from the drag, fighting gravity to keep the rig upright. The unrelenting pull of the lead dog kept the team in tandem, and the sled kept its balance, returning to the trace.

A short distance farther she was not as fortunate. A rabbit darted across the path and the dogs veered off to chase it. She lost her footing on the runners. Clinging to the handlebars, she was dragged along on her stomach. After several yards, the sled wrenched from her hands, upended, and careened away.

Once again the might and intelligence of the huge malamute steadied the dogs and brought the team to a halt after a short distance.

Her arms trembled from the strain and ached so much she thought they had been pulled out of their sockets. Mike had been flung from the seat when the sled upended, and she made out his dark form lying in the snow a few feet ahead of her.

She didn't know how to get him to the sled. If his ribs were broken as she suspected, she didn't dare pull him by the arms. The compresses had stopped the bleeding from his legs, so she decided on the lesser of two evils. Grasping him by the ankles, Sydney pulled Mike to the sled. As she shoved the sled upright, the dogs leaped and sniffed, waiting to resume the run.

Her head jerked toward the trees at the sound of a nearby yelp of a fox. The dogs took up an answering chorus. Sydney knew it wasn't a wolf. That chilling howl still echoed in her ears.

Nevertheless, she tried to hasten her movements. The challenge of getting Mike back into the seat still remained. Using the sled for support, she braced his back along the side of the sled and inched him up until she had him upright. Her chest and arms throbbed from the exertion.

With no other recourse open to her, she shoved his body backwards into the seat. After much shifting and manipulation, she got him settled comfortably once again and covered with the bearskin.

As the sled pulled away, Sydney glanced back and saw several small shapes dart from the trees and begin to lick at the blood-red snow where Mike had lain.

Tears glistened in Sydney's eyes when she finally spied the lights of Solitary. Grit led them into the town, and she halted the team in front of Claire's. Within minutes Joseph and Pasha had Mike stripped and stretched out in his own bed.

She made no effort to appear modest. Mike's naked body was as familiar to her as her own. She sponged the blood off his wounds. Two of his ribs were fractured, and Joseph wrapped them with strips Claire had torn from an old sheet.

Because of her sewing skills, the task of closing up the wound on his head fell to Sydney. She thanked God that Mike's unconsciousness enabled her to keep her concentration when she applied seven neat little stitches to the jagged laceration.

Unguent was applied to the remaining open scrapes, but time would be the only healer of the many bruises on his face and body.

The worst job still lay ahead—removing the bullets

lodged in his thighs. After sterilizing tweezers and a knife in boiling water, Joseph and Pasha set to the task.

The Indian's steady hand located the bullet in Mike's right thigh, and he extracted the small, cone-shaped piece of metal with the tweezers. The other wound proved to be more difficult. The bullet had lodged deeper in the fleshy, muscular thigh and could not be pulled out. While Pasha applied a tourniquet, Joseph probed the wound with a knife to dislodge the bullet. When the task was completed, Sydney quickly bandaged the wounds.

After all had been done for Mike that could be done at the moment, Claire stayed behind while Pasha and Joseph returned to the bar. Claire had a fire blazing and a pot of tea steeping on the hearth when Sydney joined her.

Sydney sat down before the fire. Despite the heat, she began to shiver. Clasping Sydney's hands in the warmth of her own, Claire said gently, "I'll watch Mike while you go in and take a good hot bath, honey. Then you can tell me what happened out there tonight."

Sydney did not argue. She didn't know if she shivered from the cold or from a reaction to the whole incident, but she knew she needed to take the chill off her bones.

As she lay in the water, she allowed the soothing effect of the hot liquid to ease the aches she had sustained. She thought how quickly she had forgotten her own pains over her concern for Mike.

Mike mattered to her more than anyone on earth.

A short time later, snuggled in the comfort of her nightgown and robe, Sydney sat on the rug before the fire with her knees tucked under her chin. Gratefully, she accepted the cup of tea Claire handed her. Then the motherly woman brushed out the young girl's hair as Sydney told her what had happened.

"Why don't you lie down in Bran's room and try to get some sleep?" Claire suggested when the grim tale had ended. "I'll wake you if there's any change in Mike's condition."

Sydney shook her head. "I won't be able to sleep until he's awake, Claire," she said with an awkward smile.

"I understand, honey." Claire patted Sydney's arm. "I'll keep a fire going here. Shame there's no fireplace in Mike's room. If you need anything, just sing out."

Sydney pulled up a chair and sat wrapped in a blanket at his bedside throughout the night.

Mike regained consciousness the following morning, but was in too much pain even to talk. He slipped in and out of sleep throughout the day as Sydney changed the dressings on his head and legs.

Fearing that one of his badly bruised eyes would swell shut, she kept an ice pack on the lid. The ice managed to contain the swelling, but Sydney thought Mike's face looked like he had just gone twenty rounds in the ring with the champion heavyweight pugilist, John L. Sullivan.

By the third day, Mike was coherent and allowed Sydney to shave off the beard that had grown. In truth, he would have been too weak to resist anyway.

Claire came in the afternoon to relieve Sydney so she could return to the office. Running between the house and the office, while trying to keep up the paperwork and nurse Mike at the same time, Sydney had virtually no rest for several days.

Mike was also concerned about his office work. "I can't afford to be laid up here with Bran gone," he grumbled to Claire after Sydney's departure. "This couldn't have happened at a worse time."

"Judging from the way you're busted up, Mike, my guess is that there wouldn't have been any *good* time," Claire bantered good-naturedly.

"That's not what I mean, Claire. The company has obligations right now, and there's no one to see that they're being honored. To make matters worse, I'm right in the middle of opening that new office in Seward."

"You got nothin' to worry about, Mike. Delaney seems to have the situation well in hand."

"Yeah, I know she can handle the paperwork. But she sure as hell can't drive the sledge," he grumbled.

"She's worked out an arrangement with Pasha and Rami. But Delaney probably would drive a team herself if she had to. Who do you think drove the sled that brought you back to Solitary?"

Mike looked at her quizzically. Sydney was unharmed and he was alive, which had been his first thoughts when he gained consciousness. He hadn't considered how they'd returned. "How *did* we get back to Solitary?"

"How do you think? *Delaney,*" Claire said smugly. "Colonel Kherkov kept those bastards from killing you. And Delaney brought you back."

"You're saying *she* drove me back in the sled?"

Claire nodded. "You heard me right. 'Least your hearin' is okay."

"Come on, Claire, what's the joke? Delaney's never handled a sled before."

"Well, she learned fast."

"You trying to convince me that a little bookworm from Seattle, who has never handled a seven-dog team, drove a sled for two hours in the dark by herself?"

Claire was enjoying his confusion. "I didn't say just any little bookworm, Mike. I said *Delaney.*"

"That's hard for me to believe."

"Well, you've alive today, so I guess that proves it. Right, big guy?" Claire challenged. "'Course, I imagine it would have made the job easier for Delaney if you had been at least conscious at the time. You know . . . maybe a word or two of advice . . . or even just some moral support as she was saving the life of the bullhead she was dumb enough to fall in love with?"

"Claire, I know what you're up to. Forget it. Apparently, I owe Delaney a lot, and I'll try to figure out a way to pay her back. Maybe I could set her up in that bookstore she's been dreaming about opening some day."

"Or maybe just marryin' her?" Claire interjected.

"You know how I feel on the subject of love and marriage. So get off it," he growled, closing his eyes to end the conversation.

In the past few days, Claire had quietly contained the anxiety she had suffered ever since Mike had been carried in half-dead. That pent-up tension now erupted.

"Oh, so the big boy is beyond love and marriage, is he? Well, you're dead wrong about Delaney. She ain't no Beth, Mike. Delaney's got more grit than most men twice her size. That gal drove a sled at night all by herself, not knowin' if you was alive or dead. And she didn't have no weapon either. But just to try to save the hide of a ungrateful fool like you."

"Thanks, Claire. I appreciate your coming in to cheer me up," he said as she stormed away.

Mike tried to sit up. Grabbing his ribs, he fell back as pain shot through him from over a dozen parts of his body.

He lay back, the echo of Claire's words still ringing in his ears. He knew she was right about Sydney. Hell, she drove the sled fifty miles! The gal had grit. He could still picture her round green eyes and that game little smile of hers right before that wolf attack.

Mike closed his eyes and grinned despite his pain.

Chapter 28

Sydney checked Mike's condition as soon as she closed the office. Seeing he was sleeping peacefully, she returned to the kitchen and prepared their evening meal.

He ate very little before dropping back to sleep, but his lack of appetite did not dishearten her. He still wasn't running a fever—a good sign that the only internal injuries were his ribs. And as long as he remained quiet and restful, he would heal that much faster.

Quiet and restful? Not so!

By the end of the week Mike had become a roaring bear—convinced that his bandages and vigilant nursing were shackles that chained him to the bed.

Sydney lost her last remaining bit of patience the night he refused to eat the soup she had prepared, because he claimed it wasn't salty enough.

She stood above him, her body trembling with anger. "You eat this, you boorish, insufferable, bullheaded adolescent, or I swear . . ." She shook the spoon at him to emphasize her point. ". . . I swear, Michael MacAllister, I'm going to force it down your throat." Slamming down the dish and spoon on the table next to his bed, she turned to stomp away.

Mike made a grab for her. Groaning, he fell back in pain. "Damn these bandages. If I could only stand up—"

Sydney turned with her hands on her hips and cut off

344

his threat. " 'It is hard for an empty bag to stand upright,' " she snickered with satisfaction.

"Good God, woman, suffer me not one more of your gems of wisdom," he ranted.

"Not mine, MacAllister. Benjamin Franklin's," she smirked.

"Sydney's right. Sydney's right," he mimicked. "Like hell Sydney's right!" he shouted. "Did you ever have an *original* thought, Delaney? Does one thing *ever* come out of your mouth that wasn't pinched from William Shakespeare or Henry Wadsworth Longfellow?"

Sydney was taken aback by the intensity of this latest outburst from him. Could his words be true? Was she as pedantic as he claimed?

"I dare you, Delaney. One sentence is all I ask. One gem of wisdom that is pure, unadulterated, original Sydney Delaney."

"I love you, Mike," she shouted defiantly, her chin quivering.

Mike had worked himself up to such an anger her words didn't even penetrate.

"I love you, Mike," she repeated, this time softly. "How's that for a gem of wisdom? No Shakespeare. No Longfellow. A pure, unadulterated Sydney Delaney, just as you asked."

"Ah, Syd." He closed his eyes for a fraction of a moment and when he opened them, they were filled with contrition. He raised his arm and reached out to her.

She walked over to the bed and slipped her hand into his. "Sit down, sweetheart," he said tenderly.

She lowered herself to the edge of the bed, and Mike slid his hand under the thick curtain of her hair and cupped her nape. "Why do you put up with me?" he asked, his dark eyes filled with repentance. Then he drew her head down to his.

The kiss was long and heady—made more titillating by the restraints forced upon them because of his injuries. They drew apart, and he laced his fingers through her hair.

"God, I've done nothing but lie here for a week and think about making love to you. Is it any wonder I'm half out of my mind?" he whispered hoarsely.

He kissed her again, then covered her face and eyes with quick kisses. "Slow down, MacAllister, or you'll start a fire you can't put out," she teased with breathless huskiness.

Dropping his arms, he closed his eyes. "I already have. Now something else is aching. Thank God I've discovered one part of me that is still in working condition."

"Well, I bet I know what to do about *that* ache," she said, slowly pulling down the quilt.

Startled, Mike opened his eyes, grasping her meaning. "Syd, I didn't mean . . ."

She put a finger over his mouth to shut off his words, and her gaze locked boldly with his before she lowered her head to relieve his suffering.

Later, as she sat on the bedside, Mike gently stroked her cheek with the curved knuckles of his hand. Now that the tension had eased from his body, he stared at her with awe.

"I've never known a woman like you before, Syd. You're so generous and caring. You want to please instead of being pleased. You have this inborn unselfishness . . . not only in your lovemaking, but in everything you do."

Her eyes gleamed with love as she smiled at him. "But I'm not as selfless as you think. Giving you pleasure is pleasure to *me*, Mike." She lowered her head and lightly pressed a kiss on his lips. "So now I intend for the two of us to enjoy an added pleasure." She reached for the nearby book lying on the table. "I thought I would read to you some of the poetry of James Russell Lowell."

With a long-suffering glance, Mike cast his eyes

heavenward. "Lord, the woman is a charitable lover," he groaned. "But did I mention her sadistic streak?"

The next day they played Red Dog. After losing a dozen straight hands in a row, Sydney threw down her cards in disgust.

"I haven't figured it out yet, but I think you're cheating,"

Mike threw back his head and laughed. "The reason you can't win this game, Delaney, is because you're too optimistic. You always think you can beat the draw. You have to think like I do. Develop some pessimism."

"No, thank you, Mike. Not if it means carrying pessimism to your extremes."

He eyed her cautiously. "Well, you seemed pretty downbeaten when we got back from the Indian village."

"I admit I was feeling hopeless." She smiled nervously. "You know, we humans are a strange species. The facts of life and death are very predictable. We're born young and we die old. But when that cycle is broken and we must accept that the young die too, we question what life is all about and see how vulnerable we are. And we run scared."

She shook her head and half smiled. "Lord, was I scared! The snowstorm. The wolf attack. Taitana's death. All those tragedies coming one after another in a few days made me aware of what a thin thread we have to hold on to in order to stay alive.

"And when I got back and had the time to think what it all meant, I decided I was not going to live my life just waiting for that thin thread to snap."

He had said nothing, and when she glanced over to look at him, his expression had not changed.

"Oh, you had me almost convinced that you were right, Mike. That this country was too violent and primitive. The tragic deaths of your brother and your wife. Then Taitana's death . . . the wolf attack . . . the snowstorm—they were all evidence to strengthen your argument.

"But your conclusion is not mine, Mike. Because if I thought as you do, I would have to accept that young women never die in Seattle, or Chicago, or New York. Or London, or Paris . . . or St. Petersburg, Russia. Only in Alaska."

She shook her head. "It is all very clear in my mind. You are the one who is afraid of life, not me. But don't you see, ever since Adam and Eve, man and woman have had to face the unknown together.

"I think that . . ." She paused, taking a deep breath for courage, and then continued. "I think that your objections . . . have nothing to do with the dangers. They stem from . . . guilt."

He looked at her incredulously, but she forged ahead. "You blamed yourself for the deaths of Beth and Jeff. So you made up your mind you wouldn't be responsible for anyone else's death—especially the woman you love. So you refuse to fall in love—how easy.

"Well, you aren't God, Michael MacAllister. Beth and Jeff did not die because of you. You don't have the power to determine a person's destiny. The sooner you can accept that—the sooner you and I can get on with life together."

Mike remained motionless with his arms across his chest, his thoughts once again masked behind a dark, inscrutable stare. Finally, he asked, "Are you finished?"

"Yes," she said belligerently, preparing for another argument from him.

"Well, you could have saved yourself and me that long speech because my mind is made up."

"Darn you, Mike, didn't you listen to anything I had to say? I'm not Beth. I'm a fighter. A survivor." She punched out the words desperately.

"You're right, Syd. You aren't Beth. But don't think I haven't done my share of thinking, too, in the last couple of weeks. And I've come to a few conclusions myself. I know that I was wrong about you. You do belong here. Or anywhere you wish to be. You've got the strength of character and fortitude to prevail whether you're in Solitary, Alaska . . . Chicago . . . St. Petersburg . . . and whatever other places you mentioned."

"So-o-o?" she asked hopefully, now sensing victory. Unable to restrain herself, she threw herself on the bed.

Laughing, he pulled her into his arms. "So-o-o, I'll play you another hand of Red Dog. Winner gets to pop the big question."

"What big question?" Sydney asked.

"Will you—?"

"Yes!" she answered enthusiastically.

"Yes? Yes, what?"

"Yes, I'll marry you."

"I didn't ask you," he said in mock indignation.

"But you were going to. I know you were." Suddenly she looked doubtful. "Weren't you?"

He laughed. "I'll let you know as soon as I win another hand of Red Dog."

Groaning, she threw her arms around his neck and kissed him. "Deal the cards, MacAllister," she murmured breathlessly.

The next day Sydney was so happy that her feet seemed not to touch the ground. They had planned their wedding for the following month when the preacher would once again return to Solitary.

How she wished Emily were home, so the two of them could share the excitement. However, she was comforted by the knowledge that Brandon and Emily would be back in time for the wedding.

Claire and Pasha were as excited as she was when Sydney told them the news. Grabbing a bottle of wine, they hurried back to the house and drank a toast to the engaged couple's future.

"Iz most grand day for town of Solitary. Zoon ve haf

many little MacAllisters running around beneath our feets."

"Hey, Pash," Mike groaned. "I'm still in bed. Give me a chance to get back on my feet before you make a father out of me."

Pasha looked perplexed. "How does Michael expect to make baby on his feets? Pasha think Michael in right place exactly now to make baby."

"My dear Count Pasha Eduardovich Vladimir," Sydney declared, "I'll thank you to refrain from discussing this matter any further."

When they departed, Sydney returned to her office duties. At the sound of a ship's horn, she pulled on her mantle and hurried down to the dock to meet the mail boat.

As she was rifling through the mail, a letter from the territorial governor caught her eye. She raced up the hill to the house and burst through the door.

"Mike, it's come. The letter you've been waiting for has come."

"Say a prayer, honey," he said, ripping open the envelope.

His eyes quickly scanned the typed letter, then he threw his arms in the air in jubilation. "They're coming, honey. The U. S. Navy is on its way."

She waved her arm in the air. "Hurray! 'Damn the torpedoes and full speed ahead,' " she shouted.

Laughing, she plopped down on her knees beside him. Mike pulled her into his arms. "You know what this means to me, Syd? This is what I've been trying to accomplish for the past ten years."

She smiled into his eyes. "I know, Mike. I know how much this means to you."

He kissed her and held her in his arms.

Later while he slept, Sydney had just poured herself a cup of tea when a tap sounded. She opened the door to a most unexpected visitor. Yuri Kherkov.

"Colonel Kherkov! What a pleasant surprise." She stepped aside for him to enter. "Do come in, Colonel."

"If you are certain Mr. MacAllister vould not object," he said. Hesitantly, he entered, removing his hat. His glance swept the room with interest.

"Mike is sleeping right now, Colonel Kherkov."

"Madame Claire tells me he is recovering satisfactorily from his vounds."

"Yes, thank God. And I'm sure when he does, he will want to thank you personally."

Kherkov placed a rifle on the nearby stool. "I have brought Mr. MacAllister's rifle vich was left behind. It is a fine veapon. I am sure he vould regret losing it."

"Another reason for Mike to be grateful, Yuri. May I thank you for him now?"

"I regret the unfortunate incident, Sydney."

"Unfortunate! Colonel Kherkov, those horrible men intended to kill Mike."

"Yes, that too. But also for a personal reason, Sydney, vhich has nothing to do vith Mr. MacAllister's obsession vith this otter issue."

"Frankly, in all conscience, Yuri, I cannot condone this senseless slaughter of the sea otters. It is butchery. Mike is right for fighting to end it, or at the least, to execute some control."

"The Russians are not the only foreign governments that practice this poaching, Sydney."

"You mentioned that point before. And I understand your argument, Yuri. But others doing it does not make it morally acceptable."

She sat down at the table and filled another cup. "I was just having some tea. Come join me, Colonel?"

"I am troubled to think I have dropped to such disfavor in your eyes, my little Sydney," Kherkov said, taking a seat.

"Of course you haven't, Yuri. Your intervention prevented Mike from being killed . . . and myself too, most likely. And I understand your loyalty to your government. That is to be expected."

Her eyes sparkled over the brim of her cup. "Hopefully, it soon will be resolved. Mike has received word from the U. S. government—" She cut off her words. Carried away with enthusiasm, she had almost revealed the navy's plan to him.

Kherkov's brow creased in a frown, and he set aside his cup. Glancing at his watch, he rose to his feet. "Vell, I fear that I must be departing. It behooves me to leave, my dear, but my ship vill soon be sailing. I stopped briefly to check on the condition of you and Mr. MacAllister." He kissed her hand. "A pleasure, as always, to see you, Sydney."

"And certainly more pleasant than our last encounter."

"You have my assurance, my dear, those two scoundrels are presently on their way to Siberia."

"To wreak havoc on another innocent, Colonel?" she remarked.

"Russian reprisal can often be swift and severe, my dear Sydney."

After he departed, Sydney decided it would be wise not to mention Yuri's visit to Mike. His feelings were so hostile toward the Russian colonel that she thought it would only aggravate his condition.

A week later Mike had recovered enough to be out of bed when a cruising ship of the U. S. Navy steamed into port. A naval officer entered the freight office, looking crisp in his naval uniform. He tipped his hat politely. "Captain Gerard, United States Navy, ma'am. Could you direct me to Mr. Michael MacAllister?"

"Mr. MacAllister is recovering from some recent injuries, Captain Gerard. I'll be glad to take you to him."

Mike was sitting in a chair before the fireplace when Sydney entered the house. After an introduction, the navy captain sat down. "I'm sorry to say, sir, but we

can't believe you would send me away because of an inadvertent slip of the tongue."

"No, Syd. Next time, it will be something more seri-ous. Something involving your welfare . . . or someone else's. Don't you see that? You just don't belong here. Accept that, for God's sake."

He got up and limped slowly to the door. Pausing at the entrance, he turned back. "Get out of my life, Syd. I wish you had never come to Alaska." He disappeared through the door.

His words drove a knife through her heart and her world collapsed.

The next day when she entered the house, Sydney hoped he would apologize or show a sign of contrition. He didn't. Instead, he returned to his room. Later, when she tapped on the door to see if he wanted to join her for a meal, he informed her he wasn't interested. After the third day she stopped asking him.

The arrival of an American ship bound for Seattle helped her to make her decision. She pulled on her mantle and walked down to the pier. Yuri Kherkov was just preparing to board the ship. He hurried over when he saw her.

"I would like to leave Solitary, Yuri. I want to return to Seattle. Do you know if there's space available on this ship?"

A glimmer of pain flickered in the Russian's eyes, and he took her hands. "My dear, I sincerely regret the role I played in that decision."

She nodded, paying little heed to his words. Her mind and heart were twisted together in despair.

"Are you certain that is your vish, my dear Sydney?" he asked sadly.

"Yes. The sooner the better."

"You are velcome to my cabin. I will make other ar-rangements."

She glanced up gratefully. "If you can just wait until

I pack my clothes. It won't take more than fifteen minutes."

"Of course, my dear."

She returned to the office and with tears streaming down her cheeks, she packed her valise. She would write Emily to mail her the cartons when she had an address. Then, covering Brutus, she picked up Runt and her valise.

For a moment she stood and stared at the door to the passageway. She hesitated at Mike's desk, uncertain whether she should leave him a note. Deciding against it, she walked out of the office.

Claire glanced out the window of the bar, and then took a closer look. "Pasha, come here."

"Vhat is it, darlink?" he said moving to her side.

"Isn't that Delaney getting on that ship with Kherkov?"

"Vhat?" Pasha exclaimed. He peered through the window. "Iz true."

"What the hell is goin' on?" Claire exclaimed. "Hurry and get me my wrap, Pasha. I've got to talk to Mike."

The couple hurried over to the house and burst through the door. Mike was sitting at the table with his head buried in his hands.

"Mike, where's Delaney going?" Claire asked. "We just saw her gettin' on that ship with Kherkov, and she's got the birdcage with her."

"She's going back to Seattle."

"You sent her away?" Claire asked in disbelief. "I guess I'm wrong about you, Mike. You enjoy misery, don't you?" Shaking her head, she ran after Sydney before it was too late to say good-bye. Confused, Pasha followed her.

Mike put on his parka and walked down to the wharf. The ship was already making its way out of the inlet.

Now faced with the actual loss of her, he was overcome by despair. "Oh God, Syd, I didn't mean what I said. Why did you leave? . . . You know what a bastard I am. . . . Why did you listen to me this time? . . . I felt betrayed. But I love you, Syd."

Struck with the hope that she had left a note telling him where he could find her, Mike hurried back to the office. He found a message, but not the one he hoped for.

A tiny gold whistle on a chain lay on the top of the chiffonnier. Mike clutched it in his hand.

Four weeks later Brandon MacAllister looked up and scowled when Colonel Yuri Kherkov walked into the office of the MacAllister Alaskan Freight Line. Mike jumped to his feet. Unconsciously, his hands balled into fists at his side.

"Where is she, Kherkov?" Mike demanded.

"Miss Delaney has requested I do not reveal her vereabouts."

"Then what did you come here for, Kherkov? Just to gloat?" Brandon asked.

He and Emily had not yet adjusted to the shock of returning from their honeymoon to find Sydney gone. Every night since their return, Emily had cried herself to sleep in his arms.

Yuri reached into his pocket. "Actually, I have come here to deliver some letters from Miss Delaney." He handed Mike a packet containing letters to him, Brandon and Emily, Claire and Pasha. "Sydney has asked that I pick up her cartons of books."

"Tell me where to ship them, and I'll see that she gets them," Mike said.

The Russian laughed. "Now, now, MacAllister, that vould be rather naive of me, vouldn't you say?"

"I'm not turning over those cartons to you, Kherkov," Mike said. "They belonged to her father. As long as I have them, I have her. Whenever she sends for them, all I have to do is follow the books."

"Except, MacAllister, she has sent me to get them. I believe her letter to you requests that you relinquish them to me. But if you prefer, I can call the United States marshal. He arrived on the same ship as I."

"Damn you, Kherkov. If I have to, I'll beat her whereabouts out of you."

"I am sorry. I made a promise, MacAllister. Now, the cartons?" He opened the door and motioned to several crewmen.

"It will take longer now, but I'll find her," Mike said.

Yuri stopped at his desk after the last carton had been carried away. He idly toyed with a book he carried. "Do you enjoy reading, Mr. MacAllister?" Mike's black glare was his only reply. "I am told there is a new bookstore opening soon in Seattle called The Birdcage. Unusual name for a bookstore, vouldn't you say?" the Russian said with a sly smile.

Mike's eyes flashed in disbelief and then gratitude. "I'm grateful to you, Kherkov."

"Ah ... MacAllister, I can't tell you vat measure of satisfaction I derive from knowing that."

Yuri paused with his hand on the door. "But vat I do is for the sake of our dear Sydney. I interfered in her life once. Now that guilt veighs heavily on my conscience." He shook his head. "Vat a pity. She is too good for you, MacAllister."

"I don't need you to tell me that, Kherkov," Mike said.

"I vant her happiness. And I know she vill not find it by running avay. She must face you, and then determine vat is in her heart." He sighed deeply. "So, regrettably, I must betray her again."

Kherkov's face curved into a sagacious smile. "But I am certain our precious Sydney would be the first to say that 'all's fair in love and war.' So you see, Mr.

MacAllister, there is a measure of romance in all of us."

His fingers tugged at the meticulously groomed goatee on his chin. "Hmmm . . ." he reflected. "I vonder if Mademoiselle Lily is up and about at this hour of the morning."

Chapter 29

Fourteen days later Mike approached a little corner shop on a street in Seattle. The tinkle of a bell above the doorway sounded as he entered. The room smelled of fresh paint, and several cartons stood on the floor before empty shelves.

His glance swung to the cage where Brutus was perched. The parrot's head cocked, his round eyes fixed on his adversary. But even the sight of this feathered nemesis struck a welcomed chord in Mike. He walked over and lightly jiggled the bars of the cage with his finger. "Hi, Brutus."

Mike turned at the sound of the quick patter behind him. Runt came bounding up, wagging his tail so furiously the puppy threatened to lose his balance.

Picking up the dog, he murmured affectionately, "Well, hi there, fella. How are you doing?" When Runt began to lick wildly at his face, Mike chuckled warmly, "I'm glad to see you, too."

"I'm sorry, we're not open as . . ." The words froze in Sydney's throat as she came into the room.

"Hello, Syd." His gaze lingered longingly on her face.

"Mike!" Her hand fluttered nervously to her chest. "What a surprise." She felt a rising panic. *Oh, God! It's still too soon. I'm not ready yet. How can I get through this?*

"You're looking good, Syd."

"So are you. I see your bruises have all disappeared. How are your legs feeling?"

"Coming along fine. Just takes a little time." He put down Runt, and the dog scampered away. "Looks like you've been busy."

How strange to be forcing this inane conversation with him, she thought. For the past few weeks she had done nothing except yearn for the sound of his voice—for the touch of his hand.

After a quick glance at her paint-spattered clothing, she managed a light retort. "Yes, there's a lot of work. Reminds me of when we remodeled the office after the earthquake."

He grinned. "Yeah." Their eyes met in nostalgic memory of that bygone day. "Remember the argument over whether we should have windows or not in the passageway?"

Smiling, she nodded her head. "And you were so adamant against them."

"Because I knew if we did, you'd end up hanging lace curtains at each one of them."

She glanced up sheepishly. "And you would have been right."

They broke into laughter.

As they stood smiling into one another's eyes, the image of her standing ankle deep in mud leapt to his mind. Lord, how he wanted to hold her.

Their laughter faded into an awkward silence. Finally, she said, "Somehow we always managed to find one dumb thing after another to argue over."

"They were *dumb* things, weren't they, Syd?"

Her face sobered. "Until the last one, Mike. By the way, how did you know where to find me?" she asked.

He's more handsome than I remembered, she reflected as she studied the beloved features.

Mike's fixed stare rested on her face until he became aware of her question. He shifted his glance to meet hers and finally responded to her question. "Colonel Kherkov told me."

Sydney was surprised to hear that Yuri had broken his word to her. "Well, you always said he couldn't be trusted." She tried to sound flippant.

"Why'd you leave without saying good-bye, Syd?" he suddenly asked, his voice husky with emotion.

"I thought that's what you wanted, Mike. You made your feelings very clear to me."

To ease the tension, she turned away and began to re-arrange books on a nearby shelf. "And how are Brandon and Emily?"

"Good . . . real good. They're going to have a baby."

She pivoted in surprise. "That's wonderful." Her eyes glistened with unshed tears of joy. "I'm so happy for them."

Turning away, she dusted off a shelf and began to stack it with books from a nearby carton. "And Claire and Pasha?"

"Both just the same." When she struggled to open another crate, Mike walked over. "Let me do that."

They reached for it at the same time and his hand covered hers. The brief contact felt electrifying, and a tremor raced down her spine. She jerked away her hand as if she had been burned.

Startled, they stared into each other's eyes, and she knew he had felt it too.

Fearing any further contact with him, she stepped away hurriedly and waited for him to finish opening the box. "Thank you," she said.

Mike picked up a collection of love poems from the top of the pile. " 'How do I love thee? Let me count the ways.' "

"What did you say?" She had heard him, but could not hope he meant the words for her.

Mike had not realized that he had quoted the passage aloud. "I was recalling a line from one of these poems. When I read it, I couldn't imagine anyone actually saying that to somebody." He handed her the bound copy.

Sydney hugged it to her breast. "I guess Elizabeth Barrett Browning felt the same way. It's said that she slipped these poems to her husband because she was too shy to tell him of her love. So she expressed it in the best way she knew." Her hand caressed the thin volume as she wistfully gazed into space. "Through her exquisite poetry."

"No, I guess telling someone you love them is about the hardest thing a person can do. At least for me, anyway. Too bad I can't write poetry."

Reflecting on the sensitive message of the poem, Sydney failed to hear him. Suddenly becoming aware of the prolonged silence, she snapped out of her daydream.

"Their devotion to one another is truly one of the legendary loves of our century." She returned to her task. "So what brings you all the way to Seattle, Mike?"

You, Syd, he said silently. *I came to tell you how sorry I am for all the rotten things I said to you. That life is hell without you. That I love you, Syd.*

Those were the words he wanted to say. But he could see she was getting on with her life—a life that clearly held no place for him.

"I had some business with the government. The United States has set up a conference with several foreign nations to work out a fishing agreement. Hopefully, it will help to prevent a lot of the poaching that's been going on."

She turned around and smiled. "Sounds like a step in the right direction. I'm glad you've finally got what you wanted, Mike."

His glance swept the store. "And you've got what you've always wanted—your own bookstore." He hesitated for a fraction of a moment. "Isn't that right?"

She stole a glance at him. Once again his steady gaze was fixed on her face. *I once did. But not any more, Mike. I want you. I'll want you to the day I die. Only you don't want me. I know that now. But don't worry, I'm not going to make a fool of myself. I won't embarrass you any further by throwing myself at you.*

So with pride as a foolish counselor, she forced a smile and offered a false reply. "Yes. This is what I've always wanted. Always dreamed of owning. Now that dream is finally being fulfilled. Granted, I'm only leasing the space right now, but I have an option to buy the store whenever I can afford to do so."

"Then I'm happy for you, Syd. I'm sure your bookstore will be a whopping success."

He cleared his throat. "I guess I shouldn't keep you from your work any longer. I want you to know, Syd, that I'm sorry for what I said to you in Solitary. You were right to walk out on me."

She turned to him and smiled. Her eyes glistened with the tears she fought to contain. "Well, we always were pretty hard on one another."

He reached out and gently traced a finger along her jaw. "No hard feelings, Delaney?"

Her jaw trembled under his touch. "No hard feelings, MacAllister."

She closed her eyes when he grasped her arms and drew her toward him. He pressed a light kiss to her forehead. For a long moment his gaze lingered on her face, then he dropped his hands and walked to the door. The bell sounded again as he opened it. Then he paused and looked back. "Good-bye, Syd."

She nodded. "Good-bye, Mike. Be sure and give everyone my love." Then to avoid breaking down in front of him, she sped from the room.

For several long seconds, Mike remained in the doorway, tempted to follow her and confess how much he loved her. To beg her to return with him to

Solitary, to convince her she could love him again as she once had—before he had abused and destroyed that love.

His pained glance swept the room. But she had made the message very plain to him. She had finally achieved what she had always yearned for. He knew he had no right to disrupt her life any further.

"I love you, Syd," he said, but the words fell only on the ears of Runt and Brutus, who both watched quizzically.

The trees had started to bud with the promise of spring when Sydney looked up as the bell tingled above the door. She immediately broke into a wide smile of pleasure. "Claire! Pasha!" she cried with delight.

"My little *Красота,*" Pasha exclaimed, throwing his arms around her in a bear hug.

"How I've missed you. Both of you," she declared, running into Claire's open arms. After several hugs and kisses, she stepped back, smiling. "What are the two of you doing here in Seattle?"

Claire shook her head. "Delaney, you won't believe this, but I let this crazy man talk me into headin' to the Klondike with him."

"You don't mean . . . you aren't saying . . ." Sydney broke off with a stutter.

"Vat my sweet Claire is saying is being true. Ve go to Klondike to be finding gold." To Sydney's further surprise, he pulled out the same map he had once tried to sell to everyone he encountered. "Map tell Pasha vere much gold is being. Then he vill build Claire big house."

Sydney looked to the smiling woman for confirmation. "Are you two really going to the Klondike?"

"Yes. We came here just to say good-bye to you and to see the sights of a city before goin' into that wide open country."

"But Claire, why go? You don't need the money."

"Delaney, honey, I'm just goin' to keep this damn fool from gettin' himself killed. I figure since Bran and Emily are soon to be parents, well, it might be better if I no longer owned a ... ah, you know. So I sold my business to Lily."

"Oh, but you will be returning to Solitary?"

Claire's blue eyes twinkled with warmth. "Of course! Hey, I'm goin' to be a grandmother. You don't think I'd miss seein' my grandchild do you?"

"And Pasha vill be grandpa, just like old man. But ven he finds gold, Pasha vill be most rich old man."

"Oh, it all sounds very exciting."

"Between you and me, Delaney, I think he may really be on to somethin' this time. There have been several gold strikes in the same area of this map. So what have we got to lose? Six months will get me back in plenty of time before the baby is born."

Sydney clasped Claire's hands. "Do tell me how Emily is feeling. I'm so excited for her." She pulled Claire over to a nearby table. "We'll have a cup of tea, and you can tell me all about it. I miss her so much. And Brandon, too."

In a few moments, the two were sipping tea while Pasha roamed the room looking at the books.

"Em has a little queasiness in the mornings, but the doctor says that unpleasantness will soon pass."

"Doctor?" Sydney asked, surprised.

"Oh, I've got big news to tell you, Delaney. Solitary has a doctor now. He set up office about two weeks ago."

"Why ever in Solitary?" Sydney asked. "The poor man will be starved for business."

"I don't think he much cares about the money. He's a wonderful old man. Said he's tired of practicin' in a big city. Came to Solitary because he thought Alaska sounded interestin'."

"Well, I'm glad for Emily's sake. This doctor

couldn't have come at a more opportune time," Sydney replied.

Claire eyed her cautiously. "Gotta say, it sure put Mike's mind at ease. You'd think he was the father the way he worries about Emily."

Sydney tried to hide her emotions behind a smile. "Well, you know Mike, Claire. He's convinced Alaska is no place for a woman."

Pasha came over to join them. "Is time ve be on our vay, sveetheart, or vill be missing boat."

Claire rose, and the two women embraced. "Take care of him, Claire," Sydney whispered in the woman's ear. "And yourself, too."

Claire cupped Sydney's face between her hands and gazed intently into the young woman's eyes. "Delaney, he loves you. He's miserable without you. I know Mike MacAllister better than anyone on this earth."

"Mike has to be the one to tell me, Claire. Not you. That's the only thing that could ever convince me to go back."

With their arms linked around one another's waist, they walked to the door. And after several hugs and good-bye kisses, the two women separated.

Pasha grabbed her with his usual exuberance. "Is not time for tears, *Красота*. Is being most happy time for all. And when Sydney see Pasha again, he vill be rich man."

Before departing, he laid a newspaper on the shelf. Sydney waved good-bye as they walked away. Noticing the paper Pasha had laid aside, she picked it up and was about to open the door to call him back. Then she saw the paper was folded to the classified section. The words *Solitary, Alaska,* immediately caught her attention.

Her heart lodged in her throat as she read the ad placed by the MacAllister Alaskan Freight Line calling for an office assistant. The ad clearly stated the job was offered to a male only. As much as she had tried to tell herself that Solitary was no longer any concern of hers, she discovered how much the words of that ad hurt. *Lord how they hurt!* She clutched her arms across her chest to try to ease the pain in her breast.

Tears glistened in her eyes as she laid aside the newspaper. "Well, there's no more fooling myself, Brutus. Mike didn't waste any time looking to replace me, did he?"

"I love you, Syd," the bird squawked.

"Thank you, Brutus, I'm glad somebody d—" The word froze in her throat and her head popped up. "What did you say?"

"Sydney's right. Sydney's right."

She clutched the sides of the cage. "No. That's not what you said before. What did you say at first?"

"Sydney's right. Sydney's right."

Convinced she had misunderstood him, she dropped her hands to her sides and turned away in dejection.

Sorrowfully, Sydney glanced down at Runt lying at the foot of the bird stand with his head resting on his outstretched front paws. "I guess a person hears what they want to hear, Runt." She bent down and patted his head. Two watery eyes looked up at her in commiseration, and a little tail wagged in response.

As she started to return to the storeroom, Brutus again piped, "I love you, Syd."

Sydney pivoted and rushed back to the cage. "You did say it. I heard you."

"I love you, Syd. I love you, Syd," Brutus screeched, hopping around on his perch.

Sydney's face glowed with delight as tears of happiness streaked down her cheeks. *"Mike* is the only one who ever called me Syd. You just heard it from Mike, didn't you, Brutus?"

"I love you, Syd," Brutus chirped.

"And I love you, Mike. I mean, Brutus," she cried joyously.

Seeing her change of mood, Runt hopped to his feet, jumping at her skirt. Sydney picked him up and cuddled him against her cheek. "And I love you, Runt," she murmured through her tears and laughter.

Without a moment's hesitation, she hurried to the storeroom and grabbed several of the empty cartons.

As the vessel steamed cautiously through the waters of the narrow inlet, a cold wind whipped across the gulf and tugged at the hood of the young woman standing at the ship's railing. Oblivious to the cold, her heartbeat quickened with excitement, and her eager, green-eyed gaze scanned the approaching shoreline.

The ship's whistle cut the crisp air sharply. The closer they came to the dock, the harder she trembled. The thud of the gangplank on the wharf jolted her fixed stare away from the distant building bearing the sign MacAllister Alaskan Freight Line.

"Good-bye, Miss Delaney," the ship's captain said. "I'll make certain all your *sixteen* cartons are unloaded before we depart."

"Thank you, Captain Reid."

Returning to her cabin, she firmly secured the plaid cover over Brutus' cage, and with her valise in one hand, she picked up Runt with the other. Tucking him firmly in the crook of her elbow, she picked up the birdcage.

Once on shore, she put down Runt, and he scampered away toward the familiar building. "Dear God, let him be there," she prayed as she neared the office. "I couldn't bear not to see him right away."

After sniffing around the building, Runt continued past the office and raced to the house, where he began to scratch at the door. Emily opened the door and upon seeing the puppy, she let out a cry of joy and rushed down the street into Sydney's arms.

Laughing and crying, the two women embraced for a long moment. Sydney stepped back and tightened the shawl around Emily's shoulders. "You get back into the house before you catch a chill. And Mike? Is he . . . ?"

Emily nodded and giggled with pleasure. "Yes, he's in the office." She reached out for one final hug. "Oh, Sydney, I'm so glad you're back." Her blue eyes glistening with tears, she added, "And guess what, Bran and I—"

"Are going to have a baby," Sydney finished for her. "Now get back into that house and give me a few minutes with Mike."

Emily's eyes twinkled with mischief. "Bet it'll be more than a few minutes." She grabbed the valise. "I'll take this to the house."

When she reached for the birdcage, Sydney shook her head. "You've got enough to carry. Just make sure Runt gets inside."

Sydney paused before the office, took a deep breath, and entered. Her glance immediately shifted to Mike's desk. He wasn't there.

Brandon looked up. Stunned, he grinned broadly and jumped to his feet. Sydney put a finger to her mouth to silence him as she set the cage on the desk.

"Where is he?" she mouthed.

He motioned toward one of the storerooms. Taking her into his arms, he softly whispered, "Sydney." The single word and the look in his eyes required no further message.

After giving her a hug and kiss, Brandon disappeared down the passageway leading to the house.

Sydney pulled the newspaper page out of her mantle pocket, then hung the garment on a wall peg. As she heard Mike's step nearing the stockroom door, she waited with a half-smile on her face and the folded paper in her hand.

Mike stepped out of the room and stopped in his tracks when he saw her standing before his desk. Speechless, he stared at her. Before he could find his voice, she tossed the opened newspaper onto his desk.

"My name is Sydney Delaney. I've come in response to this ad for an office assistant."

He ached to take her in his arms. To kiss her breathless. To carry her to bed and make passionate love. His beloved was back, standing before his desk again, with her chin set at that determined angle he had grown to love, her matchless green eyes sparkling with a challenge. As long as he could hold out, he would willingly play her game.

Sitting down at his desk, he locked his dark gaze with hers. "The ad clearly calls for a male, Miss Delaney."

To his further distress and a serious jolt to his loins, he saw the little vixen arch a delicate brow. "Well, I hope you'll give me the chance to convince you of the advantages of hiring a female."

"You've got five minutes," he said. He figured he could hold out that long, at least if she remained on the other side of the desk.

His fixed gaze never left her as she turned and slipped the bolt on the door. "Just a precaution," she explained with a saucy smile. "In the event anyone else would presume to apply for the position."

"I understand." He pulled out his watch and laid it on the table. "Four and a half minutes, Miss Delaney."

She raised her arms and slowly, seductively, began to pull the pins out from her hair. Mike swallowed, shifting his gaze to watch her shake her head, releasing the thick strands. The heat in his loins felt as fiery red as the flaming color of the silky curtain that dropped to her shoulders.

Sydney leaned across the desk. "My previous employer has highly complimented some of my skills."

"Then I suggest you tell me what they are, Miss Delaney, because you're quickly running out of time. You're down to under four minutes." The gleam in his dark eyes left no doubt of his intention.

She straightened up and released the buttons of her bodice then slipped it off her shoulders. The corners of his mouth curved into a barely perceptible grin at the sight of the long-sleeved underwear buttoned primly to the neck. Then the smile died and his throat went dry when his gaze came to rest on the material stretched across her breasts.

He swallowed. "Is that a one-piece garment, or two-piece, Miss Delaney?"

"One piece, Mr. MacAllister. Why?" she asked coyly.

The desire in his eyes had deepened to lust. "Because we're beginning to face a serious time pressure here," he rasped.

As she strolled around the desk, her fingers unbuttoned the underwear and she lowered herself to his lap. Her eyes were slumberous green pools of passion, holding his dark gaze. Picking up his hand, she ran her tongue across his palm, then slipped his hand into the front of her shirt.

"My former employer implied that I'm a handful. Would you agree, Mr. MacAllister?" she asked seductively.

His hand cupped her breast, and she closed her eyes with pleasure at the feel of the familiar, exciting touch.

Despite the perspiration that had begun to dot his brow, he grinned, unable to resist responding to her bawdy remark.

"I'd say it's a well-made point . . . or two," he murmured in a husky whisper. His fingers teased the nipples of her breasts to hardened peaks.

"Strange you should say that. My previous employer once expressed the same sentiment."

"I would say your previous employer was a man of remarkable discretion. Which makes me wonder why he would allow such a valuable employee to slip through his fingers." His dark eyes lit with amusement.

"You know, that same thought has crossed my mind," she said pertly. "But I can see you would never make that mistake. As a matter of fact, I can tell by your firm hold, you would never let *anything* slip through your fingers."

"Lady, you've got just about enough time for one more recommendation, then this interview is over."

Sydney could feel the bulge of his arousal, and she slipped her arms around his neck. "My previous employer also implied that I'm a great kisser. I'd like to give you a demonstration." Her mouth closed over his.

His control snapped. He took command of the kiss, driving his tongue into her mouth, probing, sweeping, dueling until breathlessness forced them apart.

His fingers laced through her hair. "Oh, God, Syd, it's been hell without you. I love you, Syd. I love you, I love you," he murmured, raining kisses on her face and eyes.

"I know. A little bird told me." She laughed lightly.

Her words fell on ears deafened by the throbbing pulse from the hot blood rushing to his brain and loins. His hands and mouth continued their ravishment of her.

She reveled in the feel of him pressing against her, the touch of his hands sweeping her body, stripping the clothes off her.

Swooping her up into his arms, he carried her into the bedroom and she helped him out of his clothes. Entwined, they fell back onto the bed.

He was hot and hard and could wait no longer. She was just as ready for him. He drove into her and felt her tighten around him.

"Mike. Oh, Mike." They clutched each other in a mindless ecstasy, their bodies shuddering with spasms as the heated liquid of his love flowed into her.

Slowly they fought their way back to their surroundings, both knowing they had much to say in the short respite before their passion would demand the return to that divine state—one body, one mind, one soul.

Mike raised his head and gazed at her lovingly. He kissed the tip of her nose, then reached out and brushed aside the strands of hair clinging to her cheeks.

"I love you, Syd."

She smiled, glowing from that simple phrase. "I know. I got your message."

"Message?"

"A little bird told me. You weren't listening."

Whatever she was saying made no sense to him. But at that moment, all that mattered was the simple phrase he had once found so hard to say. "I love you, Syd. Lord, how I love you."

His face sobered, and he brushed her cheek with his hand. "Whatever I say, whatever I do, there is nothing and no one more important to me than you. Stay with me, Syd. I can't make it without you."

His glance caressed her face. "To think I almost lost you. And not for any of the reasons I once feared. But because of my own damn stupidity and jealousy. Can you ever forgive me?"

"Don't you think the last few minutes have made that question rather superfluous, MacAllister?" she teased, brushing the hair off his forehead. " 'All's well that ends well.' "

"Oh no, Delaney! Not a quote," he groaned.

Giggling, she put her arms around his neck. "It just slipped out naturally." Then her face sobered as she gazed into his dark eyes. "But it's true, Mike. What does the past matter as long as we have the future?"

As Mike lowered his head to claim her lips, from under the plaid cover of a birdcage perched on the office desk sounded a cheery, "Sydney's right. Sydney's right."

Avon Romances—
the best in exceptional authors and unforgettable novels!

HEART OF THE WILD Donna Stephens
77014-8/$4.50 US/$5.50 Can

TRAITOR'S KISS Joy Tucker
76446-6/$4.50 US/$5.50 Can

SILVER AND SAPPHIRES Shelly Thacker
77034-2/$4.50 US/$5.50 Can

SCOUNDREL'S DESIRE Joann DeLazzari
76421-0/$4.50 US/$5.50 Can

MY LADY NOTORIOUS Jo Beverley
76785-6/$4.50 US/$5.50 Can

SURRENDER MY HEART Lois Greiman
77181-0/$4.50 US/$5.50 Can

MY REBELLIOUS HEART Samantha James
76937-9/$4.50 US/$5.50 Can

COME BE MY LOVE Patricia Watters
76909-3/$4.50 US/$5.50 Can

SUNSHINE AND SHADOW Kathleen Harrington
77058-X/$4.50 US/$5.50 Can

WILD CONQUEST Hannah Howell
77182-9/$4.50 US/$5.50 Can